UNDER THE VOLCANO

Malcolm Lowry was born in 1909 at New Brighton and died in England in 1957. He was educated at the Leys School, Cambridge, and St Catherine's College. Between school and university he went to sea, working as deckhand and trimmer for about eighteen months. His first novel, *Ultramarine*, was accepted for publication in 1932, but the typescript was stolen and the whole thing had to be rewritten from the penultimate version. It was finally published in 1933. He went to Paris that autumn, married his first wife in 1934, and wrote several short stories in Paris and Chartres before going to New York. Here he started a new novel, *In Ballast to the White Sea* which he completed in 1936. He then left for Mexico. His first marriage broke up in 1938, and in 1939 he remarried and settled in British Columbia. During 1941-4, when he was living at Dollarton, he worked on the final version of *Under the Volcano*. In 1954 he finally returned to England. During half his writing life he lived in a squatters shack, largely built by himself, near Vancouver. His *Selected Letters*, edited by H. Breit and Margerie Lowry, appeared in 1967 and *Lunar Caustic*, part of a larger, uncompleted work, appeared in 1968; Margerie Bonner Lowry and Douglas Day have completed, from Lowry's notes, the novel *Dark as the Grave Wherein My Friend is Laid* and *October Ferry to Gabriola*. All of these, together with *Ultramarine* and a collection of stories, *Hear Us O Lord From Heaven Thy Dwelling Place*, have been published in Penguins.

MALCOLM LOWRY

UNDER
THE VOLCANO

PENGUIN BOOKS
IN ASSOCIATION WITH
JONATHAN CAPE

To
MARGERIE, MY WIFE

PENGUIN BOOKS

Published by the Penguin Group
27 Wrights Lane, London W8 5TZ, England
Viking Penguin Inc., 40 West 23rd Street, New York, New York 10010, USA
Penguin Books Australia Ltd, Ringwood, Victoria, Australia
Penguin Books Canada Ltd, 2801 John Street, Markham, Ontario, Canada L3R 1B4
Penguin Books (NZ) Ltd, 182–190 Wairau Road, Auckland 10, New Zealand

Penguin Books Ltd, Registered Offices: Harmondsworth, Middlesex, England

First published by Jonathan Cape 1947
Published in Penguin Books 1962
Reprinted with letters from Jonathan Cape and Malcolm Lowry 1985
5 7 9 10 8 6 4

Penguin Books are grateful for permission to publish Jonathan Cape's letter

Made and printed in Great Britain by
Hazell Watson & Viney Limited
Member of BPCC Limited
Aylesbury, Bucks, England
Set in Linotype Granjon

Letters between Malcolm Lowry and Jonathan Cape about *Under the Volcano*

TO MALCOLM LOWRY

> Jonathan Cape
> Thirty Bedford Square
> London WC1
> 29th November 1945

Dear Malcolm Lowry,

In the letter which you sent me with your manuscript there is the sentence:

> But it would be heart-breaking to be told, when so much has been taken into account, that it should be couched in sharper or more dramatic form or something of that nature: it was created on many planes and everything in it, right down to the precise number of chapters, is there for a perfectly good reason.

Well, two readers have read it carefully, and I have read it also. The best thing that I can do is to send you a copy of one reader's report, which seems to us here to crystallize most effectively and exactly what all three of us think about it. The question is, are you on reflection inclined to consider making the revisions which the report indicates, or, after thinking it over carefully, do you still feel about it exactly the same as when you wrote to me in August last? You no doubt have a duplicate of the typescript? I will retain my copy of the typescript until I hear from you.

So that my letter should not appear ambiguous, let me say that if you decide to implement the suggestion contained in the report, I am prepared to say here and now that I will publish it and bring it out, I hope, sometime during next year. If you stand pat on your original declaration of last August that the book must remain exactly as it is, I will think again on the matter, but it does not necessarily mean I would say no. We feel here that the book has integrity and importance, but it would be a pity for it to go out as it stands, believing as we do that its favourable reception will be helped tremendously by the alterations. At the same time we believe that it would be considerably improved aesthetically if the suggestions in the report are carried out.

Yours sincerely,
Jonathan Cape

TO JONATHAN CAPE

24 Calle de Humboldt
Cuernavaca, Morelos
Mexico
[2 January 1946]

Dear Mr Cape:

Thank you very much indeed for yours of the 29th November, which did not reach me, however, until New Year's Eve, and moreover reached me here, in Cuernavaca, where, completely by chance, I happen to be living in the very tower which was the original of the house of M. Laruelle, which I had only seen previously from the outside, and that ten years ago, but which is the very place where as it happens the Consul in the *Volcano* also had a little complication with some delayed correspondence.

Passing over my feelings, which you can readily imagine, of involved triumph, I will, lest these should crystallize into a complete agraphia, get down immediately to the business in hand.

My first feeling is that the reader, a copy of whose report you sent me, could not have been (to judge from your first letter to me) as sympathetic as the reader to whom you first gave it.

On the other hand, while I distinctly agree with much this second reader very intelligently says, and while in his place I might have said much the same by way of criticism, he puts me somewhat at a loss to reply definitely to your questions *re* revisions, for reasons which I shall try to set forth, and which I am sure both you and he would agree are valid, at least for the author.

It is true that the novel gets off to a slow start, and while he is right to regard this as a fault (and while in general this may be certainly a fault in any novel) I think it possible for various human reasons that its gravity might have weighed upon him more heavily than it would weigh upon the reader *per se*, certain provisions for him having first been made. If the book anyhow were already in print and its pages not wearing the dumb pleading disparate and desperate look of the unpublished manuscript, I feel a reader's interest would tend to be very much more engaged at the outset just as, were the book already, say, an established classic, a reader's feelings would be most different: albeit he might say *God, this is tough going*, he would plod gamely on through the dark morass — indeed he might feel ashamed not to — because of the reports which had already reached his ears of the rewarding vistas further on.

Using the word *reader* in the more general sense, I suggest that whether or not the *Volcano* as it is seems tedious at the beginning depends somewhat upon that reader's state of mind and how prepared he is to grapple with the form of the book and the author's true intention. Since, while he may be prepared and equipped to do both, he cannot *know* the nature of either of these things at the start, I suggest that a little subtle but solid elucidation in a preface or a blurb might negate very largely or modify the reaction you fear — that it was your first reaction, and might well have been mine in your place, I am asking you for the moment to be generous enough to consider beside the point — if he were *conditioned*, I say, ever so slightly towards the acceptance

7

of that slow beginning as inevitable, supposing I convince you it is — slow, but perhaps not necessarily so tedious after all — the results might be surprising. If you say, well, a good wine needs no bush, all I can reply is: well, I am not talking of good wine but mescal, and quite apart from the bush, once inside the cantina, mescal needs salt and lemon to get it down, and perhaps you would not drink it at all if it were not in such an enticing bottle. If that seems beside the point too, then let me ask who would have felt encouraged to venture into the drought of *The Waste Land* without some anterior knowledge and anticipation of its poetic cases?

Some of the difficulties of approach having been cleared away therefore, I feel the first chapter for example, such as it stands, is necessary since it sets, even without the reader's knowledge, the mood and tone of the book as well as the slow melancholy tragic rhythm of Mexico itself — its sadness — and above all establishes the *terrain:* if anything here finally looks to everyone just too feeble for words I would be only too delighted to cut it, but how can you be sure that by any really serious cutting here, especially any that radically alters the form, you are not undermining the foundations of the book, the basic structure, without which your reader might not have read it at all?

I venture to suggest finally that the book is a good deal thicker, deeper, better, and a great deal more carefully planned and executed than he suspects, and that if your reader is not at fault in not spotting some of its deeper meanings or in dismissing them as pretentious or irrelevant or uninteresting where they erupt on to the surface of the book, that is at least partly because of what may be a virtue and not a fault on my side, namely that the top level of the book, for all its *longeurs*, has been by and large so compellingly designed that the reader does not want to take time off to stop and plunge beneath the surface. If this is in fact true, of how many books can you say it? And how many books of which you can say it can you say also that you were not, somewhere along the line the first time you read it, bored because you wanted to 'get on'. I do not want to make a childish comparisons, but to go to the obvious classics what about *The Idiot? The Possessed?* What about the beginning of *Moby Dick?* To say nothing of *Wuthering Heights.* E. M. Forster, I think, says somewhere that it is more of a feat to get by with the end, and in the *Volcano* at least I claim I have done this; but without the beginning, or rather the first chapter, which as it were answers it, echoes back to it over the bridge of the intervening chapters, the end — and without it the book — would lose much of its meaning.

Since I am pleading for a rereading of *Under the Volcano* in the light of certain aspects of it which may not perhaps have struck you at all, with a view to any possible alterations, and not making a defence of its every word, I had better say that for my part I feel that the main defect of *Under the Volcano*, from which the others spring, comes from something irremediable. It is that the author's equipment, such as it is, is subjective rather than objective, a better equipment, in short, for a certain kind of poet than a novelist. On the other hand I claim that just as a tailor will try to conceal the deformities of his client so I have tried, aware of this defect, to conceal in the *Volcano* as well as possible the deformities of my own mind, taking heart from the fact that since the conception of the whole thing was essentially poetical, perhaps these deformities don't matter so very much after all, even when they show! But poems often have to be read several times before their full meaning will reveal itself, explode in the mind, and it is precisely this poetical conception of the *whole* that I suggest has been, if understandably, missed. But to be more specific: your reader's main objections to the book are:

1. The long initial tedium, which I have discussed in part but will take up again later.

2. The weakness of the character drawing. This is a valid criticism. But I have not exactly attempted to draw characters in the normal sense — though s'welp me bob it's only Aristotle who thought character counted least. But here, as I shall say somewhere else, there just isn't *room:* the characters will have to wait for

another book, though I did go to incredible trouble to make my major characters seem adequate on the most *superficial* plane on which this book can be read, and I believe in some eyes the character drawing will appear the reverse of weak. (What about female readers?) The truth is that the character drawing is not only weak but virtually nonexistent, save with certain minor characters, the four main characters being intended, in one of the book's meanings, to be aspects of the same man, or of the human spirit, and two of them, Hugh and the Consul, more obviously are. I suggest that here and there what may look like unsuccessful attempts at character drawing may only be the concrete bases to the creature's lives without which again the book could not be read at all. But weak or no there is nothing I can do to improve it without reconceiving or rewriting the book, unless it is to take something out — but then, as I say, one might be thereby only removing a prop which, while it perhaps looked vexing to you in passing, was actually holding something important up.

3. 'The author has spread himself too much. The book is *much too long* and over-elaborate for its content, and could have been much more effective if only half or two thirds its present length. The author has overreached himself and is given to eccentric word-spinning and too much stream-of-consciousness stuff.' This may well be so, but I think the author may be forgiven if he asks for a fuller appraisal of that content — I say it all again — in terms of the author's intention as a whole and chapter by chapter before he can reach any agreement with anyone as to what precisely renders it over-elaborate and should therefore be cut to render that whole more effective. If the reader has not got hold of the content at first go, how can he decide then what makes it much too long, especially since his reactions may turn out to be quite different on a second reading? And not only authors perhaps but readers can overreach themselves, by reading too fast however carefully they think they are going — and what tedious book is this one has to read so fast? I believe there is such a thing as wandering attention that is the fault neither of reader nor writer: though more of this

later. As for the eccentric word-spinning, I honestly don't think there is much that is not in some way thematic. As for the 'stream-of-consciousness stuff', many techniques have been employed, and while I did try to cut mere 'stuff' to a minimum, I suspect that your reader would finally agree, if confronted with the same problems, that most of it could be done in no other way: a lot of the so-called 'stuff' I feel to be justified simply on poetical or dramatic grounds: and I think you would be surprised to find how much of what at first sight seems unnecessary even in this 'stuff' is simply disguised, honest-to-God exposition, the author trying to proceed on Henry James' dictum that what is not vivid is not represented, what is not represented is not art.

To return to the criticisms on the first and second page of your reader's report:

1. 'Flashbacks of the character's past lives and past and present thoughts and emotions . . . (are) often tedious and unconvincing.' These flashbacks are necessary however, I feel: where they are really tedious or unconvincing, I should be glad to cut of course, but I feel it only fair to the book that this should be done only after what I shall say later (and have already said) has been taken into account. That which may seem inorganic in itself might prove right in terms of the whole churrigueresque structure I conceived and which I hope may begin soon to loom out of the fog for you like Borda's horrible–beautiful cathedral in Taxco.

2. 'Mexican local colour heaped on in shovelfuls . . . is very well done and gives one an astonishing sense of the place and the atmosphere.' Thank you very much, but if you will excuse my saying so I did not heap the local colour, whatever that is, on in shovelfuls. I am delighted he likes it but take issue because what he says implies carelessness. I hope to convince you that, just as I said in my first letter, all that is there is there for a reason. And what about the use of Nature, of which he says nothing?

3. 'The mescal-inspired phantasmagoria, or heebie-jeebies, to which Geoffrey has succumbed . . . is impressive but I think too long, wayward and elaborate. On account of (3) the book inevitably

recalls . . . *The Lost Weekend.*' I will take this in combination with your reader's last and welcome remarks *re* the book's virtues, and the last sentence of the report in which he says: 'Everything should be concentrated on the drunk's inability to rise to the occasion of Yvonne's return, on his delirious consciousness (which is very well done) and on the local colour, which is excellent throughout.' I do not want to quibble, but I do seem to detect something like a contradiction here. Here is my mescal-inspired phantasmagoria, which is impressive but already too long, wayward and elaborate — to say nothing of too much eccentric word-spinning and stream-of-consciousness stuff — and yet on the other hand, I am invited to concentrate still *more* upon it, since all this can be after all nothing but the delirious consciousness (which is very well done) — and I would like very much to know how I can concentrate still more upon a delirious consciousness without making it still more long-wayward-elaborate, and since that is the way of delirious consciousnesses, without investing it with still more stream-of-consciousness stuff: moreover here too is my local colour, and although this is already 'heaped on in shovelfuls' (if excellent throughout) I am invited to concentrate still more upon it and this without calling in the aid of some yet large long-handled scoop-like implement used to lift and throw earth, coal, grain and so forth: nor do I see either how I can very well concentrate very much more than I have on the drunk's inability to rise to the occasion of Yvonne's return without incurring the risk of being accused of heaping on the mescal-inspired phantasmagoria with — at least! — a snow plough. Having let me have my fun, I must say that I admit the critical probity in your reader's last remarks but that it would be impossible to act on his suggestions without writing another book, possibly a better one, but still, another. I respect what he says, for what he seems to be saying is (like Yeats, when he cut nearly all the famous but irrelevent lines out of the *Ballad of Reading Gaol* and thereby, unfortunately for my thesis, much improved it): a work of art should have but one subject. Perhaps it will be seen that the *Volcano*, after all, *has* but one

12

subject. This brings me to the unhappy (for me) subject of the *Lost Weekend*. Mr Jackson likewise obeys your reader's aesthetic and does to my mind an excellent job within the limits he set himself. Your reader could not know, of course, that it should have been the other way round — that it was *The Lost Weekend* that should have inevitably recalled the *Volcano*; whether this matters or not in the long run, it happens to have a very desiccating effect on me. I began the *Volcano* in 1936, the same year having written, in New York, a novelette of about 100 pages about an alcoholic entitled *The Last Address*, which takes place mostly in the same hospital ward where Don Birnam spends an interesting afternoon. This — it was too short I thought to publish separately or I would have sent it to you for it was and is, I believe, remarkably good — was accepted and paid for by *Story Magazine*, who were publishing novelettes at that time, but was never published because they had meantime changed their policy back to shorter things again. It was however, in spite of Zola, accepted as more or less pioneer work in that field, and nine years and two months ago when I was here in this same town in Mexico I conceived the *Volcano* and I decided really to go to town on the poetical possibilities of that subject. I had written a 40,000-word version by 1937 that Arthur Calder-Marshall liked, but it was not thorough or honest enough. In 1939 I volunteered to come to England but was told to remain in Canada, and in 1940, while waiting to be called up, I rewrote the entire book in six months, but it was no damn good, a failure, except for the drunk passages about the Consul, but even some of them did not seem to me good enough. I also rewrote *The Last Address* in 1940–41 and rechristened it *Lunar Caustic*, and conceived the idea of a trilogy entitled *The Voyage That Never Ends* for your firm (nothing less than a trilogy would do) with the *Volcano* as the first, infernal part, a much amplified *Lunar Caustic* as the second, purgatorial part, and an enormous novel I was also working on called *In Ballast to the White Sea* (which I lost when my house burned down as I believe I wrote you) as the paradisal third part, the whole to concern the battering the human spirit takes (doubtless because it is overreaching itself) in its ascent towards its true purpose. At the end of 1941 I laid aside *In Ballast* – of which there were 1000 pages of eccentric word-spinning by this time – and decided to take this mescal-inspired phantasmagoria the *Volcano* by the throat and really do something about it, it having become a spiritual thing by this time. I also told my wife that I would probably cut my throat if during this period of the world's drunkenness someone else had the same sober idea. I worked for two more years, eight hours a day, and had just ascetically completed all the drunken parts to my satisfaction and there were but three other chapters to rewrite when one day round about New Year's '44, I picked up an American review of *The Lost Weekend*. At first I thought it must be *The Last Week End*, by my old pal John (*Volunteer in Spain*) Sommerfield, a very strange book in which figured in some decline no less a person than myself, and I am still wondering what John thinks about this: but doubtless the old boy ascribes it to the capitalist system. *The Lost Weekend* did not appear in Canada till about April '44, and after reading the book it became extremely hard for the time being to go on writing and having faith in mine. I could still congratulate myself upon having *In Ballast* up my sleeve however, but only a month or so later that went completely west with my house. My wife saved the MSS of the *Volcano*, God knows how, while I was doing something about the forest, and the book was finished over a year ago in Niagara-on-the-Lake, Ontario. We returned to British Columbia to rebuild our house and since we had some serious setbacks and accidents in doing so it took some time to get the typescript in order. Meantime, however, this *Lost Weekend* business on top of everything else had somewhat got me down. The only way I can look upon it is as a form of punishment. My own worst fault in the past has been precisely lack of integrity, and that is particularly hard to face in one's own work. Youth plus booze plus hysterical indentifications plus vanity plus self-deception plus no work plus more booze. But now, when this ex-pseudo author climbs down from his cross in his little

Oberammergau where he has been hibernating all these years to offer something really original and terrific to atone for his sins, it turns out that somebody from Brooklyn has just done the same thing better. Or has he not? And how many times has this author not been told that *that* theme of all themes couldn't sell, that nothing was duller than dipsomania! Anyway Papa Henry James would certainly have agreed that all this was a turn of the screw. But I think it not unreasonable to suppose either that he might have added that, for that matter, the *Volcano* was, so to say, a couple of turns of the screw on *The Lost Weekend* anyway. At all events I've tried to give you some of the reasons why I can't turn the *Volcano* into simply a kind of *quid pro quo* of the thing, which is what your reader's suggestions would tend to make it, or, if that's unfair to your reader, what I would then tend to make it. These reasons may be briefly crystallized. 1. Your reader wants me to do what I wanted to do myself (and still sometimes regret not having done) but did not do because 2. *Under the Volcano*, such as it is, is better. After this long digression, to return to the last page of your reader's report: I agree:

A. It is worth my while — and I am anxious — to make the book as effective as possible. But I think it only fair to the book that the lengths which have been gone to already to make it effective as possible *in its own terms* should be appreciated by someone who sees the whole.

B. Cuts should possibly be made in some of the passages indicated, but with the same reservations.

I disagree that:

A. Hugh's past is of little interest

B. or relevance

for reasons I shall set forth. One, which may seem odd, is: There is not a single part of this book I have not submitted to Flaubert's acid test of reading aloud or having read aloud, frequently to the kind of people one would expect to loathe it, and nearly always to people who were not afraid of speaking their minds. Chapter 6, which concerns Hugh's past life, always convulsed people with laughter, so much so that often the reader could not go on. Apart from anything else, then, and there is much else — what about its humour? This does not take care of its relevance, which I shall point out; but to refer back to something I said before, I submit that the real reason why your reader found this chapter of no interest or relevance was perhaps that I had built better than I knew in the previous chapter, and he wanted to skip and get on to the Consul again. Actually this chapter is the heart of the book and if cuts are to be made in it they should be made on the advice of someone who, having seen what the author is driving at, has at least an inspiration equivalent to that of the author who created it.

I had wanted to give in the following pages a kind of synopsis of the *Volcano* chapter by chapter, but since my spare copy of the MSS has not reached me from Canada I will simply suggest as well as I can some of its deeper meanings, and something of the form and intention that was in the author's mind, and that which he feels should be taken into account, should alterations be necessary. The twelve chapters should be considered as twelve blocks, to each of which I have devoted over a period of years a great deal of labour, and I hope to convince you that whatever cuts may be made there must still be twelve chapters. Each chapter is a unity in itself and all are related and interrelated. Twelve is a universal unit. To say nothing of the 12 labours of Hercules, there are 12 hours in a day, and the book is concerned with a single day as well as, though very incidentally, with time: there are 12 months in a year, and the novel is enclosed by a year; while the deeply buried layer of the novel or poem that attaches itself to myth, does so to the Jewish Cabbala where the number 12 is of the highest symbolic importance. The Cabbala is used for poetical purposes because it represents man's spiritual aspiration. The Tree of Life, which is its emblem, is a kind of complicated ladder with Kether, or Light, at the top and an extremely unpleasant abyss some way above the middle. The Consul's spiritual domain in this regard is probably the Qliphoth, the world of shells and demons, represented by the Tree of Life upside down — all this is not important at all to the understanding of the book; I just mention it in passing to hint that, as Henry James says, 'There are depths.' But also, because I have to have my 12: it is as if I hear a clock slowly striking midnight for Faust; as I think of the slow progression of the chapters, I feel it destined to have 12 chapters and nothing more nor less will satisfy me. For the rest, the book is written on numerous planes with provision made, it was my fond hope, for almost every kind of reader, my approach with all humility being opposite, I felt, to that of Mr Joyce, i.e., a simplifying, as far as possible, of what originally suggested itself in far more baffling, complex and esoteric terms, rather than the other way round. The novel can be read simply as a story which you can skip if you want. It can be read as a story you will get more out of if you don't skip. It can be regarded as a kind of symphony, or in another way as a kind of opera — or even a horse opera. It is hot music, a poem, a song, a tragedy, a comedy, a farce, and so forth. It is superificial, profound, entertaining and boring, according to taste. It is a prophecy, a political warning, a cryptogram, a preposterous movie, and a writing on the wall. It can even be regarded as a sort of machine: it works too, believe me, as I have found out. In case you think I mean it to be everything but a novel I better say that after all it is intended to be and, though I say so myself, a deeply serious one too. But it is also I claim a work of art somewhat different from the one you suspected it was, and more successful too, even though according to its own lights.

This novel then is concerned principally, in Edmund Wilson's words (speaking of Gogol), with the forces in man which cause him to be terrified of himself. It is also concerned with the guilt of man, with his remorse, with his ceaseless struggling toward the light under the weight of the past, and with his doom. The allegory is that of the Garden of Eden, the Garden representing the world, from which we ourselves run perhaps slightly more danger of being ejected than when I wrote the book. The drunkenness of the Consul is used on one plane to symbolize the universal drunkenness of mankind during the war, or during the period immediately preceding it, which is almost the same thing, and what profundity and final meaning there is in his fate should be seen also in its universal relationship to the ultimate fate of mankind.

Since it is Chapter 1 that I believe to be chiefly responsible for your reader's charge of tedium, and since, as I've said, I believe that a reader needs only a little flying start for this apparent tedium to be turned into an increasing suspense from the outset, I will devote more space to this first chapter than to any other, unless it is the sixth, saying also in passing that I believe it will become clear on a second reading that nearly all the material in 1 is necessary, and if one should try to eliminate this chapter entirely, or chop up all the material in it and stuff it in here and there into the book in wedges and blocks — I even tried it once — it would not only take a very long time but the results would be nowhere near as effective, while it would moreover buckle the very form of the book, which is to be considered like that of a wheel, with 12 spokes, the motion of which is something like that, conceivably, of time itself.

Under the Volcano

(*Note:* the book opens in the Casino de la Selva. Selva means wood and this strikes the opening chord of the *Inferno* — remember, the book was planned and still is a kind of Inferno, with Purgatorio and Paradiso to follow, the tragic protagonist in each, like Tchitchikov in *Dead Souls*, becoming slightly better — in the middle of our life . . . in a dark wood, etc., this chord being struck again in 6, the middle and heart of the book where Hugh, in the middle of his life, recalls at the beginning of that chapter Dante's words: the chord is struck again remotely toward the end of 7 where the Consul enters a gloomy cantina called El Bosque, which also means the wood (both of these places being by the way real, one here, the other in Oaxaca), while the chord is resolved in

9, in the chapter concerning Yvonne's death, where the wood becomes real, and dark.)

The scene is Mexico, the meeting place, according to some, of mankind itself, pyre of Bierce and springboard of Hart Crane, the age-old arena of racial and political conflicts of every nature, and where a colourful native people of genius have a religion that we can roughly describe as one of death, so that it is a good place, at least as good as Lancashire or Yorkshire, to set our drama of a man's struggle between the powers of darkness and light. Its geographical remoteness from us, as well as the closeness of its problems to our own, will assist the tragedy each in its own way We can see it as the world itself, or the Garden of Eden, or both at once. Or we can see it as a kind of timeless symbol of the world on which we can place the Garden of Eden, the Tower of Babel and indeed anything else we please. It is paradisal: it is unquestionably infernal. It is, in fact, Mexico, the place of the pulques and chinches, and it is important to remember that when the story opens it is November 1939, not November 1938, the Day of the Dead, and precisely one year after the Consul has gone down the barranca, the ravine, the abyss that man finds himself looking into now (to quote the Archbishop of York) the worse one in the Cabbala, the still unmentionably worse one in the Qliphoth. or simply down the drain, according to taste.

I have spoken already of one reason why I consider this chapter necessary more or less as it is, for the terrain, the mood, the sadness of Mexico, etc., but before I go on to mention any more I must say I fail to see what is wrong with this opening, as Dr Vigil and M. Laruelle, on the latter's last day in the country, discuss the Consul. After their parting the ensuing exposition is perhaps hard to follow and you can say that it is a melodramatic fault that by concealing the true nature of the death of Yvonne and the Consul I have created suspense by false means: myself, I believe the concealment is organic, but even were it not, the criterion by which most critics condemn such devices seems to me to be that of pure reporting, and against the kind of novel they admire I am in rebellion, both revolutionary and reactionary at once. You can say too that it is a gamey and outworn trick to begin at the end of the book: it certainly is: I like it in this case and there is moreover a deep motive for it, as I have partially explained, and as I think you will see shortly. During Laruelle's walk we have to give some account of who he is; this is done as clearly as possible and if it could be achieved in a shorter or more masterly fashion I would be only too willing to take advice: a second reading however will show you what thematic problems we are also solving on the way — not to say what hams, that have to be there, are being hung in the window. Meanwhile the story is unfolding as the Mexican evening deepens into night: the reader is told of the love of M. Laruelle for Yvonne, the chord of tragic love is struck in the farewell visit at sunset to the Palace of Maximilian, where Hugh and Yvonne are to stand (or have stood) in the noonday in Chapter 4 and while M. Laruelle leans over the fateful ravine we have, in his memory, the Taskerson episode. (Taskerson crops up again in 5, in 7 the Consul sings the Taskerson song to himself, and even in 12 he is still trying to walk with the Taskerson 'erect manly carriage'.) The Taskerson episode in this Chapter 1 — damned by implication by your reader — may be unsound if considered seriously in the light of a psychological etiology for the Consul's drinking or downfall, but I have a sincere and not unjustified conviction that it is very funny in itself, and justified in itself musically and artistically at this point as relief, as also for another reason: is it not precisely in this particular passage that your reader may have acquired the necessary *sympathy* with Geoffrey Firmin that enabled him to read past Chapter 2 and into 3 without being beset by the tedium there instead — and hence to become much more interested as he went on? Your reader has omitted the possibility of the poor author's having any wit anywhere. If you do not believe this Taskerson incident is funny, try reading it aloud. I think that wit might seem slightly larger on a second reading: also the drunken man on horseback, who now appears to interrupt M. Laruelle's reverie, by hurtling on up the Calle Nicaragua, might have a larger significance: and still more on a third reading. This drunken horseman is by implication the first appearance of the Consul himself as a symbol of mankind. Here also, as if tangentially (even if your reader saw it as but another shovelful of local colour) is also struck the chord of Yvonne's death in 11; true, this horse is not riderless as yet, but it may well be soon: here man and the force he will release are for the moment fused. (Since by the way there is no suggestion in your reader's report that he has read the rather important Chapter 11, in which there is incidentally some of the action he misses, I had better say at this point that Yvonne is finally killed by a panic-stricken horse in 11 that the Consul drunkenly releases in a thunderstorm in 12 (the 2 chapters overlapping in time at this juncture) in the erroneous, fuddled yet almost praiseworthy belief he is doing somebody a good turn.) M. Laruelle now, avoiding the house where I am writing this letter (which is one thing that must certainly be cut if I am not to spend my patrimony sending it airmail), goes gloomily toward the local movie. In the cinema and the bar, people are taking refuge from the storm as in the world they are creeping into bomb shelters, and the lights have gone out as they have gone out in the world. The movie playing is *Las Manos de Orlac*, the same film that had been playing exactly a year before when the Consul was killed, but the man with the bloody hands in the poster, via the German origin on the picture, symbolizes the *guilt* of mankind, which relates him also to M. Laruelle and the Consul again, while he is also more particularly a foreshadowing of the thief who takes the money from the dying man by the roadside in Chapter 8, and whose hands are also covered with blood. Inside the cinema cantina we hear more of the Consul from the cinema manager, Bustamente, much of which again may engage our sympathy for the Consul and our interest in him. It should not be forgotten that it is the Day of the Dead and

21

that on that day in Mexico the dead are supposed to commune with the living. Life however is omnipresent: but meantime there have been both political (the German film star Maria Landrock) and historical (Cortez and Moctezuma) notes being sounded in the background; and while the story itself is being unfolded, the themes and counterthemes of the book are being stated. Finally Bustamente comes back with the book of Elizabethan plays M. Laruelle has left there eighteen months before, and the theme of Faust is struck. Laruelle had been planning to make a modern movie of Faust but for a moment the Consul himself seems like his Faust, who had sold his soul to the devil. We now hear more of the Consul, his gallant war record, and of a war crime he has possibly committed against some German submarine officers – whether he is really as much to blame as he tells himself, he is, in a sense, paid back in coin for it at the end of the book and you may say that here the Consul is merely being established in the Grecian manner as a fellow of some stature, so that his fall may be tragic: it could be cut, I suppose, even though this is exactly as I see the Consul – but do we not look at him with more interest thereafter? We also hear that the Consul has been suspected of being an English spy, or 'espider', and though he suffers dreadfully from the mania of persecution, and you feel sometimes, quite objectively, that he is indeed being followed throughout the book, it is as if the Consul himself is not aware of this and is afraid of something quite different: for lack of an object therefore it was the writer's reasonable hope that this first sense of being followed might settle on the reader and haunt him instead. At the moment however Bustamente's sympathy for him should arouse *our* sympathy. This sympathy I feel should be very considerably increased by the Consul's letter which Laruelle reads, and which was never posted, and this letter I believe important: his tortured cry is not answered until in the last chapter, 12, when, in the Farolito, the Consul finds Yvonne's letters he has lost and never really read until this time just before his death. M. Laruelle burns the Consul's letter, the act of which is poetically balanced by the

22

flight of vultures ('like burnt papers floating from a fire') at the end of 3, and also by the burning of the Consul's MSS in Yvonne's dying dream in 11: the storm is over: and —

Outside in the dark tempestuous night backwards revolved the luminous wheel.

This wheel is of course the Ferris wheel in the square, but it is, if you like, also many other things: it is Buddha's wheel of the law (see 7), it is eternity, it is the instrument of eternal recurrence, the eternal return, and it is the form of the book; or superficially it can be seen simply in an obvious movie sense as the wheel of time whirling backwards until we have reached the year before and Chapter 2 and in this sense, if we like, we can look at the rest of the book through Laruelle's eyes, as if it were his creation.

(*Note:* In the Cabbala, the misuse of magical powers is compared to drunkenness or the misuse of wine, and termed, if I remember rightly, in Hebrew *sōd*, which gives us our parallel. There is a kind of attribute of the word *sōd* also which implies garden or a neglected garden, I seem to recall too, for the Cabbala is sometimes considered as the garden itself, with the Tree of Life, which is related of course to that Tree the forbidden fruit of which gave one the knowledge of good and evil, and ourselves the legend of Adam and Eve, planted within it. Be these things as they may — and they are certainly at the root of most of our knowledge, the wisdom of our religious thought, and most of our inborn superstitions as to the origin of man — William James if not Freud would certainly agree with me when I say that the agonies of the drunkard find their most accurate poetic analogue in the agonies of the mystic who has abused his powers. The Consul here of course has the whole thing wonderfully and drunkenly mixed up: mescal in Mexico is a hell of a drink but it is still a drink you can get at any cantina, more readily I dare say than Scotch these days at the dear old Horseshoe. But mescal is also a drug, taken in the form of buttons, and the transcending of its effects is one of the well-known ordeals that occultists have to go through. It would appear that the Consul has fuddledly come to confuse the two, and he is perhaps not far wrong.)

Final note on Chapter 1: If this chapter is to be cut, can it not be done then with such wisdom as to make the chapter and the book itself better? I feel the chapter makes a wonderful entity and must be cut, if at all, by someone who at least sees its potentialities in terms of the whole book. I myself don't see much wrong with it. Against the charge of appalling pretentiousness, which is the most obvious one to be made by anyone who has read this letter, I feel I go clear; because these other meanings and danks and darks are not stressed at all: it is only if the reader himself, prompted by instinct or curiosity, cares to invoke them that they will raise their demonic heads from the abyss, or peer at him from above. But even if he is not prompted by anything, new meanings will certainly reveal themselves if he reads this book again. I hope you will be good enough not to remind me that the same might be said of *Orphan Annie* or *Jemima Puddleduck*.

2

You are now back on exactly the same day the year before – the Day of the Dead 1938 – and the story of Yvonne's and the Consul's last day begins at seven o'clock in the morning on her arrival. I do not see any difficulties here. The mysterious contrapuntal dialogue in the Bella Vista bar you hear is supplied by Weber, you will later see if you watch and listen carefully, the smuggler who flew Hugh down to Mexico, and who is mixed up with the local thugs – as your reader calls them – and Sinarchistas in the Farolito in Parián who finally shoot the Consul. The chord of *no se puede vivir sin amar*, the writing in gold leaf outside M. Laruelle's house (where I am writing this letter, with my back to the degenerate machicolation, and even if you do not believe in my wheels – the wheel shows up in this chapter in the flywheel in the printer's shop – and so on, you must admit this is funny, as also that it is quite funny that the same movie happens to be playing in town as was playing here nine years ago, not *Las Manos de Orlac* as it happens but *La Tragedia de Mayerling*), is struck ironically by the bartender with his 'absolutamente necesario', the recurring notices for the boxing match symbolize the conflict between Yvonne and the Consul. The chapter is a sort of bridge, it was written with extreme care; it too is absolutamente necesario, I think you would agree yourself on a second reading: it is an entity, a unity in itself, as are all the other chapters; it is, I claim, dramatic, amusing, and within its limits I think is entirely successful. I don't see any opportunity for cuts either.

3

I think will improve on a second reading and still more on a third. But since I believe your reader was impressed by it I will pass over it quickly. Word-spinning flashback while the Consul is lying down flat on his face in the Calle Nicaragua is really very careful exposition. This chapter was first written in 1940 and completed in 1942 long before Jackson went Lostweekending. Cuts should be made with great sympathy ('compliments of the Venezuelan Government' bit might go for instance) by someone – or by the author in conjunction with someone – who is prepared for the book to sink slowly at a not distant date into the action of the mind, and who is not necessarily put off by this. The scene between the Consul and Yvonne where he is impotent is balanced by scene between Consul and Maria in the last chapter: meanings of the Consul's impotence are practically inexhaustible The dead man with hat over head the Consul sees in the garden is man by the wayside in Chapter 8. This can happen in really super DTs. Paracelsus will bear me out.

Necessary, I feel, much as it is, especially in view of my last sentence *re* 3 about the action of the mind. In this there is another kind of action. There is movement and swiftness, it is a contrast, it supplies a needed *ozone*. It gives a needed, also, sympathy and understanding of Mexico and her problems and people from a material viewpoint. If the very beginning seems slightly ridiculous you can read it as satire, but on a second reading I think the whole will improve vastly. We have now the countermovement of the Battle of the Ebro being lost, while no one does anything about it, which is a kind of correlative of the scene by the roadside in 8, the victim of which here first makes his appearance outside the cantina La Sepultura, with his horse tethered near, that will kill Yvonne. Man's political aspirations, as opposed to his spiritual, come into view, and Hugh's sense of guilt balances the Consul's. If part of it must be cut, let it be done with a view to the whole — and with genius at least, I feel like saying — and let it not be cut so that it bleeds. Almost everything in it is relevant even down to the horses, the dogs, the river, and the small talk about the local movie. And what is not, as I say, supplies a needed ozone. For myself I think this ride through the Mexican morning sunlight is one of the best things in the book, and if Hugh strikes you as himself slightly preposterous, there is importance to the theme in the passage *re* his passionate desire for *goodness* at the close.

5

Is a contrast in the reverse direction, the opening words having an ironic bearing on the last words of 4. The book is now fast sinking into the action of the mind, and away from normal action, and yet I believe that by now your reader was really interested, *too* interested in fact here in the Consul to be able to cope with 6. Here at all events the most important theme of the book appears: *'Le gusta este jardin?'* on the sign. The Consul slightly mistranslates this sign, but 'You like this garden? Why is it yours? We evict those who destroy!' will have to stand (while we will point out elsewhere that the real translation can be in a certain sense even more more horrifying). The garden is the Garden of Eden, which he even discusses with Mr Quincy. It is the world too. It also has all the cabbalistic attributes of 'garden'. (Though all this is buried far down in the book, so that if you don't want to bother about it, you needn't. I wish that Hugh I'Anson Fausset, however, one of your own writers, one whose writings I very much admire and some of whose writings have had a very formative influence on my own life, could read the *Volcano*.) On the surface I am going to town here on the subject of the drunkard and I hope do well and amusingly. Parián again is death. Word-spinning phantasmagoria somewhere toward end of first part is necessary. It should be clear that the Consul has a blackout and that the second part in the bathroom is concerned with what he remembers half deliriously of the missing hour. Most of what he remembers is again disguised exposition and drama which carries on the story to the question: shall they go to Guanajuato (life) or Tomalin, which of course involves Parián (death). For the rest the Consul at one point identifies himself with the infant Horus, about which or whom the less said the better; some mystics believe him responsible for this last war, but I need another language I guess to explain what I mean. Perhaps Mr Fausset would explain, but at all events you don't have to think about it because the passage is only short, and reads like quite good lunacy. The rest I think is perfectly good clean DTs such as your reader would approve of. This was first written in 1937. Final revision was made in March 1943. This too is an entity in itself. Possible objection could be to the technique of the second part but I believe it is a subtle way to do a difficult thing. Cuts might be made here, I guess, but they would have to be inspired at least as much as the chapter was.

Here we come to the heart of the book which, instead of going into high delirious gear of the Consul, returns instead, surprisingly although inevitably if you reflect, to the uneasy, but healthy, systole-diastole of Hugh. In the middle of our life . . . and the theme of the Inferno is stated again, then follows the enormously long *straight* passage. This passage is the one your reader claims has little or no interest or relevance and I maintain he skipped because of a virtue on my side, namely he was more interested in the Consul himself. But here the guilt theme, and the theme of man's guilt, takes on a new shade of meaning. Hugh may be a bit of a fool but he none the less typifies the sort of person who may make or break our future: in fact he is the future in a certain sense. He is Everyman tightened up a screw, for he is just beyond being mediocre. And he is the youth of Everyman. Moreover his frustrations with his music, with the sea, in his desire to be good and decent, his self-deceptions, triumphs, defeats and dishonesties (and once more I point out that a much needed ozone blows into the book here with the sea air) his troubles with his guitar, are everyone's frustrations, triumphs, defeats, dishonesties and troubles with their *quid pro quo* of a guitar. And his desire to be a composer or musician is everyone's innate desire to be a poet of life in some way, while his desire to be accepted at sea is everyone's desire, conscious or unconscious, to be a part – even if it doesn't exist – of the brotherhood of man. He is revealed as a frustrated fellow whose frustrations might just as well have made him a drunk too, just like the Consul. (Who was frustrated as a poet – as who is not? – this indeed is another thing that binds us all together, but for whose drunkenness no satisfactory etiology is ever given unless it is in 7. 'But the cold world shall not know.') Hugh feels he has betrayed himself by betraying his brother and also betrayed the brotherhood of man by having been at one time an anti-Semite. But when, in the middle of the chapter, which is also the middle of the book, his thoughts are interrupted by

Geoffrey's call of 'Help' you can receive, I claim, upon rereading, a *frisson* of a quite different calibre to that received when reading such pieces as 'William Wilson' or other stories about doppelgängers. Hugh and the Consul are the same person, but within a book which obeys not the laws of other books, but those it creates as it goes along. I have reason to believe that much of this long straight passage is extremely funny anyway and will cause people to laugh aloud. We now proceed into the still greater nonsense and at the same time far more desperate seriousness of the shaving scene. Hugh shaves the corpse — but I cannot be persuaded that nonetheless much of this is not very hilarious indeed. We are then introduced to Geoffrey's room, with his picture of his old ship the *Samaritan* (and the theme is struck remotely again of the man by the wayside in 8) upon which ship it has been mentioned before in 1, etc., that he either has committed or imagines he has, but was certainly made in part responsible for, a crime against a number of German submarine officers — valid at least as any crime we may have committed in the past against Germany in general, that ugsome child of Europe whose evil and destructive energy is so much responsible for all our progress. At the same time he shows Hugh his alchemistic books, and we are for a moment, if in a pseudo-farcical situation, standing before the evidence of what is no less than the magical basis of the world. You do not believe the world has a magical basis, especially while the Battle of the Ebro is going on, or worse, bombs are dropping in Bedford Square? Well, perhaps I don't either. But the point is that Hitler *did*. And Hitler was another pseudo black magician out of the same drawer as Amfortas in the *Parsifal* he so much admired, and who has had the same inevitable fate. And if you don't believe that a British general actually told me that the real reason why Hitler destroyed the Polish Jews was to prevent their cabbalistic knowledge being used against him you can let me have my point on poetical grounds, I repeat, since it is made at a very sunken level of the book and is not very important here anyway. Saturn lives at 63, and Bahomet lives next door, however, and don't say I didn't tell you!

The rest of the chapter, and all this is probably too long, takes Hugh and the Consul and Yvonne, meeting Laruelle on the way (I hope dramatically) up to the house where I am now writing you this letter: the point about the postcard the Consul receives (from the same tiny bearded postman who delivered your delayed letter to me on New Year's Eve) is that it was posted about a year before in 1937 not long after she left, or was sent away by the Consul (following her affair with Laruelle but probably so that the Consul could drink in peace), and that its tone would seem to suggest that her going away was only a final thing in the Consul's mind, that really they loved each other all the time, had just had a lover's quarrel, and in spite of M. Laruelle, the whole thing was absolutely unnecessary. The chapter closes with a dying fall, like the end of some guitar piece of Ed Lang's, or conceivably Hugh's (and in this respect the brackets earlier might represent the 'breaks') — oddly but rightly, I felt, the path theme of Dante, however, reappearing and fading with the vanishing road.

I believe on rereading this chapter it will seem to have much more relevance than before and its humour will appear as more considerable. On the other hand this is undoubtedly the juiciest area for your surgeon's knife. The middle part of the shaving scene was written in 1937, as was the very end, that much comprising the whole chapter then. The new version was done in 1943 but I had not quite finally revised it in 1944 when my house burned down. The final revisions I made later in 1944 comprised the first work I had been able to do since the fire, in which several pages of this chapter and notes for cuts were lost, and it well may be the job is shaky or forced here and there. This is the first point in the book where I can be persuaded to share your reader's objections, I think, to any extent. Some of it may be in a kind of bad taste. On the other hand I feel it deserves a careful rereading — I say again and again in the light of the form and intention I have indicated, bearing in mind that the journalistic style of the first part is intended to represent Hugh himself. In brief, I could stand even slashing cuts were your surgeon to say, 'This would be more effective if such and such were done,' and I saw he was taking everything into account. If a major operation by a sympathetic surgeon will save the patient's life, OK, but, even though I do live in Mexico, I'm damned if I'm going to help him cut out his heart. (And then, when he's dead, 'just flop it back in again anyhow', as the nurse said to me having just attended the post mortem.)

7

Here we come to seven, the fateful, the magic, the lucky good-bad number and the scene in the tower, where I write this letter. By a coincidence I moved to the tower on January 7 – I was living in another apartment in the same house, but downstairs, when I got your letter. My house burned down on June 7; when I returned to the burned site someone had branded, for some reason, the number 7 on a burned tree; why was I not a philosopher? Philosophy has been dying since the days of Duns Scotus, though it continues underground, if quacking slightly. Boehme would support me when I speak of the passion for order even in the smallest things that exist in the universe: 7 too is the number on the horse that will kill Yvonne and 7 the hour when the Consul will die – I believe the intention of this chapter to be quite clear and that it is one your reader approves of and I think too it is probably one of the best in the book. It was first written in 1936, rewritten in 1937, 1940, 1941, 1943, and finally 1944. Parallels with *The Lost Weekend* I think are most in evidence in this chapter. One long one that does not appear and which was written long before the *LWE* I hoiked out with a heavy heart, but imbued with the spirit of competition, then added something else to my telephone scene to outdo him. I was particularly annoyed because my telephone scene in 3 and this one before I revised it, as I have said, were written long before Jackson's book appeared. Another

31

parallel toward the end when he had his drink before him he doesn't pick it up will have to stand: it was written in 1937 anyway. I allowed myself also in the conversation in the middle with Laruelle a little of the Consul's professional contempt for the belief that the D Ts is the end of everything and I think if you ever publish the book you might do me justice by saying that this begins where Jackson leaves off. If there must be cuts here again I say they should be made by someone who appreciates this chapter as an entity right down to the bit about Samaritana mia and with reference to the whole book. There were the usual thicknesses and obliquities, stray cards from the tarot pack, and odd political and mystical chords and dissonances being sounded here and there in this chapter but I won't go into them: but there is also, above all, the continued attention to the *story*. The horseman, first seen in 4 and who is to be the man by the roadside, is seen again going up the hill, and whose horse, with the number 7 on it, will kill Yvonne. This chapter constitutes almost the Consul's last chance and if the book has been read carefully I feel you should have a fine sense of doom by this time. *Es inevitable le muerte del Papa* is quite possibly just an anachronism, but I feel it must stand for I hold this a fine ending.

(Notes *re* local colour heaped on in shovelfuls: this chapter is a good example and every damn thing in it is organic. The madman futilely and endlessly throwing a bicycle tyre in front of him, the man stuck half way up the slippery pole — these are projections of the Consul and of the futility of his life, and at the same time are *right*, are *true*, are what one sees here. Life is a forest of symbols, as Baudelaire said, but I won't be told you can't see the wood for the trees here!)

8

Here the book, so to speak, goes into reverse — or, more strictly speaking, it begins to go downhill, though not, by any means, I hope, in the sense of deteriorating! Downhill (the first word), toward the abyss. I think it one of the better chapters; though it needs reading carefully, I feel the reader will be well rewarded. Man dying by the roadside with his horse branded No. 7 near is, of course, the chap who'd been sitting outside the pulquería in 4, had appeared singing in 7 when the Consul identified himself with him. He is, obviously, mankind himself, mankind dying — then, in the Battle of the Ebro, or now, in Europe, while we do nothing, or if we would, have put ourselves in a position where we *can* do nothing, but talk, while he goes on dying — in another sense he is the Consul too. I claim the chapter proceeds well on its own account while these meanings are revealed without being too much laboured. I think the meaning is obvious, intentionally so, almost, in a sense, like a cartoon, and on one plane as over-simplified as journalism, intentionally too, for it is through Hugh's eyes. The story on the top plane is being carried on normally however, and while the local political significance would be clear to anyone who knows Mexico, the wider political and religious significance must be self-evident to anyone. It was the first chapter written in the book; the incident by the roadside, based on a personal experience, was the germ of the book. I feel that some wag not too unlike your reader might tell me at this point that I would do better to reduce the book back to this original germ so that we could all have it printed in O'Brien's *Best Short Stories of 1946*, with luck, instead of as a novel, and against this resourceful notion I can only cite the example of Beethoven, who also was somewhat inclined to overspread himself I seem to think, even though most of his themes are actually so simple they could be played by just rolling an orange down the black keys. The chapter is more apropos now than then, in 1936: then there were no deputies — though I invented them in 1941: now there are; in fact one is living in an apartment downstairs. I don't think it can be cut: but if it must be, it should be done with the same reservations I have made elsewhere. As for the *xopilotes*, the vultures, I should add that they are more than merely cartoon birds: they are real in these parts, in fact one is looking at me as I write, none too pleasantly either: they fly through the whole book and in 11 become as it were archetypal, Promethean fowl. Once considered by ornithologists the first of birds, all I can say is that they are more than likely to be the last.

9

This chapter was originally written in 1937 but then it was through Hugh's eyes. Then it was rewritten as through the Consul's eyes. And now – as it must be for sake of balance, if you reflect – it is through Yvonne's eyes. Possibly it could have been seen just as well through the bull's eyes, but it reads very well aloud and I think is among other things a successful and colourful entity in itself and musically speaking ought to be an exceedingly good contrast to 8 and 10. Readers might disagree about flashbacks here – some think it good, others suspecting a belated attempt to draw character and at that a meretricious one – though I feel many of your *feminine* readers might approve. The flashbacks are not here though either for their own sake, or particularly for the sake of character, which as I said was my last consideration as it was Aristotle's – since there isn't *room*, for one thing. (It was, I think, one of your own writers, and a magnificent one, Sean O'Faolain, who put this heretical notion even further into my headpiece about the comparative unimportance of character anyway. Since he is a wonderful character drawer himself, his words bore weight with me. Were not Hamlet and Laertes, he says, at the final moment, almost the same person? The novel then, he went on to argue, should reform itself by drawing upon its ancient Aeschylean and tragic heritage. There are a thousand writers who can draw adequate characters till all is blue for one who can tell you anything new about hell fire. And I am telling you something new about hell fire. I see the pitfalls— it can be an easy way out of hard work, an invitation to eccentric word-spinning and laboured phantasmagorias, and subjective inferior masterpieces that on closer investigation turn out not even to be bona fide documents but like my own *Ultramarine*, to be apparently translated with a windmill out of the unoriginal Latvian, but just the same in our Elizabethan days we used to have at least passionate poetic writing about things that will always mean something and not just silly ass style and semicolon technique: and in this sense I am trying to remedy a deficiency, to strike a blow, to fire a shot for you as it were, roughly in the direction, say, of another Renaissance: it will probably go straight through my brain but that is another matter. Possibly too the Renaissance is already in full swing but if so I have heard nothing of this in Canada.) No, the real point of this chapter is Hope, with a capital H, for this note must be struck in order to stress the later downfall. Though even the capacity of the intelligent reader for suspending his disbelief is enormous I didn't intend that this feeling of hope should be experienced by the reader in quite the ordinary way, though he can if he wants to. I intended somehow the feeling of hope per se to transcend even one's interest in the characters. Since these characters are in one way 'Things', as that French philosopher of the absurd fellow has it, or even if you believe in them you know perfectly well that they are ditched anyhow, this hope should be, rather, a transcendent, a universal hope. The novel meanwhile is, as it were, teetering between past and future – between despair (the past) and hope – hence these flashbacks (some of them could doubtless be cut slightly but I don't think I could do it). Shall the Consul, once more, go forward and be reborn, as if previously to Guanajuato – is there a chance that he may be, at any rate on the top level? – or shall he sink back into degeneracy and Parián and extinction. He is one aspect of Everyman (just as Yvonne is so to speak the eternal woman, as in *Parsifal*, Kundry, whoever she was, angel and destroyer both). The other aspect of Everyman is

35

of course Hugh who all this time is somewhat preposterously subduing the bull: in short, though with intentional absurdity — the whole book for that matter can be seen as a kind of gruesome and serious absurdity, just like the world in fact — he conquers the animal forces of nature which the Consul later lets loose. The threads of the various themes of the book begin to be drawn together. The close of the chapter, with the Indian carrying his father, is a restatement and universalizing of the theme of humanity struggling on under the eternal tragic weight of the past. But it is also Freudian (man eternally carrying the psychological burden of his father), Sophoclean, Oedipean, what have you, which relates the Indian to the Consul again.

If cuts are made those things and the fact that it is a unity in itself, as usual, should be taken into account. It was finally completed as it stands in 1944.

10

This was first written in '36–'37 and rewritten at various periods up to 1943. This final version was written after my fire, in the summer and fall of 1944, and I dare say this is another obvious candidate for your surgeon's knife. Nothing I wrote after the fire save most of 11 has quite the integrity of what I wrote before it but though this chapter seems absolutely interminable, indeed intolerable, when read aloud, I submit it to be a considerable inspiration and one of the best of the lot. The opening train theme is related to Freudian death dreams and also to 'A corpse will be transported by express' of the beginning of 2 and I can't see that it is not extremely thrilling in its gruesome fashion. Passage that follows *re* the 'Virgin for those who have nobody with' ties up with opening pages of Chapter 1 and were written previously, as was the humorous menu section. I can see valid objections though to the great length of some of the Tlaxcala stuff from the folder: but I was absolutely unable to resist it. I cut and cut as it was, I even sacrificed two good points, namely that Tlaxcala is probably the only capital in the world where black magic is still a working proposition, and that it is also the easiest place in the world to get a divorce in, and then could cut no more: I thought it too good, while the constant repetition of churrigueresque 'of an overloaded style' seemed to be a suggestion that the book was satirizing itself. This Tlaxcala folder part has a quite different effect when read with the eyes, as it will be (I hope) — then you can of course get it much more swiftly; and I had originally thought it would possibly go quicker still if some experiment were made with the typesetting such as the occasional use of black letter for the headings juxtaposed with anything from cursive down to diamond type for the rest and back again according to the reader's interest or the Consul's state of delirium: some simplification of this suggestion might be extremely effective but I do not see how it can be very popular with you and is perhaps a little much anyway. At all events I believe there are strange evocations and explosions here that have merit in themselves even if you are not closely following what is happening, much as, even if you can't make out what Harpo is saying, the sound of the words themselves may be funny. Revelations such as that Pulquería, which is a kind of Mexican pub, is also the name of Raskolnikov's mother should doubtless not be taken too seriously, but the whole Tlaxcala business *does* have an underlying deep seriousness. Tlaxcala, of course, just like Parián, is death: but the Tlaxcalans were Mexico's traitors — here the Consul is giving way to the forces within him that are betraying himself, that indeed have now finally betrayed him, and the general plan of the whole phantasmagoric thing seems to me to be right. Dialogue here brings in the theme of war, which is of course related to the Consul's self-destruction. This chapter was finally completed about a year before atom bombs, etc. But if it does so happen that man is now in danger of finding himself in the evil position of the black magician of old who discovered suddenly that all the elements of the universe were against him, the old Consul might be given credit for pointing out as much in a crazy passage where he even names the elements uranium plutonium, and so forth; undoubtedly it is of no interest as prophecy any more, but I can't say it dates! This little bit is, of course, thematic, if you reflect. At the end of this chapter the volcanoes, which have been getting closer throughout, are used as a symbol of approaching war. In spite of its apparent chaos this chapter has been written very carefully and with attention to every word. It, too, is an entity in itself, and if it must be cut I ask that the cutter see it also as an entity and in its place in the book. Though I suggest it is dramatically extremely powerful, regarded in a certain light, I am more disposed to have this chapter and Chapter 6 cut than any other, if cuts there must be, and if in the case of this chapter it is merely rendered more dramatic and more powerful.

II

This was the last chapter I wrote and [it] was completed in late 1944, though I had had its conception in mind for a long time. My object was to pull out here all the stops of Nature, to go to town, as it were, on the natural elemental beauty of the world and the stars, and through the latter to relate the book, as it was related through the wheel at the end of Chapter 1, to eternity. Here the wheel appears in another guise, the wheel of the motion of the stars and constellations themselves through the universe. And here again appears the dark wood of Dante, this time as a real wood and not just a cantina or the name of one. Here again too appears the theme of the Day of the Dead, the scene in the cemetery balancing the scene of the mourners at the opening of the book, but this time it has tremendously more human emphasis. The chapter again acts as a double contrast to the lesser horrors of 10 and the worse ones of 12. On the surface Hugh and Yvonne are simply searching for the Consul, but such a search would have added meaning to anyone who knows anything of the Eleusinian mysteries, and the same esoteric idea of this kind of search also appears in Shakespeare's *Tempest*. Here however all the meanings

38

of the book have to be blended somehow in an unpretentious and organic manner in the interest of the tale itself and this was no mean task, especially as Yvonne had to be killed by a horse in a thunderstorm, and Hugh left holding a guitar in a dark wood, singing drunken songs of revolutionary Spain. Could Thomas Hardy do as much? I suspect your reader, who doesn't even mention the very important fact of Yvonne's death, of not reading this chapter at all — and I take this again as a compliment that he was too interested in what happened to the Consul to do more than glance at it. Be that as it may, I feel passionately that the chapter comes off, partly because I came to believe so absolutely in it. Actually someone being killed by a horse in a thunderstorm is nothing like so unusual an occurrence as you might suppose in these parts, where the paths in the forests are narrow and horses when they do get frightened become more wildly panic-stricken than did the ancestors of their riders who thought the horses Cortez sent against them were supernatural beings. I feel that this chapter like all the rest calls for a sympathetic rereading. It is quite short and I don't think can be cut at all and is *absolutely necessary*. Yvonne's dying visions hark back to her first thought at the beginning of Chapter 2 and also to Chapter 9, but the very end of the chapter has practically stepped outside the bounds of the book altogether. Yvonne imagines herself gathered up and swept up to the stars: a not dissimilar idea appears at the end of one of Julian Green's books, but my notion came obviously from *Faust*, where Marguerite is hauled up to heaven on pulleys, while the devil hauls Faust down to hell. Here Yvonne imagines herself voyaging straight up through the stars to the Pleiades, while the Consul is, simultaneously and incidentally, being cast straight down the abyss. The horse of course is the evil force that the Consul has released. But by this time you know the humbler aspect of this horse. It is no less than the horse you last heard of in 10 and that first appeard in 4, likewise riderless, during Hugh and Yvonne's ride, outside the pulquería La Sepultura.

(Note: Is it too much to say that all these chords, struck and resolved, while no reader can possibly apprehend them on first or even fourth reading, consciously, nevertheless vastly contribute *unconsciously* to the final weight of the book?)

12

This chapter was first written at the beginning of 1937 and I think is definitely the best of the lot. I have scarcely changed it since 1940— though I made some slight additions and subtractions in 1942 and substituted the passage 'How alike are the groans of love to the groans of the dying', etc., in 1944, for another one not so good. I do think it deserves more than rereading carefully and that it is not only not fair to say it merely recalls *The Lost Weekend* but ridiculous. In any event, I believe, it goes even on the superficial plane a good deal further than that in terms of human agony, and, as his book does, it can widen, I think, one's knowledge of hell. In fact the feeling you are supposed to get from this chapter is an almost Biblical one. Hasn't the guy had enough suffering? Surely we've reached the end now. But no. Apparently it's only just starting. All the strands of the book, political, esoteric, tragic, comical, religious, and what not are here gathered together and in the Farolito in Parián we are standing amid the confusion of tongues of Biblical prophecy. Parián, as I have said, has represented death all along, but this, I would like the reader to feel, is far worse than that. This chapter is the easterly tower, Chapter 1 being the westerly, at each end of my churrigueresque Mexican cathedral, and all the gargoyles of the latter are repeated with interest in this. While the doleful bells of one echo the doleful bells of the other, just as the hopeless letters of Yvonne the Consul finally finds here answer the hopeless letter of the Consul M. Laruelle reads precisely a year later in Chapter 1. Possibly you did not find much to criticize in this chapter but I believe it will immeasurably improve when the whole is taken into account. The slightly ridiculous horse that the Consul releases which kills

40

Yvonne is of course the destructive force we have heard of before, some fifteen times, I am afraid, in this letter and suggested first in 1, and which his own final absorption by the powers of evil releases. There was a half-humorous foreshadowing of his action in 7, in terms of a quotation from Goethe, when Laruelle and he were passed by the horse and its rider, who waved at them and rode off singing. There still remain passages of humour in this chapter and they are necessary because after all we are expected to believe and not believe and then again to believe: the humour is a kind of bridge between the naturalistic and the transcendental and then back to the naturalistic again, though that humour I feel always remains true to the special reality created by the chapter itself. I am so inordinately proud of this chapter that you will be surprised when I say that I think it possible that it too can be cut here and there, though the deadly flat tempo of the beginning seems to me essential and important. I don't think the chapter's final effect should be depressing: I feel you should most definitely get your katharsis, while there is even a hint of redemption for the poor old Consul at the end, who realizes that he is after all part of humanity: and indeed, as I have said before, what profundity and final meaning there is in his fate should be seen also in its universal relationship to the ultimate fate of mankind.

> You like this garden?
> Why is it yours?
> We evict those who destroy!

Reading all this over I am struck among other things such as that writers can always grow fancy and learned about their books and say almost anything at all, as Sherwood Anderson once said in another context, by how much stress is laid on the esoteric element. This does not of course matter two hoots in a hollow if the whole thing is not good art, and to make it such was the whole of my labour. The esoteric business was only a deep-laid anchor anyway but I think I may be forgiven for bringing it in evidence since your reader never saw that the book had any such significance at all. That is right too; I don't care whether the reader does or doesn't see it, but the meaning is there just the same and I might have stressed another element of the book just as well. For they are all involved with each other and their fusion is the book. I believe it more than comes off, on the whole, and because of this belief I am asking you for this re-evaluation of it as it was conceived and upon its own terms. Though I would be grievously disappointed were you not to publish it I can scarcely do otherwise than this, believing as I do that the things that stand in the way of its appreciation are largely superficial. On the other hand I am extremely sensible of the honour you do me by considering it and I do not wish to be vain or stubborn about cuts, even large ones, where a more piercing and maturer eye than mine can see the advantage to the *whole*, the wound being drawn together. I can hope only that I have made some case for a further look at the thing being worth while. Whether it sells or not seems to me either way a risk. But there is something about the destiny of the creation of the book that seems to tell me it just might go *on* selling a very long time. Whether this is the same kind of delusion, at best, that beset another of your authors, Herman Melville, when he wrote such berserk pieces as *Pierre* remains to be seen, but certain it is in that case that no major alterations could have altered its destiny, prevented its plates from being burned, or its author from becoming a customs inspector. I was reading somewhere of that internal basic use of time which makes or breaks a motion picture, and which is the work of the director or cutter. It depends on the speed at which one scene moves and on the amount of footage devoted to another: and it depends also on what sequences are placed between others, because the way movies are made allows you to shift whole sequences about. I believe that the reader whose report you sent me was at least impressed to the extent that he read the book creatively, but too much so, as if he were already a director and cutter combined of some *potential* work, without stopping to ask himself how far it had already been directed and cut, and what internal basic use of time, and so on, was making him as interested as he was.

But what, I repeat, of the reaction of your first reader? There is a certain disparity in tone between your letters of October 15 (received in Canada Nov. 2) and that of 29th Nov. (received here in Mexico Dec. 31) i.e., in your first one you do not mention any criticisms but simply say that your reader was greatly impressed and that it was a long time since you had begun to read a book with such hope and expectation as in reading *Under the Volcano* and seizing, perhaps too hastily, on this, I can deduce only that your first reader was tremendously more sympathetic towards it??? You also said, 'I will send you a cable when I have finished reading it so it is possible you may get a cable before receiving this letter.' Of course I now see why you found this extremely difficult or impossible but at that time I waited and waited in vain for that cable as you can only wait in winter in the Canadian Wilderness, unless it is in Reckmondwike, Yorks. When therefore I received your letter of 29th Nov. here on New Year's Eve, with your second reader's report, it produced, together with the sense of triumph, one of those barranca-like drops in spirits peculiar to authors and it is to this I must attribute the time I've taken to reply. Talk about turning the accomplishment of many years into an hour glass — but I never heard of it being turned into a mescal glass before, and a small one at that! However after puzzling my brains, I decided that however your own feelings might lean x-ward or y-ward of the crystallization of reaction, you were putting me, as you had every right to do, on the spot. In short, you were saying: 'If this book is any damn good as it is he'll explain why!' I was being invited, I thought, if necessary, to do battle. So here is the battle. For taking such a long time about it I sincerely apologize but it has been a difficult letter to write.

I have now received your second letter with a copy of the report and I thank you for this. On your twenty-fifth anniversary I heartily congratulate you. It seems to me that among other things your firm has done more international good than any other. For myself, my first school prize was *The Hairy Ape*, ourselves being allowed to choose our own prizes when they were books, so with your volume of O'Neill's plays containing *The Hairy Ape*, complete with Latin inscription inside, I was therefore presented by the Headmaster on Prize Day. Those O'Neill volumes with the labels, I guess, sent me to sea and everywhere else, but also for the Melville volumes, the O'Brien books, Hugh I'Anson Fausset, and among lesser known things the strange Leo Steni novels, and Calder-Marshall's *About Levy*, for these and hundreds of other things besides I am eternally grateful. When I was looking in '28 or '29 for some work in England by the American Conrad Aiken sure enough I found *Costumes by Eros* published by your firm and this led to a lasting and valuable friendship. (I believe him indisputably one of the world's nine or ten greatest living writers and I mention in passing that ⅔ of his stuff has never had a fair hearing in England and is probably just lying around somewhere. I believe him to be living now at his old English home again at Jeakes House, Rye, Sussex.) All this by the way.

I have spoken of thinking of the book as like some Mexican churrigueresque cathedral: but that is probably just confusing, the more especially since I have been quoting Aristotle at you, and the book has in its odd way a severe classical pattern – you can even see the German submarine officers taking revenge on the Consul in the form of the *sinarquistas* and semi-facist *brutos* at the end, as I said before. No – please put all that down to the local tropic fever which just recently has been sending my temperature up too far. No. The book should be seen as essentially *trochal*, I repeat, the form of it as a wheel so that, when you get to the end, if you have read carefully, you should want to turn back to the beginning again, where it is not impossible, too, that your eye might alight once more upon Sophocles' *Wonders are many, and none is more wonderful than man* – just to cheer you up. For the book was so designed, counterdesigned and interwelded that it could be read an indefinite number of times and still not have yielded all its meanings or its drama or its poetry: and it is upon this fact that I base my hope in it, and in that hope that, with all its faults, and now with all the redundancies of my letter, I have offered it to you.

Yours very sincerely,
Malcolm Lowry

WONDERS are many, and none is more wonderful than man; the power that crosses the white sea, driven by the stormy south wind, making a path under surges that threaten to engulf him; and Earth, the eldest of the gods, the immortal, unwearied, doth he wear, turning the soil with the offspring of horses, as the ploughs go to and fro from year to year.

And the light-hearted race of birds, and the tribes of savage beasts, and the sea-brood of the deep, he snares in the meshes of his woven toils, he leads captive, man excellent in wit. And he masters by his arts the beast whose lair is in the wilds, who roams the hills; he tames the horse of shaggy mane, he puts the yoke upon its neck, he tames the tireless mountain bull.

And speech, and wind-swift thought, and all the moods that mould a state, hath he taught himself; and how to flee the arrows of the frost, when it is hard lodging under the clear sky, and the arrows of the rushing rain; yea, he hath resource for all; without resource he meets nothing that must come; only against Death shall he call for aid in vain; but from baffling maladies he hath devised escape.

SOPHOCLES – *Antigone*

Now I blessed the condition of the dog and toad, yea, gladly would I have been in the condition of the dog or horse, for I knew they had no soul to perish under the everlasting weight of Hell or Sin, as mine was like to do. Nay, and though I saw this, felt this, and was broken to pieces with it, yet that which added to my sorrow was, that I could not find with all my soul that I did desire deliverance.

JOHN BUNYAN – *Grace Abounding for the Chief of Sinners*

WER immer strebend sich bemüht, den können wir erlösen.
Whosoever unceasingly strives upward ... him can we save.

GOETHE

I

Two mountain chains traverse the republic roughly from north to south, forming between them a number of valleys and plateaux. Overlooking one of these valleys, which is dominated by two volcanoes, lies, six thousand feet above sea-level, the town of Quauhnahuac. It is situated well south of the Tropic of Cancer, to be exact, on the nineteenth parallel, in about the same latitude as the Revillagigedo Islands to the west in the Pacific, or very much farther west, the southernmost tip of Hawaii – and as the port of Tzucox to the east on the Atlantic seaboard of Yucatan near the border of British Honduras, or very much farther east, the town of Juggernaut, in India, on the Bay of Bengal.

The walls of the town, which is built on a hill, are high, the streets and lanes tortuous and broken, the roads winding. A fine American-style highway leads in from the north but is lost in its narrow streets and comes out a goat track. Quauhnahuac possesses eighteen churches and fifty-seven *cantinas*. It also boasts a golf course and no fewer than four hundred swimming-pools, public and private, filled with the water that ceaselessly pours down from the mountains, and many splendid hotels.

The Hotel Casino de la Selva stands on a slightly higher hill just outside the town, near the railway station. It is built far back from the main highway and surrounded by gardens and terraces which command a spacious view in every direction. Palatial, a certain air of desolate splendour pervades it. For it is no longer a Casino. You may not even dice for drinks in the bar. The ghosts of ruined gamblers haunt it. No one ever seems to swim in the magnificent Olympic pool. The springboards stand empty and mournful. Its jai-alai courts are grass-grown and deserted. Two tennis courts only are kept up in the season.

Towards sunset on the Day of the Dead in November 1939, two men in white flannels sat on the main terrace of the Casino drinking *anís*. They had been playing tennis, followed by billiards, and their rackets, rainproofed, screwed in their presses – the doctor's triangular, the other's quadrangular – lay on the parapet before them. As the processions winding from the cemetery down the hillside behind the hotel came closer the plangent sounds of their chanting were borne to the two men; they turned to watch the mourners, a little later to be visible only as the melancholy lights of their candles, circling among the distant trussed cornstalks. Dr Arturo Díaz Vigil pushed the bottle of Anís del Mono over to M. Jacques Laruelle, who now was leaning forward intently.

Slightly to the right and below them, below the gigantic red evening, whose reflection bled away in the deserted swimming pools scattered everywhere like so many mirages, lay the peace and sweetness of the town. It seemed peaceful enough from where they were sitting. Only if one listened intently, as M. Laruelle was doing now, could one distinguish a remote confused sound – distinct yet somehow inseparable from the minute murmuring, the tintinnabulation of the mourners – as of singing, rising and falling, and a steady trampling – the bangs and cries of the *fiesta* that had been going on all day.

M. Laruelle poured himself another *anís*. He was drinking *anís* because it reminded him of absinthe. A deep flush had suffused his face, and his hand trembled slightly over the bottle, from whose label a florid demon brandished a pitchfork at him.

' – I meant to persuade him to go away and get *déalcoholisé*,' Dr Vigil was saying. He stumbled over the word in French and continued in English. 'But I was so sick myself that day after the ball that I suffer, physical, really. That is very bad, for we doctors must comport ourselves like apostles. You remember, we played tennis that day too. Well, after I lookèd the Consul in his garden I sended a boy down to see if he would come for a few minutes and knock my door, I would appreciate it to him, if not, please write me a note, if drinking have not killèd him already.'

M. Laruelle smiled.

'But they have gone,' the other went on, 'and yes, I think to ask you too that day if you had lookèd him at his house.'

'He was at my house when you telephoned, Arturo.'

'Oh, I know, but we got so horrible drunkness that night before, so *perfecta*mente *borracho*, that it seems to me, the Consul is as sick as I am.' Dr Vigil shook his head. 'Sickness is not only in body, but in that part used to be call : soul. Poor your friend he spend his money on earth in such continuous tragedies.'

M. Laruelle finished his drink. He rose and went to the parapet; resting his hands one on each tennis racket, he gazed down and around him : the abandoned jai-alai courts, their bastions covered with grass, the dead tennis courts, the fountain, quite near in the centre of the hotel avenue, where a cactus farmer had reined up his horse to drink. Two young Americans, a boy and a girl, had started a belated game of ping-pong on the veranda of the annex below. What had happened just a year ago today seemed already to belong in a different age. One would have thought the horrors of the present would have swallowed it up like a drop of water. It was not so. Though tragedy was in the process of becoming unreal and meaningless it seemed one was still permitted to remember the days when an individual life held some value and was not a mere misprint in a communiqué. He lit a cigarette. Far to his left, in the northeast, beyond the valley and the terraced foothills of the Sierra Madre Oriental, the two volcanoes, Popocatepetl and Ixtaccihuatl, rose clear and magnificent into the sunset. Nearer, perhaps ten miles distant, and on a lower level than the main valley, he made out the village of Tomalín, nestling behind the jungle, from which rose a thin blue scarf of illegal smoke, someone burning wood for carbon. Before him, on the other side of the American highway, spread fields and groves, through which meandered a river, and the Alcapancingo road. The watchtower of a prison rose over a wood between the river and the road which lost itself farther on where the purple hills of a Doré Paradise sloped away into the distance. Over in the town the lights of Quauhnahuac's one cinema, built on an incline and standing out sharply, suddenly came on, flickered off, came on again. '*No se puede vivir sin amar*,' M. Laruelle said ... 'As that *estúpido* inscribed on my house.'

'Come, *amigo*, throw away your mind,' Dr Vigil said behind him.

' – But *hombre*, Yvonne came back! That's what I shall never understand. She came back to the man!' M. Laruelle returned to the table where he poured himself and drank a glass of Tehuacan mineral water. He said:

'*Salud y pesetas.*'

'*Y tiempo para gastarlas*,' his friend returned thoughtfully.

M. Laruelle watched the doctor leaning back in the steamer chair, yawning, the handsome, impossibly handsome, dark imperturbable Mexican face, the kind deep brown eyes, innocent too, like the eyes of those wistful beautiful Oaxaqueñan children one saw in Tehuantepec (that ideal spot where the women did the work while the men bathed in the river all day), the slender small hands and delicate wrists, upon the back of which it was almost a shock to see the sprinkling of coarse black hair. 'I threw away my mind long ago, Arturo,' he said in English, withdrawing his cigarette from his mouth with refined nervous fingers on which he was aware he wore too many rings. 'What I find more – ' M. Laruelle noted the cigarette was out and gave himself another *anís*.

'*Con permiso.*' Dr Vigil conjured a flaring lighter out of his pocket so swiftly it seemed it must have been already ignited there, that he had drawn a flame out of himself, the gesture and the igniting one movement; he held the light for M. Laruelle. 'Did you never go to the church for the bereavèd here,' he asked suddenly, 'where is the Virgin for those who have nobody with?'

M. Laruelle shook his head.

'Nobody go there. Only those who have nobody them with,' the doctor said, slowly. He pocketed the lighter and looked at his watch, turning his wrist upwards with a neat flick. '*Allons-nous-en*,' he added, '*vámonos*,' and laughed yawningly with a series of nods that seemed to carry his body forward until his head was resting between his hands. Then he rose and joined M. Laruelle at the parapet, drawing deep breaths. 'Ah, but this is the hour I love, with the sun coming down, when all the man began to sing and all the dogs to shark – '

M. Laruelle laughed. While they had been talking the sky had grown wild and stormy to the south; the mourners had left the slope of the hill. Sleepy vultures, high overhead, deployed down-wind. 'About eight-thirty then, I might go to the *cine* for an hour.'

'*Bueno*. I will see you this night then, in the place where you know. Remember, I still do not believe you are leaving tomorrow.' He held out his hand which M. Laruelle grasped firmly, loving him. 'Try and come tonight, if not, please understand I am always interested in your health.'

'*Hasta la vista.*'

'*Hasta la vista.*'

– Alone, standing beside the highway down which he had driven four years before on the last mile of that long, insane, beautiful journey from Los Angeles, M. Laruelle also found it hard to believe he was really going. Then the thought of to-morrow seemed well-nigh overwhelming. He had paused, un-decided which way to walk home, as the little overloaded bus – *Tomalín Zócalo* – jounced past him downhill towards the *barranca* before climbing into Quauhnahuac. He was loth to take the same direction tonight. He crossed the street, making for the station. Although he would not be travelling by train the sense of departure, of its imminence, came heavily about him again as, childishly avoiding the locked points, he picked his path over the narrow-gauge lines. Light from the setting sun glanced off the oil tanks on the grass embankment beyond. The platform slept. The tracks were vacant, the signals up. There was little to suggest that any train ever arrived at this station, let alone left it :

QUAUHNAHUAC

Yet a little less than a year ago the place had been the scene of a parting he would never forget. He had not liked the Consul's half-brother at their first encounter when he'd come with Yvonne and the Consul himself to M. Laruelle's house in the Calle Nicaragua, any more, he felt now, than Hugh had liked

53

him. Hugh's odd appearance – though such was the over-whelming effect of meeting Yvonne again, he did not obtain even the impression of oddity so strongly that he was able later in Parián immediately to recognize him – had merely seemed to caricature the Consul's amiable half-bitter description of him. So this was the child M. Laruelle vaguely remembered hearing about years before! In half an hour he'd dismissed him as an irresponsible bore, a professional indoor Marxman, vain and self-conscious really, but affecting a romantic extroverted air. While Hugh, who for various reasons had certainly not been 'prepared' by the Consul to meet M. Laruelle, doubtless saw him as an even more precious type of bore, the elderly aesthete, a confirmedly promiscuous bachelor, with a rather unctuous possessive manner towards women. But three sleepless nights later an eternity had been lived through: grief and bewilder-ment at an unassimilable catastrophe had drawn them together. In the hours which followed his response to Hugh's telephone call from Parián M. Laruelle learned much about Hugh: his hopes, his fears, his self-deceptions, his despairs. When Hugh left, it was as if he had lost a son.

Careless of his tennis clothes, M. Laruelle climbed the em-bankment. Yet he was right, he told himself, as reaching the top he paused for breath, right, after the Consul had been 'dis-covered' (though meantime the grotesquely pathetic situation had developed where there was not, on probably the first occa-sion when one had been so urgently needed, a British Consul in Quauhnahuac to appeal to), right in insisting Hugh should waive all conventional scruples and take every advantage of the curious reluctance of the 'police' to hold him – their anxiety, it all but appeared, to be rid of him just when it seemed highly logical they should detain him as a witness, at least in one as-pect of what now at a distance one could almost refer to as the 'case' – and at the earliest possible moment join that ship pro-videntially awaiting him at Vera Cruz. M. Laruelle looked back at the station; Hugh left a gap. In a sense he had decamped with the last of his illusions. For Hugh, at twenty-nine, still dreamed, even then, of changing the world (there was no other way of saying this) through his actions – just as Laruelle, at forty-two, had still then not quite given up hope of changing it through the great films he proposed somehow to make. But today these dreams seemed absurd and presumptuous. After all he had made great films as great films went in the past. And so far as he knew they had not changed the world in the slightest. However he had acquired a certain identity with Hugh. Like Hugh he was going to Vera Cruz; and like Hugh too, he did not know if his ship would ever reach port ...

M. Laruelle's way led through half-cultivated fields bordered by narrow grass paths, trodden by cactus farmers coming home from work. It was thus far a favourite walk, though not taken since before the rains. The leaves of cacti attracted with their freshness; green trees shot by evening sunlight might have been weeping willows tossing in the gusty wind which had sprung up; a lake of yellow sunlight appeared in the distance below pretty hills like loaves. But there was something baleful now about the evening. Black clouds plunged up to the south. The sun poured molten glass on the fields. The volcanoes seemed terrifying in the wild sunset. M. Laruelle walked swiftly, in the good heavy tennis shoes he should have already packed, swinging his tennis racket. A sense of fear had possessed him again, a sense of being, after all these years, and on his last day here, still a stranger. Four years, almost five, and he still felt like a wanderer on another planet. Not that that made it any the less hard to be leaving, even though he would soon, God willing, see Paris again. Ah well! He had few emotions about the war, save that it was bad. One side or the other would win. And in either case life would be hard. Though if the Allies lost it would be harder. And in either case one's own battle would go on.

How continually, how startlingly, the landscape changed! Now the fields were full of stones: there was a row of dead trees. An abandoned plough, silhouetted against the sky, raised its arms to heaven in mute supplication; another planet, he reflected again, a strange planet where, if you looked a little farther, beyond the Tres Marías, you would find every sort of landscape at once, the Cotswolds, Windermere, New Hampshire, the meadows of the Eure-et-Loire, even the grey dunes of

Cheshire, even the Sahara, a planet upon which, in the twinkling of an eye, you could change climates, and, if you cared to think so, in the crossing of a highway, three civilizations; but beautiful, there was no denying its beauty, fatal or cleansing as it happened to be, the beauty of the Earthly Paradise itself.

Yet in the Earthly Paradise, what had he done? He had made few friends. He had acquired a Mexican mistress with whom he quarrelled, and numerous beautiful Mayan idols he would be unable to take out of the country, and he had –

M. Laruelle wondered if it was going to rain: it sometimes, though rarely, did at this time of year, as last year for instance, it rained when it should not. And those were storm clouds in the south. He imagined he could smell the rain, and it ran in his head he would enjoy nothing better than to get wet, soaked through to the skin, to walk on and on through this wild country in his clinging white flannels getting wetter and wetter and wetter. He watched the clouds: dark swift horses surging up the sky. A black storm breaking out of its season! That was what love was like, he thought; love which came too late. Only no sane calm succeeded it, as when the evening fragrance or slow sunlight and warmth returned to the surprised land! M. Laruelle hastened his steps still farther. And let such love strike you dumb, blind, mad, dead – your fate would not be altered by your simile. *Tonnerre de dieu* ... It slaked no thirst to say what love was like which came too late.

The town was almost directly to his right now and above him, for M. Laruelle had been walking gradually downhill since leaving the Casino de la Selva. From the field he was crossing he could see, over the trees on the slope of the hill, and beyond the dark castled shape of Cortez Palace, the slowly revolving Ferris wheel, already lit up, in the square of Quauhnahuac; he thought he could distinguish the sound of human laughter rising from its bright gondolas and, again, that faint intoxication of voices singing, diminishing, dying in the wind, inaudible finally. A despondent American tune, the *St Louis Blues*, or some such, was borne across the fields to him, at times a soft wind-blown surge of music from which skimmed a spray of gabbling, that seemed not so much to break against as to be thumping the walls and towers of the outskirts; then with a moan it would be sucked back into the distance. He found himself in the lane that led away through the brewery to the Tomalín road. He came to the Alcapancingo road. A car was passing and as he waited, face averted, for the dust to subside, he recalled that time motoring with Yvonne and the Consul along the Mexican lake-bed, itself once the crater of a huge volcano, and saw again the horizon softened by dust, the buses whizzing past through the whirling dust, the shuddering boys standing on the backs of the lorries holding on for grim death, their faces bandaged against the dust (and there was a magnificence about this, he always felt, some symbolism for the future, for which such truly great preparation had been made by a heroic people, since all over Mexico one could see those thundering lorries with those young builders in them, standing erect, their trousers flapping hard, legs planted wide, firm) and in the sunlight, on the round hill, the lone section of dust advancing, the dust-darkened hills by the lake like islands in driving rain. The Consul, whose old house M. Laruelle now made out on the slope beyond the *barranca*, had seemed happy enough too then, wandering around Cholula with its three hundred and six churches and its two barber shops, the 'Toilet' and the 'Harem', and climbing the ruined pyramid later, which he had proudly insisted was the original Tower of Babel. How admirably he had concealed what must have been the babel of his thoughts !

Two ragged Indians were approaching M. Laruelle through the dust; they were arguing, but with the profound concentration of university professors wandering in summer twilight through the Sorbonne. Their voices, the gestures of their refined grimy hands, were unbelievably courtly, delicate. Their carriage suggested the majesty of Aztec princes, their faces obscure sculpturings on Yucatecan ruins :

' – *perfectamente borracho* –
' – *completamente fantástico* –'
'*Sí, hombre, la vida impersonal* –'
'*Claro, hombre* –'
'*¡Positivamente!*'

57

'Buenas noches.'
'Buenas noches.'

They passed into the dusk. The Ferris wheel sank from sight: the sounds of the fair, the music, instead of coming closer, had temporarily ceased. M. Laruelle looked into the west; a knight of old, with tennis racket for shield and pocket torch for scrip, he dreamed a moment of battles the soul survived to wander there. He had intended turning down another lane to the right, that led past the model farm where the Casino de la Selva grazed its horses, directly into his street, the Calle Nicaragua. But on a sudden impulse he turned left along the road running by the prison. He felt an obscure desire on his last night to bid farewell to the ruin of Maximilian's Palace.

To the south an immense archangel, black as thunder, beat up from the Pacific. And yet, after all, the storm contained its own secret calm ... His passion for Yvonne (whether or not she'd ever been much good as an actress was beside the point, he'd told her the truth when he said she would have been more than good in any film he made) had brought back to his heart, in a way he could not have explained, the first time that alone, walking over the meadows from Saint Près, the sleepy French village of backwaters and locks and grey disused watermills where he was lodging, he had seen, rising slowly and wonderfully and with boundless beauty above the stubble fields blowing with wildflowers, slowly rising into the sunlight, as centuries before the pilgrims straying over those same fields had watched them rise, the twin spires of Chartres Cathedral. His love had brought a peace, for all too short a while, that was strangely like the enchantment, the spell, of Chartres itself, long ago, whose every side-street he had come to love and café where he could gaze at the Cathedral eternally sailing against the clouds, the spell not even the fact he was scandalously in debt there could break. M. Laruelle walked on swiftly towards the Palace. Nor had any remorse for the Consul's plight broken that other spell fifteen years later here in Quauhnahuac! for that matter, M. Laruelle reflected, what had reunited the Consul and himself for a time, even after Yvonne left, was not, on either side, remorse. It was perhaps, partly, more the desire for that illusory comfort, about as satisfying as biting on an aching tooth, to be derived from the mutual unspoken pretence that Yvonne was still here.

– Ah, but all these things might have seemed a good enough reason for putting the whole earth between themselves and Quauhnahuac! Yet neither had done so. And now M. Laruelle could feel their burden pressing upon him from outside, as if somehow it had been transferred to these purple mountains all around him, so mysterious, with their secret mines of silver, so withdrawn, yet so close, so still, and from these mountains emanated a strange melancholy force that tried to hold him here bodily, which was its weight, the weight of many things, but mostly that of sorrow.

He passed a field where a faded blue Ford, a total wreck, had been pushed beneath a hedge on a slope : two bricks had been set under its front wheels against involuntary departure. What are you waiting for, he wanted to ask it, feeling a sort of kinship, an empathy, for those tatters of ancient hood flapping ... *Darling, why did I leave? Why did you let me?* It was not to M. Laruelle that these words on that long-belated postcard of Yvonne's had been addressed, that postcard which the Consul must have maliciously put under his pillow some time on that last morning – but how could one ever be sure when? – as though the Consul had calculated it all, *knowing* M. Laruelle would discover it at the precise moment that Hugh, distraughtly, would call from Parián. Parián! To his right towered the prison walls. Up on the watchtower, just visible above them, two policemen peered east and west with binoculars. M. Laruelle crossed a bridge over the river, then took a short cut through a wide clearing in the woods evidently being laid out as a botanical garden. Birds came swarming out of the southeast : small, black, ugly birds, yet too long, something like monstrous insects, something like crows, with awkward long tails, and an undulating, bouncing, laboured flight. Shatterers of the twilight hour, they were flapping their way feverishly home, as they did every evening, to roost within the fresno trees in the *zócalo*, which until nightfall would ring with their incessant drilling mechanic screech. Straggling, the obscene

59

concourse hushed and peddled by. By the time he reached the Palace the sun had set.

In spite of his *amour propre* he immediately regretted having come. The broken pink pillars, in the half-light, might have been waiting to fall down on him : the pool, covered with green scum, its steps torn away and hanging by one rotting clamp, to close over his head. The shattered evil-smelling chapel, over-grown with weeds, the crumbling walls, splashed with urine, on which scorpions lurked – wrecked entablature, sad archivolt, slippery stones covered with excreta – this place, where love had once brooded, seemed part of a nightmare. And Laruelle was tired of nightmares. France, even in Austrian guise, should not transfer itself to Mexico, he thought. Maximilian had been un-lucky in his palaces too, poor devil. Why did they have to call that other fatal palace in Trieste also the Miramar, where Car-lotta went insane, and everyone who ever lived there from the Empress Elizabeth of Austria to the Archduke Ferdinand had met with a violent death? And yet, how they must have loved this land, these two lonely empurpled exiles, human beings finally, lovers out of their element – their Eden, without either knowing quite why, beginning to turn under their noses into a prison and smell like a brewery, their only majesty at last that of tragedy. Ghosts. Ghosts, as at the Casino, certainly lived here. And a ghost who still said : 'It is our destiny to come here, Carlotta. Look at this rolling glorious country, its hills, its valleys, its volcanoes beautiful beyond belief. And to think that it is ours ! Let us be good and constructive and make ourselves worthy of it !' Or there were ghosts quarrelling : 'No, you loved yourself, you loved your misery more than I. You did this deliberately to us.' 'I ?' 'You always had people to look after you, to love you, to use you, to lead you. You listened to every-one save me, who really loved you.' 'No, you're the only person I've ever loved.' 'Ever? You loved only yourself.' 'No, it was you, always you, you must believe me, please : you must re-member how we were always planning to go to Mexico. Do you remember? ... Yes, you are right. I had my chance with you. Never a chance like that again !' And suddenly they were weeping together, passionately, as they stood.

But it was the Consul's voice, not Maximilian's, M. Laruelle could almost have heard in the Palace: and he remembered as he walked on, thankful he had finally struck the Calle Nicaragua even at its farthest end, the day he'd stumbled upon the Consul and Yvonne embracing there; it was not very long after their arrival in Mexico and how different the Palace had seemed to him then! M. Laruelle slackened his pace. The wind had dropped. He opened his English tweed coat (bought however from High Life, pronounced Eetchleef, Mexico City) and loosened his blue polka-dotted scarf. The evening was unusually oppressive. And how silent. Not a sound, not a cry reached his ears now. Nothing but the clumsy suction of his footsteps ... Not a soul in sight. M. Laruelle felt slightly chafed too, his trousers bound him. He was getting too fat, had already got too fat in Mexico, which suggested another odd reason some people might have for taking up arms, that would never find its way into the newspapers. Absurdly, he swung his tennis racket in the air, through the motions of a serve, a return: but it was too heavy, he had forgotten about the press. He passed the model farm on his right, the buildings, the fields, the hills shadowy now in the swiftly gathering gloom. The Ferris wheel came into view again, just the top, silently burning high on the hill, almost directly in front of him, then the trees rose up over it. The road, which was terrible and full of pot-holes, went steeply downhill here; he was approaching the little bridge over the *barranca*, the deep ravine. Half-way across the bridge he stopped; he lit a new cigarette from the one he'd been smoking, and leaned over the parapet, looking down. It was too dark to see the bottom, but: here was finality indeed, and cleavage! Quauhnahuac was like the times in this respect, wherever you turned the abyss was waiting for you round the corner. Dormitory for vultures and city Moloch! When Christ was being crucified, so ran the sea-borne, hieratic legend, the earth had opened all through this country, though the coincidence could hardly have impressed anyone then! It was on this bridge the Consul had once suggested to him he make a film about Atlantis. Yes, leaning over just like this, drunk but collected, coherent, a little mad, a little impatient – it was one of those occasions when the Consul had drunk himself sober – he had spoken to him about the spirit of the abyss, the god of storm, *'huracán'*, that 'testified so suggestively to intercourse between opposite sides of the Atlantic'. Whatever he had meant.

Though it was not the first occasion the Consul and he had stood looking into an abyss. For there had always been, ages ago – and how could one now forget it? – the 'Hell Bunker': and that other encounter there which seemed to bear some obscure relation to the later one in Maximilian's Palace ... Had his discovery of the Consul here in Quauhnahuac really been so extraordinary, the discovery that his old English playmate – he could scarcely call him 'schoolmate' – whom he hadn't seen for nearly a quarter of a century was actually living in his street, and had been, without his knowledge, for six weeks? Probably not; probably it was just one of those meaningless correspondences that might be labelled : 'favourite trick of the gods'. But how vividly, again, that old seaside holiday in England came back to him!

– M. Laruelle, who had been born in Languion, in the Moselle country, but whose father, a rich philatelist of remote habits, had moved to Paris, usually spent his summer holidays as a boy with his parents in Normandy. Courseulles, in Calvados, on the English Channel, was not a fashionable resort. Far from it. There were a few windy battered pensions, miles of desolate sand-dunes, and the sea was cold. But it was to Courseulles, nevertheless, in the sweltering summer of 1911, that the family of the famous English poet, Abraham Taskerson, had come, bringing with them the strange little Anglo-Indian orphan, a broody creature of fifteen, so shy and yet so curiously self-contained, who wrote poetry that old Taskerson (who'd stayed at home) apparently encouraged him with, and who sometimes burst out crying if you mentioned in his presence the word 'father' or 'mother'. Jacques, about the same age, had felt oddly attracted to him : and since the other Taskerson boys – at least six, mostly older and, it would appear, all of a tougher breed, though they were in fact collateral relatives of young Geoffrey Firmin – tended to band together and leave the lad alone, he saw a great deal of him. They wandered together along the shore with a couple of old 'cleeks' brought from England and some wretched gutta-percha golf balls, to be driven on their last afternoon gloriously into the sea. 'Joffrey' became 'The Old Bean'. Laruelle *mère*, to whom, however, he was 'that beautiful English young poet', liked him too. Taskerson *mère* had taken a fancy to the French boy: the upshot was Jacques was asked to spend September in England with the Taskersons, where Geoffrey would be staying till the commencement of his school term. Jacques's father, who planned sending him to an English school till he was eighteen, consented. Particularly he admired the erect manly carriage of the Taskersons ... And that was how M. Laruelle came to Leasowe.

It was a kind of grown-up, civilized version of Courseulles on the English north-west coast. The Taskersons lived in a comfortable house whose back garden abutted on a beautiful, undulating golf course bounded on the far side by the sea. It looked like the sea; actually it was the estuary, seven miles wide, of a river: white horses westward marked where the real sea began. The Welsh mountains, gaunt and black and cloudy, with occasionally a snow peak to remind Geoff of India, lay across the river. During the week, when they were allowed to play, the course was deserted: yellow ragged sea poppies fluttered in the spiny sea grass. On the shore were the remains of an antediluvian forest with ugly black stumps showing, and farther up an old stubby deserted lighthouse. There was an island in the estuary, with a windmill on it like a curious black flower, which you could ride out to at low tide on a donkey. The smoke of freighters outward bound from Liverpool hung low on the horizon. There was a feeling of space and emptiness. Only at week-ends did a certain disadvantage appear in their site: although the season was drawing to a close and the grey hydropathic hotels along the promenades were emptying, the golf course was packed all day with Liverpool brokers playing foursomes. From Saturday morning till Sunday night a continuous hail of golf balls flying out of bounds bombarded the roof. Then it was a pleasure to go out with Geoffrey into the town, which was still full of laughing pretty girls, and walk through the sunlit windy streets or to look at one of the comical

Pierrot shows on the beach. Or best of all they would sail on the marine lake in a borrowed twelve-foot yacht managed expertly by Geoffrey.

For Geoffrey and he were – as at Courseulles – left much to themselves. And Jacques now understood more clearly why he'd seen so little of the Taskersons in Normandy. Those boys were unprecedented, portentous walkers. They thought nothing of walking twenty-five or thirty miles in a day. But what seemed stranger still, considering none was above school age, they were also unprecedented, portentous drinkers. In a mere five-mile walk they would stop at as many 'pubs' and drink a pint or two of powerful beer in each. Even the youngest, who had not turned fifteen, would get through his six pints in an afternoon. And if anyone was sick, so much the better for him. That made room for more. Neither Jacques, who had a weak stomach – though he was used to a certain amount of wine at home – nor Geoffrey, who disliked the taste of beer, and besides attended a strict Wesleyan school, could stand this medieval pace. But indeed the whole family drank inordinately. Old Taskerson, a kindly sharp man, had lost the only one of his sons who'd inherited any degree of literary talent; every night he sat brooding in his study with the door open, drinking hour after hour, his cats on his lap, his evening newspaper crackling distant disapproval of the other sons, who for their part sat drinking hour after hour in the dining-room. Mrs Taskerson, a different woman at home, where she perhaps felt less necessity of making a good impression, sat with her sons, her pretty face flushed, half disapproving too, but nevertheless cheerfully drinking everyone else under the table. It was true the boys usually had a head start. – Not that they were the sort ever to be seen staggering about outside in the street. It was a point of honour with them that, the drunker they became, the more sober they should appear. As a rule they walked fabulously upright, shoulders thrown back, eyes front, like guardsmen on duty, only, towards the end of the day, very very slowly, with that same 'erect manly carriage', in short, that had so impressed M. Laruelle's father. Even so it was by no means an unusual occurrence in the morning to discover the entire household sleeping on the dining-room floor. Yet no one seemed to feel any the worse for it. And the pantry was always bulging with barrels of beer to be tapped by anyone who did. Healthy and strong, the boys ate like lions. They devoured appalling messes of fried sheep's stomachs and pudding known as black or blood puddings, a sort of conglomerate offal rolled in oatmeal that Jacques feared might be intended at least partly for his benefit – *boudin*, don't you know, Jacques – while the Old Bean, now often referred to as 'that Firmin', sat bashful and out of place, his glass of pale bitter untouched, shyly trying to make conversation with Mr Taskerson.

It was difficult at first to understand what 'that Firmin' was doing at all with such an unlikely family. He had no tastes in common with the Taskerson lads and he was not even at the same school. Yet it was easy to see that the relatives who sent him had acted with the best of motives. Geoffrey's 'nose was always in a book', so that 'Cousin Abraham', whose work had a religious turn, should be the 'very man' to assist him. While as for the boys themselves they probably knew as little about them as Jacques's own family: they won all the language prizes at school, and all the athletic ones: surely these fine hearty fellows would be 'just the thing' to help poor Geoffrey over his shyness and stop him 'wool-gathering' about his father and India. Jacques's heart went out to the poor Old Bean. His mother had died when he was a child, in Kashmir, and, within the last year or so, his father, who'd married again, had simply, yet scandalously, disappeared. Nobody in Kashmir or elsewhere knew quite what had happened to him. One day he had walked up into the Himalayas and vanished, leaving Geoffrey, at Srinagar, with his half-brother, Hugh, then a baby in arms, and his stepmother. Then, as if that were not enough, the stepmother died too, leaving the two children alone in India. Poor Old Bean. He was really, in spite of his queerness, so touched by any kindness done to him. He was even touched by being called 'that Firmin'. And he was devoted to old Taskerson. M. Laruelle felt that in his way he was devoted to all the Taskersons and would have defended them to the death. There was something disarmingly helpless and at the same time so loyal about him. And after all, the Taskerson boys had, in their monstrous bluff English fashion, done their best not to leave him out and to show him their sympathy on his first summer holiday in England. It was not their fault if he could not drink seven pints in fourteen minutes or walk fifty miles without dropping. It was partly due to them that Jacques himself was here to keep him company. And they *had* perhaps partly succeeded in making him overcome his shyness. For from the Taskersons the Old Bean had at least learned, as Jacques with him, the English art of 'picking up girls'. They had an absurd Pierrot song, sung preferably in Jacques's French accent.

Jacques and he walked along the promenade singing :

> Oh we allll WALK ze wibberlee wobberlee WALK
> And we alll TALK ze wibberlee wobberlee TALK
> And we alll WEAR wibberlee wobberlee TIES
> And-look-at-all-ze-pretty-girls-with-wibberlee-
>   wobberlee eyes. Oh
> We allll SING ze wibberlee wobberlee SONG
> Until ze day is dawn-ing,
> And-we-all-have-zat-wibberlee-wobberlee-wobberlee-
>   wibberlee-wibberlee-wobberlee feeling
> In ze morning.

Then the ritual was to shout 'Hi' and walk after some girl whose admiration you imagined, if she happened to turn round, you had aroused. If you really had and it was after sunset you took her walking on the golf course, which was full, as the Taskersons put it, of good 'sitting-out places'. These were in the main bunkers or gulleys between dunes. The bunkers were usually full of sand, but they were windproof, and deep; none deeper than the 'Hell Bunker'. The Hell Bunker was a dreaded hazard, fairly near the Taskersons' house, in the middle of the long sloping eighth fairway. It guarded the green in a sense, though at a great distance, being far below it and slightly to the left. The abyss yawned in such a position as to engulf the third shot of a golfer like Geoffrey, a naturally beautiful and graceful player, and about the fifteenth of a duffer like Jacques. Jacques and the Old Bean had often decided that the Hell Bunker would be a nice place to take a girl, though wherever you took one, it was understood nothing very serious happened. There was, in general, about the whole business of 'picking up' an air of innocence. After a while the Old Bean, who was a virgin to put it mildly, and Jacques, who pretended he was not, fell into the habit of picking up girls on the promenade, walking to the golf course, separating there, and meeting later. There were, oddly, fairly regular hours at the Taskersons'. M. Laruelle didn't know to this day why there was no understanding about the Hell Bunker. He had certainly no intention of playing Peeping Tom on Geoffrey. He had happened with his girl, who bored him, to be crossing the eighth fairway towards Leasowe Drive when both were startled by voices coming from the bunker. Then the moonlight disclosed the bizarre scene from which neither he nor the girl could turn their eyes. Laruelle would have hurried away but neither of them – neither quite aware of the sensible impact of what was occurring in the Hell Bunker – could control their laughter. Curiously, M. Laruelle had never remembered what anyone said, only the expression on Geoffrey's face in the moonlight and the awkward grotesque way the girl had scrambled to her feet, then, that both Geoffrey and he behaved with remarkable aplomb. They all went to a tavern with some queer name, as 'The Case is Altered'. It was patently the first time the Consul had ever been into a bar on his own initiative; he ordered Johnny Walkers all round loudly, but the waiter, encountering the proprietor, refused to serve them and they were turned out as minors. Alas, their friendship did not for some reason survive these two sad, though doubtless providential, little frustrations. M. Laruelle's father had meantime dropped the idea of sending him to school in England. The holiday fizzled out in desolation and equinoctial gales. It had been a melancholy dreary parting at Liverpool and a dreary melancholy journey down to Dover and back home, lonesome as an onion peddler, on the sea-swept channel boat to Calais –

M. Laruelle straightened, instantly becoming aware of activity, to step just in time from the path of a horseman who had reined up sideways across the bridge. Darkness had fallen like the House of Usher. The horse stood blinking in the leaping headlights of a car, a rare phenomenon so far down the Calle Nicaragua, that was approaching from the town, rolling like a ship on the dreadful road. The rider of the horse was so drunk he was sprawling all over his mount, his stirrups lost, a feat in itself considering their size, and barely managing to hold on by the reins, though not once did he grasp the pommel to steady himself. The horse reared wildly, rebellious – half fearful, half contemptuous, perhaps, of its rider – then it catapulted in the direction of the car : the man, who seemed to be falling straight backwards at first, miraculously saved himself only to slip to one side like a trick rider, regained the saddle, slid, slipped, fell backwards – just saving himself each time, but always with the reins, never with the pommel, holding them in one hand now, the stirrups still unrecovered as he furiously beat the horse's flanks with the machete he had withdrawn from a long curved scabbard. Meantime the headlights had picked out a family straggling down the hill, a man and a woman in mourning, and two neatly dressed children, whom the woman drew in to the side of the road as the horseman fled on, while the man stood back against the ditch. The car halted, dimming its lights for the rider, then came towards M. Laruelle and crossed the bridge behind him. It was a powerful silent car, of American build, sinking deeply on its springs, its engine scarcely audible, and the sound of the horse's hooves rang out plainly, receding now, slanting up the ill-lit Calle Nicaragua, past the Consul's house, where there would be a light in the window M. Laruelle didn't want to see – for long after Adam had left the garden the light in Adam's house burned on – and the gate was mended, past the school on the left, and the spot where he had met Yvonne with Hugh and Geoffrey that day – and he imagined the rider as not pausing even at Laruelle's own house, where his trunks lay mountainous and still only half packed, but galloping recklessly round the corner into the Calle Tierra del Fuego and on, his eyes wild as those soon to look on death, through the town – and this too, he thought suddenly, this maniacal vision of senseless frenzy, but controlled, not quite uncontrolled, somehow almost admirable, this too, obscurely, was the Consul ...

M. Laruelle passed up the hill: he stood, tired, in the town below the square. He had not, however, climbed the Calle Nicaragua. In order to avoid his own house he had taken a cut to the left just beyond the school, a steep broken circuitous path that wound round behind the *zócalo*. People stared at him curiously as he sauntered down the Avenida de la Revolución, still encumbered with his tennis racket. This street, pursued far enough, would lead back to the American highway again and the Casino de la Selva; M. Laruelle smiled: at this rate he could go on travelling in an eccentric orbit round his house for ever. Behind him now, the fair, which he'd given scarcely a glance, whirled on. The town, colourful even at night, was brilliantly lit, but only in patches, like a harbour. Windy shadows swept the pavements. And occasional trees in the shadow seemed as if drenched in coal dust, their branches bowed beneath a weight of soot. The little bus clanged by him again, going the other way now, braking hard on the steep hill, and without a tail light. The last bus to Tomalín. He passed Dr Vigil's windows on the far side: *Dr Arturo Díaz Vigil, Médico Cirujano y Partero, Facultad de México, de la Escuela Médico Militar, Enfermedades de Niños, Indisposiciones nerviosas* – and how politely all this differed from the notices one encountered in the *mingitorios*! – *Consultas de 12 a 2 y 4 a 7*. A slight overstatement, he thought. Newsboys ran past selling copies of *Quauhnahuac Nuevo*, the pro-Almazán, pro-Axis sheet put out, they said, by the tiresome Unión Militar. *Un avión de combate Francés derribado por un caza Alemán. Los trabajadores de Australia abogan por la paz. ¿Quiere Vd?* – a placard asked him in a shop window – *vestirse con elegancia y a la última moda de Europa y los Estados Unidos?* M. Laruelle walked on down the hill. Outside the barracks two soldiers, wearing French army helmets and grey faded purple uniforms laced and interlaced with green lariats, paced on sentry duty. He crossed the street. Approaching the cinema he became conscious all was not as it should be, that there was a strange unnatural excitement in the air, a kind of fever. It had grown on the instant much cooler. And the cinema was dark, as though no picture were playing tonight. On the other hand a large group of people, not a queue, but evidently some of the patrons from the *cine* itself, who had come prematurely flooding out, were standing on the pavement and under the arcature listening to a loudspeaker mounted on a van blaring the Washington Post March. Suddenly there was a crash of thunder and the street lights twitched off. So the lights of the *cine* had gone already. Rain, M. Laruelle thought. But his desire to get wet had deserted him. He put his tennis racket under his coat and ran. A troughing wind all at once engulfed the street, scattering old newspapers and blowing the naphtha flares on the tortilla stands flat : there was a savage scribble of lightning over the hotel opposite the cinema, followed by another peal of thunder. The wind was moaning, everywhere people were running, mostly laughing, for shelter. M. Laruelle could hear the thunderclaps crashing on the mountains behind him. He just reached the theatre in time. The rain was falling in torrents.

He stood, out of breath, under the shelter of the theatre entrance which was, however, more like the entrance to some gloomy bazaar or market. Peasants were crowding in with baskets. At the box office, momentarily vacated, the door left half open, a frantic hen sought admission. Everywhere people were flashing torches or striking matches. The van with the loudspeaker slithered away into the rain and thunder. *Las Manos de Orlac*, said a poster : *6 y 8.30. Las Manos de Orlac, con Peter Lorre.*

The street lights came on again, though the theatre still remained dark. M. Laruelle fumbled for a cigarette. The hands of Orlac ... How, in a flash, that had brought back the old days of the cinema, he thought, indeed his own delayed student days, the days of the *Student of Prague*, and Wiene and Werner Krauss and Karl Grüne, the Ufa days when a defeated Germany was winning the respect of the cultured world by the pictures she was making. Only then it had been Conrad Veidt in *Orlac*. Strangely, that particular film had been scarcely better than the present version, a feeble Hollywood product he'd seen some years before in Mexico City or perhaps – M. Laruelle looked around him – perhaps at this very theatre. It was not impossible. But so far as he remembered not even Peter Lorre had been able to salvage it and he didn't want to see it again . . . Yet what a complicated endless tale it seemed to tell, of tyranny and sanctuary, that poster looming above him now, showing the murderer Orlac! An artist with a murderer's hands; that was the ticket, the hieroglyphic of the times. For really it was Germany itself that, in the gruesome degradation of a bad cartoon, stood over him. – Or was it, by some uncomfortable stretch of the imagination, M. Laruelle himself?

The manager of the *cine* was standing before him, cupping, with that same lightning-swift, fumbling-thwarting courtesy exhibited by Dr Vigil, by all Latin Americans, a match for his cigarette: his hair, innocent of raindrops, which seemed almost lacquered, and a heavy perfume emanating from him, betrayed his daily visit to the *peluquería*; he was impeccably dressed in striped trousers and a black coat, inflexibly *muy correcto*, like most Mexicans of his type, despite earthquake and thunderstorm. He threw the match away now with a gesture that was not wasted, for it amounted to a salute. 'Come and have a drink,' he said.

'The rainy season dies hard,' M. Laruelle smiled as they elbowed their way through into a little *cantina* which abutted on the cinema without sharing its frontal shelter. The *cantina*, known as the Cervecería XX, and which was also Vigil's 'place where you know', was lit by candles stuck in bottles on the bar and on the few tables along the walls. The tables were all full.

'*Chingar*,' the manager said, under his breath, preoccupied, alert, and gazing about him: they took their places standing at the end of the short bar where there was room for two. 'I am very sorry the function must be suspended. But the wires have decomposed. *Chingado*. Every blessed week something goes wrong with the lights. Last week it was much worse, really terrible. You know we had a troupe from Panama City here trying out a show for Mexico.'

'Do you mind my – '

'No, *hombre*,' laughed the other – M. Laruelle had asked Sr Bustamente, who'd now succeeded in attracting the barman's attention, hadn't he seen the *Orlac* picture here before and if so had he revived it as a hit. '¿ – *uno* – ?'

71

M. Laruelle hesitated: '*Tequila*,' then corrected himself: '*No, anís – anís, por favor, señor.*'

'*Y una – ah – gaseosa,*' Sr Bustamente told the barman. '*No, señor,*' he was fingering appraisingly, still preoccupied, the stuff of M. Laruelle's scarcely wet tweed jacket. '*Compañero*, we have not revived it. It has only returned. The other day I show my latest news here too: believe it, the first newsreels from the Spanish war, that have come back again.'

'I see you get some modern pictures still though,' M. Laruelle (he had just declined a seat in the *autoridades* box for the second showing, if any) glanced somewhat ironically at a garish three-sheet of a German film star, though the features seemed carefully Spanish, hanging behind the bar: *La simpatiquísima y encantadora María Landrock, notable artista alemana que pronto habremos de ver en sensacional Film.*

'*– un momentito, señor. Con permiso . . .*'

Sr Bustamente went out, not through the door by which they had entered, but through a side entrance behind the bar immediately on their right, from which a curtain had been drawn back, into the cinema itself. M. Laruelle had a good view of the interior. From it, exactly indeed as though the show were in progress, came a beautiful uproar of bawling children and hawkers selling fried potatoes and frijoles. It was difficult to believe so many had left their seats. Dark shapes of pariah dogs prowled in and out of the stalls. The lights were not entirely dead: they glimmered, a dim reddish orange, flickering. On the screen, over which clambered an endless procession of torchlit shadows, hung, magically projected upside down, a faint apology for the 'suspended function'; in the *autoridades* box three cigarettes were lit on one match. At the rear where reflected light caught the lettering SALIDA of the exit he just made out the anxious figure of Sr Bustamente taking to his office. Outside it thundered and rained. M. Laruelle sipped his water-clouded *anís* which was first greenly chilling then rather nauseating. Actually it was not at all like absinthe. But his tiredness had left him and he began to feel hungry. It was already seven o'clock. Though Vigil and he would probably dine later at the Gambrinus or Charley's Place. He selected, from a saucer, a quarter lemon and sucked it reflectively, reading a calendar which, next to the enigmatic María Landrock, behind the bar portrayed the meeting of Cortez and Moctezuma in Tenochtitlán : *El último Emperador Azteca,* it said below, *Moctezuma y Hernán Cortés representativo de la raza hispaña, quedan frente a frente: dos razas y dos civilizaciones que habían llegado a un alto grado de perfección se mezclan para integrar el núcleo de nuestra nacionalidad actual.* But Sr Bustamente was coming back, carrying, in one uplifted hand above a press of people by the curtain, a book ...

M. Laruelle, conscious of shock, was turning the book over and over in his hands. Then he laid it on the bar counter and took a sip of *anís. 'Bueno, muchas gracias, señor,'* he said.

'*De nada,*' Sr Bustamente answered in a lowered tone; he waved aside with a sweeping somehow inclusive gesture, a sombre pillar advancing bearing a tray of chocolate skulls. 'Don't know how long, maybe two, maybe three years *aquí.*'

M. Laruelle glanced in the flyleaf again, then shut the book on the counter. Above them the rain slammed on the cinema roof. It was eighteen months since the Consul had lent him the thumbed maroon volume of Elizabethan plays. At that time Geoffrey and Yvonne had been separated for perhaps five months. Six more must elapse before she would return. In the Consul's garden they drifted gloomily up and down among the roses and the plumbago and the waxplants 'like dilapidated *préservatifs*', the Consul had remarked with a diabolical look at him, a look at the same time almost official, that seemed now to have said : 'I know, Jacques, you may never return the book, but suppose I lend it you precisely for that reason, that some day you may be sorry you did not. Oh, I shall forgive you then, but will you be able to forgive yourself? Not merely for not having returned it, but because the book will by then have become an emblem of what even now it is impossible to return.' M. Laruelle had taken the book. He wanted it because for some time he had been carrying at the back of his mind the notion of making in France a modern film version of the Faustus story with some such character as Trotsky for its protagonist : as a matter of fact he had not opened the volume till this minute.

Though the Consul had several times asked him for it later he had missed it that same day when he must have left it behind in the cinema. M. Laruelle listened to the water booming down the gutters beneath the one jalousie door of the Cervecería XX which opened into a side-street in the far left-hand corner. A sudden thunderclap shook the whole building and the sound echoed away like coal sliding down a chute.

'You know, *señor*,' he said suddenly, 'that this isn't my book.'

'I know,' Sr Bustamente replied, but softly, almost in a whisper: 'I think your *amigo*, it was his.' He gave a little confused cough, an *appoggiatura*. 'Your *amigo*, the *bicho* – ' Sensitive apparently to M. Laruelle's smile he interrupted himself quietly. 'I did not mean bitch; I mean *bicho*, the one with the blue eyes.' Then, as if there were any longer doubt of whom he spoke, he pinched his chin and drew downward from it an imaginary beard. 'Your *amigo* – ah – Señor Firmin. *El Cónsul*. The *Americano*.'

'No. He wasn't American.' M. Laruelle tried to raise his voice a little. It was hard, for everyone in the *cantina* had stopped talking and M. Laruelle noticed that a curious hush had also fallen in the theatre. The light had now completely failed and he stared over Sr Bustamente's shoulder past the curtain into a graveyard darkness, stabbed by flashes of torchlight like heat lightning, but the vendors had lowered their voices, the children had stopped laughing and crying while the diminished audience sat slackly and bored yet patient before the dark screen, suddenly illuminated, swept, by silent grotesque shadows of giants and spears and birds, then dark again, the men along the right-hand balcony, who hadn't bothered to move or come downstairs, a solid frieze carved into the wall, serious, moustachioed men, warriors waiting for the show to begin, for a glimpse of the murderer's bloodstained hands.

'No?' Sr Bustamente said softly. He took a sip of his *gaseosa*, looking too into the dark theatre and then, preoccupied again, around the *cantina*. 'But was it true, then, he was a Consul? For I remember him many time sitting here drinking: and often, the poor guy, he have no socks.'

74

M. Laruelle laughed shortly. 'Yes, he was the British Consul here.' They spoke subduedly in Spanish, and Sr Bustamente despairing for another ten minutes of the lights, was persuaded to a glass of beer while M. Laruelle himself took a soft drink.

But he had not succeeded in explaining the Consul to the gracious Mexican. The lights had dimly come on again both in the theatre and the *cantina*, though the show had not recommenced, and M. Laruelle sat alone at a vacated corner table of the Cervecería XX with another *anís* before him. His stomach would suffer for it: it was only during the last year he had been drinking so heavily. He sat rigidly, the book of Elizabethan plays closed on the table, staring at his tennis racket propped against the back of the seat opposite he was keeping for Dr Vigil. He felt rather like someone lying in a bath after all the water has run out, witless, almost dead. Had he only gone home he might have finished his packing by now. But he had not been able to even make the decision to say good-bye to Sr Bustamente. It was still raining, out of season, over Mexico, the dark waters rising outside to engulf his own *zacualí* in the Calle Nicaragua, his useless tower against the coming of the second flood. Night of the Culmination of the Pleiades! What, after all, was a Consul that one was mindful of him? Sr Bustamente, who was older than he looked, had remembered the days of Porfirio Díaz, the days when, in America, every small town along the Mexican border harboured a 'Consul'. Indeed Mexican Consuls were to be found even in villages hundreds of miles from that border. Consuls were expected to look after the interests of trade between countries – were they not? But towns in Arizona that did not do ten dollars' worth of trade a year with Mexico had Consuls maintained by Díaz. Of course, they were not Consuls but spies. Sr Bustamente knew because before the revolution his own father, a liberal and a member of the Ponciano Arriaga, had been held for three months in prison at Douglas, Arizona (in spite of which Sr Bustamente himself was going to vote for Almazán), on the orders of a Díaz-maintained Consul. Was it not then reasonable to suppose, he had hinted, without offence, and perhaps not altogether seriously, Señor Firmin was such a Consul, not, it was true, a Mexican

Consul, nor of quite the same breed as those others, but an English Consul who could scarcely claim to have the interests of British trade at heart in a place where there were no British interests and no Englishmen, the less so when it was considered that England had severed diplomatic relations with Mexico?

Actually Sr Bustamente seemed half convinced that M. Laruelle had been taken in, that Señor Firmin had really been a sort of spy, or, as he put it, spider. But nowhere in the world were there people more human or readily moved to sympathy than the Mexicans, vote as they might for Almazán. Sr Bustamente was prepared to be sorry for the Consul even as a spider, sorry in his heart for the poor lonely dispossessed trembling soul that had sat drinking here night after night, abandoned by his wife (though she came back, M. Laruelle almost cried aloud, that was the extraordinary thing, she came back!) and possibly, remembering the socks, even by his country, and wandering hatless and *desconsolado* and beside himself around the town pursued by other spiders who, without his ever being quite certain of it, a man in dark glasses he took to be a loafer here, a man lounging on the other side of the road he thought was a peon there, a bald boy with ear-rings swinging madly on a creaking hammock there, guarded every street and alley entrance, which even a Mexican would no longer believe (because it was not true, M. Laruelle said) but which was still quite possible, as Sr Bustamente's father would have assured him, let him start something and find out, just as his father would have assured him that he, M. Laruelle, could not cross the border in a cattle truck, say, without 'their' knowing it in Mexico City before he arrived and having already decided what 'they' were going to do about it. Certainly Sr Bustamente did not know the Consul well, though it was his habit to keep his eyes open, but the whole town knew him by sight, and the impression he gave, or gave that last year anyway, apart from being always *muy borracho* of course, was of a man living in continual terror of his life. Once he had run into the *cantina* El Bosque, kept by the old woman Gregorio, now a widow, shouting something like ' *Sanctuario!* ' that people were after him, and the widow, more terrified than he, had hidden him in the back room for half

76

the afternoon. It was not the widow who'd told him that but Señor Gregorio himself before he died, whose brother was his, Sr Bustamente's, gardener, because Señora Gregorio was half English or American herself and had had some difficult explanations to make both to Señor Gregorio and his brother Bernardino. And yet, if the Consul were a 'spider', he was one no longer and could be forgiven. After all, he was *simpático* himself. Had he not seen him once in this very bar give all his money to a beggar taken by the police?

– But the Consul also was not a coward, M. Laruelle had interrupted, perhaps irrelevantly, at least not the kind to be craven about his life. On the contrary he was an extremely brave man, no less than a hero in fact, who had won, for conspicuous gallantry in the service of his country during the last war, a coveted medal. Nor with all his faults was he at bottom a vicious man. Without knowing quite why M. Laruelle felt he might have actually proved a great force for good. But Sr Bustamente had never said he was a coward. Almost reverently Sr Bustamente pointed out that being a coward and afraid for one's life were two different things in Mexico. And certainly the Consul was not vicious but an *hombre noble*. Yet might not just such a character and distinguished record as M. Laruelle claimed was his have precisely qualified him for the excessively dangerous activities of a spider? It seemed useless to try and explain to Sr Bustamente that the poor Consul's job was merely a retreat, that while he had intended originally to enter the Indian Civil Service, he had in fact entered the Diplomatic Service only for one reason and another to be kicked downstairs into ever remoter consulships, and finally into the sinecure in Quauhnahuac as a position where he was least likely to prove a nuisance to the Empire, in which, with one part of his mind at least, M. Laruelle suspected he so passionately believed.

But why had all this happened? he asked himself now. ¿*Quién sabe?* He risked another *anís*, and at the first sip a scene, probably rather inaccurate (M. Laruelle had been in the artillery during the last war, survived by him in spite of Guillaume Apollinaire's being for a time his commanding officer), was conjured to his mind. A dead calm on the line, but the s.s. *Samaritan*, if she should have been on the line, was actually far north of it. Indeed for a steamer bound from Shanghai to Newcastle, New South Wales, with a cargo of antimony and quicksilver and wolfram she had for some time been steering a rather odd course. Why, for instance, had she emerged into the Pacific Ocean out of the Bungo Strait in Japan south of Shikoku and not far from the East China Sea? For days now, not unlike a stray sheep on the immeasurable green meadows of waters, she had been keeping an offing from various interesting islands far out of her path. Lot's Wife and Arzobispo. Rosario and Sulphur Island. Volcano Island and St Augustine. It was somewhere between Guy Rock and the Euphrosyne Reef that she first sighted the periscope and sent her engines full speed astern. But when the submarine surfaced she hove to. An unarmed merchantman, the *Samaritan* put up no fight. Before the boarding party from the submarine reached her, however, she suddenly changed her temper. As if by magic the sheep turned to a dragon belching fire. The U-boat did not even have time to dive. Her entire crew was captured. The *Samaritan*, who had lost her captain in the engagement, sailed on, leaving the submarine burning helplessly, a smoking cigar aglow on the vast surface of the Pacific.

And in some capacity obscure to M. Laruelle – for Geoffrey had not been in the merchant service but, arrived via the yacht club and something in salvage, a naval lieutenant, or God knows perhaps by that time a lieutenant-commander – the Consul had been largely responsible for this escapade. And for it, or gallantry connected with it, he had received the British Distinguished Service Order or Cross.

But there was a slight hitch apparently. For whereas the submarine's crew became prisoners of war when the *Samaritan* (which was only one of the ship's names, albeit that the Consul liked best) reached port, mysteriously none of her officers was among them. Something had happened to those German officers, and what had happened was not pretty. They had, it was said, been kidnapped by the *Samaritan*'s stokers and burned alive in the furnaces.

M. Laruelle thought of this. The Consul loved England and

as a young man may have subscribed – though it was doubtful, this being rather more in those days the prerogative of non-combatants – to the popular hatred of the enemy. But he was a man of honour and probably no one supposed for a moment he had ordered the *Samaritan*'s stokers to put the Germans in the furnace. None dreamed that such an order given would have been obeyed. But the fact remained the Germans had been put there and it was no use saying that was the best place for them. Someone must take the blame.

So the Consul had not received his decoration without first being court-martialled. He was acquitted. It was not at all clear to M. Laruelle why he and no one else should have been tried. Yet it was easy to think of the Consul as a kind of more lachrymose pseudo 'Lord Jim' living in a self-imposed exile, brooding, despite his award, over his lost honour, his secret, and imagining that a stigma would cling to him because of it throughout his whole life. Yet this was far from the case. No stigma clung to him evidently. And he had shown no reluctance in discussing the incident with M. Laruelle, who years before had read a guarded article concerning it in the *Paris-Soir*. He had even been enormously funny about it. 'People simply did not go round', he said, 'putting Germans in furnaces.' It was only once or twice during those later months when drunk that to M. Laruelle's astonishment he suddenly began proclaiming not only his guilt in the matter but that he'd always suffered horribly on account of it. He went much further. No blame attached to the stokers. No question arose of any order given them. Flexing his muscles he sardonically announced the single-handed accomplishment himself of the deed. But by this time the poor Consul had already lost almost all capacity for telling the truth and his life had become a quixotic oral fiction. Unlike 'Jim' he had grown rather careless of his honour and the German officers were merely an excuse to buy another bottle of mescal. M. Laruelle told the Consul as much, and they quarrelled grotesquely, becoming estranged again – when bitterer things had not estranged them – and remained so till the last – indeed at the very last it had been wickedly, sorrowfully worse than ever – as years before at Leasowe.

> Then will I headlong fly into the earth:
> Earth, gape! it will not harbour me!

M. Laruelle had opened the book of Elizabethan plays at random and for a moment he sat oblivious of his surroundings, gazing at the words that seemed to have the power of carrying his own mind downward into a gulf, as in fulfilment on his own spirit of the threat Marlowe's Faustus had cast at his despair. Only Faustus had not said quite that. He looked more closely at the passage. Faustus had said: 'Then will I headlong run into the earth', and 'O, no, it will not – ' That was not so bad. Under the circumstances to run was not so bad as to fly. Intaglioed in the maroon leather cover of the book was a golden faceless figurine also running, carrying a torch like the elongated neck and head and open beak of the sacred ibis. M. Laruelle sighed, ashamed of himself. What had produced the illusion, the elusive flickering candlelight, coupled with the dim, though now less dim, electric light, or some correspondence, maybe, as Geoff liked to put it, between the subnormal world and the abnormally suspicious? How the Consul had delighted in the absurd game too: sortes Shakespeareanae ... *And what wonders I have done all Germany can witness. Enter Wagner, solus ... Ick sal you wat suggen, Hans. Dis skip, dat comen from Candy, is als vol, by God's sacrament, van sugar, almonds, cambrick, end alle dingen, towsand, towsand ding.* M. Laruelle closed the book on Dekker's comedy, then, in the face of the barman who was watching him, strained dishcloth over his arm, with quiet amazement, shut his eyes, and opening the book again twirled one finger in the air, and brought it down firmly upon a passage he now held up to the light:

> Cut is the branch that might have grown full straight,
> And burnèd is Apollo's laurel bough,
> That sometimes grew within this learnèd man,
> Faustus is gone: regard his hellish fall –

Shaken, M. Laruelle replaced the book on the table, closing it with the fingers and thumb of one hand, while with the other hand he reached to the floor for a folded sheet of paper that had fluttered out of it. He picked the paper up between two fingers and unfolded it, turning it over. *Hotel Bella Vista*, he read. There were really two sheets of uncommonly thin hotel notepaper that had been pressed flat in the book, long but narrow and crammed on both sides with meaningless writing in pencil. At first glance it did not appear a letter. But there was no mistaking, even in the uncertain light, the hand, half crabbed, half generous, and wholly drunken, of the Consul himself, the Greek e's, flying buttresses of d's, the t's like lonely wayside crosses save where they crucified the entire word, the words themselves slanting steeply downhill, though the individual characters seemed as if resisting the descent, braced, climbing the other way. M. Laruelle felt a qualm. For he saw now that it was indeed a letter of sorts, though one that the writer undoubtedly had little intention, possibly no capability for the further tactile effort, of posting:

... Night: and once again, the nightly grapple with death, the room shaking with daemonic orchestras, the snatches of fearful sleep, the voices outside the window, my name being continually repeated with scorn by imaginary parties arriving, the dark's spinnets. As if there were not enough real noises in these nights the colour of grey hair. Not like the rending tumult of American cities, the noise of the unbandaging of great giants in agony. But the howling pariah dogs, the cocks that herald dawn all night, the drumming, the moaning that will be found later white plumage huddled on telegraph wires in back gardens or fowl roosting in apple trees, the eternal sorrow that never sleeps of great Mexico. For myself I like to take my sorrow into the shadow of old monasteries, my guilt into cloisters and under tapestries, and into the misericordes of unimaginable *cantinas* where sad-faced potters and legless beggars drink at dawn, whose cold jonquil beauty one rediscovers in death. So that when you left, Yvonne, I went to Oaxaca. There is no sadder word. Shall I tell you, Yvonne, of the terrible jouney there through the desert over the narrow gauge railway on the rack of a third-class carriage bench, the child whose life its mother and I saved by rubbing its belly with tequila out of my bottle, or of how, when I went to my room in the hotel where we once were happy, the noise of slaughtering below in the kitchen drove me out into the glare of the street, and later, that night, there was a vulture sitting in the washbasin? Horrors portioned to a giant nerve! No, my secrets are of the grave and must be kept. And this is how I sometimes think

81

of myself, as a great explorer who has discovered some extraordinary land from which he can never return to give his knowledge to the world: but the name of this land is hell.

It is not Mexico of course but in the heart. And today I was in Quauhnahuac as usual when I received from my lawyers news of our divorce. This was as I invited it. I received other news too: England is breaking off diplomatic relations with Mexico and all her Consuls – those, that is, who are English – are being called home. These are kindly and good men, for the most part, whose name I suppose I demean. I shall not go home with them. I shall perhaps go home but not to England, not to that home. So, at midnight, I drove in the Plymouth to Tomalín to see my Tlaxcaltecan friend Cervantes the cockfighter at the Salón Ofélia. And thence I came to the Farolito in Parián where I sit now in a little room off the bar at four-thirty in the morning drinking *ochas* and then *mescal* and writing this on some Bella Vista notepaper I filched the other night, perhaps because the writing paper at the Consulate, which is a tomb, hurts me to look at. I think I know a good deal about physical suffering. But this is worst of all, to feel your soul dying. I wonder if it is because tonight my soul has really died that I feel at the moment something like peace.

Or is it because right through hell there is a path, as Blake well knew, and though I may not take it, sometimes lately in dreams I have been able to see it? And here is one strange effect my lawyer's news has had upon me. I seem to see now, between mescals, this path, and beyond it strange vistas, like visions of a new life together we might somewhere lead. I seem to see us living in some northern country, of mountains and hills and blue water; our house is built on an inlet and one evening we are standing, happy in one another, on the balcony of this house, looking over the water. There are sawmills half hidden by trees beyond and under the hills on the other side of the inlet, what looks like an oil refinery, only softened and rendered beautiful by distance.

It is a light blue moonless summer evening, but late, perhaps ten o'clock, with Venus burning hard in daylight, so we are certainly somewhere far north, and standing on this balcony, when from beyond along the coast comes the gathering thunder of a long many-engined freight train, thunder because though we are separated by this wide strip of water from it, the train is rolling eastward and the changing wind veers for the moment from an easterly quarter, and we face east, like Swedenborg's angels, under a sky clear save where far to the north-east over distant mountains whose purple has faded, lies a mass of almost pure white clouds, suddenly, as by light in an alabaster lamp, illumined from within by gold lightning, yet you can hear no thunder, only the roar of the great train with its engines and its wide shunting echoes as it advances from the hills into the mountains: and then all at once a fishing-boat with tall gear comes running round the point like a white giraffe, very swift and stately, leaving directly behind it a long silver scalloped rim of wake, not visibly moving inshore, but now stealing ponderously beachward towards us, this scrolled silver rim of wash striking the shore first in the distance, then spreading all along the curve of beach, its growing thunder and commotion now joined to the diminishing thunder of the train, and now breaking reboant on our beach, while the floats, for there are timber diving floats, are swayed together, everything jostled and beautifully ruffled and stirred and tormented in this rolling sleeked silver, then little by little calm again, and you see the reflection of the remote white thunderclouds in the water, and now the lightning within the white clouds in deep water, as the fishing-boat itself with a golden scroll of travelling light in its silver wake beside it reflected from the cabin vanishes round the headland, silence, and then again, within the white white distant alabaster thunderclouds beyond the mountains, the thunderless gold lightning in the blue evening, un-earthly ...

And as we stand looking all at once comes the wash of another unseen ship, like a great wheel, the vast spokes of the wheel whirl-ing across the bay –

(Several mescals later.) Since December 1937, and you went, and it is now I hear the spring of 1938, I have been deliberately strug-gling against my love for you. I dared not submit to it. I have grasped at every root and branch which would help me across this abyss in my life by myself but I can deceive myself no longer. If I am to survive I need your help. Otherwise, sooner or later, I shall fall. Ah, if only you had given me something in memory to hate you for so finally no kind thought of you would ever touch me in this terrible place where I am! But instead you sent me those letters. Why did you send the first ones to Wells Fargo in Mexico City, by the way? Can it be you didn't realize I was still here? – Or – if in Oaxaca – that Quauhnahuac was still my base. That is very peculiar. It would have been so easy to find out too. And if you'd only written me *right away* also, it might have been different – sent me a postcard even, out of the common anguish of our separa-tion, appealing simply to *us*, in spite of all, to end the absurdity immediately – somehow, anyhow – and saying we loved each other, something, or a telegram, simple. But you waited too long – or so it seems now, till after Christmas – Christmas! – and the New Year, and then what you sent I couldn't read. No: I have scarcely been once free enough from torment or sufficiently sober to apprehend more than the governing design of any of these letters. But I could, can feel them. I think I have some of them on me. But they are too painful to read, they seem too long digested. I shall not attempt it now. I cannot read them. They break my heart. And they came too late anyway. And now I suppose there will be no more.

Alas, but why have I not pretended at least that I had read them, accepted some meed of retraction in the fact that they were sent? And why did I not send a telegram or some word immediately? Ah, why not, why not, why not? For I suppose you would have come back in due course if I had asked you? But this is what it is to live in hell. I could not, cannot ask you. I could not, cannot send a telegram. I have stood here, and in Mexico City, in the Compañía Telegráfica Mexicana, and in Oaxaca, trembling and sweltering in the post office and writing telegrams all afternoon, when I had drunk enough to steady my hand, without having sent one. And I once had some number of yours and actually called you long distance to Los Angeles though without success. And another time the telephone broke down. Then why do I not come to America myself? I am too ill to arrange about the tickets, to suffer the shaking delirium of the endless weary cactus plains. And why go to America to die? Perhaps I would not mind being buried in the United States. But I think I would prefer to die in Mexico.

Meantime do you see me as still working on the book, still trying to answer such questions as: Is there any ultimate reality, external, conscious, and ever-present, etc. etc., that can be realized by any such means that may be acceptable to all creeds and religions and suitable to all climes and countries? Or do you find me between Mercy and Understanding, between Chesed and Binah (but still at Chesed) – my equilibrium, and equilibrium is all, precarious – balancing, teetering over the awful unbridgeable void, the all-but-unretraceable path of God's lightning back to God? as if I ever were in Chesed! More like the Qliphoth. When I should have been producing obscure volumes of verse entitled the Triumph of Humpty Dumpty or the Nose with the Luminous Dong! Or at best, like Clare, 'weaving fearful vision' ... A frustrated poet in every man. Though it is perhaps a good idea under the circumstances to pretend at least to be proceeding with one's great work on 'Secret Knowledge', then one can always say when it never comes out that the title explains this deficiency.

– But alas for the Knight of Sorry Aspect! For oh, Yvonne, I am so haunted continuously by the thought of your songs, of your warmth and merriment, of your simplicity and comradeship, of your abilities in a hundred ways, your fundamental sanity, your untidiness, your equally excessive neatness – the sweet beginnings of our marriage. Do you remember the Strauss song we used to sing? Once a year the dead live for one day. Oh come to me again as once in May. The Generalife Gardens and the Alhambra Gardens. And shadows of our fate at our meeting in Spain. The Hollywood bar in Granada. Why Hollywood? And the nunnery there: why Los Angeles? And in Malaga, the Pensión México. And yet nothing can ever take the place of the unity we once knew and which Christ alone knows must still exist somewhere. Knew even in Paris – before Hugh came. Is this an illusion too? I am being completely maudlin certainly. But no one can take your place; I ought to know by now, I laugh as I write this, whether I love you or not ... Sometimes I am possessed by a most powerful feeling, a despairing bewildered jealousy which, when deepened by drink, turns into a desire to destroy myself by my own imagination – not at least to be the prey of – ghosts –

(Several mescalitos later and dawn in the Farolito) ... Time is a fake healer anyhow. How can anyone presume to tell me about you? You cannot know the sadness of my life. Endlessly haunted waking and sleeping by the thought that you may need my help, which I cannot give, as I need yours, which you cannot, seeing you in visions and in every shadow, I have been compelled to write this, which I shall never send, to ask you what we can do. Is not that extraordinary? And yet – do we not owe it ourselves, to that self we created, apart from us, to try again? Alas, what has happened to the love and understanding we once had! What is going to happen to it – what is going to happen to our hearts? Love is the only thing which gives meaning to our poor ways on earth: not precisely a discovery, I am afraid. You will think I am mad, but this is how I drink too, as if I were taking an eternal sacrament. Oh Yvonne, we cannot allow what we created to sink down to oblivion in this dingy fashion –

Lift up your eyes unto the hills, I seem to hear a voice saying. Sometimes, when I see the little red mail plane fly in from Acapulco at seven in the morning over the strange hills, or more probably hear, lying trembling, shaking, and dying in bed (when I am in

85

bed at that time) – just a tiny roar and gone – as I reach out babbling for the glass of *mescal*, the drink that I can never believe even
in raising to my lips is real, that I have had the marvellous foresight to put within easy reach the night before, I think that you
will be on it, on that plane every morning as it goes by, and will
have come to save me. Then the morning goes by and you have
not come. But oh, I pray for this now, that you will come. On
second thoughts I do not see why from Acapulco. But for God's
sake, Yvonne, hear me, my defences are down, at the moment they
are down – and there goes the plane, I heard it in the distance
then, just for an instant, beyond Tomalín – come back, come back.
I will stop drinking, anything. I am dying without you. For Christ
Jesus' sake Yvonne come back to me, hear me, it is a cry, come
back to me, Yvonne, if only for a day . . .

M. Laruelle began very slowly to fold up the letter again,
smoothing the creases carefully between finger and thumb,
then almost without thinking he had crumpled it up. He sat
holding the crumpled paper in one fist on the table staring,
deeply abstracted, around him. In the last five minutes the
scene within the *cantina* had wholly changed. Outside the
storm seemed over but the Cervecería XX meantime had filled
with peasants, evidently refugees from it. They were not sitting at the tables, which where empty – for while the show had
still not recommenced most of the audience had filed back into
the theatre, now fairly quiet as in immediate anticipation of it –
but crowded by the bar. And there was a beauty and a sort of
piety about this scene. In the *cantina* both the candles and the
dim electric lights still burned. A peasant held two little girls
by the hand while the floor was covered with baskets, mostly
empty and leaning against each other, and now the barman
was giving the younger of the two children an orange : someone went out, the little girl sat on the orange, the jalousie door
swung and swung and swung. M. Laruelle looked at his watch
– Vigil would not come for half an hour yet – and again at
the crumpled pages in his hand. The fresh coolness of rain-
washed air came through the jalousie into the *cantina* and he
could hear the rain dripping off the roofs and the water still
rushing down the gutters in the street and from the distance
once more the sounds of the fair. He was about to replace the

crumpled letter in the book when, half absently, yet on a sudden definite impulse, he held it into the candle flame. The flare lit up the whole *cantina* with a burst of brilliance in which the figures at the bar – that he now saw included besides the little children and the peasants who were quince or cactus farmers in loose white clothes and wide hats, several women in mourning from the cemeteries and dark-faced men in dark suits with open collars and their ties undone – appeared, for an instant, frozen, a mural : they had all stopped talking and were gazing round at him curiously, all save the barman who seemed momentarily about to object, then lost interest as M. Laruelle set the writhing mass in an ashtray, where beautifully conforming it folded upon itself, a burning castle, collapsed, subsided to a ticking hive through which sparks like tiny red worms crawled and flew, while above a few grey wisps of ashes floated in the thin smoke, a dead husk now, faintly crepitant . . .

Suddenly from outside, a bell spoke out, then ceased abruptly : *dolente . . . dolore!*

Over the town, in the dark tempestuous night, backwards revolved the luminous wheel.

... 'A corpse will be transported by express !'

The tireless resilient voice that had just lobbed this singular remark over the Bella Vista bar window-sill into the square was, though its owner remained unseen, unmistakable and achingly familiar as the spacious flower-boxed balconied hotel itself, and as unreal, Yvonne thought.

'But why, Fernando, why should a corpse be transported by express, do you suppose?'

The Mexican taxi-driver, familiar too, who'd just picked up her bags – there'd been no taxi at the tiny Quauhnahuac airfield though, only the bumptious station wagon that insisted on taking her to the Bella Vista – put them down again on the pavement as to assure her : I know why you're here, but no one's recognized you except me, and I won't give you away. '*Sí señora,*' he chuckled. '*Señora – El Cónsul.*' Sighing, he inclined his head with a certain admiration towards the bar window. '*¡Qué hombre!*'

' – on the other hand, damn it, Fernando, why shouldn't it? Why shouldn't a corpse be transported by express?'

'*Absolutamente necesario.*'

' – just a bunch of Alladamnbama farmers!'

The last was yet another voice. So the bar, open all night for the occasion, was evidently full. Ashamed, numb with nostalgia and anxiety, reluctant to enter the crowded bar, though equally reluctant to have the taxi-driver go in for her, Yvonne, her consciousness so lashed by wind and air and voyage she still seemed to be travelling, still sailing into Acapulco harbour yesterday evening through a hurricane of immense and gorgeous butterflies swooping seaward to greet the *Pennsylvania* – at first it was as though fountains of multicoloured stationery were being swept out of the saloon lounge – glanced defensively round the square, really tranquil in the midst of this commotion, of the butterflies still zigzagging overhead or past the heavy open ports, endlessly vanishing astern, *their* square, motionless and brilliant in the seven o'clock morning sunlight, silent yet somehow poised, expectant, with one eye half open already, the merry-go-rounds, the Ferris wheel, lightly dreaming, looking forward to the *fiesta* later – the ranged rugged taxis too that were looking forward to something else, a taxi strike that afternoon, she'd been confidentially informed. The *zócalo* was just the same in spite of its air of slumbering Harlequin. The old bandstand stood empty, the equestrian statue of the turbulent Huerta rode under the nutant trees wild-eyed evermore, gazing over the valley beyond which, as if nothing had happened and it was November 1936 and not November 1938, rose, eternally, her volcanoes, her beautiful, beautiful volcanoes. Ah, how familiar it all was: Quauhnahuac, her town of cold mountain water swiftly running. Where the eagle stops! Or did it really mean, as Louis said, near the wood? The trees, the massive shining depths of these ancient fresno trees, how had she ever lived without them? She drew a deep breath, the air had yet a hint about it of dawn, the dawn this morning at Acapulco – green and deep purple high above and gold scrolled back to reveal a river of lapis where the horn of Venus burned so fiercely she could imagine her dim shadow cast from its light on the airfield, the vultures floating lazily up there above the brick-red horizon into whose peaceful foreboding the little plane of the Compañía Mexicana de Aviación had ascended, like a minute red demon, winged emissary of Lucifer, the windsock below streaming out its steadfast farewell.

She took in the *zócalo* with a long final look – the untenanted ambulance that might not have moved since she'd last been here, outside the Servicio de Ambulancia within Cortez Palace, the huge paper poster strung between two trees which said *Hotel Bella Vista Gran Baile Noviembre 1938 a Beneficio de la Cruz Roja. Los Mejores Artistas del radio en acción. No falte Vd,* beneath which some of the guests were returning home, pallid and exhausted as the music that struck up at this moment and reminded her the ball was still proceeding – then entered the bar silently, blinking, myopic in the swift leathery perfumed alcoholic dusk, the sea that morning going in with her, rough and pure, the long dawn rollers advancing, rising, and crashing down to glide, sinking, in colourless ellipses over the sand, while early pelicans hunting turned and dived, dived and turned and dived again into the spume, moving with the precision of planets, the spent breakers racing back to their calm; flotsam was scattered all along the beach : she had heard, from the small boats tossing in the Spanish Main, the boys, like young Tritons, already beginning to blow on their mournful conch shells . . .

The bar was empty, however.

Or rather it contained one figure. Still in his dress clothes, which weren't particularly dishevelled, the Consul, a lock of fair hair falling over his eyes and one hand clasped in his short pointed beard, was sitting sideways with one foot on the rail of an adjacent stool at the small right-angled counter, half leaning over it and talking apparently to himself, for the barman, a sleek dark lad of about eighteen, stood at a little distance against a glass partition that divided the room (from yet another bar, she remembered now, giving on a side-street) and didn't have the air of listening. Yvonne stood there silently by the door, unable to make a move, watching, the roar of the plane still with her, the buffeting of wind and air as they left the sea behind, the roads below still climbing and dropping, the little towns still steadily passing with their humped churches. Quauhnahuac with all its cobalt swimming pools rising again obliquely to meet her. But the exhilaration of her flight, of mountain piled on mountain, the terrific onslaught of sunlight while the earth turned yet in shadow, a river flashing, a gorge winding darkly beneath, the volcanoes abruptly wheeling into view from the glowing east, the exhilaration and the longing had left her. Yvonne felt her spirit that had flown to meet this man's as if already sticking to the leather. She saw she was mistaken about the barman : he was listening after all. That is, while he mightn't understand what Geoffrey (who was, she noticed, wearing no socks) was talking about, he was waiting, his towelled hands overhauling the glasses ever more slowly, for an opening to say or do something. He set the glass he was drying down. Then he picked up the Consul's cigarette, which was consuming itself in an ashtray at the counter edge, inhaled it deeply, closing his eyes with an expression of playful ecstasy, opened them and pointed, scarcely exhaling now the slow billowing smoke from his nostrils and mouth, at an advertisement for *Cafeaspirina*, a woman wearing a scarlet brassière lying on a scrolled divan, behind the upper row of *tequila añejo* bottles. '*Absolutamente necesario,*' he said, and Yvonne realized it was the woman, not the *Cafeaspirina,* he meant (the Consul's phrase doubtless) was absolutely necessary. But he hadn't attracted the Consul's attention, so he closed his eyes again with the same expression, opened them, replaced the Consul's cigarette, and, still exuding smoke, pointed once more to the advertisement – next to it she noticed one for the local cinema, simply, *Las Manos de Orlac, con Peter Lorre* – and repeated: '*Absolutamente necesario.*'

'A corpse, whether adult or child,' the Consul had resumed, after briefly pausing to laugh at this pantomime, and to agree, with a kind of agony, '*Sí, Fernando, absolutamente necesario*' – and it is a ritual, she thought, a ritual between them, as there were once rituals between us, only Geoffrey has gotten a little bored with it at last – resumed his study of a blue and red Mexican National Railways time-table. Then he looked up abruptly and saw her, peering shortsightedly about him before recognizing her, standing there, a little blurred probably because the sunlight was behind her, with one hand thrust through the handle of her scarlet bag resting on her hip, standing there as she knew he must see her, half jaunty, a little diffident.

Still holding the time-table the Consul built himself to his feet as she came forward. ' – *Good* God.'

Yvonne hesitated but he made no move towards her; she slipped quietly on to a stool beside him; they did not kiss.

'Surprise party. I've come back ... My plane got in an hour ago.'

' – when Alabama comes through we ask nobody any questions,' came suddenly from the bar on the other side of the glass partition: 'We come through with heels flying!'

' – From Acapulco, Hornos ... I came by boat, Geoff, from San Pedro – Panama Pacific. The *Pennsylvania*. Geoff – '

' – bull-headed Dutchmen! The sun parches the lips and they crack. Oh Christ, it's a shame! The horses all go away kicking in the dust! I wouldn't have it. They plugged 'em too. They don't miss it. They shoot first and ask questions later. You're goddam right. And that's a nice thing to say. I take a bunch of goddamned farmers, then ask them no questions. Righto! – smoke a cool cigarette – '

'Don't you love these early mornings?' The Consul's voice, but not his hand, was perfectly steady as now he put the time-table down. 'Have, as our friend next door suggests,' he inclined his head towards the partition, 'a – ' the name on the trembling, offered, and rejected cigarette package struck her: Alas! ' – '

The Consul was saying with gravity: 'Ah, Hornos. – But why come via Cape Horn? It has a bad habit of wagging its tail, sailors tell me. Or does it mean ovens?'

' – *Calle Nicaragua, cincuenta dos*.' Yvonne pressed a *tostón* on a dark god by this time in possession of her bags who bowed and disappeared obscurely.

'What if I didn't live there any longer.' The Consul, sitting down again, was shaking so violently he had to hold the bottle of whisky he was pouring himself a drink from with both hands. 'Have a drink?'

' – '

Or should she? She should: even though she hated drinking in the morning she undoubtedly should: it was what she had made up her mind to do if necessary, not to have one drink alone but a great many drinks with the Consul. But instead she could feel the smile leaving her face that was struggling to keep back the tears she had forbidden herself on any account, thinking and knowing Geoffrey knew she was thinking: 'I was prepared for this, I was prepared for it.' 'You have one and I'll cheer,' she found herself saying. (As a matter of fact she had been prepared for almost anything. After all, what could one expect? She had told herself all the way down on the ship, a ship because she would have time on board to persuade herself her journey was neither thoughtless nor precipitate, and on the plane when she knew it was both, that she should have warned him, that it was abominably unfair to take him by surprise.) 'Geoffrey,' she went on, wondering if she seemed pathetic sitting there, all her carefully thought-out speeches, her plans and tact so obviously vanishing in the gloom, or merely repellent – she felt slightly repellent – because she wouldn't have a drink. 'What have you done? I wrote you and wrote you. I wrote till my heart broke. What have you done with your – '

' – life,' came from beyond the glass partition. 'What a life! Christ, it's a shame! Where I come from they don't run. We're going through busting this way – '

' – No. I thought of course you'd returned to England, when you didn't answer. What have you done? Oh Geoff – have you resigned from the service?'

' – went down to Fort Sale. Took your shoeshot. And took your Brownings. – Jump, jump, jump, jump, jump – see, get it – '

'I ran into Louis in Santa Barbara. He said you were still here.'

' – and like hell you can, you can't do it, and that's what you do in Alabama!'

'Well, actually I've only been away once.' The Consul took a long shuddering drink, then sat down again beside her. 'To Oaxaca. – Remember Oaxaca?'

' – Oaxaca? – '

' – Oaxaca. – '

– The word was like a breaking heart, a sudden peal of stifled bells in a gale, the last syllables of one dying of thirst in the desert. Did she remember Oaxaca! The roses and the great tree, was that, the dust and the buses to Etla and Nochitlán? and : *'damas acompañadas de un caballero, gratis!'* Or at night their cries of love, rising into the ancient fragrant Mayan air, heard only by ghosts? In Oaxaca they had found each other once. She was watching the Consul who seemed less on the defensive than in process while straightening out the leaflets on the bar of changing mentally from the part played for Fernando to the part he would play for her, watching him almost with amazement : 'Surely this cannot be us,' she cried in her heart suddenly. 'This cannot be us – say that it is not, somebody, this cannot be *us* here!' – Divorce. What did the word really mean? She'd looked it up in the dictionary, on the ship: to sunder, to sever. And divorced meant: sundered, severed. Oaxaca meant divorce. They had not been divorced there but that was where the Consul had gone when she left, as if into the heart of the sundering, of the severance. Yet they had loved one another! But it was as though their love were wandering over some desolate cactus plain, far from here, lost, stumbling and falling, attacked by wild beasts, calling for help – dying, to sigh at last, with a kind of weary peace: Oaxaca –

–'The strange thing about this little corpse, Yvonne,' the Consul was saying, 'is that it must be accompanied by a person holding its hand: no, sorry. Apparently not its hand, just a first-class ticket.' He held up, smiling, his own right hand which shook as with a movement of wiping chalk from an imaginary blackboard. 'It's really the shakes that make this kind of life insupportable. But they will stop: I was only drinking enough so they would. Just the necessary, the therapeutic drink.' Yvonne looked back at him. '–but the shakes are the worst of course,' he was going on. 'You get to like the other after a while, and I'm really doing very well, I'm much better than I was six months ago, very much better than I was, say, in Oaxaca' – noticing a curious familiar glare in his eyes that always frightened her, a glare turned inward now like one of those sombrely brilliant cluster-lamps down the hatches of the *Pennsylvania* on the work of unloading, only this was a work of spoliation: and she felt a sudden dread lest this glare, as of old, should swing outward, turn upon her.

'God knows I've seen you like this before,' her thoughts were saying, her love was saying, through the gloom of the bar, 'too many times for it to be a surprise anyhow. You are denying me again. But this time there is a profound difference. This is like an ultimate denial – oh Geoffrey, why can't you turn back? Must you go on and on for ever into this stupid darkness, seeking it, even now, where I cannot reach you, ever on into the darkness of the sundering, of the severance! – Oh Geoffrey, why do you do it!'

'But look here, hang it all, it is not altogether darkness,' the Consul seemed to be saying in reply to her, gently, as he produced a half-filled pipe and with the utmost difficulty lit it, and as her eyes followed his as they roved around the bar, not meeting those of the barman, who had gravely, busily effaced himself into the background, 'you misunderstand me if you think it is altogether darkness I see, and if you insist on thinking so, how can I tell you why I do it? But if you look at that sunlight there, ah, then perhaps you'll get the answer, see, look at the way it falls through the window: what beauty can compare to that of a *cantina* in the early morning? Your volcanoes outside? Your stars – Ras Algethi? Antares raging south south-east? Forgive me, no. Not so much the beauty of this one necessarily, which, a regression on my part, is not perhaps properly a *cantina,* but think of all the other terrible ones where people go mad that will soon be taking down their shutters, for not even the gates of heaven, opening wide to receive me, could fill me with such celestial complicated and hopeless joy as the iron screen that rolls up with a crash, as the unpadlocked jostling jalousies which admit those whose souls tremble with the drinks they carry unsteadily to their lips. All mystery, all hope, all disappointment, yes, all disaster, is here, beyond those swinging doors. And, by the way, do you see that old woman from Tarasco sitting in the corner, you didn't before, but do you now?' his eyes asked her, gazing round him with the bemused unfocused brightness of a lover's, his love asked her, 'how, unless you drink as I do, can you hope to understand the beauty of an old woman from Tarasco who plays dominoes at seven o'clock in the morning?'

It was true, it was almost uncanny, there *was* someone else in the room she hadn't noticed until the Consul, without a word, had glanced behind them: now Yvonne's eyes came to rest on the old woman, who was sitting in the shadow at the bar's one table. On the edge of the table her stick, made of steel with some animal's claw for a handle, hung like something alive. She had a little chicken on a cord which she kept under her dress over her heart. The chicken peeped out with pert, jerky, sidelong glances. She set the little chicken on a table near her where it pecked among the dominoes, uttering tiny cries. Then she replaced it, drawing her dress tenderly over it. But Yvonne looked away. The old woman with her chicken and the dominoes chilled her heart. It was like an evil omen.

– 'Talking of corpses' – the Consul poured himself another whisky and was signing a chit book with a somewhat steadier hand while Yvonne sauntered towards the door – 'personally I'd like to be buried next to William Blackstone –' He pushed the book back for Fernando, to whom mercifully he had not attempted to introduce her. 'The man who went to live among the Indians. You know who he was, of course?' The Consul stood half turned towards her, doubtfully regarding this new drink he had not picked up.

' – Christ, if you want it, Alabama, go ahead and take it ... I don't want it. But if you wish it, you go and take it.'

'*Absolutamente necesario –*'

The Consul left half of it.

Outside, in the sunlight, in the backwash of tabid music from the still-continuing ball, Yvonne waited again, casting nervous glances over her shoulder at the main entrance of the hotel from which belated revellers like half-dazed wasps out of a hidden nest issued every few moments while, on the instant, correct, abrupt, army and navy, consular, the Consul, with scarce a tremor now, found a pair of dark glasses and put them on.

'Well,' he said, 'the taxis seem to have all disappeared. Shall we walk?'

'Why what's happened to the car?' So confused by apprehension of meeting any acquaintance was she, Yvonne had almost taken the arm of another man wearing dark glasses, a ragged young Mexican leaning against the hotel wall to whom the Consul, slapping his stick over his wrist and with something enigmatic in his voice observed : '*Buenas tardes, señor.*' Yvonne started forward quickly. 'Yes, let's walk.'

The Consul took her arm with courtliness (the ragged Mexican with the dark glasses had been joined, she noticed, by another man with a shade over one eye and bare feet who had been leaning against the wall farther down, to whom the Consul also remarked '*Buenas tardes*', but there were no more guests coming out of the hotel, only the two men who'd politely called 'Buenas' after them standing there nudging each other as if to say: 'He said "Buenas tardes", what a card he is!') and they set off obliquely through the square. The fiesta wouldn't start till much later and the streets that remembered so many other Days of the Dead were fairly deserted. The bright banners, the paper streamers, flashed: the great wheel brooded under the trees, brilliant, motionless. Even so the town around and below them was already full of sharp remote noises like explosions of rich colour. ¡Box! said an advertisement. ARENA TOMALÍN. Frente al Jardín Xicotancatl. Domingo 8 de Noviembre de 1938. 4 Emocionantes Peleas.

Yvonne tried to keep herself from asking:

'Did you smack the car up again?'

'As a matter of fact I've lost it.'

'Lost it!'

'It's a pity because – but look here, dash it all, aren't you terribly tired, Yvonne?'

'Not in the least! I should think you're the one to be –'

– ¡Box! Preliminar a 4 Rounds. EL TURCO (Gonzalo Calderón de Par. de 52 kilos) vs EL OSO (de Par. de 53 kilos).

'I had a million hours of sleep on the boat! And I'd far rather walk, only –'

'Nothing. Just a touch of rheumatiz. – O is it the sprue? I'm glad to get some circulation going in the old legs.'

– ¡Box! Evento Especial a 5 rounds, en los que el vencedor pasará al grupo de Semi-Finales. TOMA AGUERO (El Invencible Indio de Quauhnahuac de 57 kilos, que acaba de llegar de la Capital de la República). ARENA TOMALÍN. Frente al Jardín Xicotancatl.

'It's a pity about the car because we might have gone to the boxing,' said the Consul, who was walking almost exaggeratedly erect.

'I hate boxing.'

' – But that's not till next Sunday anyhow ... I heard they had some kind of a bullthrowing on today over at Tomalín. – Do you remember –'

'No!'

The Consul, with no more recognition than she, held up one finger in dubious greeting to an individual resembling a carpenter, running past them wagging his head and carrying a sawed length of grained board under his arm and who threw, almost chanted, a laughing word at him that sounded like: '¡Mescalito!'

The sunlight blazed down on them, blazed on the eternal ambulance whose headlights were momentarily transformed into a blinding magnifying glass, glazed on the volcanoes – she could not look at them now. Born in Hawaii, she'd had volcanoes in her life before, however. Seated on a park bench under a tree in the square, his feet barely touching the ground, the little public scribe was already crashing away on a giant typewriter.

'I am taking the only way out, semicolon,' the Consul offered cheerfully and soberly in passing. 'Good-bye, full stop. Change of paragraph, change of chapter, change of worlds – '

The whole scene about her – the names on the shops surrounding the square: *La China Poblana, hand-embroidered dresses*, the advertisements: *Baños de la Libertad, Los mejores de la Capital y los únicos en donde nunca falta el agua, Estufas especiales para Damas y Caballeros:* and *Sr Panadero: Si quiere hacer buen pan exija las harinas 'Princesa Donaji'* – striking Yvonne as so strangely familiar all over again and yet so sharply strange after the year's absence, the severance of thought and body, mode of being, became almost intolerable for a moment. 'You might have made use of him to answer some of *my* letters,' she said.

'Look, do you remember what Maria used to call it?' The Consul, with his stick, was indicating through the trees the little American grocery store, catercorner to Cortez Palace. 'Peegly Weegly.'

'I won't,' Yvonne thought, hurrying on and biting her lips. 'I won't cry.'

The Consul had taken her arm. 'I'm sorry, I never thought.'

They emerged on the street again: when they had crossed it she was grateful for the excuse suggested by the printer's shop window for readjustment. They stood, as once, looking in. The shop, adjacent to the Palace, but divided from it by the breadth of a steep narrow street desperate as a winze, was opening early. From the mirror within the window an ocean creature so drenched and coppered by sun and winnowed by sea-wind and spray looked back at her she seemed, even while making the fugitive motions of Yvonne's vanity, somewhere beyond human grief charioting the surf. But the sun turned grief to poison and a glowing body only mocked the sick heart, Yvonne knew, if the sun-darkened creature of waves and sea margins and windows did not! In the window itself, on either side of this abstracted gaze of her mirrored face, the same brave wedding invitations she remembered were ranged, the same touched-up prints of extravagantly floriferous brides, but this time there was something she hadn't seen before, which the Consul now pointed out with a murmur of 'Strange', peering closer: a photographic enlargement, purporting to show the disintegration of a glacial deposit in the Sierra Madre, of a great rock split by forest fires. This curious, and curiously sad picture – to which the nature of the other exhibits lent an added ironic poignance – set behind and above the already spinning flywheel of the presses, was called : *La Despedida*.

They moved on past the front of Cortez Palace, then down its blind side began to descend the cliff that traversed it widthways. Their path made the short cut to the Calle Tierra del Fuego which curved below to meet them but the cliff was little better than a rubbish heap with smouldering debris and they had to pick their way carefully. Yvonne breathed more freely though, now they were leaving the centre of the town behind. La Despedida, she thought. The Parting! After the damp and detritus had done their work both severed halves of that blasted rock would crumble to earth. It was inevitable, so it said on the picture ... Was it really? Wasn't there some way of saving the poor rock whose immutability so short a time ago no one would have dreamed of doubting! Ah, who would have thought of it then as other than a single integrated rock? But granted it had been split, was there no way before total disintegration should set in of at least saving the severed halves? There was no way. The violence of the fire which split the rock apart had

99

also incited the destruction of each separate rock, cancelling the power that might have held them unities. Oh, but why – by some fanciful geologic thaumaturgy, couldn't the pieces be welded together again! She longed to heal the cleft rock. She was one of the rocks and she yearned to save the other, that both might be saved. By a superlapidary effort she moved herself nearer it, poured out her pleas, her passionate tears, told all her forgiveness : the other rock stood unmoved. 'That's all very well,' it said, 'but it happens to be your fault, and as for myself, I propose to disintegrate as I please!'

' – in Tortu,' the Consul was saying, though Yvonne was not following, and now they had come out in the Calle Tierra del Fuego itself, a rough narrow dusty street that, deserted, looked quite unfamiliar. The Consul was beginning to shake again.

'Geoffrey, I'm so thirsty, why don't we stop and have a drink?'

'Geoffrey, let's be reckless this once and get tight together before breakfast!'

Yvonne said neither of these things.

– The Street of the Land of Fire! To their left, raised high above road level, were uneven sidewalks with rough steps hewn in them. The whole little thoroughfare, slightly humpbacked in the centre where the open sewers had been filled in, was banked sharply down to the right as though it had once sideslipped in an earthquake. On this side one-storied houses with tiled roofs and oblong barred windows stood flush with the street but seemingly below it. On the other, above them, they were passing small shops, sleepy, though mostly opening or, like the 'Molino para Nixtamal, Morelense', open : harness shops, a milk shop under its sign Lechería (brothel, someone insisted it meant, and she hadn't seen the joke), dark interiors with strings of tiny sausages, chorizos, hanging over the counters where you could also buy goat cheese or sweet quince wine or cacao, into one of which the Consul was now, with a 'momentito', disappearing. 'Just go on and I'll catch you up. I won't be a jiffy.'

Yvonne walked on past the place a short distance, then

retraced her steps. She had not entered any of these shops since their first week in Mexico and the danger of being recognized in the *abarrotes* was slight. Nevertheless, repenting her tardy impulse to follow the Consul in, she waited outside, restless as a little yacht turning at anchor. The opportunity to join him ebbed. A mood of martyrdom stole upon her. She wanted the Consul to see her, when he emerged, waiting there, abandoned and affronted. But glancing back the way they had come she forgot Geoffrey an instant. – It was unbelievable. She was in Quauhnahuac again! There was Cortez Palace and there, high on the cliff, a man standing gazing over the valley who from his air of martial intentness might have been Cortez himself. The man moved, spoiling the illusion. Now he looked less like Cortez than the poor young man in the dark glasses who'd been leaning against the wall of the Bella Vista.

'*You-are-a-man-who-like-much-Vine!*' now issued powerfully from the *abarrotes* into the peaceful street, followed by a roar of incredibly good-humoured but ruffianly male laughter. 'You are – *diablo!*' There was a pause in which she heard the Consul saying something. '*Eggs!*' the good-humoured voice exploded again. 'You – *two diablos! You tree diablos.*' The voice crackled with glee. '*Eggs!*' Then: 'Who is the beautiful *layee?* – Ah, you are – ah *five diablos*, you ah – *Eggs!*' ludicrously followed the Consul, who appeared at this moment, calmly smiling, on the pavement above Yvonne.

'In Tortu', he was saying as, steadier again, he fell into step beside her, 'the ideal University, where no application whatsoever, so I have heard on good authority, nothing, not even athletics, is allowed to interfere with the business of – look out! ... drinking.'

It came sailing out of nowhere, the child's funeral, the tiny lace-covered coffin followed by the band: two saxophones, bass guitar, a fiddle, playing of all things '*La Cucaracha*', the women behind, very solemn, while several paces back a few hangers-on were joking, straggling along in the dust almost at a run.

They stood to one side while the little cortège slanted by swiftly in the direction of the town, then walked on in silence not looking at one another. The banking of the street now became less acute and the sidewalks and the shops dropped away. To the left there was only a low blank wall with vacant lots behind it, whereas to the right the houses had turned into low open shanties filled with black carbon. Yvonne's heart, that had been struggling with an insufferable pang, suddenly missed a beat. Though one might not think it they were approaching the residental district, their own terrain.

'Do look where you're going, Geoffrey !' But it was Yvonne who had stumbled rounding the right-angled corner into the Calle Nicaragua. The Consul regarded her without expression as she stared up into the sun at the bizarre house opposite them near the head of their street, with two towers and a connecting catwalk over the ridgepole, at which someone else, a peon with his back turned, was also gazing curiously.

'Yes, it's still there, it hasn't budged an inch,' he said, and now they had passed the house to their left with its inscription on the wall she didn't want to see and were walking down the Calle Nicaragua.

'Yet the street looks different somehow.' Yvonne relapsed into silence again. Actually she was making a tremendous effort to control herself. What she could not have explained was that recently in her picture of Quauhnahuac this house hadn't been here at all ! On the occasions imagination had led her with Geoffrey down the Calle Nicaragua lately, never once, poor phantoms, had they been confronted with Jacques's *zacuali*. It had vanished some time before, leaving not a trace, it was as if the house had never existed, just as in the mind of a murderer, it may happen, some prominent landmark in the vicinity of his crime becomes obliterated, so that on returning to the neighbourhood, once so familiar, he scarcely knows where to turn. But the Calle Nicaragua didn't really look different. Here it was, still cluttered up with large grey loose stones, full of the same lunar potholes, and in that well-known state of frozen eruption that resembled repair but which in fact only testified facetiously to the continued deadlock betwen the Municipality and the property owners here over its maintenance. Calle Nicaragua ! – the name, despite everything, sang plangently within her : only that ridiculous shock at Jacques's house could account for her feeling, with one part of her mind, calm as she did about it.

The road, broad, sidewalkless, ran with increasing steepness downhill, mostly between high walls overhung by trees, though at the moment there were more little carbon shanties to their right, down to a leftward curve some three hundred yards away where roughly the same distance again above their own house it was lost from sight. Trees blocked the view beyond of low rolling hills. Nearly all the large residences were on their left, built far back from the road towards the *barranca* in order to face the volcanoes across the valley. She saw the mountains again in the distance through a gap between two estates, a small field bounded by a barbed-wire fence and overflowing with tall spiny grasses tossed wildly together as by a big wind that had abruptly ceased. There they were, Popocatepetl and Ixtaccihuatl, remote ambassadors of Mauna Loa, Mokuaweoweo : dark clouds now obscured their base. The grass, she thought, wasn't as green as it should be at the end of the rains : there must have been a dry spell, though the gutters on either side of the road were brimful of rushing mountain water and –

'And he's still there too. He hasn't budged an inch either.' The Consul without turning was nodding back in the direction of M. Laruelle's house.

'Who – who hasn't – ' Yvonne faltered. She glanced behind her : there was only the peon who had stopped looking at the house and was going into an alleyway.

'Jacques.'

'Jacques!'

'That's right. In fact we've had terrific times together. We've been slap through everything from Bishop Berkeley to the four o'clock *mirabilis jalapa*.'

'You do *what*?'

'The Diplomatic Service.' The Consul had paused and was lighting his pipe. 'Sometimes I really think there's something to be said for it.'

' – '

He stopped to float a match down the brimming gutter and

somehow they were moving, even hurrying on : she heard be-
musedly the swift angry click and crunch of her heels on
the road and the Consul's seemingly effortless voice at her
shoulder.

'For instance had you ever been British attaché to the White
Russian Embassy in Zagreb in 1922, and I've always thought a
woman like you would have done very well as attaché to the
White Russian Embassy in Zagreb in 1922, though God knows
how it managed to survive that long, you might have acquired
a certain, I don't say technique exactly, but a mien, a mask, a
way, at any rate, of throwing a look into your face at a moment's notice of sublime dishonest detachment.'

' – '

'Although I can very well see how it strikes you – how the
picture of our implied indifference, Jacques's and mine that is,
I mean, strikes you, as being even more indecent than that, say,
Jacques shouldn't have left when you did or that we shouldn't
have dropped the friendship.'

' – '

'But had you, Yvonne, ever been on the bridge of a British
Q-ship, and I've always thought a woman like you would have
been very good on the bridge of a British Q-ship – peering at
the Tottenham Court Road through a telescope, only figura-
tively speaking of course, day in and day out, counting the
waves, you might have learnt – '

'Please look where you're going!'

'Though had you of course ever been Consul to Cuckolds-
haven, that town cursed by the lost love of Maximilian and
Carlotta, then, why then – '

– ¡BOX! ARENA TOMALÍN. EL BALÓN *vs* EL REDONDILLO.

'But I don't think I finished about the little corpse. What is
really so astonishing about him is that he has to be checked,
actually checked, to the U.S. Border of Exit. While the charges
for him are equivalent to two adult passengers – '

' – '

'However since you don't seem to want to listen to me, here's
something else perhaps I ought to tell you.'

' – '

104

'Something else, I repeat, very important, that perhaps I ought to tell you.'

'Yes. What is it?'

'About Hugh.'

Yvonne said at last:

'You've heard from Hugh. How is he?'

'He's staying with me.'

– |BOX! ARENA TOMALÍN. FRENTE AL JARDIN XICOTAN-CATL. *Domingo 8 de Noviembre de 1938. 4 Emocionantes Peleas.* EL BALÓN *vs* EL REDONDILLO.

Las Manos de Orlac. Con Peter Lorre.

'*What!*' Yvonne stopped dead.

'It seems he's been in America this time on a cattle ranch,' the Consul was saying rather gravely as somehow, anyhow, they moved on, but this time more slowly. 'Why, heaven knows. It couldn't be he was learning to ride, but still, he turned up about a week ago in a distinctly unpukka outfit, looking like Hoot S. Hart in the *Riders to the Purple Sage*. Apparently he'd teleported himself, or been deported, from America by cattle-truck. I don't pretend to know how the Press get by in these matters. Or maybe it was a bet ... Anyhow he got as far as Chihuahua with the cattle, and some gun-running gun-toting pal by the name of – Weber? – I forget, anyway, I didn't meet him, flew him the rest of the way.' The Consul knocked out his pipe on his heel, smiling. 'It seems everyone comes flying to see me these days.'

'But – but *Hugh* – I don't understand – '

'He'd lost his clothes *en route* but it wasn't carelessness, if you can believe it, only that they wanted to make him pay higher duty at the border than they were worth, so quite naturally he left them behind. He hadn't lost his passport however, which was unusual perhaps because he's still somehow with – though I haven't the foggiest in what capacity – the London *Globe* ... Of course you knew he's become quite famous lately. For the second time, in case you weren't aware of the first.'

'Did he know about our divorce?' Yvonne managed to ask.

The Consul shook his head. They walked on slowly, the Consul looking at the ground.

'Did you tell him?'

The Consul was silent, walking more and more slowly. 'What did I say?' he said at length.

'Nothing, Geoff.'

'Well, he knows now that we're separated, of course.' The Consul decapitated a dusty coquelicot poppy growing by the side of the gutter with his stick. 'But he expected us both to be here. I gather he had some idea we might let – but I avoided telling him the divorce had gone through. That is, I think I did. I meant to avoid it. So far as I know, honestly, I hadn't got around to telling him when he left.'

'Then he's not staying with you any longer.'

The Consul burst out in a laugh that became a cough. 'Oh yes he is! He most certainly is ... In fact, I nearly passed out altogether under the stress of his salvage operations. Which is to say he's been trying to "straighten me out". Can't you see it? Can't you recognize his fine Italian hand? And he almost literally succeeded right off with some malevolent strychnine compound he produced. But', just for one moment the Consul seemed to have difficulty placing one foot before another, 'to be more concrete, actually he did have a better reason for staying than to play Theodore Watts Dunton. To my Swinburne.' The Consul decapitated another poppy. 'Mute Swinburne. He'd got wind of some story while vacationing on the ranch and came after it here like a red rag after a bull. Didn't I tell you that? ... Which – didn't I say so before? – is why he's gone off to Mexico City.'

After a while Yvonne said weakly, scarcely hearing herself speak : 'Well, we may have a little time together, mayn't we?'

'¿Quien sabé?'

'But you mean he's in the City now,' she covered hastily.

'Oh, he's throwing up the job – he might be home now. At any rate he'll be back today, I think. He says he wants "action". Poor old chap, he's wearing a very popular front indeed these days.' Whether the Consul was being sincere or not he added, sympathetically enough, it sounded, 'And God alone knows what will be the end of that romantic little urge in him.'

'And how will he feel', Yvonne asked bravely all at once, 'when he sees you again?'

'Yes, well, not much difference, not enough time to show, but I'd just been about to say', the Consul went on with a slight hoarseness, 'that the terrific times, Laruelle's and mine, I mean, ceased on the advent of Hugh.' He was poking at the dust with his stick, making little patterns for a minute as he went along, like a blind man. 'They were mostly mine because Jacques has a weak stomach and is usually sick after three drinks and after four he would start to play the Good Samaritan, and after five Theodore Watts Dunton too ... So that I appreciated, so to speak, a change of technique. At least to the extent that I find I shall be grateful now, on Hugh's behalf, if you'd say nothing to him – '

'Oh – '

The Consul cleared his throat. 'Not that I have been drinking much of course in his absence, and not that I'm not absolutely cold stone sober now, as you can readily see.'

'Oh yes indeed,' Yvonne smiled, full of thoughts that had already swept her a thousand miles in frantic retreat from all this. Yet she was walking on slowly beside him. And deliberately as a climber on a high unguarded place looks up at the pine trees above on the precipice and comforts himself by saying: 'Never mind about the drop below me, how very much worse if I were on top of one of those pines up there!' she forced herself out of the moment: she stopped thinking: or she thought about the street again, remembering her last poignant glimpse of it – and how even more desperate things had seemed then! – at the beginning of that fateful journey to Mexico City, glancing back from the now lost Plymouth as they turned the corner, crashing, crunching down on its springs into the potholes, stopping dead, then crawling, leaping forward again, keeping in, it didn't matter on which side, to the walls. They were higher than she recalled and covered with bougainvillea; massive smouldering banks of bloom. Over them she could see the crests of trees, their boughs heavy and motionless, and occasionally a watch-tower, the eternal mirador of Parián state, set among them, the houses invisible here below the walls and from on top too, she'd once taken the trouble to find out, as if shrunken down inside their patios, the miradors cut off, floating above like lonely rooftrees of the soul. Nor could you distinguish the houses much better through the wrought-iron lacework of the high gates, vaguely reminiscent of New Orleans, locked in these walls on which were furtively pencilled lovers' trysts, and which so often concealed less Mexico than a Spaniard's dream of home. The gutter on the right ran underground a while and another of those low shanties built on the street frowned at her with its dark open sinister bunkers – where Maria used to fetch their carbon. Then the water tumbled out into the sunlight and on the other side, through a gap in the walls, Popocatepetl emerged alone. Without her knowing it they had passed the corner and the entrance to their house was in sight.

The street was now absolutely deserted and save for the gushing murmurous gutters that now became like two fierce little streams racing each other, silent: it reminded her, confusedly, of how in her heart's eye, before she'd met Louis, and when she'd half imagined the Consul back in England, she'd tried to keep Quauhnahuac itself, as a sort of safe footway where his phantom could endlessly pace, accompanied only by her own consoling unwanted shadow, above the rising waters of possible catastrophe.

Then since the other day Quauhnahuac had seemed, though emptied still, different – purged, swept clean of the past, with Geoffrey here alone, but now in the flesh, redeemable, wanting her help.

And here Geoffrey indeed was, not only not alone, not only not wanting her help, but living in the midst of her blame, a blame by which, to all appearances, he was curiously sustained –

Yvonne gripped her bag tightly, suddenly lightheaded and barely conscious of the landmarks the Consul, who seemed recovered in spirits, was silently indicating with his stick: the country lane to the right, and the little church that had been turned into a school with the tombstones and the horizontal bar in the playground, the dark entrance in the ditch – the high walls on both sides had temporarily disappeared altogether – to the abandoned iron mine running under the garden.

To and fro from school ..
Popocatepetl
It was your shining day ...

The Consul hummed. Yvonne felt her heart melting. A sense
of a shared, a mountain peace seemed to fall between them; it
was false, it was a lie, but for a moment it was almost as though
they were returning home from marketing in days past. She
took his arm, laughing, they fell into step. And now here were
the walls again, and their drive sloping down into the street
where no one had allayed the dust, already paddled by early
bare feet, and now here was their gate, off its hinges and lying
just beyond the entrance, as for that matter it always had lain,
defiantly, half hidden under the bank of bougainvillea.

'There now, Yvonne. Come along, darling ... We're almost
home!'

'Yes.'

'Strange – ' the Consul said.

A hideous pariah dog followed them in.

THE tragedy, proclaimed, as they made their way up the crescent of the drive, no less by the gaping potholes in it than by the tall exotic plants, livid and crepuscular through his dark glasses, perishing on every hand of unnecessary thirst, staggering, it almost appeared, against one another, yet struggling like dying voluptuaries in a vision to maintain some final attitude of potency, or of a collective desolate fecundity, the Consul thought distantly, seemed to be reviewed and interpreted by a person walking at his side suffering for him and saying: 'Regard: see how strange, how sad, familiar things may be. Touch this tree, once your friend: alas, that that which you have known in the blood should ever seem so strange! Look up at that niche in the wall over there on the house where Christ is still, suffering, who would help you if you asked him: you cannot ask him. Consider the agony of the roses. See, on the lawn Concepta's coffee beans, you used to say they were María's, drying in the sun. Do you know their sweet aroma any more? Regard: the plantains with their queer familiar blooms, once emblematic of life, now of an evil phallic death. You do not know how to love these things any longer. All your love is the *cantinas* now: the feeble survival of a love of life now turned to poison, which only is not wholly poison, and poison has become your daily food, when in the tavern –'

'Has Pedro gone too then?' Yvonne was holding his arm tightly but her voice was almost natural, he felt.

'Yes, thank God!'

'How about the cats?'

'*¡Perro!*' the Consul, removing his glasses, said amiably to the pariah dog that had appeared familiarly at heel. But the animal cowered back down the drive. 'Though the garden's a rajah mess, I'm afraid. We've been virtually without a gardener at all for months. Hugh pulled up a few weeds. He cleaned out

the swimming-pool too ... Hear it? It ought to be full today.'
The drive widened to a small arena then debouched into a path
cutting obliquely across the narrow sloping lawn, islanded by
rose beds, to the 'front' door, actually at the back of the low
white house which was roofed with imbricated flower-pot-
coloured tiles resembling bisected drainpipes. Glimpsed through
the trees, with its chimney on the far left, from which rose a
thread of dark smoke, the bungalow looked an instant like a
pretty little ship lying at anchor. 'No. Skullduggery and su-
ings for back wages have been my lot. And leaf-cutter ants,
several species. The house was broken into one night when I
was out. And flood: the drains of Quauhnahuac visited us and
left us with something that smelt like the Cosmic Egg till recently. Never mind though, maybe you can –'

Yvonne disengaged her arm to lift a tentacle from a trumpet
vine growing across the path:

'Oh Geoffrey! Where're my camellias? –'

'God knows.' The lawn was divided by a dry runnel parallel
with the house bridged by a spurious plank. Between floribun-
dia and rose a spider wove an intricate web. With pebbly cries
a covey of tyrant flycatchers swept over the house in quick dark
flight. They crossed the plank and they were on the 'stoop'.

An old woman with a face of a highly intellectual black
gnome the Consul always thought (mistress to some gnarled
guardian of the mine beneath the garden once, perhaps), and
carrying the inevitable mop, the *trapeador* or American hus-
band, over her shoulder, shuffled out of the 'front' door, scraping her feet – the shuffling and the scraping however seemingly
unidentified, controlled by separate mechanisms. 'Here's Concepta,' the Consul said. Yvonne: Concepta. Concepta, Señora
Firmin.' The gnome smiled a childlike smile that momentarily
transformed its face into an innocent girl's. Concepta wiped
her hands on her apron: she was shaking hands with Yvonne
as the Consul hesitated, seeing now, studying with sober interest (though at this point all at once he felt more pleasantly
'tight' than at any time since just before that blank period last
night) Yvonne's luggage on the stoop before him, three bags
and a hatbox so bespangled with labels they might have burst

forth into a kind of bloom, to be saying too, here is your history: Hotel Hilo Honolulu, Villa Carmona Granada, Hotel Theba Algeciras, Hotel Peninsula Gibraltar, Hotel Nazareth Galilee, Hôtel Manchester Paris, Cosmo Hotel London, the s.s. *Ile de France*, Regis Hotel Canada, Hotel Mexico D.F. – and now the new labels, the newest blossoms: Hotel Astor New York, the Town House Los Angeles, s.s. *Pennsylvania*, Hotel Mirador Acapulco, the Compañía Mexicana de Aviación. '*¿El otro señor?*' he was saying to Concepta who shook her head with delighted emphasis. 'Hasn't returned yet. All right, Yvonne, I dare say you want your old room. Anyhow Hugh's in the back one with the machine.'

'The machine?'

'The mowing machine.'

' – *por qué no, agua caliente,*' Concepta's soft musical humorous voice rose and fell as she shuffled and scraped off with two of the bags.

'So there's hot water for you, which is a miracle!'

On the other side of the house the view was suddenly spacious and windy as the sea.

Beyond the *barranca* the plains rolled up to the very foot of the volcanoes into a barrier of murk above which rose the pure cone of old Popo, and spreading to the left of it like a University City in the snow the jagged peaks of Ixtaccihuatl, and for a moment they stood on the porch without speaking, not holding hands, but with their hands just meeting, as though not quite sure they weren't dreaming this, each of them separately on their far bereaved cots, their hands but blown fragments of their memories, half afraid to commingle, yet touching over the howling sea at night.

Immediately below them the small chuckling swimming-pool was still filling from a leaky hose connected with a hydrant, though it was almost full; they had painted it themselves once, blue on the sides and the bottom; the paint had scarcely faded and mirroring the sky, aping it, the water appeared a deep turquoise. Hugh had trimmed about the pool's edges but the garden sloped off beyond into an indescribable confusion of briars from which the Consul averted his eyes: the pleasant evanescent feeling of tightness was wearing off ...

He glanced absently round the porch which also embraced briefly the left side of the house, the house Yvonne hadn't yet entered at all, and now as in answer to his prayer Concepta was approaching them down its length. Concepta's gaze was fixed steadfastly on the tray she was carrying and she glanced neither to right nor left, neither at the drooping plants, dusty and gone to seed on the low parapet, nor at the stained hammock, nor the bad melodrama of the broken chair, nor the disembowelled day-bed, nor the uncomfortable stuffed Quixotes tilting their straw mounts on the house wall, shuffling slowly nearer them through the dust and dead leaves she hadn't yet swept from the ruddy tiled floor.

'Concepta knows my habits, you see.' The Consul regarded the tray now on which were two glasses, a bottle of Johnny Walker, half full, a soda siphon, a *jarro* of melting ice, and the sinister-looking bottle, also half full, containing a dull red concoction like bad claret, or perhaps cough mixture. 'However this is the strychnine. Will you have a whisky and soda? ... The ice seems to be for your benefit anyway. Not even a straight wormwood?' The Consul shifted the tray from the parapet to a wicker table Concepta had just brought out.

'Good heavens, not for me, thank you.'

' – A straight whisky then. Go ahead. What have you got to lose?'

'... Let me have some breakfast first!'

' – She might have said yes for once', a voice said in the Consul's ear at this moment with incredible rapidity, 'for now of course poor old chap you want horribly to get drunk all over again don't you the whole trouble being as we see it that Yvonne's long-dreamed-of coming alas but put away the anguish my boy there's nothing in it', the voice gabbled on, 'has in itself created the most important situation in your life save one namely the far more important situation it in turn creates of your having to have five hundred drinks in order to deal with it,' the voice he recognized of a pleasant and impertinent familiar, perhaps horned, prodigal of disguise, a specialist in casuistry, and who added severely, 'but are you the man to weaken and have a drink at this critical hour Geoffrey Firmin you are not you will fight it have already fought down this temptation have you not you have not then I must remind you did you not last night refuse drink after drink and finally after a nice little sleep even sober up altogether you didn't you did you didn't you did we know afterwards you did you were only drinking enough to correct your tremor a masterly self-control she does not and cannot appreciate !'

'I don't feel you believe in the strychnine somehow,' the Consul said, with quiet triumph (there was an immense comfort however in the mere presence of the whisky bottle) pouring himself from the sinister bottle a half-tumblerful of his mixture. I have resisted temptation for two and a half minutes at least: my redemption is sure. 'Neither do I believe in the strychnine, you'll make me cry again, you bloody fool Geoffrey Firmin, I'll kick your face in, O idiot!' That was yet another familiar and the Consul raised his glass in token of recognition and drank half its contents thoughtfully. The strychnine – he had ironically put some ice in it – tasted sweet, rather like *cassis*; it provided perhaps a species of subliminal stimulus, faintly perceived: the Consul, who was still standing, was aware too of a faint feeble wooing of his pain, contemptible. . . .

'But can't you see you *cabrón* that she is thinking that the first thing you think of after she has arrived home like this is a drink even if it is only a drink of strychnine the intrusive necessity for which and juxtaposition cancels its innocence so you see you might as well in the face of such hostility might you not start now on the whisky instead of later not on the *tequila* where is it by the way all right all right we know where it is that would be the beginning of the end though a damned good end perhaps but whisky the fine old healthful throat-smarting fire of your wife's ancestors *nació 1820 y siguiendo tan campante* and afterwards you might perhaps have some beer good for you too and full of vitamins for your brother will be here and it is an occasion and this is perhaps the whole point for celebration of course it is and while drinking the whisky and later the beer you could nevertheless still be tapering off *poco a poco* as you must but everyone knows it's dangerous to attempt it too quickly still keeping up Hugh's good work of straightening you out of course you would!' It was his first familiar again and the Consul sighing put the tumbler down on the tray with a defiantly steady hand.

'What was that you said?' he asked Yvonne.

'I said three times,' Yvonne was laughing, 'for Pete's sake have a decent drink. You don't have to drink that stuff to impress me ... I'll just sit here and cheer.'

'*What?*' She was sitting on the parapet gazing over the valley with every semblance of interested enjoyment. It was dead calm in the garden itself. But the wind must have suddenly changed; Ixta had vanished while Popocatepetl was almost wholly obscured by black horizontal columns of cloud, like smoke drawn across the mountain by several trains running parallel. 'Will you say that again?' The Consul took her hand.

They were embracing, or so it all but seemed, passionately: somewhere, out of the heavens, a swan, transfixed, plummeted to earth. Outside the *cantina* El Puerto del Sol in Independencia the doomed men would be already crowding into the warmth of the sun, waiting for the shutters to roll up with a crash of trumpets ...

'No, I'll stick to the old medicine, thanks.' The Consul had almost fallen backwards on to his broken green rocking-chair. He sat soberly facing Yvonne. This was the moment then, yearned for under beds, sleeping in the corners of bars, at the edge of dark woods, lanes, bazaars, prisons, the moment when – but the moment, stillborn, was gone: and behind him the *ursa horribilis* of the night had moved nearer. What had he done? Slept somewhere, that much was certain. *Tak* : *tok* : *help*: *help* : the swimming-pool ticked like a clock. He had slept: what else? His hand searching in his dress trousers pockets felt the hard edge of a clue. The card he brought to light said:

Arturo Díaz Vigil
Médico Cirujano y Partero
Enfermedades de Niños
Indisposiciones Nerviosas
Consultas de 12 a 2 y de 4 a 7
Av. Revolución Numero 8.

' – Have you really come back? Or have you just come to see me?' the Consul was asking Yvonne gently as he replaced the card.

'Here I am, aren't I?' Yvonne said merrily, even with a slight note of challenge.

'Strange,' the Consul commented, half trying to rise for the drink Yvonne had ratified in spite of himself and the quick voice that protested: 'You bloody fool Geoffrey Firmin, I'll kick your face in if you do, if you have a drink I'll cry, O idiot!' 'Yet it's awfully courageous of you. What if – I'm in a frightfully jolly mess, you know.'

'But you look *amazingly* well I thought. You've no *idea* how well you look.' (The Consul had absurdly flexed his biceps, feeling them: 'Still strong as a horse, so to speak, strong as a horse!') 'How do I look?' She seemed to have said. Yvonne averted her face a little, keeping it in profile.

'Didn't I say?' The Consul watched her. 'Beautiful ... Brown.' Had he said that? 'Brown as a berry. You've been swimming,' he added. 'You look as though you've had plenty of sun ... There's been plenty of sun here too of course,' he went on. 'As usual ... Too much of it. In spite of the rain ... Do you know, I don't like it.'

'Oh yes you do, really,' she had apparently replied. 'We could get out in the sun, you know.'

'Well – '

The Consul sat on the broken green rocker facing Yvonne. Perhaps it was just the soul, he thought, slowly emerging out of the strychnine into a form of detachment, to dispute with Lucretius, that grew older, while the body could renew itself many times unless it had acquired an unalterable habit of age. And perhaps the soul thrived on its sufferings, and upon the sufferings he had inflicted on his wife her soul had not only thrived but flourished. Ah, and not only upon the sufferings he had inflicted. What of those for which the adulterous ghost named Cliff he imagined always as just a morning coat and a pair of striped pyjamas open at the front, had been responsible? And the child, strangely named Geoffrey too, she had had by the ghost, two years before her first ticket to Reno, and which would now be six, had it not died at the age of as many months as many years ago, of meningitis, in 1932, three years before they themselves had met, and been married in Granada, in Spain? There Yvonne was at all events, bronzed and youthful and ageless: she had been at fifteen, she'd told him (that is, about the time she must have been acting in those Western pictures M. Laruelle, who had not seen them, adroitly assured one had influenced Eisenstein or somebody), a girl of whom people said, 'She is not pretty but she is going to be beautiful': at twenty they still said so, and at twenty-seven when she'd married him it was still true, according to the category through which one perceived such things of course: it was equally true of her now, at thirty, that she gave the impression of someone who is still going to be, perhaps just about to be, 'beautiful': the same tilted nose, the small ears, the warm brown eyes, clouded now and hurt-looking, the same wide, full-lipped mouth, warm too and generous, the slightly weak chin. Yvonne's was the same fresh bright face that could collapse, as Hugh would say, like a heap of ashes, and be grey. Yet she was changed. Ah yes indeed! Much as the demoted skipper's lost command, seen through the bar-room window lying out in harbour, is changed. She was no longer his: someone had doubtless approved her smart slate-blue travelling suit: it had not been he.

Suddenly with a quietly impatient gesture Yvonne pulled her hat off, and shaking her brown sunbleached hair rose from the parapet. She settled herself on the daybed, crossing her unusually beautiful and aristocratic long legs. The daybed emitted a rending guitar crash of chords. The Consul found his dark glasses and put them on almost playfully. But it had struck him with remote anguish that Yvonne was still waiting for the courage to enter the house. He said consularly in a deep false voice:

'Hugh ought to be here before very long if he comes back by the first bus.'

'What time is the first bus?'

'Half past ten, eleven.' What did it matter? Chimes sounded from the city. Unless of course it seemed utterly impossible, one dreaded the hour of anyone's arrival unless they were bringing liquor. What if there had been no liquor in the house, only the strychnine? Could he have endured it? He would be even now stumbling through the dusty streets in the growing heat of the day after a bottle; or have dispatched Concepta. In some tiny bar at a dusty alley corner, his mission forgotten, he would drink all morning celebrating Yvonne's coming while she slept. Perhaps he would pretend to be an Icelander or a visitor from the Andes or Argentina. Far more than the hour of Hugh's arrival was to be dreaded the issue that was already bounding after him at the gait of Goethe's famous church bell in pursuit of the child truant from church. Yvonne twisted her wedding-ring round her finger, once. Did she still wear it for love or for one of two kinds of convenience, or both? Or, poor girl, was it merely for his, for *their* benefit? The swimming-pool ticked on. *Might a soul bathe there and be clean or slake its drought?*

'It's still only eight-thirty.' The Consul took off his glasses again.

'Your eyes, you poor darling – they've got such a glare,' Yvonne burst out with: and the church bell was nearer; now it had loped, clanging, over a stile and the child had stumbled.

'A touch of the goujeers ... Just a touch.' *Die Glocke Glocke tönt nicht mehr* ... The Consul traced a pattern on one of the porch tiles with his dress shoes in which his sockless feet (sockless not because as Sr Bustamente the manager of the local cinema would have it, he'd drunk himself into a position where he could afford no socks, but because his whole frame was so neuritic with alcohol he found it impossible to put them on) felt swollen and sore. They would not have, but for the strychnine, damn the stuff, and this complete cold ugly sobriety it had let him down into! Yvonne was sitting on the parapet again leaning against a pillar. She bit her lips, intent on the garden:

'Geoffrey this place is a wreck!'

'Mariana and the moated grange isn't in it.' The Consul was winding his wrist-watch. '... But look here, suppose for the sake of argument you abandoned a besieged town to the enemy and then somehow or other not very long afterwards you go back to it – there's something about my analogy I don't like, but never mind, suppose you do it – then you can't very well expect to invite your soul into quite the same green graces, with quite the same dear old welcome here and there, can you, eh?'

'But I didn't abandon – '

'Even, I wouldn't say, if that town seems to be going about its business again, though in a somewhat stricken fashion, I admit, and its trams running more or less on schedule.' The Consul strapped his watch firmly on his wrist. 'Eh?'

' – Look at the red bird on the tree-twigs, Geoffrey! I never saw a cardinal as big as that before.'

'No.' The Consul, all unobserved, secured the whisky bottle, uncorked it, smelt its contents, and returned it to the tray gravely, pursing his lips: 'You wouldn't have. Because it isn't a cardinal.'

'Of course that's a cardinal. Look at its red breast. It's like a bit of flame!' Yvonne, it was clear to him, dreaded the approaching scene as much as he, and now felt under some compulsion to go on talking about anything until the perfect inappropriate moment arrived, that moment too when, unseen by her, the awful bell would actually touch the doomed child with giant protruding tongue and hellish Wesleyan breath. 'There, on the hibiscus!'

The Consul closed one eye. 'He's a coppery-tailed trogon I believe. And he has no red breast. He's a solitary fellow who probably lives way off in the Canyon of the Wolves over there, away off from those other fellows with ideas, so that he can have peace to meditate about not being a cardinal.'

'I'm sure it's a cardinal and lives right here in this garden!'

'Have it your own way. *Trogon ambiguus ambiguus* is the exact name, I think, the ambiguous bird! Two ambiguities ought to make an affirmative and this is it, the coppery-tailed trogon, not the cardinal.' The Consul reached out towards the tray for his empty strychnine glass, but forgetting midway what he proposed to put in it, or whether it wasn't one of the bottles he wanted first, if only to smell, and not the glass, he dropped his hand and leaned still farther forward, turning the movement into one of concern for the volcanoes. He said :

'Old Popeye ought to be coming out again pretty soon.'

'He seems to be completely obliterated in spinach at the moment – ' Yvonne's voice quivered.

The Consul struck a match against their old jest for the cigarette he had somehow failed to place between his lips : after a little, finding himself with a dead match, he put it in his pocket.

For a time they confronted each other like two mute unspeaking forts.

The water still trickling into the pool – God, how deadeningly slowly – filled the silence between them ... There was something else : the Consul imagined he still heard the music of the ball, which must have long since ceased, so that this silence was pervaded as with a stale thudding of drums. Pariah : that meant drums too. *Parián*. It was doubtless the almost tactile absence of the music however, that made it so peculiar the trees should be apparently shaking to it, an illusion investing not only the garden but the plains beyond, the whole scene before his eyes, with horror, the horror of an intolerable unreality. This must be not unlike, he told himself, what some insane person suffers at those moments when, sitting benignly in the asylum grounds, madness suddenly ceases to be a refuge and becomes incarnate in the shattering sky and all his surroundings in the presence of which reason, already struck dumb, can only bow the head. Does the madman find solace at such moments, as his thoughts like cannonballs crash through his brain, in the exquisite beauty of the madhouse garden or of the neighbouring hills beyond the terrible chimney? Hardly, the Consul felt. As for this particular beauty he knew it dead as his marriage and as wilfully slaughtered. The sun shining brilliantly now on all the world before him, its rays picking out the timber-line of Popocatepetl as its summit like a gigantic surfacing whale shouldered out of the clouds again, all this could not lift his spirit. The sunlight could not share his burden of conscience, of sourceless sorrow. It did not know him. Down to his left beyond the plantains the gardener at the Argentinian ambassador's week-end residence was slashing his way through some tall grasses, clearing the ground for a badminton court, yet something about this innocent enough occupation contained a horrible threat against him. The broad leaves of the plantains themselves dropping gently seemed menacingly savage as the stretched wings of pelicans, shaking before they fold. The movements of some more little red birds in the garden, like animated rosebuds, appeared unbearably jittery and thievish. It was as though the creatures were attached by sensitive wires to his nerves. When the telephone rang his heart almost stopped beating.

As a matter of fact the telephone was ringing clearly and the Consul left the porch for the dining-room where, afraid of the furious thing, he started to speak into the receiver, then, sweating, into the mouthpiece, talking rapidly – for it was a trunk-call – not knowing what he was saying, hearing Tom's muted voice quite plainly but turning his questions into his own answers, apprehensive lest at any moment boiling oil pour into his eardrums or his mouth : 'All right. Good-bye ... Oh, say, Tom, what was the origin of that silver rumour that appeared in the papers yesterday denied by Washington? I wonder where it came from ... What started it? Yes. All right. Good-bye. Yes, I have, terrible. Oh they did! Too bad. But after all they own it. Or don't they? Good-bye. They probably will. Yes, that's all right, that's all right. Good-bye; good-bye!' ... Christ. What does he want to ring me up at this hour of the morning for. What time is it in America? Erikson 43?

Christ ... He hung up the receiver the wrong way and returned to the porch : no Yvonne; after a moment he heard her in the bathroom ...

The Consul was guiltily climbing the Calle Nicaragua.

It was as if he were toiling up some endless staircase between houses. Or perhaps even old Popeye itself. Never had it seemed such a long way to the top of this hill. The road with its tossing broken stones stretched on for ever into the distance like a life of agony. He thought : 900 pesos = 100 bottles of whisky = 900 ditto tequila. Argal : one should drink neither tequila nor whisky but mescal. It was hot as a furnace too out on the street and the Consul sweated profusely. Away! Away! He was not going very far away, nor to the top of the hill. There was a lane branching to the left before you reached Jacques's house, leafy, no more than a cart-track at first, then a switchback, and somewhere along that lane to the right, not five minutes' walk, at a dusty corner, waited a cool nameless *cantina* with horses probably tethered outside, and a huge white tom cat sleeping below the counter of whom a *whiskerando* would say: 'He ah work all night mistair and sleep all day!' And this *cantina* would be open.

This was where he was going (the lane was plainly in sight now, a dog guarding it) to have in peace a couple of necessary drinks unspecified in his mind, and be back again before Yvonne had finished her bath. It was just possible too of course that he might meet –

But suddenly the Calle Nicaragua rose up to meet him.

The Consul lay face downward on the deserted street.

– Hugh, is that you old chap lending the old boy a hand? Thank you so much. For it is perhaps indeed your turn these days to lend a hand. Not that I haven't always been delighted to help you! I was even delighted in Paris that time you arrived from Aden in a fix over your *carte d'identité* and the passport you so often seem to prefer travelling without and whose number I remember to this day is 21312. It perhaps gave me all the more pleasure in that it served a while to take my mind from my own tangled affairs and moreover proved to my satisfaction, though some of my colleagues were even then beginning to doubt it, that I was still not so divorced from life as to be incapable of discharging such duties with dispatch. Why do I say this? – Is it in part that you should see that I also recognize how close Yvonne and I had already been brought to disaster before your meeting! Are you listening, Hugh – do I make myself clear? Clear that I forgive you, as somehow I have never wholly been able to forgive Yvonne, and that I can still love you as a brother and respect you as a man. Clear, that I would help you, ungrudgingly, again. In fact ever since Father went up into the White Alps alone and failed to return, though they happened to be the Himalayas, and more often than I care to think these volcanoes remind me of them, just as this valley does of the Valley of the Indus, and as those old turbaned trees in Taxco do of Srinigar, and just as Xochimilco – are you listening, Hugh? – of all places when I first came here, reminded me of those houseboats on the Shalimar you cannot remember,

and your mother, my step-mother died, all those dreadful things
seeming to happen at once as though the in-laws of catastrophe
had suddenly arrived from nowhere, or, perhaps, Damchok,
and moved in on us bag and baggage – there has been all too
little opportunity to act, so to say, as a brother to you. Mind you
I have perhaps acted as a father : but you were only an infant
then, and seasick, upon the P. and O., the old erratic *Cocanada*.
But after that and once back in England there were too many
guardians, too many surrogates in Harrogate, too many estab-
lishments and schools, not to mention the war, the struggle to
win which, for as you say rightly it is not yet over, I continue
in a bottle and you with the ideas I hope may prove less calamitous to you than did our father's to him, or for that matter
mine to myself. However all this may be – still there, Hugh,
lending a hand? – I ought to point out in no uncertain terms
that I never dreamed for a moment such a thing as did happen
would or could happen. That I had forfeited Yvonne's trust did
not necessarily mean she had forfeited mine, of which one had
a rather different conception. And that I trusted you goes without saying. Far less could I have dreamed you would attempt
morally to justify yourself on the grounds that I was absorbed
in a debauch : there are certain reasons too, to be revealed only
at the day of reckoning, why you should not have stood in
judgement upon me. Yet I am afraid – are you listening, Hugh?
– that long before that day what you did impulsively and have
tried to forget in the cruel abstraction of youth will begin to
strike you in a new and darker light. I am sadly afraid that you
may indeed, precisely because you are a good and simple person at bottom and genuinely respect more than most the prin-
ciples and decencies that might have prevented it, fall heir, as
you grow older and your conscience less robust, to a suffering
on account of it more abominable than any you have caused me.
How may I help you? How ward it off? How shall the murdered man convince his assassin he will not haunt him? Ah,
the past is filled up quicker than we know and God has little
patience with remorse ! Yet does this help, what I am trying to
tell you, that *I* realize to what degree I brought all this upon
myself? Help, that I am admitting moreover that to have cast

Yvonne upon you in that fashion was a reckless action, almost, I was going to say, a clownish one, inviting in return the inevitable bladder on the brain, the mouthful and heartful of sawdust. I sincerely hope so ... Meantime, however, old fellow, my mind, staggering under the influence of the last half-hour's strychnine, of the several therapeutic drinks before that, of the numerous distinctly untherapeutic drinks with Dr Vigil before that, you must meet Dr Vigil, I say nothing of his friend Jacques Laruelle to whom for various reasons I have hitherto avoided introducing you – please remind me to get back my Elizabethan plays from him – of the two days' and one night's continuous drinking before that, of the seven hundred and seventy-five and a half – but why go on? My mind, I repeat, must somehow, drugged though it is, like Don Quixote avoiding a town invested with his abhorrence because of his excesses there, take a clear cut around – did I say Dr Vigil? – '

'I say I say what's the matter there?' The English 'King's Parade' voice, scarcely above him, called out from behind the steering wheel, the Consul saw now, of an extremely long low car drawn up beside him, murmurous: an M.G. Magna, or some such.

'Nothing.' The Consul sprang to his feet instantly sober as a judge. 'Absolutely all right.'

'Can't be all right, you were lying right down in the road there, what?' The English face, now turned up toward him, was rubicund, merry, kindly, but worried, above the English striped tie, mnemonic of a fountain in a great court.

The Consul brushed the dust from his clothes; he sought for wounds in vain; there was not a scratch. He saw the fountain distinctly. *Might a soul bathe there and be clean or slake its drought?*

'All right, apparently,' he said, 'thanks very much.'

'But damn it all I say you were lying right down in the road there, might have run over you, there must be something wrong, what? No?' The Englishman switched his engine off. 'I say, haven't I seen you before or something.'

' – '

' – '

'Trinity.' The Consul found his own voice becoming involuntarily a little more 'English'. 'Unless – '

'Caius.'

'But you're wearing a Trinity tie – ' the Consul remarked with a polite note of triumph.

'Trinity? ... Yes. It's my cousin's, as a matter of fact.' The Englishman peered down his chin at the tie, his red merry face become a shade redder. 'We're going to Guatemala ... Wonderful country this. Pity about all this oil business, isn't it? Bad show. – Are you sure there's no bones broken or anything, old man?'

'No. There are no bones broken,' the Consul said. But he was trembling.

The Englishman leaned forward fumbling as for the engine switch again. 'Sure you're all right? We're staying at the Bella Vista Hotel, not leaving until this afternoon. I could take you along there for a little shuteye ... Deuced nice pub I must say but deuced awful row going on all night. I suppose you were at the ball – is that it? Going the wrong way though, aren't you? I always keep a bottle of something in the car for an emergency ... No. Not Scotch. Irish. Burke's Irish. Have a nip? But perhaps you'd – '

'Ah ...' The Consul was taking a long draught. 'Thanks a million.'

'Go ahead ... Go ahead ...'

'Thanks.' The Consul handed back the bottle. 'A million.'

'Well, cheerio.' The Englishman restarted his engine. 'Cheerio man. Don't go lying down in roads. Bless my soul you'll get run over or run in or something, damn it all. Dreadful road too. Splendid weather, isn't it?' The Englishman drove away up the hill, waving his hand.

'If you're ever in any kind of a jam yourself,' the Consul cried after him recklessly, 'I'm – wait, here's my card – '

'Bungho!'

– It was not Dr Vigil's card the Consul still held in his hand: but it was certainly not his own. *Compliments of the Venezuelan Government.* What was this? *The Venezuelan Government will appreciate* ... Wherever could this have sprung from? *The*

Venezuelan Government will appreciate an acknowledgement
to the Mnisterio de Relaciones Exteriores. Caracas, Venezuela.
Well, now, Caracas – well, why not?

Erect as Jim Taskerson, he thought, married now too, poor
devil – restored, the Consul glided down the Calle Nicaragua.

Within the house there was the sound of bathwater running
out : he made a lightning toilet. Intercepting Concepta (though
not before he had added a tactful strychnine to her burden) with
the breakfast tray, the Consul, innocently as a man who has
committed a murder while dummy at bridge, entered Yvonne's
room. It was bright and tidy. A gaily coloured Oaxaqueñan
serape covered the low bed where Yvonne lay half asleep with
her head resting on one hand.

'How!'

'How!'

A magazine she'd been reading dropped to the floor. The
Consul, inclined slightly forward over the orange juice and
ranchero eggs, advanced boldly through a diversity of powerless emotions.

'Are you comfortable there?'

'Fine, thanks.' Yvonne accepted the tray smiling. The magazine was the amateur astronomy one she subscribed to and from
the cover the huge domes of an observatory, haloed in gold and
standing out in black silhouette like roman helmets, regarded
the Consul waggishly. ' "The Mayas",' he read aloud, ' "were
far advanced in observational astronomy. But they did not suspect a Copernican system." ' He threw the magazine back on
the bed and sat easily in his chair, crossing his legs, the tips of
his fingers meeting in a strange calm, his strychnine on the
floor beside him. 'Why should they? ... What I like though
are the "vague" years of the old Mayans. And their "pseudo
years", mustn't overlook them! And their delicious names for
the months. Pop. Uo. Zip. Zotz. Tzec. Xul. Yaxkin.'

'Mac,' Yvonne was laughing. 'Isn't there one called Mac?'

'There's Yax and Zac. And Uayeb : I like that one most of
all, the month that only lasts five days.'

'In receipt of yours dated Zip the first ! – '

'But where does it all get you in the end?' The Consul sipped his strychnine that had yet to prove its adequacy as a chaser to the Burke's Irish (now perhaps in the garage at the Bella Vista). 'The knowledge, I mean. One of the first penances I ever imposed on myself was to learn the philosophical section of *War and Peace* by heart. That was of course before I could dodge about in the rigging of the Cabbala like a St Jago's monkey. But then the other day I realized that the only thing I remembered about the whole book was that Napoleon's leg twitched – '

'Aren't you going to eat anything yourself? You must be starved.'

'I partook.'

Yvonne who was herself breakfasting heartily asked :

'How's the market?'

'Tom's a bit fed up because they've confiscated some property of his in Tlaxcala, or Puebla, he thought he'd got away with. They haven't my number yet, I'm not sure where I really do stand in that regard, now I've resigned the service – '

'So you – '

'By the by I must apologize for still being in these duds – dusty too – bad show, I might have put on a blazer at least for your benefit !' The Consul smiled inwardly at his accent, now become for undivulgeable reasons almost uncontrolledly 'English'.

'So you really have resigned !'

'Oh absolutely! I'm thinking of becoming a Mexican subject, of going to live among the Indians, like William Blackstone. But for one's habit of making money, don't you know, all very mysterious to you, I suppose, outside looking in – ' The Consul stared round mildly at the pictures on the wall, mostly water-colours by his mother depicting scenes in Kashmir : a small grey stone enclosure encompassing several birch trees and a taller poplar was Lalla Rookh's tomb, a picture of wild torrential scenery, vaguely Scottish, the gorge, the ravine at Gugganvir; the Shalimar looked more like the Cam than ever : a distant view of Nanga Parbat from Sind valley could have been painted on the porch here, Nanga Parbat might well have passed for old Popo . . . ' – outside looking in,' he repeated, 'the result of so much worry, speculation, foresight, alimony, seigniorage – '

'But –' Yvonne had laid aside her breakfast tray and taken a cigarette from her own case beside the bed and lit it before the Consul could help her.

'One might have already done so!'

Yvonne lay back in bed smoking ... In the end the Consul scarcely heard what she was saying – calmly, sensibly, courageously – for his awareness of an extraordinary thing that was happening in his mind. He saw in a flash, as if these were ships on the horizon, under a black lateral abstract sky, the occasion for desperate celebration (it didn't matter he might be the only one to celebrate it) receding, while at the same time, coming closer, what could only be, what was – Good God! – his salvation ...

'*Now?*' he found he had said gently. 'But we can't very well go away *now* can we, what with Hugh and you and me and one thing and another, don't you think? It's a little unfeasible, isn't it?' (For his salvation might not have seemed so large with menace had not the Burke's Irish whiskey chosen suddenly to tighten, if almost imperceptibly, a screw. It was the soaring of this moment, conceived of as continuous, that felt itself threatened.) 'Isn't it?' he repeated.

'I'm sure Hugh'd understand –'

'But that's not quite the point!'

'Geoffrey, this house has become somehow evil –'

'– I mean it's rather a dirty trick –'

Oh Jesus ... The Consul slowly assumed an expression intended to be slightly bantering and at the same time assured, indicative of a final consular sanity. For this was it. Goethe's church bell was looking him straight between the eyes; fortunately, he was prepared for it. 'I remember a fellow I helped out in New York once', he was saying with apparent irrelevance, 'in some way, an out of work actor he was. "Why Mr Firmin," he said, "it isn't naturel here." That's exactly how he pronounced it: naturel. "Man wasn't intended for it," he complained. "All the streets are the same as this Tenth or Eleventh Street in Philadelphia too ..."' The Consul could feel his English accent leaving him and that of a Bleecker Street mummer taking its place. '"But in Newcastle, Delaware, now that's another thing again! Old cobbled roads ... And Charleston: old Southern stuff ... But oh my God this city – the noise! the chaos! If I could only get out! If only I knew where you could get to!"' The Consul concluded with passion, with anguish, his voice quivering – though as it happened he had never met any such person, and the whole story had been told him by Tom, he shook violently with the emotion of the poor actor.

'What's the use of escaping', he drew the moral with complete seriousness, 'from ourselves?'

Yvonne had sunk back in bed patiently. But now she stretched forward and stabbed out her cigarette in the tray of a tall grey tin-work ashstand shaped like an abstract representation of a swan. The swan's neck had become slightly unravelled but it bowed gracefully, tremulously at her touch as she answered:

'All right, Geoffrey: suppose we forget it until you're feeling better: we can cope with it in a day or two, when you're sober.'

'But good lord!'

The Consul sat perfectly still staring at the floor while the enormity of the insult passed into his soul. As if, as if, he were not sober now! Yet there was some elusive subtlety in the impeachment that still escaped him. For he was not sober. No, he was not, not at this very moment he wasn't! But what had that to do with a minute before, or half an hour ago? And what right had Yvonne to assume it, assume either that he was not sober now, or that, far worse, in a day or two he *would* be sober? And even if he were not sober now, by what fabulous stages, comparable indeed only to the paths and spheres of the Holy Cabbala itself, had he reached *this* stage again, touched briefly once before this morning, this stage at which alone he could, as she put it, 'cope', this precarious precious stage, so arduous to maintain, of being drunk in which alone he was sober! What right had she, when he had sat suffering the tortures of the damned and the madhouse on her behalf for fully twenty-five minutes on end without having a decent drink, even to hint that he was anything but, to her eyes, sober? Ah, a woman could not know the perils, the complications, yes, the *importance* of a drunkard's life! From what conceivable standpoint of rectitude did she imagine she could judge what was anterior to her arrival? And she knew nothing whatever of what all too recently he had gone through, his fall in the Calle Nicaragua, his aplomb, coolness, even bravery there — the Burke's Irish whiskey! What a world! And the trouble was she had now spoiled the moment. Because the Consul now felt that he might have been capable, remembering Yvonne's 'perhaps I'll have one after breakfast', and all that implied, of saying, in a minute (but for her remark and yes, in spite of any salvation), 'Yes, by all means you are right: let us go!' But who could agree with someone who was so certain you were going to be sober the day after tomorrow? It wasn't as though either, upon the most superficial plane, it were not well known that no one could tell when he was drunk. Just like the Taskersons: God bless them. He was not the person to be seen reeling about in the street. True he might lie down in the street, if need be, like a gentleman, but he would not reel. Ah, what a world it was, that trampled down the truth and drunkards alike! A world full of bloodthirsty people, no less! Bloodthirsty, did I hear you say bloodthirsty, Commander Firmin?

'But my lord, Yvonne, surely you know by this time I can't get drunk however much I drink,' he said almost tragically, taking an abrupt swallow of strychnine. 'Why, do you think I *like* swilling down this awful *nux vomica* or belladonna or whatever it is of Hugh's?' The Consul got up with his empty glass and began to walk around the room. He was not so much aware of having done by default anything fatal (it wasn't as if, for instance, he'd thrown his whole life away) as something merely foolish, and at the same time, as it were, sad. Yet there seemed a call for some amends. He either thought or said:

'Well, tomorrow perhaps I'll drink beer only. There's nothing like beer to straighten you out, and a little more strychnine, and then the next day just beer — I'm sure no one will object if I drink beer. This Mexican stuff is particularly full of vitamins, I gather ... For I can see it really is going to be somewhat of an occasion, this reunion of us all, and then perhaps when my nerves are back to normal again, I'll go off it completely. And then, who knows,' he brought up by the door, 'I might get down to work again and finish my book!'

But the door was still a door and it was shut: and now ajar. Through it, on the porch he saw the whisky bottle, slightly smaller and emptier of hope than the Burke's Irish, standing forlornly. Yvonne had not opposed a snifter: he had been unjust to her. Yet was that any reason why he should be unjust also to the bottle? Nothing in the world was more terrible than an empty bottle! Unless it was an empty glass. But he could wait: yes, sometimes he knew when to leave it alone. He wandered back to the bed thinking or saying:

'Yes: I can see the reviews now. Mr Firmin's sensational new data on Atlantis! The most extraordinary thing of its kind since Donnelly! Interrupted by his untimely death ... Marvellous. And the chapters on the alchemists! Which beat the Bishop of Tasmania to a frazzle. Only that's not quite the way they'll put it. Pretty good, eh? I might even work in something about Coxcox and Noah. I've got a publisher interested too; in Chicago – interested but not concerned, if you understand me, for it's really a mistake to imagine such a book could ever become popular. But it's amazing when you come to think of it how the human spirit seems to blossom in the shadow of the *abattoir*! How – to say nothing of all the poetry – not far enough below the stockyards to escape altogether the reek of the porterhouse of tomorrow, people can be living in cellars the life of the old alchemists of Prague! Yes: living among the cohobations of Faust himself, among the litharge and agate and hyacinth and pearls A life which is amorphous, plastic and crystalline. What am ' talking about? Copula Maritalis? Or from alcohol to alkahest Can you tell me? ... Or perhaps I might get myself another job, first of course being sure to insert an advertisement in the *Universal*: will accompany corpse to any place in the east!'

Yvonne was sitting up half reading her magazine, her nightgown slightly pulled aside showing where her warm tan faded into the white skin of her breast, her arms outside the covers and one hand turned downward from the wrist hanging over the edge of the bed listlessly: as he approached she turned this hand palm upward in an involuntary movement, of irritation perhaps, but it was like an unconscious gesture of appeal: it was more : it seemed to epitomize, suddenly, all the old supplication, the whole queer secret dumb show of incommunicable tendernesses and loyalties and eternal hopes of their marriage. The Consul felt his tearducts quicken. But he had also felt a sudden peculiar sense of embarrassment, a sense, almost, of indecency that he, a stranger, should be in her room. This room! He went to the door and looked out. The whisky bottle was still there.

But he made no motion towards it, none at all, save to put on his dark glasses. He was conscious of new aches here and there, of, for the first time, the impact of the Calle Nicaragua. Vague images of grief and tragedy flickered in his mind. Somewhere a butterfly was flying out to sea : lost. La Fontaine's duck had loved the white hen, yet after escaping together from the dreadful farmyard through the forest to the lake it was the duck that swam : the hen, following, drowned. In November 1895, in convict dress, from two o'clock in the afternoon till half past, handcuffed, recognized, Oscar Wilde stood on the centre platform at Clapham Junction ...

When the Consul returned to the bed and sat down on it Yvonne's arms were under the covers while her face was turned to the wall. After a while he said with emotion, his voice grown hoarse again :

'Do you remember how the night before you left we actually made a date like a couple of strangers to meet for dinner in Mexico City?'

Yvonne gazed at the wall :

'You didn't keep it.'

'That was because I couldn't remember the name of the restaurant at the last moment. All I knew was that it was in the Via Dolorosa somewhere. It was the one we'd discovered together the last time we were in the city. I went into all the restaurants in the Via Dolorosa looking for you and not finding you I had a drink in each one.'

'Poor Geoffrey.'

'I must have phoned back the Hotel Canada from each restaurant. From the *cantina* of each restaurant. God knows how many times, for I thought you might have returned there. And each time they said the same thing, that you'd left to meet me, but they didn't know where. And finally they became pretty damned annoyed. I can't imagine why we stayed at the Canada instead of the Regis – do you remember how they kept mistaking me there, with my beard, for that wrestler? ... Anyhow, there I was wandering around from place to place, wrestling, and thinking all the while I could prevent you from going the next morning, if I could only find you !'

'Yes.'

(If you could only find her ! Ah, how cold it was that night, and bitter, with a howling wind and wild steam blowing from the pavement gratings where the ragged children were making to sleep early under their poor newspapers. Yet none was more homeless than you, as it grew later and colder and darker, and still you had not found her ! And a sorrowful voice seemed to be wailing down the street at you with the wind calling its name : Via Dolorosa, Via Dolorosa ! And then somehow it was early the next morning directly after she had left the Canada – you brought one of her suitcases down yourself though you didn't see her off – and you were sitting in the hotel bar drinking *mescal* with ice in it that chilled your stomach, you kept swallowing the lemon pips, when suddenly a man with the look of an executioner came from the street dragging two little fawns shrieking with fright into the kitchen. And later you heard them screaming, being slaughtered probably. And you thought : better not remember what you thought. And later still, after Oaxaca, when you had returned here to Quauhnahuac, through the anguish of that return – circling down from the Tres Marías in the Plymouth, seeing the town below through the mist, and then the town itself, the landmarks, your soul dragged past them as at the tail of a runaway horse – when you returned here –)

'The cats had died', he said, 'when I got back – Pedro insisted it was typhoid. Or rather, poor old Oedipuss died the very day you left apparently, he'd already been thrown down the *barranca* while little Pathos was lying in the garden under the plantains when I arrived looking even sicker than when we first picked her out of the gutter; dying, though no one could make out what of: Maria claimed it was a broken heart – '

'Cheery little matter,' Yvonne answered in a lost hard tone with her face still turned to the wall.

'Do you remember your song, I won't sing it: "No work has been done by the little cat, no work has been done by the big cat, no work has been done, by an-y-one!"' the Consul heard himself ask; tears of sorrow came to his eyes, he removed his dark glasses quickly and buried his face on her shoulder. No, but Hugh, she began – 'Never mind Hugh,' he had not meant to elicit this, to thrust her back against the pillows; he felt her body stiffen, becoming hard and cold. Yet her consent did not seem from weariness only, but to a solution for one shared instant beautiful as trumpets out of a clear sky ...

But he could feel now, too, trying the prelude, the preparatory nostalgic phrases on his wife's senses, the image of his possession, like that jewelled gate the desperate neophyte, Yesod-bound, projects for the thousandth time on the heavens to permit passage of his astral body, fading, and slowly, inexorably, that of a *cantina*, when in dead silence and peace it first opens in the morning, taking its place. It was one of those *cantinas* that would be opening now, at nine o'clock: and he was queerly conscious of his own presence there with the angry tragic words, the very words which might soon be spoken, glaring behind him. This image faded also: he was where he was, sweating now, glancing once – but never ceasing to play the prelude, the little one-fingered introduction to the unclassifiable composition that might still just follow – out of the window at the drive, fearful himself lest Hugh appear there, then he imagined he really saw him at the end of it coming through the gap, now that he distinctly heard his step in the gravel ... No one. But now, now he wanted to go, passionately he wanted to go, aware that the peace of the *cantina* was changing to its first fevered preoccupation of the morning: the political exile in the corner discreetly sipping orange crush, the accountant arriving, accounts gloomily surveyed, the iceblock dragged in by a brigand with an iron scorpion, the one bartender slicing lemons, the other, sleep in his eyes, sorting beer bottles. And now, now he wanted to go, aware that the place was filling with people not at any other time part of the *cantina's* community at all, people eructating, exploding, committing nuisances, lassoes over their shoulders, aware too of the debris from the night before, the dead matchboxes, lemon peel, cigarettes open like tortillas, the dead packages of them swarming in filth and sputum. Now that the clock over the mirror would say a little past nine, and the news-vendors of *La Prensa* and *El Universal* were stamping in, or standing in the corner at this very moment before the crowded grimed *mingitorio* with the shoe-blacks who carried their shoe-stools in their hands, or had left them balanced between the burning foot-rail and the bar, now he wanted to go! Ah none but he knew how beautiful it all was, the sunlight, sunlight, sunlight flooding the bar of El Puerto del Sol, flooding the watercress and oranges, or falling in a single golden line as if in the act of conceiving a God, falling like a lance straight into a block of ice —

'Sorry, it isn't any good I'm afraid.' The Consul shut the door behind him and a small rain of plaster showered on his head. A Don Quixote fell from the wall. He picked up the sad straw knight . . .

And then the whisky bottle: he drank fiercely from it.

He had not forgotten his glass however, and into it he was now pouring himself chaotically a long drink of his strychnine mixture, half by mistake, he'd meant to pour the whisky. 'Strychnine is an aphrodisiac. Perhaps it will take immediate effect. It still may not be too late.' He had sunk through, it almost felt, the green cane rocking-chair.

He just managed to reach his glass left on the tray and held it now in his hands, weighing it, but — for he was trembling again, not slightly, but violently, like a man with Parkinson's disease or palsy — unable to bring it to his lips. Then without drinking he set it on the parapet. After a while, his whole body quaking, he rose deliberately and poured, somehow, into the other unused tumbler Concepta had not removed, about a half quartern of whisky. *Nació 1820 y siguiendo tan campante. Siguiendo.* Born 1896 and still going flat. I love you, he murmured, gripping the bottle with both hands as he replaced it on the tray. He now brought the tumbler filled with whisky back to his chair and sat with it in his hands, thinking. Presently without having drunk from this glass either he set it on the parapet next to his strychnine. He sat watching both the glasses. Behind him in the room he heard Yvonne crying.

' – Have you forgotten the letters Geoffrey Firmin the letters she wrote till her heart broke why do you sit there trembling why do you not go back to her now she will understand after all it hasn't always been that way toward the end perhaps but you could laugh at this you could laugh at it why do you think she is weeping it is not for that alone you have done this to her my boy the letters you not only have never answered you didn't you did you didn't you did then where is your reply but have never really read where are they now they are lost Geoffrey Firmin lost or left somewhere even we do not know where – '

The Consul reached forward and absentmindedly managed a sip of whisky; the voice might have been either of his familiars or –

Hullo, good morning.

The instant the Consul saw the thing he knew it an hallucination and he sat, quite calmly now, waiting for the object shaped like a dead man and which seemed to be lying flat on its back by his swimming-pool, with a large sombrero over its face, to go away. So the 'other' had come again. And now gone, he thought : but no, not quite, for there was still something there, in some way connected with it, or here, at his elbow, or behind his back, in front of him now; no, that too, whatever it was, was going : perhaps it had only been the coppery-tailed trogon stirring in the bushes, his 'ambiguous bird' that was now departing quickly on creaking wings, like a pigeon once it was in flight, heading for its solitary home in the Canyon of the Wolves, away from the people with ideas.

'Damn it, I feel pretty well,' he thought suddenly, finishing his half quartern. He stretched out for the whisky bottle, failed to reach it, rose again and poured himself another finger. 'My hand is much steadier already.' He finished this whisky and taking the glass and the bottle of Johnny Walker, which was fuller than he'd imagined, crossed the porch to its farthest corner and placed them in a cupboard. There were two old golf balls in the cupboard. 'Play with me I can still carry the eighth green in three. I am tapering off,' he said. 'What am I talking about? Even I know I am being fatuous.'

'I shall sober up.' He returned and poured some more strychnine into the other glass, filling it, then moved the strychnine bottle from the tray into a more prominent position on the parapet. 'After all I have been out all night: what could one expect?'

'I am too sober. I have lost my familiars, my guardian angels. I am straightening out,' he added, sitting down again opposite the strychnine bottle with his glass. 'In a sense what happened was a sign of my fidelity, my loyalty; any other man would have spent this last year in a very different manner. At least I have no disease,' he cried in his heart, the cry seeming to end on a somewhat doubtful note, however. 'And perhaps it's fortunate I've had some whisky since alcohol is an aphrodisiac too. One must never forget either that alcohol is a food. How can a man be expected to perform his marital duties without food? Marital? At all events I am progressing, slowly but surely. Instead of immediately rushing out to the Bella Vista and getting drunk as I did the last time all this happened and we had that disastrous quarrel about Jacques and I smashed the electric-light bulb, I have stayed here. True, I had the car before and it was easier. But here I am. I am not escaping. And what's more I intend to have a hell of a sight better time staying.' The Consul sipped his strychnine, then put his glass on the floor.

'The will of man is unconquerable. Even God cannot conquer it.'

He lay back in his chair. Ixtaccihuatl and Popocatepetl, that image of the perfect marriage, lay now clear and beautiful on the horizon under an almost pure morning sky. Far above him a few white clouds were racing windily after a pale gibbous moon. Drink all morning, they said to him, drink all day. This is life!

Enormously high too, he noted some vultures waiting, more graceful than eagles as they hovered there like burnt papers floating from a fire which suddenly are seen to be blowing swiftly upward, rocking.

The shadow of an immense weariness stole over him ... The Consul fell asleep with a crash.

4

DAILY GLOBE intelube londres presse collect following yester-days head-coming antisemitic campaign mexpress propetition see tee emma mex-workers confederation proexpulsion exmexico quote small jewish textile manufacturers unquote learned today perreliable source that german legation mexcity actively behind the campaign etstatement that legation gone length sending antisemitic propaganda mexdept interiorwards borne out pro-pamphlet possession local newspaperman stop pamphlet asserts jews influence unfavourably any country they live etemphasises quote their belief absolute power etthat they gain their ends without conscience or consideration unquote stop Firmin.

Reading it over once more, the carbon of his final dispatch (sent that morning from the Oficina Principal of the Compañía Telegráfica Mexicana Esq., San Juan de Letrán e Independencia, México, D.F.), Hugh Firmin less than sauntered, so slowly did he move, up the drive towards his brother's house, his brother's jacket balanced on his shoulder, one arm thrust almost to the elbow through the twin handles of his brother's small gladstone bag, his pistol in the checkered holster lazily slapping his thigh : eyes in my feet, I must have, as well as straw, he thought, stopping on the edge of the deep pothole, and then his heart and the world stopped too; the horse half over the hurdle, the diver, the guillotine, the hanged man falling, the murderer's bullet, and the cannon's breath, in Spain or China frozen in mid-air, the wheel, the piston, poised –

Yvonne, or something woven from the filaments of the past that looked like her, was working in the garden, and at a little distance appeared clothed entirely in sunlight. Now she stood up straight – she was wearing yellow slacks – and was squinting at him, one hand raised to shield her eyes from the sun.

Hugh jumped over the pothole to the grass; disentangling

himself from the bag he knew an instant's paralysed confusion, and reluctance to meet the past. The bag, decanted on the faded rustic seat, disgorged into its lid a bald toothbrush, a rusty safety-razor, his brother's shirt, and a second-hand copy of Jack London's *Valley of the Moon,* bought yesterday for fifteen centavos at the German bookstore opposite Sandborns in Mexico City. Yvonne was waving.

And he was advancing (just as on the Ebro they were retreating) the borrowed jacket still somehow balanced, half slung on his shoulder, his broad hat in one hand, the cable, folded, still somehow in the other.

'Hullo, Hugh. Gosh, I thought for a moment you were Bill Hodson – Geoffrey said you were here. How nice to see you again.'

Yvonne brushed the dirt from her palms and held out her hand, which he did not grip, nor even feel at first, then dropped as if carelessly, becoming conscious of a pain in his heart and also of a faint giddiness.

'How absolutely something or other. When did you get here?'

'Just a little while ago.' Yvonne was plucking the dead blossoms from some potted plants resembling zinnias, with fragrant delicate white and crimson flowers, that were ranged on a low wall; she took the cable Hugh had for some reason handed her along to the next flower pot: 'I hear you've been in Texas. Have you become a drugstore cowboy?'

Hugh replaced his ten-gallon Stetson on the back of his head, laughing down, embarrassed, at his high-heeled boots, the too-tight trousers tucked inside them. 'They impounded my clothes at the border. I meant to buy some new ones in the City but somehow never got around to it ... You look awfully well!'

'And you!'

He began to button his shirt, which was open to the waist, revealing, above the two belts, the skin more black than brown with sun; he patted the bandolier below his lower belt, which slanted diagonally to the holster resting on his hip-bone and attached to his right leg by a flat leather thong, patted the thong (he was secretly enormously proud of his whole outfit), then the breast pocket of his shirt, where he found a loose rolled cigarette he was lighting when Yvonne said :

'What's this, the new message from Garcia?'

'The C.T.M.,' Hugh glanced over his shoulder at his cable, 'the Confederation of Mexican Workers, have sent a petition. They object to certain Teutonic huggermugger in this state. As I see it, they are right to object.' Hugh gazed about the garden; where was Geoff? Why was she here? She is too casual. Are they not separated or divorced after all? What is the point? Yvonne handed back the cable and Hugh slipped it into the pocket of his jacket. 'That', he said, climbing into it, since they were now standing in the shade, 'is the last cable I send the *Globe.*'

'So Geoffrey – ' Yvonne stared at him : she pulled the jacket down at the back (knowing it Geoff's), the sleeves were too short : her eyes seemed hurt and unhappy, but vaguely amused : her expression as she went on paring blossoms managed to be both speculative and indifferent ; she asked :

'What's all this I hear about you travelling on a cattle truck?'

'I entered Mexico disguised as a cow so they'd think I was a Texan at the border and I wouldn't have to pay any head tax. Or worse,' Hugh said, 'England being *persona non grata* here, so to speak, after Cárdenas's oil shindig. Morally of course we're at war with Mexico, in case you didn't know – where's our ruddy monarch?'

' – Geoffrey's asleep,' Yvonne said, not meaning plastered by any chance, Hugh thought. 'But doesn't your paper take care of those things?'

'Well. It's *muy complicado* ... I'd sent my resignation in to the *Globe* from the States but they hadn't replied – here, let me do that – '

Yvonne was trying to thrust back a stubborn branch of bougainvillea blocking some steps he hadn't noticed before.

'I take it you heard we were in Quauhnahuac?'

'I'd discovered I might kill several birds with one stone by coming to Mexico ... Of course it was a surprise you *weren't* here – '

140

'Isn't the garden a *wreck*?' Yvonne said suddenly.

'It looks quite beautiful to me, considering Geoffrey hasn't had a gardener for so long.' Hugh had mastered the branch – they are losing the Battle of the Ebro because I did that – and there were the steps; Yvonne grimaced, moving down them, and halted near the bottom to inspect an oleander that looked reasonably poisonous, and was even still in bloom:

'And your friend, was he a cattleman or disguised as a cow too?'

'A smuggler, I think. Geoff told you about Weber, eh?' Hugh chuckled. 'I strongly suspect him of running ammunition. Anyhow I got into an argument with the fellow in a dive in El Paso and it turned out he'd somehow arranged to go as far as Chihuahua by cattle truck, which seemed a good idea, and then fly to Mexico City. Actually we did fly, from some place with a weird name, like Cusihuriachic, arguing all the way down, you know – he was one of these American semi-Fascist blokes, been in the Foreign Legion, God knows what. But Parián was where he really wanted to go so he sat us down conveniently in the field here. It was quite a trip.'

'Hugh, how like you!'

Yvonne stood below smiling up at him, hands in the pockets of her slacks, feet wide apart like a boy. Her breasts stood up under her blouse embroidered with birds and flowers and pyramids she had probably bought or brought for Geoff's benefit, and once more Hugh felt the pain in his heart and looked away.

'I probably should have shot the *bastardo* out of hand: only he was a decent sort of swine – '

'You can see Parián from here sometimes.'

Hugh was offering the thin air a cigarette. 'Isn't it rather indefatigably English or something of Geoff's to be asleep?' He followed Yvonne down the path. 'Here, it's my last machine-made one.'

'Geoffrey was at the Red Cross Ball last night. He's pretty tired, poor dear.' They walked on together, smoking, Yvonne pausing every few steps to uproot some weed or other until, suddenly, she stopped, gazing down at a flower-bed that was completely, grossly strangled by a coarse green vine. 'My God, this used to be a beautiful garden. It was like Paradise.'

'Let's get the hell out of it then. Unless you're too tired for a walk.' A snore, ricocheting, agonized, embittered, but controlled, single, was wafted to his ears: the muted voice of England long asleep.

Yvonne glanced hastily around as if fearful Geoff might come catapulting out of the window, bed and all, unless he was on the porch, and hesitated. 'Not a bit,' she said brightly, warmly. 'Let's do ...' She started down the path before him. 'What are we waiting for?'

Unconsciously, he had been watching her, her bare brown neck and arms, the yellow slacks, and the vivid scarlet flowers behind her, the brown hair circling her ears, the graceful swift movements of her yellow sandals in which she seemed to dance, to be floating rather than walking. He caught up with her and once more they walked on together, avoiding a long-tailed bird that glided down to alight near them like a spent arrow.

The bird swaggered ahead of them now down the cratered drive, through the gateless gateway, where it was joined by a crimson and white turkey, a pirate attempting to escape under full sail, and into the dusty street. They were laughing at the birds, but the things they might have gone on to say under somewhat different circumstances, as: I wonder what's happened to our bikes, or, do you remember, in Paris, that café, with the tables up the trees, in Robinson, remained unspoken.

They turned to the left, away from the town. The road declined sharply below them. At the bottom rose purple hills. Why is this not bitter, he thought, why is it not indeed, it was already: Hugh was aware for the first time of the other gnawing, as the Calle Nicaragua, the walls of the large residences left behind, became an almost unnavigable chaos of loose stones and potholes. Yvonne's bicycle wouldn't have been much use here.

'What on earth were *you* doing in Texas, Hugh?'

'Stalking Okies. That is, I was after them in Oklahoma. I thought the *Globe* ought to be interested in Okies. Then I went down to this ranch in Texas. That's where I'd heard about these chaps from the dust bowl not being allowed to cross the border.'

'What an old Nosey Parker you are!'

'I landed in Frisco just in time for Munich.' Hugh stared over to the left where in the distance the latticed watchtower of the Alcapancingo prison had just appeared with little figures on top gazing east and west through binoculars.

'They're just playing. The police here love to be mysterious, like you. Where were you before that? We must have just missed each other in Frisco.'

A lizard vanished into the bougainvillea growing along the roadbank, wild bougainvillea now, an overflux, followed by a second lizard. Under the bank gaped a half-shored-in hole, another entrance to the mine perhaps. Precipitous fields fell away down to their right, tilting violently at every angle. Far beyond them, cupped by hills, he made out the old bull-ring and again he heard Weber's voice in the plane, shouting, yelling in his ear, as they passed the pinch-bottle of *habanero* between them:'*Quauhnahuac! That's where they crucified the women in the bull-rings during the revolution and set the bulls at them. And that's a nice thing to say! The blood ran down the gutters and they barbecued the dogs in the market place. They shoot first and ask questions later! You're goddamn right –* ' But there was no revolution in Quauhnahuac now and in the stillness the purple slopes before them, the fields, even the watchtower and the bull-ring, seemed to be murmuring of peace, of paradise indeed. 'China,' he said.

Yvonne turned, smiling, though her eyes were troubled and perplexed : 'What about the war?' she said.

'That was the point. I fell out of an ambulance with three dozen beer bottles and six journalists on top of me and that's when I decided it might be healthier to go to California.' Hugh glanced suspiciously at a billy goat which had been following them on their right along the grass margin between the road and a wire fence, and which now stood there motionless, regarding them with patriarchal contempt. 'No, they're the lowest form of animal life, except possibly – look out! – my God, I knew it – ' The goat had charged and Hugh felt the sudden intoxicating terrified incidence and warmth of Yvonne's body as the animal missed them, skidded, slithered round the abrupt leftward bend the road took at this point over a low stone bridge, and disappeared beyond up a hill, furiously trailing its tether. 'Goats,' he said, twisting Yvonne firmly out of his arms. 'Even when there are no wars think of the damage they do,' he went on, through something nervous, mutually dependent still, about their mirth. 'I mean journalists, not goats. There's no punishment on earth fit for them. Only the Malebolge ... And here is the Malebolge.'

The Malebolge was the *barranca*, the ravine which wound through the country, narrow here – but its momentousness successfully prescinded their minds from the goat. The little stone bridge on which they stood crossed it. Trees, their tops below them, grew down into the gulch, their foliage partly obscuring the terrific drop. From the bottom came a faint chuckling of water.

'This ought to be about the place, if Alcapancingo's over there,' Hugh said, 'where Bernal Díaz and his Tlaxcalans got across to beat up Quauhnahuac. Superb name for a dance-band: Bernal Díaz and his Tlaxcalans ... Or didn't you get around to Prescott at the University of Hawaii?'

'Mm hm,' Yvonne said, meaning yes or no to the meaningless question, and peering down the ravine with a shudder.

'I understand it made even old Díaz's head swim.'

'I shouldn't wonder.'

'You can't see them, but it's chock full of defunct newspapermen, still spying through keyholes and persuading themselves they're acting in the best interests of democracy. But I'd forgotten you didn't read the papers. Eh?' Hugh laughed. 'Journalism equals intellectual male prostitution of speech and writing, Yvonne. That's one point on which I'm in complete agreement with Spengler. Hullo.' Hugh looked up suddenly at a sound, unpleasantly familiar, as of a thousand carpets being simultaneously beaten in the distance: the uproar, seeming to emanate from the direction of the volcanoes, which had almost imperceptibly come into view on the horizon, was followed presently by the prolonged *twang-piiing* of its echo.

'Target practice,' Yvonne said. 'They're at it again.'

Parachutes of smoke were drifting over the mountains; they

watched a minute in silence. Hugh sighed and started to roll a cigarette.

'I had an English friend fighting in Spain, and if he's dead I expect he's still there.' Hugh licked the fold of paper, sealed it and lit it, the cigarette drawing hot and fast. 'As a matter of fact he was reported dead twice but he turned up again the last two times. He was there in thirty-six. While they were waiting for Franco to attack he lay with his machine-gun in the library at University City reading De Quincey, whom he hadn't read before. I may be exaggerating about the machine-gun though: I don't think they had one between them. He was a Communist and approximately the best man I've ever met. He had a taste for Vin Rosé d'Anjou. He also had a dog named Harpo, back in London. You probably wouldn't have expected a Communist to have a dog named Harpo – or would you?'

'Or would you?'

Hugh put one foot up on the parapet and regarded his cigarette that seemed bent, like humanity, on consuming itself as quickly as possible.

'I had another friend who went to China, but didn't know what to make of that, or they didn't of him, so he went to Spain too as a volunteer. He was killed by a stray shell before seeing any action at all. Both these fellows had perfectly good lives at home. They hadn't robbed the bank.' He was lamely silent.

'Of course we left Spain about a year before it started, but Geoffrey used to say there was far too much sentiment about this whole business of going to die for the Loyalists. In fact, he said he thought it would be much better if the Fascists just won and got it over with – '

'He has a new line now. He says *when* the Fascists win there'll only be a sort of "freezing" of culture in Spain – by the way, is that the moon up there? – well, freezing anyway. Which will presumably thaw at some future date when it will be discovered, if you please, simply to have been in a state of suspended animation. I dare say it's true as far as that goes. Incidentally, did you know *I* was in Spain?'

'No,' Yvonne said, startled.

'Oh yes. I fell out of an ambulance there with only two dozen beer bottles and five journalists on top of me, all heading for Paris. That wasn't so very long after I last saw you. The thing was, just as the Madrid show was really getting under way, as it turned out, it seemed all up, so the *Globe* told me to beat it . . . And like a heel I went, though they sent me back again afterwards for a time. I didn't go to China until after Brihuega.'

Yvonne gave him an odd look, then said:

'Hugh, you're not thinking of going back to Spain *now* are you, by any chance?'

Hugh shook his head, laughing: he meticulously dropped his ravaged cigarette down the ravine. '*¿Cui bono?* To stand in for the noble army of pimps and experts, who've already gone home to practise the little sneers with which they propose to discredit the whole thing – the first moment it becomes fashionable not to be a Communist fence. *No, muchas gracias*. And I'm completely through with newspaper work, it isn't a pose.' Hugh put his thumbs under his belt. 'So – since they got the Internationals out five weeks ago, on the twenty-eighth of September to be precise – two days before Chamberlain went to Godesberg and neatly crimped the Ebro offensive – and with half the last bunch of volunteers still rotting in gaol in Perpignan, how do you suppose one could get in anyway, at this late date?'

'Then what did Geoffrey mean by saying that you "wanted action" and all that? . . . And what's this mysterious other purpose you came down here for?'

'It's really rather tedious,' Hugh answered. 'As a matter of fact I'm going back to sea for a while. If all goes well I'll be sailing from Vera Cruz in about a week. As quartermaster, you knew I had an A.B.'s ticket didn't you? Well, I might have got a ship in Galveston but it's not so easy as it used to be. Anyway it'll be more amusing to sail from Vera Cruz. Havana, perhaps Nassau and then, you know, down to the West Indies and São Paulo. I've always wanted to take a look at Trinidad – might be some real fun coming out of Trinidad one day. Geoff helped me with a couple of introductions but no more than that, I didn't want to make him responsible. No, I'm merely fed to the teeth with myself, that's all. Try persuading the world not to cut its throat for half a decade or more, like me, under one name or another, and it'll begin to dawn on you that even *your* behaviour's part of its plan. I ask you, what do we know?'

And Hugh thought: the s.s. *Noemijolea*, 6,000 tons, leaving Vera Cruz on the night of 13–14 (?) November 1938, with antimony and coffee, bound for Freetown, British West Africa, will proceed thither, oddly enough, from Tzucox on the Yucatan coast, and also in a north-easterly direction: in spite of which she will still emerge through the passages named Windward and Crooked into the Atlantic Ocean: where after many days out of sight of land she will make eventually the mountainous landfall of Madeira: whence, avoiding Port Lyautey and carefully keeping her destination in Sierra Leone some 1,800 miles to the south-east, she will pass, with luck, through the straits of Gibraltar. Whence again, negotiating, it is profoundly to be hoped, Franco's blockade, she will proceed with the utmost caution into the Mediterranean Sea, leaving first Cape de Gata, then Cape de Palos, then Cape de la Nao, well aft: thence, the Pityusae Isles sighted, she will roll through the Gulf of Valencia and so northwards past Carlos de la Rápita, and the mouth of the Ebro until the rocky Garraf coast looms abaft the beam where finally, still rolling, at Vallcara, twenty miles south of Barcelona, she will discharge her cargo of T.N.T. for the hard-pressed Loyalist armies and probably be blown to smithereens –

Yvonne was staring down the *barranca*, her hair hanging over her face: 'I know Geoff sounds pretty foul sometimes,' she was saying, 'but there's one point where I do agree with him, these romantic notions about the International Brigade – '

But Hugh was standing at the wheel: Potato Firmin or Columbus in reverse: below him the foredeck of the *Noemijolea* lay over in the blue trough and spray slowly exploded through the lee scuppers into the eyes of the seaman chipping a winch: on the forecastle head the look-out echoed one bell, struck by Hugh a moment before, and the seaman gathered up his tools: Hugh's heart was lifting with the ship, he was aware that the officer on duty had changed from white to blue for

winter but at the same time of exhilaration, the limitless puri-
fication of the sea –

Yvonne flung back her hair impatiently and stood up. 'If
they'd stayed out of it the war would have been over long ago!'

'Well, there ain't no brigade no mo',' Hugh said absently,
for it was not a ship he was steering now, but the world, out of
the Western Ocean of its misery. 'If the paths of glory lead but
to the grave – I once made such an excursion into poetry – then
Spain's the grave where England's glory led.'

'Fiddlesticks!'

Hugh suddenly laughed, not loud, probably at nothing at
all: he straightened himself with a swift movement and jumped on the parapet.

'Hugh!'

'My God! Horses,' Hugh said, glancing and stretching himself to his full mental height of six feet two (he was five feet
eleven).

'Where?'

He was pointing. 'Over there.'

'Of course,' Yvonne said slowly, 'I'd forgotten – they belong
to the Casino de la Selva: they put them out there to pasture
or something. If we go up the hill a ways we'll come to the
place – '

... On a gentle slope to their left now, colts with glossy coats
were rolling in the grass. They turned off the Calle Nicaragua
along a narrow shady lane leading down one side of the paddock. The stables were part of what appeared to be a model
dairy farm. It stretched away behind the stables on level ground
where tall English-looking trees lined either side of a grassy
wheel-rutted avenue. In the distance a few rather large cows,
which, however, like Texas longhorns, bore a disturbing resemblance to stags (you've got your cattle again, I see, Yvonne
said) were lying under the trees. A row of shining milkpails
stood outside the stables in the sun. A sweet smell of milk and
vanilla and wild flowers hung about the quiet place. And the
sun was over all.

'Isn't it an adorable farm?' Yvonne said. 'I believe it's some
government experiment. I'd love to have a farm like that.'

' – perhaps you'd like to hire a couple of those greater kudus over there instead?'

Their horses proved two pesos an hour apiece. '*Muy correcto*,' the stable boy's dark eyes flashed good-humouredly at Hugh's boots as he turned swiftly to adjust Yvonne's deep leather stirrups. Hugh didn't know why, but this lad reminded him of how, in Mexico City, if you stand at a certain place on the Paseo de la Reforma in the early morning, suddenly everyone in sight will seem to be running, laughing, to work, in the sunlight, past the statue of Pasteur ... '*Muy* in*correcto*,' Yvonne surveyed her slacks : she swung, swung twice into the saddle. 'We've never ridden together before, have we?' She leaned forward to pat her mare's neck as they swayed forward.

They ambled up the lane, accompanied by two foals, which had followed their mothers out of the paddock, and an affectionate scrubbed woolly white dog belonging to the farm. After a while the lane branched off into a main road. They seemed to be in Alcapancingo itself, a sort of straggling suburb. The watchtower, nearer, taller, bloomed above a wood, through which they just made out the high prison walls. On the other side, to their left, Geoffrey's house came in sight, almost a bird's-eye view, the bungalow crouching, very tiny, before the trees, the long garden below descending steeply, parallel with which on different levels obliquely climbing the hill, all the other gardens of the contiguous residences, each with its cobalt oblong of swimming-pool, also descended steeply towards the *barranca*, the land sweeping away at the top of the Calle Nicaragua back up to the pre-eminence of Cortez Palace. Could that white dot down there be Geoffrey himself? Possibly to avoid coming to a place where, by the entrance to the public garden, they must be almost directly opposite the house, they trotted into another lane that inclined to their right. Hugh was pleased to see that Yvonne rode cowboy-fashion, jammed to the saddle, and not, as Juan Cerillo put it, 'as in gardens'. The prison was now behind them and he imagined themselves jogging into enormous focus for the inquisitive binoculars up there on the watchtower; '*Guapa*,' one policeman would say. '*Ah, muy hermosa*,' another might call, delighted with Yvonne and smacking his lips. The world was always within the binoculars of the police. Meantime the foals, which perhaps were not fully aware that a road was a means of getting somewhere and not, like a field, something to roll on or eat, kept straying into the undergrowth on either hand. Then the mares whinnied after them anxiously and they scrambled back again. Presently the mares grew tired of whinnying, so in a way he had learned Hugh whistled instead. He had pledged himself to guard the foals but actually the dog was guarding all of them. Evidently trained to detect snakes, he would run ahead then double back to make sure all were safe before loping on once more. Hugh watched him a moment. It was certainly hard to reconcile this dog with the pariahs one saw in town, those dreadful creatures that seemed to shadow his brother everywhere.

'You do sound astonishingly like a horse,' Yvonne said suddenly. 'Wherever did you learn that?'

'Wh-wh-wh-wh-wh-wh-wh-wh-wheeee-u,' Hugh whistled again. 'In Texas.' Why had he said Texas? He had learned the trick in Spain, from Juan Cerillo. Hugh took off his jacket and laid it across the horse's withers in front of the saddle. Turning round as the foals came obediently plunging out of the bushes he added:

'It's the wheee-u that does it. The dying fall of the whinny.'

They passed the goat, two fierce cornucopias over a hedge. There could be no mistaking it. Laughing they tried to decide if it had turned off the Calle Nicaragua at the other lane or at its juncture with the Alcapancingo road. The goat was cropping at the edge of a field and lifted towards them, now, a Machiavellian eye, but did not move farther, watching them. *I may have missed that time. I am still on the warpath however.*

The new lane, peaceful, quite shady, deep-rutted, and despite the dry spell full of pools, beautifully reflecting the sky, wandered on between clumps of trees and broken hedges screening indeterminate fields, and now it was as though they were a company, a caravan, carrying, for their greater security, a little world of love with them as they rode along. Earlier it had promised to be too hot: but just enough sun warmed them, a soft breeze caressed their faces, the countryside on either hand smiled upon them with deceptive innocence, a drowsy hum rose up from the morning, the mares nodded, there were the foals, here was the dog, and it is all a bloody lie, he thought : we have fallen inevitably into it, it is as if, upon this one day in the year, the dead come to life, or so one was reliably informed on the bus, this day of visions and miracles, by some contrariety we have been allowed for one hour a glimpse of what never was at all, of what never can be since brotherhood was betrayed, the image of our happiness, of that it would be better to think could not have been. Another thought struck Hugh. And yet I do not expect, ever in my life, to be happier than I am now. No peace I shall ever find but will be poisoned as these moments are poisoned –

('Firmin, you are a poor sort of good man.' The voice might have come from an imaginary member of their caravan, and Hugh pictured Juan Cerillo distinctly now, tall, and riding a horse much too small for him, without stirrups, so that his feet nearly touched the ground, his wide ribboned hat on the back of his head, and a typewriter in a box slung around his neck resting on the pommel; in one free hand he held a bag of money, and a boy was running along beside him in the dust. Juan Cerillo ! He had been one of the fairly rare overt human symbols in Spain of the generous help Mexico had actually given; he had returned home before Brihuega. Trained as a chemist, he worked for a Credit Bank in Oaxaca with the Ejido, delivering money on horseback to finance the collective effort of remote Zapotecan villages; frequently beset by bandits murderously yelling *Viva el Cristo Rey*, shot at by enemies of Cárdenas in reverberating church towers, his daily job was equally an adventure in a human cause, which Hugh had been invited to share. For Juan had written, express, his letter in a bravely stamped envelope of thumbnail size – the stamps showed archers shooting at the sun – written that he was well, back at work, less than a hundred miles away, and now as each glimpse of the mysterious mountains seemed to mourn this opportunity lost to Geoff and the *Noemijolea*, Hugh seemed to hear his good friend rebuking him. It was the same plangent voice that had said once, in Spain, of his horse left in Cuicatlán :

'My poor horse, she will be biting, biting all the time.'
But now it spoke of the Mexico of Juan's childhood, of the year
Hugh was born. Juarez had lived and died. Yet was it a country with free speech, and the guarantee of life, liberty, and the
pursuit of happiness? A country of brilliantly muralled schools,
and where even each little cold mountain village had its stone
open-air stage, and the land was owned by its people free to
express their native genius? A country of model farms: of
hope? – It was a country of slavery, where human beings were
sold like cattle, and its native peoples, the Yaquis, the Papagos,
the Tomasachics, exterminated through deportation, or reduced
to worse than peonage, their lands in thrall or the hands of
foreigners. And in Oaxaca lay the terrible Valle Nacional where
Juan himself, a bona-fide slave aged seven, had seen an older
brother beaten to death, and another, bought for forty-five pesos,
starved to death in seven months, because it was cheaper this
should happen, and the slave-holder buy another slave, than
simply have one slave better fed merely worked to death in a
year. All this spelt Porfirio Díaz: *rurales* everywhere, *jefes
políticos*, and murder, the extirpation of liberal political institutions, the army an engine of massacre, an instrument of exile.
Juan knew this, having suffered it; and more. For later in the
revolution, his mother was murdered. And later still Juan himself killed his father, who had fought with Huerta, but turned
traitor. Ah, guilt and sorrow had dogged Juan's footsteps too,
for he was not a Catholic who could rise refreshed from the
cold bath of confession. Yet the banality stood: that the past
was irrevocably past. And conscience had been given man to
regret it only in so far as that might change the future. For
man, every man, Juan seemed to be telling him, even as Mexico,
must ceaselessly struggle upward. What was life but a warfare
and a stranger's sojourn? Revolution rages too in the *tierra
caliente* of each human soul. No peace but that must pay full
toll to hell –)
  'Is that so?'
  'Is that so?'
  They were all plodding downhill towards a river – even the
dog, lulled in a woolly soliloquy, was plodding – and now they

were in it, the first cautious heavy step forward, then the hesitation, then the surging onward, the lurching surefootedness below one that was yet so delicate there derived a certain sensation of lightness, as if the mare were swimming, or floating through the air, bearing one across with the divine surety of a Cristoferus, rather than by fallible instinct. The dog swam ahead, fatuously important; the foals, nodding solemnly, swayed along behind up to their necks : sunlight sparkled on the calm water, which further downstream where the river narrowed broke into furious little waves, swirling and eddying close inshore against black rocks, giving an effect of wildness, almost of rapids; low over their heads an ecstatic lightning of strange birds manoeuvred, looping-the-loop and immelmaning at unbelievable speed, aerobatic as new-born dragon-flies. The opposite shore was thickly wooded. Beyond the gently sloping bank, a little to the left of what was apparently the cavernous entrance to the continuation of their lane, stood a *pulquería*, decorated, above its wooden twin swing-doors (which from a distance looked not unlike the immensely magnificent chevrons of an American army sergeant), with gaily coloured fluttering ribbons. *Pulques Finos*, it said in faded blue letters on the oyster-white adobe wall : *La Sepultura*. A grim name : but doubtless it had some humorous connotation. An Indian sat with his back against the wall, his broad hat half down over his face, rested outside in the sunshine. His horse, or a horse, was tethered near him to a tree and Hugh could see from midstream the number seven branded on its rump. An advertisement for the local cinema was stuck on the tree : *Las Manos de Orlac con Peter Lorre*. On the roof of the *pulquería* a toy windmill, of the kind one saw in Cape Cod, Massachusetts, was twirling restlessly in the breeze. Hugh said :

'Your horse doesn't want to drink, Yvonne, just to look at her reflection. Let her. Don't yank at her head.'

'I wasn't. I know that too,' Yvonne said, with an ironic little smile.

They zigzagged slowly across the river; the dog, swimming like an otter, had almost reached the opposite bank. Hugh became aware of a question in the air.

'– you're our house guest, you know.'

'*Por favor.*' Hugh inclined his head.

'– would you like to have dinner out and go to a movie? Or will you brave Concepta's cooking?'

'What what?' Hugh had been thinking, for some reason, of his first week at his public school in England, a week of not knowing what one was supposed to do or to answer to any question, but of being carried on by a sort of pressure of shared ignorance into crowded halls, activities, marathons, even exclusive isolations, as when he had found himself once riding on horseback with the headmaster's wife, a reward, he was told, but for what he had never found out. 'No, I think I should hate to go to a movie, thank you very much,' he laughed.

'It's a strange little place – you might find it fun. The newsreels used to be about two years old and I shouldn't think it's changed any. And the same features come back over and over again. *Cimarron* and the *Gold Diggers of 1930* and oh – last year we saw a travelogue, *Come to Sunny Andalusia*, by way of news from Spain – '

'Blimey,' Hugh said.

'And the lighting is *always* failing.'

'I think I've seen the Peter Lorre movie somewhere. He's a great actor but it's a lousy picture. Your horse doesn't want to drink, Yvonne. It's all about a pianist who has a sense of guilt because he thinks his hands are a murderer's or something and keeps washing the blood off them. Perhaps they really are a murderer's, but I forget.'

'It sounds creepy.'

'I know, but it isn't.'

On the other side of the river their horses did want to drink and they paused to let them. Then they rode up the bank into the lane. This time the hedges were taller and thicker and twined with convolvulus. For that matter they might have been in England, exploring some little-known bypath of Devon or Cheshire. There was little to contradict the impression save an occasional huddled conclave of vultures up a tree. After climbing steeply through woodland the lane levelled off. Presently they reached more open country and fell into a canter. – Christ, how marvellous this was, or rather Christ, how he wanted to be deceived about it, as must have Judas, he thought – and here it was again, damn it – if ever Judas had a horse, or borrowed, stole one more likely, after that Madrugada of all Madrugadas, regretting then that he had given the thirty pieces of silver back – what is that to us, see thou to that, the *bastardos* had said – when now he probably wanted a drink, thirty drinks (like Geoff undoubtedly would this morning), and perhaps even so he had managed a few on credit, smelling the good smells of leather and sweat, listening to the pleasant clopping of the horses' hooves and thinking, how joyous all this could be, riding on like this under the dazzling sky of Jerusalem – and forgetting for an instant, so that it really *was* joyous – how splendid it all might be had I only not betrayed that man last night, even though I know perfectly well I was going to, how good indeed, if only it had not happened though, if only it were not so absolutely necessary to go out and hang oneself –

And here indeed it was again, the temptation, the cowardly, the future-corruptive serpent: trample on it, stupid fool. Be Mexico. Have you not passed through the river? In the name of God be dead. And Hugh actually did ride over a dead garter snake, embossed on the path like a belt to a pair of bathing trunks. Or perhaps it was a Gila monster.

They had emerged on the outermost edge of what looked like a spacious, somewhat neglected park, spreading down on their right, or what had once been a huge grove, planted with lofty majestic trees. They reined in and Hugh, behind, rode slowly by himself for a while ... The foals separated him from Yvonne, who was staring blankly ahead as if insensible to their surroundings. The grove seemed to be irrigated by artificially banked streams, which were choked with leaves – though by no means all the trees were deciduous and underneath were frequent dark pools of shadow – and was lined with walks. Their lane had in fact become one of these walks. A noise of shunting sounded on the left; the station couldn't be far off; probably it was hidden behind that hillock over which hung a plume of white steam. But a railway track, raised above scrub-land, gleamed through the trees to their right; the line apparently made a wide detour round the whole place. They rode past a dried-up fountain below some broken steps, its basin filled with twigs and leaves. Hugh sniffed : a strong raw smell, he couldn't identify at first, pervaded the air. They were entering the vague precincts of what might have been a French château. The building, half hidden by trees, lay in a sort of courtyard at the end of the grove, which was closed by a row of cypresses growing behind a high wall, in which a massive gate, straight ahead of them, stood open. Dust was blowing across the gap. *Cervecería Quauhnahuac* : Hugh now saw written in white letters on the side of the château. He hallooed and waved at Yvonne to halt. So the château was a brewery, but of a very odd type – one that hadn't quite made up its mind not to be an open-air restaurant and beer garden. Outside in the courtyard two or three round tables (more likely to provide against the occasional visits of semi-official 'tasters'), blackened and leaf covered, were set beneath immense trees not quite familiar enough for oaks, not quite strangely tropical either, which were perhaps not really very old, but possessed an indefinable air of being immemorial, of having been planted centuries ago by some emperor, at least, with a golden trowel. Under these trees, where their cavalcade stopped, a little girl was playing with an armadillo.

Out of the brewery itself, which at close quarters appeared quite different, more like a mill, sliced, oblong, which emitted a sudden mill-like clamour, and on which flitted and slid mill-wheel-like reflections of sunlight on water, cast from a nearby stream, out of a glimpse of its very machinery, now issued a pied man, visored, resembling a gamekeeper, bearing two foaming tankards of dark German beer. They had not dismounted and he handed the beer up to them.

'God, that's cold,' Hugh said, 'good though.' The beer had a piercing taste, half metallic, half earthy, like distilled loam. It was so cold that it hurt.

'*Buenos días, muchacha.*' Yvonne, tankard in hand, was smiling down at the child with the armadillo. The gamekeeper vanished through an ostiole back into the machinery; closing away its clamour from them, as might an engineer on ship-board. The child was crouching on her haunches holding the armadillo and apprehensively eyeing the dog, who however lay at a safe distance watching the foals inspect the rear of the plant. Each time the armadillo ran off, as if on tiny wheels, the little girl would catch it by its long whip of a tail and turn it over. How astonishingly soft and helpless it appeared then! Now she righted the creature and set it going once more, some engine of destruction perhaps that after millions of years had come to this. '*¿Cuánto?*' Yvonne asked.

Catching the animal again the child piped:

'*Cincuenta centavos.*'

'You don't really want it, do you?' Hugh – like General Winfield Scott, he thought privately, after emerging from the ravines of the Cerro Gordo – was sitting with one leg athwart the pommel.

Yvonne nodded in jest: 'I'd adore it. It's perfectly sweet.'

'You couldn't make a pet of it. Neither can the kid: that's why she wants to sell it.' Hugh sipped his beer. 'I know about armadillos.'

'Oh so do I!' Yvonne shook her head mockingly, opening her eyes very wide. 'But everything!'

'Then you know that if you let the thing loose in your garden it'll merely tunnel down into the ground and never come back.'

Yvonne was still half-mockingly shaking her head, her eyes wide. 'Isn't he a darling?'

Hugh swung his leg back and sat now with his tankard propped on the pommel looking down at the creature with its big mischievous nose, iguana's tail, and helpless speckled belly, a Martian infant's toy. '*No, muchas gracias,*' he said firmly to the little girl who, indifferent, did not retreat. 'It'll not only never come back, Yvonne, but if you try to stop it it will do its damnedest to pull you down the hole too.' He turned to her, eyebrows raised, and for a time they watched each other in silence. 'As your friend W. H. Hudson, I think it was, found out to his cost,' Hugh added. A leaf fell off a tree somewhere behind them with a crash, like a sudden footstep. Hugh drank

157

a long cold draught. 'Yvonne,' he said, 'do you mind if I ask you straight out if you *are* divorced from Geoff or not?'

Yvonne choked on her beer; she wasn't holding the reins at all, which were looped round her pommel, and her horse gave a small lurch forward, then halted before Hugh had time to reach for the bridle.

'Do you mean to go back to him or what? Or have you already gone back?' Hugh's mare had also taken a sympathetic step forward. 'Forgive my being so blunt, but I feel in a horribly false position. – I'd like to know precisely what the situation is.'

'So would I.' Yvonne did not look at him.

'Then you don't know whether you *have* divorced him or not?'

'Oh, I've – divorced him,' she answered unhappily.

'But you don't know whether you've gone back to him or not?'

'Yes. No ... Yes. I've gone back to him all right all right.'

Hugh was silent while another leaf fell, crashed and hung tilted, balanced in the undergrowth. 'Then wouldn't it be rather simpler for you if I went away immediately,' he asked her gently, 'instead of staying on a little while as I'd hoped? – I'd been thinking of going to Oaxaca for a day or two anyhow – '

Yvonne had raised her head at the word Oaxaca. 'Yes,' she said. 'Yes, it might. Though, oh Hugh, I don't like to say it, only – '

'Only what?'

'Only please don't go away till we've talked it over. I'm so frightened.'

Hugh was paying for the beers, which were only twenty centavos; thirty less than the armadillo, he thought. 'Or do you want another?' He had to raise his voice above the renewed clamour of the plant : *dungeons: dungeons: dungeons:* it said.

'I can't finish this one. You finish it for me.'

Their cavalcade moved off again slowly, out of the courtyard, through the massive gate into the road beyond. As by common consent they turned right, away from the railway station. A *camión* was approaching behind them from the town and Hugh reined in beside Yvonne while the dog herded the foals along the ditch. The bus – *Tomalín : Zócalo* – disappeared, clanging round a corner.

'That's one way to get to Parián.' Yvonne averted her face from the dust.

'Wasn't that the Tomalín bus?'

'Just the same it's the easiest way to get to Parián. I think there is a bus goes straight there, but from the other end of the town, and by another road, from Tepalzanco.'

'There seems to be something sinister about Parián.'

'It's a very dull place actually. Of course it's the old capital of the state. Years ago there used to be a huge monastery there, I believe – rather like Oaxaca in that respect. Some of the shops and even the *cantinas* are part of what were once the monks' quarters. But it's quite a ruin.'

'I wonder what Weber sees in it,' Hugh said. They left the cypresses and the plant behind. Having come, unwarned, to a gateless level-crossing they turned right once more, this time heading homeward.

They were riding abreast down the railway lines Hugh had seen from the grove, flanking the grove in almost the opposite direction to the way they had approached. On either side a low embankment sloped to a narrow ditch, beyond which stretched scrub-land. Above them telegraph wires twanged and whined : *guitarra guitarra guitarra* : which was, perhaps, a better thing to say than *dungeons*. The railway – a double track but of narrow gauge – now divagated away from the grove, for no apparent reason, then wandered back again parallel to it. A little farther on, as if to balance matters, it made a similar deviation towards the grove. But in the distance it curved away in a wide leftward sweep of such proportions one felt it must logically come to involve itself again with the Tomalín road. This was too much for the telegraph poles that strode straight ahead arrogantly and were lost from sight.

Yvonne was smiling. 'I see you look worried. There's really a story for your *Globe* in this line.'

'I can't make out what sort of damn thing it is at all.'

'It was built by you English. Only the company was paid by the kilometre.'

Hugh laughed loudly. 'How marvellous. You don't mean it was laid out in this cockeyed fashion just for the sake of the extra mileage, do you?'

'That's what they say. Though I don't suppose it's true.'

'Well, well. I'm disappointed. I'd been thinking it must be some delightful Mexican whimsey. It certainly gives one to think however.'

'Of the capitalist system?' There was again a hint of mockery about Yvonne's smile.

'It reminds one of some story in *Punch* ... Did you know there was a place called Punch in Kashmir by the by?' (Yvonne murmured, shaking her head.) ' – Sorry, I've forgotten what I was going to say.'

'What do you think about Geoffrey?' Yvonne asked the question at last. She was leaning forward, resting on the pommel, watching him sideways. 'Hugh, tell me the truth. Do you think there's any – well – hope for him?' Their mares were picking their way delicately along this unusual lane, the foals keeping farther ahead than before, glancing round from time to time for approbation at their daring. The dog ran ahead of the foals though he never failed to dodge back periodically to see all was well. He was sniffing busily for snakes among the metals.

'About his drinking, do you mean?'

'Do you think there's anything I can do?'

Hugh looked down at some blue wildflowers like forget-me-nots that had somehow found a place to grow between the sleepers on the track. These innocents had their problem too: what is this frightful dark sun that roars and strikes at our eyelids every few minutes? Minutes? Hours more likely. Perhaps even days: the lone semaphores seemed permanently up, it might be sadly expeditious to ask about trains oneself. 'I dare say you've heard about his "strychnine", as he calls it,' Hugh said. 'The journalist's cure. Well, I actually got the stuff by prescription from some guy in Quauhnahuac who knew you both at one time.'

'Dr Guzmán?'

'Yes, Guzmán. I think that was the name. I tried to persuade him to see Geoff. But he refused to waste time on him. He said simply that so far as he knew there was nothing wrong with Papa and never had been save that he wouldn't make up his mind to stop drinking. That seems plain enough and I dare say it's true.'

The track sank level with the scrub-land, then below it, so that the embankments were now above them.

'It *isn't* drinking, somehow,' Yvonne said suddenly. 'But why does he do it?'

'Perhaps now you've come back like this he'll stop.'

'You don't sound very hopeful.'

'Yvonne, listen to me. So obviously there are a thousand things to say and there isn't going to be time to say most of them. It's difficult to know where to begin. I'm almost completely in the dark. I wasn't even sure you were divorced till five minutes ago. I don't know – ' Hugh clicked his tongue at his horse but held her back. 'As for Geoff,' he went on, 'I simply have no idea what he's been doing or how much he's been drinking. Half the time you can't tell when he's tight anyway.'

'You couldn't say that if you were his *wife*.'

'Wait a minute. – My attitude towards Geoff was simply the one I'd take towards some brother scribe with a godawful hangover. But while I've been in Mexico City I've been saying to myself : *¿Cui bono?* What's the good? Just sobering him up for a day or two's not going to help. Good God, if our civilization were to sober up for a couple of days it'd die of remorse on the third – '

'That's *very* helpful,' Yvonne said. 'Thank you.'

'Besides after a while one begins to feel, if a man can hold his liquor as well as that why shouldn't he drink?' Hugh leaned over and patted her horse. 'No, seriously, why don't both of you get out, though? Out of Mexico. There's no reason for you to stay any longer, is there? Geoff loathed the consular service anyway.' For a moment Hugh watched one of the foals standing silhouetted against the sky on top of the embankment. 'You've got money.'

'You'll forgive me when I tell you this, Hugh. It wasn't because I didn't want to see you. But I tried to get Geoffrey to leave this morning before you came back.'

'It was no go, eh?'

'Maybe it wouldn't have worked anyhow. We tried it before, this getting away and starting all over. But Geoffrey said something this morning about going on with his book – for the life of me I don't know whether he's still writing one or not, he's never done any work on it since I've known him, and he's never let me see scarcely any of it, still, he keeps all those reference books with him – and I thought –'

'Yes,' Hugh said, 'how much does he really know about all this alchemy and cabbala business? How much does it mean to him?'

'That's just what I was going to ask you. I've never been able to find out – '

'Good lord, I don't know ... ' Hugh added with almost avuncular relish : 'Maybe he's a black magician!'

Yvonne smiled absently, flicking her reins against the pommel. The track emerged into the open and once more the embankments sloped down on either side. High overhead sailed white sculpturings of clouds, like billowing concepts in the brain of Michelangelo. One of the foals had strayed from the track into the scrub. Hugh repeated the ritual of whistling, the foal hauled itself back up the bank and they were a company again, trotting smartly along the meandering selfish little railroad. 'Hugh,' Yvonne said, 'I had an idea coming down on the boat ... I don't know whether – I've always dreamed of having a farm somewhere. A real farm, you know, with cows and pigs and chickens – and a red barn and silos and fields of corn and wheat.'

'What, no guinea-fowl? I might have a dream like that in a week or two,' Hugh said. 'Where does the farm come in?'

'Why – Geoffrey and I might buy one.'

'*Buy* one?'

'Is that so fantastic?'

'I suppose not, but where?' Hugh's pint-and-a-half of strong beer was beginning to take pleasurable effect, and all at once he gave a guffaw that was more like a sneeze. 'I'm sorry,' he said, 'it was just the notion of Geoff among the alfalfa, in overalls and a straw hat, soberly hoeing, that got me a moment.'

'It wouldn't have to be as soberly as all that. I'm not an ogre.' Yvonne was laughing too, but her dark eyes, that had been shining, were opaque and withdrawn.

'But what if Geoff hates farms? Perhaps the mere sight of a cow makes him seasick.'

'Oh no. We often used to talk about having a farm in the old days.'

'Do you *know* anything about farming?'

'No.' Yvonne abruptly, delightfully, dismissed the possibility, leaning forward and stroking her mare's neck. 'But I wondered if we mightn't get some couple who'd lost their own farm or something actually to run it for us and live on it.'

'I wouldn't have thought it exactly a good point in history to begin to prosper as the landed gentry, but still maybe it is. Where's this farm to be?'

'Well ... What's to stop us going to Canada, for instance?'

'... *Canada?* ... Are you serious? Well, why not, but –'

'Perfectly.'

They had now reached the place where the railway took its wide leftward curve and they descended the embankment. The grove had dropped behind but there was still thick woodland to their right (above the centre of which had appeared again the almost friendly landmark of the prison watchtower) and stretching far ahead. A road showed briefly along the margin of the woods. They approached this road slowly, following the single-minded thrumming telegraph poles and picking a difficult course through the scrub.

'I mean why Canada more than British Honduras? Or even Tristan da Cunha? A little lonely perhaps, though an admirable place for one's teeth, I've heard. Then there's Gough Island, hard by Tristan. That's uninhabited. Still, you might colonize it. Or Sokotra, where the frankincense and myrrh used to come from and the camels climb like chamois – my favourite island in the Arabian Sea.' But Hugh's tone though amused was not altogether sceptical as he touched on these fantasies, half to himself, for Yvonne rode a little in front; it was as if he were after all seriously grappling with the problem of Canada while at the same time making an effort to pass off the situation as possessing any number of adventurous whimsical solutions. He caught up with her.

'Hasn't Geoffrey mentioned his genteel Siberia to you lately?' she said. 'You surely haven't forgotten he owns an island in British Columbia?'

'On a lake, isn't it? Pineaus Lake. I remember. But there isn't any house on it, is there? And you can't graze cattle on fircones and hardpan.'

'That's not the point, Hugh.'

'Or would you propose to camp on it and have your farm elsewhere?'

'Hugh, listen – '

'But suppose you could only buy your farm in some place like Saskatchewan,' Hugh objected. An idiotic verse came into his head, keeping time with the horse's hooves:

> Oh take me back to Poor Fish River,
> Take me back to Onion Lake,
> You can keep the Guadalquivir,
> Como you may likewise take.
> Take me back to dear old Horsefly,
> Aneroid or Gravelburg. . . .

'In some place with a name like Product. Or even Dumble,' he went on. 'There must be a Dumble. In fact I know there's a Dumble.'

'All right. Maybe it *is* ridiculous. But at least it's better than sitting here doing nothing!' Almost crying, Yvonne angrily urged her horse into a brief wild canter, but the terrain was too rough; Hugh reined in beside her and they halted together.

'I'm awfully, dreadfully sorry.' Contrite, he took her bridle. 'I was just being more than unusually bloody stupid.'

'Then you *do* think it's a good idea?' Yvonne brightened slightly, even contriving again an air of mockery.

'Have you ever been to Canada?' he asked her.

'I've been to Niagara Falls.'

They rode on, Hugh still holding her bridle. 'I've never been to Canada at all. But a Canuck in Spain, a fisherman pal of mine with the Macs-Paps, used to keep telling me it was the most terrific place in the world. British Columbia, at any rate.'

'That's what Geoffrey used to say too.'

'Well, Geoff's liable to be vague on the subject. But here's what McGoff told me. This man was a Pict. Suppose you land in Vancouver, as seems reasonable. So far not so good. McGoff didn't have much use for modern Vancouver. According to him it has a sort of Pango Pango quality mingled with sausage and mash and generally a rather Puritan atmosphere. Everyone fast asleep and when you prick them a Union Jack flows out of the hole. But no one in a certain sense lives there. They merely as it were pass through. Mine the country and quit. Blast the land to pieces, knock down the trees and send them rolling down Burrard Inlet ... As for drinking, by the way, that is beset,' Hugh chuckled, 'everywhere beset by perhaps favourable difficulties. No bars, only beer parlours so uncomfortable and cold that serve beer so weak no self-respecting drunkard would show his nose in them. You have to drink at home, and when you run short it's too far to get a bottle – '

'But – ' They were both laughing.

'But wait a minute.' Hugh looked up at the sky of New Spain. It was a day like a good Joe Venuti record. He listened to the faint steady droning of the telegraph poles and the wires above them that sang in his heart with his pint-and-a-half of beer. At this moment the best and easiest and most simple thing in the world seemed to be the happiness of these two people in a new country. And what counted seemed probably the swiftness with which they moved. He thought of the Ebro. Just as a long-planned offensive might be defeated in its first few days by unconsidered potentialities that have now been given time to mature, so a sudden desperate move might succeed precisely because of the number of potentialities it destroys at one fell swoop ...

'The thing to do', he went on, 'is to get out of Vancouver as fast as possible. Go down one of the inlets to some fishing village and buy a shack slap spang on the sea, with only foreshore rights, for, say a hundred dollars. Then live on it this winter for about sixty a month. No phone. No rent. No consulate. Be a squatter. Call on your pioneer ancestors. Water from the well. Chop your own wood. After all, Geoff's as strong as a horse. And perhaps he'll be able really to get down to his book and you can have your stars and the sense of the seasons again; though you can sometimes swim late as November. And get to know the real people : the Seine fishermen, the old boatbuilders, the trappers, according to McGoff the last truly free people left in the world. Meantime you can get your island fixed up and find out about your farm, which previously you'll have used a a decoy for all you're worth, if you still want it by then – '

'Oh Hugh, *yes* – '

He all but shook her horse with enthusiasm. 'I can see your shack now. It's between the forest and the sea and you've got a pier going down to the water over rough stones, you know, covered with barnacles and sea anemones and starfish. You'll have to go through the woods to the store.' Hugh saw the store in his mind's eye. *The woods will be wet. And occasionally a tree will come crashing down. And sometimes there will be a fog and that fog will freeze. Then your whole forest will become a crystal forest. The ice crystals on the twigs will grow like leaves. Then pretty soon you'll be seeing the jack-in-the-pulpits and then it will be spring.*

They were galloping ... Bare level plain had taken the place of the scrub and they'd been cantering briskly, the foals prancing delightedly ahead, when suddenly the dog was a shoulder-shrugging streaking fleece, and as their mares almost imperceptibly fell into the long untrammelled undulating strides, Hugh felt the sense of change, the keen elemental pleasure one experienced too on board a ship which, leaving the choppy waters of the estuary, gives way to the pitch and swing of the open sea. A faint carillon of bells sounded in the distance, rising and falling, sinking back as if into the very substance of the day. Judas had forgotten; nay, Judas had been, somehow, redeemed.

They were galloping parallel to the road which was hedgeless and on ground level, then the thudding regular thunder of the hooves struck abruptly hard and metallic and dispersed and they were clattering on the road itself; it bore away to the right skirting the woods round a sort of headland jutting into the plain.

'We're on the Calle Nicaragua again,' Yvonne shouted gaily, 'almost!'

At a full gallop they were approaching the Malebolge once more, the serpentine *barranca*, though at a point much farther up than where they'd first crossed it; they were trotting side by side over a white-fenced bridge: then, all at once, they were in the ruin. Yvonne was in it first, the animals seeming to be checked less by the reins than by their own decision, possibly nostalgic, possibly even considerate, to halt. They dismounted. The ruin occupied a considerable stretch of the grassy roadside on their right hand. Near them was what might once have been a chapel, with grass on which the dew still sparkled growing through the floor. Elsewhere were the remains of a wide stone porch with low crumbled balustrades. Hugh, who had quite lost his bearings, secured their mares to a broken pink pillar that stood apart from the rest of the desuetude, a meaningless mouldering emblem.

'What is all this ex-splendour anyway?' he said.

'Maximilian's Palace. The summer one, I think. I believe all that grove effect by the brewery was once part of his grounds too.' Yvonne looked suddenly ill at ease.

'Don't you want to stop here?' he had asked her.

'Sure. It's a good idea. I'd like a cigarette,' she said hesitantly. 'But we'll have to stroll down a ways for Carlotta's favourite view.'

'The emperor's mirador certainly has seen better days.' Hugh, rolling Yvonne a cigarette, glanced absently round the place, which appeared so reconciled to its own ruin no sadness touched it; birds perched on the blasted towers and dilapidated masonry over which clambered the inevitable blue convolvulus; the foals with their guardian dog resting near were meekly grazing in the chapel: it seemed safe to leave them . . .

'Maximilian and Carlotta, eh?' Hugh was saying. 'Should Juarez have had the man shot or not?'

'It's an awfully tragic story.'

167

'He should have had old thingmetight, Díaz, shot at the same time and made a job of it.'

They came to the headland and stood gazing back the way they had come, over the plains, the scrub, the railway, the Tomalín road. It was blowing here, a dry steady wind. Popocatepetl and Ixtaccihuatl. There they lay peacefully enough beyond the valley; the firing had ceased. Hugh felt a pang. On the way down he'd entertained a quite serious notion of finding time to climb Popo, perhaps even with Juan Cerillo –

'There's your moon for you still,' he pointed it out again, a fragment blown out of the night by a cosmic storm.

'Weren't those wonderful names', she said, 'the old astronomers gave the places on the moon?'

'The Marsh of Corruption. That's the only one I can remember.'

'Sea of Darkness ... Sea of Tranquillity ...'

They stood side by side without speaking, the wind tearing cigarette smoke over their shoulders; from here the valley too resembled a sea, a galloping sea. Beyond the Tomalín road the country rolled and broke its barbarous waves of dunes and rocks in every direction. Above the foothills, spiked along their rims with firs, like broken bottles guarding a wall, a white onrush of clouds might have been poised breakers. But behind the volcanoes themselves he saw now that storm clouds were gathering. 'Sokotra,' he thought, 'my mysterious island in the Arabian Sea, where the frankincense and myrrh used to come from, and no one has ever been – '

There was something in the wild strength of this landscape, once a battlefield, that seemed to be shouting at him, a presence born of that strength whose cry his whole being recognized as familiar, caught and threw back into the wind, some youthful password of courage and pride – the passionate, yet so nearly always hypocritical, affirmation of one's soul perhaps, he thought, of the desire to be, to do, good, what was right. It was as though he were gazing now beyond this expanse of plains and beyond the volcanoes out to the wide rolling blue ocean itself, feeling it in his heart still, the boundless impatience, the immeasurable longing.

5

BEHIND them walked the only living thing that shared their pilgrimage, the dog. And by degrees they reached the briny sea. Then, with souls well disciplined they reached the northern region, and beheld, with heaven aspiring hearts, the mighty mountain Himavat ... Whereupon the lake was lapping, the lilacs were blowing, the chenars were budding, the mountains were glistening, the waterfalls were playing, the spring was green, the snow was white, the sky was blue, the fruit blossoms were clouds: and he was still thirsty. Then the snow was not glistening, the fruit blossoms were not clouds, they were mosquitoes, the Himalayas were hidden by dust, and he was thirstier than ever. Then the lake was blowing, the snow was blowing, the waterfalls were blowing, the fruit blossoms were blowing, the seasons were blowing – blowing away – he was blowing away himself, whirled by a storm of blossoms into the mountains, where now the rain was falling. But this rain, that fell only on the mountains, did not assuage his thirst. Nor was he after all in the mountains. He was standing, among cattle, in a stream. He was resting, with some ponies, knee-deep beside him in the cool marshes. He was lying face downward drinking from a lake that reflected the white-capped ranges, the clouds piled five miles high behind the mighty mountain Himavat: the purple chenars and a village nestling among the mulberries. Yet his thirst still remained unquenched. Perhaps because he was drinking, not water, but lightness, and promise of lightness – how could he be drinking promise of lightness? Perhaps because he was drinking, not water, but certainty of brightness – how could he be drinking certainty of brightness? Certainty of brightness, promise of lightness, of light, light, light, and again, of light, light, light, light, light!

... The Consul, an inconceivable anguish of horripilating hangover thunderclapping about his skull, and accompanied by

169

a protective screen of demons gnattering in his ears, became aware that in the horrid event of his being observed by his neighbours it could hardly be supposed he was just sauntering down his garden with some innocent horticultural object in view. Nor even that he was sauntering. The Consul, who had waked a moment or two ago on the porch and remembered everything immediately, was almost running. He was also lurching. In vain he tried to check himself, plunging his hands, with an extraordinary attempt at nonchalance, in which he hoped might appear more than a hint of consular majesty, deeper into the sweat-soaked pockets of his dress trousers. And now, rheumatisms discarded, he really was running ... Might he not, then, be reasonably suspected of a more dramatic purpose, of having assumed, for instance, the impatient buskin of a William Blackstone leaving the Puritans to dwell among the Indians, or the desperate mien of his friend Wilson when he so magnificently abandoned the University Expedition to disappear, likewise in a pair of dress trousers, into the jungles of darkest Oceania, never to return? Not very reasonably. For one thing, if he continued much farther in this present direction towards the bottom of his garden any such visioned escape into the unknown must shortly be arrested by what was, for him, an unscalable wire fence. 'Do not be so foolish as to imagine you have no object, however. We warned you, we told you so, but now that in spite of all our pleas you have got yourself into this deplorable – ' He recognized the tone of one of his familiars, faint among the other voices as he crashed on through the metamorphoses of dying and reborn hallucinations, like a man who does not know he has been shot from behind. ' – condition,' the voice went on severely, 'you have to do something about it. Therefore we are leading you towards the accomplishment of this something.' 'I'm not going to drink,' the Consul said, halting suddenly. 'Or am I? Not mescal anyway.' 'Of course not, the bottle's just there, behind that bush. Pick it up.' 'I can't,' he objected – 'That's right, just take one drink, just the necessary, the therapeutic drink: perhaps two drinks.' 'God,' the Consul said. 'Ah. Good. God. Christ.' 'Then you can say it doesn't count.' 'It doesn't. It isn't mescal.' 'Of course not, it's tequila.

You might have another.' 'Thanks, I will.' The Consul palsiedly readjusted the bottle to his lips. 'Bliss. Jesus. Sanctuary ... Horror,' he added. ' – Stop. Put that bottle down, Geoffrey Firmin, what are you doing to yourself?' another voice said in his ear so loudly he turned round. On the path before him a little snake he had thought a twig was rustling off into the bushes and he watched it a moment through his dark glasses, fascinated. It was a real snake all right. Not that he was much bothered by anything so simple as snakes, he reflected with a degree of pride, gazing straight into the eyes of a dog. It was a pariah dog and disturbingly familiar. '*Perro*,' he repeated, as it still stood there – but had not this incident occurred, was it not now, as it were, occurring an hour or two ago, he thought in a flash. Strange. He dropped the bottle which was of white corrugated glass – Tequila Añejo de Jalisco, it said on the label – out of sight into the undergrowth, looking about him. All seemed normal again. Anyway, both snake and dog had gone. And the voices had ceased ...

The Consul now felt himself in a position to entertain, for a minute, the illusion that all really was 'normal'. Yvonne would probably be asleep: no point in disturbing her yet. And it was fortunate he'd remembered about the almost full tequila bottle: now he had a chance to straighten up a little, which he never could have done on the porch, before greeting her again. There was altogether too much difficulty involved, under the circumstances, in drinking on the porch; it was a good thing a man knew where to have a quiet drink when he wanted it, without being disturbed, etc. etc. ... All these thoughts were passing through his mind – which, so to say, nodding gravely, accepted them with the most complete seriousness – while he gazed back up his garden. Oddly enough, it did not strike him as being nearly so 'ruined' as it had earlier appeared. Such chaos as might exist even lent an added charm. He liked the exuberance of the unclipped growth at hand. Whereas farther away, the superb plantains flowering so finally and obscenely, the splendid trumpet vines, brave and stubborn pear trees, the papayas planted around the swimming-pool and beyond, the low white bungalow itself covered by bougainvillea, its long porch like the

171

bridge of a ship, positively made a little vision of order, a vision, however, which inadvertently blended at this moment, as he turned by accident, into a strangely subaqueous view of the plains and the volcanoes with a huge indigo sun multitudinously blazing south-south-east. Or was it north-north-west? He noted it all without sorrow, even with a certain ecstasy, lighting a cigarette, an Alas (though he repeated the word 'Alas' aloud mechanically), then, the alcohol sweat pouring off his brows like water, he began to walk down the path towards the fence separating his garden from the little new public one beyond that truncated his property.

In this garden, which he hadn't looked at since the day Hugh arrived, when he'd hidden the bottle, and which seemed carefully and lovingly kept, there existed at the moment certain evidence of work left uncompleted : tools, unusual tools, a murderous machete, an oddly shaped fork, somehow nakedly impaling the mind, with its twisted tines glittering in the sunlight, were leaning against the fence, as also was something else, a sign uprooted or new, whose oblong pallid face stared through the wire at him. *¿Le gusta este jardín?* it asked . . .

¿LE GUSTA ESTE JARDÍN?
¿QUE ES SUYO?
¡EVITE QUE SUS HIJOS LO DESTRUYAN!

The Consul stared back at the black words on the sign without moving. You like this garden? Why is it yours? We evict those who destroy! Simple words, simple and terrible words, words which one took to the very bottom of one's being, words which, perhaps a final judgement on one, were nevertheless unproductive of any emotion whatsoever, unless a kind of colourless cold, a white agony, an agony chill as that iced mescal drunk in the Hotel Canada on the morning of Yvonne's departure.

However he was drinking tequila again now – and with no very clear idea how he'd returned so quickly and found the bottle. Ah, the subtle bouquet of pitch and teredos! Careless of being observed this time, he drank long and deeply, then stood – and he had been observed too, by his neighbour Mr Quincey, who was watering flowers in the shade of their common fence to the left beyond the briars – stood facing his bungalow once more. He felt hemmed in. Gone was the little dishonest vision of order. Over his house, above the spectres of neglect that now refused to disguise themselves, the tragic wings of untenable responsibilities hovered. Behind him, in the other garden, his fate repeated softly: 'Why is it yours? ... Do you like this garden? ... We evict those who destroy!' Perhaps the sign didn't mean quite that – for alcohol sometimes affected the Consul's Spanish adversely (or perhaps the sign itself, inscribed by some Aztec, was wrong) – but it was near enough. Coming to an abrupt decision he dropped the tequila into the under-growth again and turned back towards the public garden, walking with an attempted 'easy' stride.

Not that he had any intention of 'verifying' the words on the sign, which certainly seemed to have more question marks than it should have; no, what he wanted, he now saw very clearly, was to talk to someone: that was necessary: but it was more, merely, than that; what he wanted involved something like the grasping, at this moment, of a brilliant opportunity, or more accurately, of an opportunity to be brilliant, an opportunity evinced by that apparition of Mr Quincey through the briars which, now upon his right, he must circumvent in order to reach him. Yet this opportunity to be brilliant was, in turn, more like something else, an opportunity to be admired; even, and he could at least thank the tequila for such honesty, how-ever brief its duration, to be loved. Loved precisely for what was another question: since he'd put it to himself he might answer: loved for my reckless and irresponsible appear-ance, or rather for the fact that, beneath that appearance, so obviously burns the fire of genius, which, not so obviously, is not my genius but in an extraordinary manner that of my old and good friend, Abraham Taskerson, the great poet, who once spoke so glowingly of my potentialities as a young man.

And what he wanted then, ah then (he had turned right without looking at the sign and was following the path along the wire fence), what he wanted then, he thought, casting one yearning glance at the plains – and at this moment he could have sworn that a figure, the details of whose dress he did not have time to make out before it departed, but apparently in some kind of mourning, had been standing, head bowed in deepest anguish, near the centre of the public garden – what you want then, Geoffrey Firmin, if only as an antidote against such routine hallucinations, is, why it is, nothing less than to drink; to drink, indeed, all day, just as the clouds once more bid you, and yet not quite; again it is more subtle than this; you do not wish merely to drink, but to drink in a particular place and in a particular town.

Parián! ... It was a name suggestive of old marble and the gale-swept Cyclades. The Farolito in Parián, how it called to him with its gloomy voices of the night and early dawn. But the Consul (he had inclined right again leaving the wire fence behind) realized he wasn't yet drunk enough to be very sanguine about his chances of going there; the day offered too many immediate – pitfalls! It was the exact word ... He had almost fallen into the *barranca*, an unguarded section of whose hither bank – the ravine curved sharply down here towards the Alcapancingo road to curve again below and follow its direction, bisecting the public garden – added at this juncture a tiny fifth side to his estate. He paused, peeping, tequila-unafraid, over the bank. Ah the frightful cleft, the eternal horror of opposites! Thou mighty gulf, insatiate cormorant, deride me not, though I seem petulant to fall into thy chops. One was, come to that, always stumbling upon the damned thing, this immense intricate donga cutting right through the town, right, indeed, through the country, in places a two-hundred-foot sheer drop into what pretended to be a churlish river during the rainy season, but which, even now, though one couldn't see the bottom, was probably beginning to resume its normal role of general Tartarus and gigantic jakes. It was, perhaps, not so frightening here: one might even climb down, if one wished, by easy stages of course, and taking the occasional swig of tequila on the way, to visit the cloacal Prometheus who doubtless inhabited it. The Consul walked on more slowly. He had come face to face with his house again and simultaneously to the path skirting Mr

174

Quincey's garden. On his left beyond their common fence, now at hand, the green lawns of the American, at the moment being sprinkled by innumerable small whizzing hoses, swept down parallel with his own briars. Nor could any English turf have appeared smoother or lovelier. Suddenly overwhelmed by sentiment, as at the same time by a violent attack of hiccups, the Consul stepped behind a gnarled fruit tree rooted on his side but spreading its remnant of shade over the other, and leaned against it, holding his breath. In this curious way he imagined himself hidden from Mr Quincey, working farther up, but he soon forgot all about Quincey in spasmodic admiration of his garden ... Would it happen at the end, and would this save one, that old Popeye would begin to seem less desirable than a slag-heap in Chester-le-Street, and that mighty Johnsonian prospect, the road to England, would stretch out again in the Western Ocean of his soul? And how peculiar that would be! How strange the landing at Liverpool, the Liver Building seen once more through the misty rain, that murk smelling already of nosebags and Caegwyrle Ale – the familiar deep-draughted cargo steamers, harmoniously masted, still sternly sailing outward bound with the tide, worlds of iron hiding their crews from the weeping black-shawled women on the piers : Liverpool, whence sailed so often during the war under sealed orders those mysterious submarine catchers Q-boats, fake freighters turning into turreted men-of-war at a moment's notice, obsolete peril of submarines, the snouted voyagers of the sea's unconscious ...

'Dr Livingstone, I presume.'

'Hicket,' said the Consul, taken aback by the premature rediscovery, at such close quarters, of the tall slightly stooping figure, in khaki shirt and grey flannel trousers, sandalled, immaculate, grey-haired, complete, fit, a credit to Soda Springs, and carrying a watering-can, who was regarding him distastefully through horn-rimmed spectacles from the other side of the fence. 'Ah, good morning, Quincey.'

'What's good about it?' the retired walnut grower asked suspiciously, continuing his work of watering his flower beds, which were out of range of the ceaselessly swinging hoses.

The Consul gestured towards his briars, and perhaps unconsciously also in the direction of the tequila bottle. 'I saw you from over there ... I was just out inspecting my jungle, don't you know.'

'You are doing *what?*' Mr Quincey glanced at him over the top of the watering-can as if to say: I have seen all this going on; I know all about it because I am God, and even when God was much older than you are he was nevertheless up at this time and fighting it, if necessary, while you don't even know whether you're up or not yet, and even if you have been out all night you are certainly not fighting it, as I would be, just as I would be ready to fight anything or anybody else too, for that matter, at the drop of a hat!

'And I'm afraid it really is a jungle too,' pursued the Consul, 'in fact I expect Rousseau to come riding out of it at any moment on a tiger.'

'What's that?' Mr Quincey said, frowning in a manner that might have meant: And God never drinks before breakfast either.

'On a tiger,' the Consul repeated.

The other gazed at him a moment with the cold sardonic eye of the material world. 'I expect so,' he said sourly. 'Plenty tigers. Plenty elephants too ... Might I ask you if the next time you inspect your jungle you'd mind being sick on your own side of the fence?'

'Hicket,' answered the Consul simply. 'Hicket,' he snarled, laughing, and, trying to take himself by surprise, he thwacked himself hard in the kidneys, a remedy which, strangely, seemed to work. 'Sorry I gave that impression, it was merely this damned hiccups! – '

'So I observe,' Mr Quincey said, and perhaps he too had cast a subtle glance towards the ambush of the tequila bottle.

'And the funny thing is,' interrupted the Consul, 'I scarcely touched anything more than Tehuacan water all night ... By the way; how did you manage to survive the ball?'

Mr Quincey stared at him evenly, then began to refill his watering can from a hydrant nearby.

'Just Tehuacan,' the Consul continued. 'And a little *gaseosa*.

That ought to take you back to dear old Soda Springs, eh? – tee hee! – yes, I've cut liquor right out these days.'

The other resumed his watering, sternly moving on down the fence, and the Consul, not sorry to leave the fruit tree, to which he had noticed clinging the sinister carapace of a seven-year locust, followed him step by step.

'Yes, I'm on the wagon now,' he commented, 'in case you didn't know.'

'The funeral wagon, I'd say, Firmin,' Mr Quincey muttered testily.

'By the way, I saw one of those little garter snakes just a moment ago,' the Consul broke out.

Mr Quincey coughed or snorted but said nothing.

'And it made me think ... Do you know, Quincey, I've often wondered whether there isn't more in the old legend of the Garden of Eden, and so on, than meets the eye. What if Adam wasn't really banished from the place at all? That is, in the sense we used to understand it – ' The walnut grower had looked up and was fixing him with a steady gaze that seemed, however, directed at a point rather below the Consul's midriff – 'What if his punishment really consisted', the Consul continued with warmth, 'in his having to *go on living there*, alone, of course – suffering, unseen, cut off from God ... Or perhaps', he added, in more cheerful vein, 'perhaps Adam was the first property owner and God, the first agrarian, a kind of Cárdenas, in fact – tee hee! – kicked him out. Eh? Yes,' the Consul chuckled, aware, moreover, that all this was possibly not so amusing under the existing historical circumstances, 'for it's obvious to everyone these days – don't you think so, Quincey? – that the original sin was to be an owner of property ...'

The walnut grower was nodding at him, almost imperceptibly, but not it seemed in any agreement; his *realpolitik* eye was still concentrated upon that same spot below his midriff and looking down the Consul discovered his open fly. *Licentia vatum* indeed! 'Pardon me, *j'adoube*,' he said, and making the adjustment continued, laughing, returning to his first theme mysteriously unabashed by his recusancy. 'Yes, indeed. Yes ... And of course the real *reason* for that punishment – his being

177

forced to go on living in the garden, I mean, might well have been that the poor fellow, who knows, secretly loathed the place! Simply hated it, and had done so all along. *And that the Old Man found this out –*'

'Was it my imagination, or did I see your wife up there a while ago?' patiently said Mr Quincey.

' – and no wonder! To hell with the place! Just think of all the scorpions and leafcutter ants – to mention only a few of the abominations he must have had to put up with! What?' the Consul exclaimed as the other repeated his question. 'In the garden? Yes – that is, no. How do you know? No, she's asleep as far as I –'

'Been away quite a time, hasn't she?' the other asked mildly, leaning forward so that he could see, more clearly, the Consul's bungalow. 'Your brother still here?'

'Brother? Oh. you mean Hugh ... No, he's in Mexico City.'

'I think you'll find he's got back.'

The Consul now glanced up at the house himself. 'Hicket,' he said briefly, apprehensively.

'I think he went out with your wife,' the walnut grower added.

' – Hullo-hullo-look-who-comes-hullo-my-little-snake-in-the-grass-my-little-anguish-in-herba – ' the Consul at this moment greeted Mr Quincey's cat, momentarily forgetting its owner again as the grey, meditative animal, with a tail so long it trailed on the ground, came stalking through the zinnias: he stooped, patting his thighs – 'hello-pussy-my-little-Priapusspuss, my-little-Oedipusspusspuss,' and the cat, recognizing a friend and uttering a cry of pleasure, wound through the fence and rubbed against the Consul's legs, purring. 'My little Xicotancatl.' The Consul stood up. He gave two short whistles while below him the cat's ears twirled. 'She thinks I'm a tree with a bird in it,' he added.

'I wouldn't wonder,' retorted Mr Quincey, who was refilling his watering can at the hydrant.

'Animals not fit for food and kept only for pleasure, curiosity, or whim – eh? – as William Blackstone said – you've heard of him of course! – ' The Consul was somehow on his haunches

178

half talking to the cat, half to the walnut grower, who had paused to light a cigarette. 'Or was that another William Blackstone?' He addressed himself now directly to Mr Quincey, who was paying no attention. 'He's a character I've always liked. I think it was William Blackstone. Or so Abraham ... Anyway, one day he arrived in what is now, I believe – no matter – somewhere in Massachusetts. And lived there quietly among the Indians. After a while the Puritans settled on the other side of the river. They invited him over; they said it was healthier on that side, you see. Ah, these people, these fellows with ideas,' he told the cat, 'old William didn't like them – no he didn't – so he went back to live among the Indians, so he did. But the Puritans found him out, Quincey, trust them. Then he disappeared altogether – God knows where ... *Now*, little cat', the Consul tapped his chest indicatively, and the cat, its face swelling, body arched, important, stepped back, 'the Indians are in here.'

'They sure are,' sighed Mr Quincey, somewhat in the manner of a quietly exacerbated sergeant-major, 'along with all those snakes and pink elephants and them tigers you were talking about.'

The Consul laughed, his laughter having a humourless sound, as though the part of his mind that knew all this essentially a burlesque of a great and generous man once his friend knew also how hollow the satisfaction afforded him by the performance. 'Not real Indians ... And I didn't mean in the garden; but in *here*.' He tapped his chest again. 'Yes, just the final frontier of consciousness, that's all. Genius, as I'm so fond of saying,' he added, standing up, adjusting his tie and (he did not think further of the tie) squaring his shoulders as if to go with a decisiveness that, also borrowed on this occasion from the same source as the genius and his interest in cats, left him abruptly as it had been assumed, ' – genius will look after itself.'

Somewhere in the distance a clock was striking; the Consul still stood there motionless. 'Oh, Yvonne, can I have forgotten you already, on this of all days?' Nineteen, twenty, twenty-one strokes. By his watch it was a quarter to eleven. But the clock hadn't finished: it struck twice more, two wry, tragic notes:

bing-bong: whirring. The emptiness in the air after filled with whispers: *alas, alas*. Wings, it really meant.

'Where's your friend these days – I never can remember his name – that French fellow?' Mr Quincey had asked a moment ago.

'Laruelle?' The Consul's voice came from far away. He was aware of vertigo; closing his eyes wearily he took hold of the fence to steady himself. Mr Quincey's words knocked on his consciousness – or someone actually was knocking on a door – fell away, then knocked again, louder. Old De Quincey; the knocking on the gate in Macbeth. Knock, knock, knock: who's there? Cat. Cat who? Catastrophe. Catastrophe who? Catastrophysicist. What, is it you, my little popocat? Just wait an eternity till Jacques and I have finished murdering sleep? Katabasis to cat abysses. Cat hartes atratus ... Of course, he should have know it, these were the final moments of the retiring of the human heart, and of the final entrance of the fiendish, the night insulated – just as the real De Quincey (that mere drug fiend, he thought opening his eyes – he found he was looking straight over towards the tequila bottle) imagined the murder of Duncan and the others insulated, self-withdrawn into a deep syncope and suspension of earthly passion ... But where had Quincey gone? And my God, who was this advancing behind the morning paper to his rescue across the lawn, where the breath of the hoses had suddenly failed as if by magic, if not Dr Guzmán?

If not Guzmán, if not, it could not be, but it was, it certainly was no less a figure than that of his companion the night before, Dr Vigil; and what on earth would he be doing here? As the figure approached closer the Consul felt an increasing uneasiness. Quincey was his patient doubtless. But in that case why wasn't the doctor in the house? Why all this secretive prowling about the garden? It could only mean one thing: Vigil's visit had somehow been timed to coincide with his own probable visit to the tequila (though he had fooled them neatly there), with the object, naturally, of spying upon him, of obtaining some information about him, some clue to the nature of which might all too conceivably be found within the pages of that accusing newspaper: 'Old Samaritan case to be reopened, Commander Firmin believed in Mexico.' 'Firmin found guilty, acquitted, cries in box.' 'Firmin innocent, but bears guilt of world on shoulders.' 'Body of Firmin found drunk in bunker', such monstrous headlines as these indeed took instant shape in the Consul's mind, for it was not merely *El Universal* the doctor was reading, it was his fate; but the creatures of his more immediate conscience were not to be denied, they seemed silently to accompany that morning paper too, withdrawing to one side (as the doctor came to a standstill, looking about him) with averted heads, listening, murmuring now: 'You cannot lie to us. We know what you did last night.' What *had* he done though? He saw again clearly enough – as Dr Vigil, recognized him with a smile, closed his paper and hastened towards him – the doctor's consulting-room in the Avenida de la Revolución, visited for some drunken reason in the early hours of the morning, macabre with its pictures of ancient Spanish surgeons, their goat faces rising queerly from ruffs resembling ectoplasm, roaring with laughter as they performed inquisitorial operations; but since all this was retained as a mere vivid setting completely detached from his own activity, and since it was about all he did remember, he could scarcely take comfort from not seeming to appear within it in any vicious role. Not so much comfort, at least, as had just been afforded him by Vigil's smile, nor half so much as was now afforded him when the doctor, upon reaching the spot lately vacated by the walnut grower, halted, and, suddenly, bowed to him profoundly from the waist; bowed once, twice, thrice, mutely yet tremendously assuring the Consul that after all no crime had been committed during the night so great he was still not worthy of respect.

Then, simultaneously, the two men groaned.

'*Qué t –*' began the Consul.

'*Por favor,*' broke in the other hoarsely, placing a well-manicured though shaky finger to his lips, and with a slightly worried look up the garden.

The Consul nodded. 'Of course. You're looking so fit, I see *you* can't have been at the ball last night,' he added loudly and loyally, following the other's gaze, though Mr Quincey, who after all could not have been so fit, was still nowhere to be seen.

He had probably been turning off the hoses at the main hydrant – and how absurd to have suspected a 'plan' when it was so patently an informal call and the doctor had just happened to notice Quincey working in the garden from the drive. He lowered his voice. 'All the same, might I take this opportunity of asking you what you prescribe for a slight case of katzenjammer?'

The doctor gave another worried look down the garden and began to laugh quietly, though his whole body was shaking with mirth, his white teeth flashed in the sun, even his immaculate blue suit seemed to be laughing. 'Señor,' he began, biting off his laughter short on his lips, like a child, with his front teeth. 'Señor Firmin, *por favor*, I am sorry, but I must comport myself here like,' he looked round him again, catching his breath, 'like an apostle. You mean, *señor*,' he went on more evenly, 'that you are feeling fine this morning, quite like the cat's pyjamas.'

'Well: hardly,' said the Consul, softly as before, casting a suspicious eye for his part in the other direction at some maguey growing beyond the *barranca*, like a battalion moving up a slope under machine-gun fire. 'Perhaps that's an overstatement. To put it more simply, what would you do for a case of chronic, controlled, all-possessing, and inescapable delirium tremens?'

Dr Vigil started. A half-playful smile hovered at the corner of his lips as he contrived rather unsteadily to roll up his paper into a neat cylindrical tube. 'You mean, not cats –' he said, and he made a swift rippling circular crawling gesture in front of his eyes with one hand, 'but rather –'

The Consul nodded cheerfully. For his mind was at rest. He had caught a glimpse of those morning headlines, which seemed entirely concerned with the Pope's illness and the Battle of the Ebro.

'– *progresión*,' the doctor was repeating the gesture more slowly with his eyes closed, his fingers crawling separately, curved like claws, his head shaking idiotically. '– *a ratos!*' he pounced. '*Sí*,' he said, pursing his lips and clapping his hand to his forehead in a motion of mock horror. '*Sí*,' he repeated. 'Tereebly . . . More alcohol is perhaps best,' he smiled.

'Your doctor tells me that in my case delirium tremens may

not prove fatal,' the Consul, triumphantly himself at last, informed Mr Quincey, who came up just at this moment.

And at the next moment, though not before there had passed between himself and the doctor a barely perceptible exchange of signals, a tiny symbolic mouthward flick of the wrist on the Consul's side as he glanced up at his bungalow, and upon Vigil's a slight flapping movement of the arms extended apparently in the act of stretching, which meant (in the obscure language known only to major adepts in the Great Brotherhood of Alcohol), 'Come up and have a spot when you've finished,' 'I shouldn't, for if I do I shall be "flying", but on second thoughts perhaps I will' – it seemed he was back drinking from his bottle of tequila. And, the moment after, that he was drifting slowly and powerfully through the sunlight back towards the bungalow itself. Accompanied by Mr Quincey's cat, who was following an insect of some sort along his path, the Consul floated in an amber glow. Beyond the house, where now the problems awaiting him seemed already on the point of energetic solution, the day before him stretched out like an illimitable rolling wonderful desert in which one was going, though in a delightful way, to be lost : lost, but not so completely he would be unable to find the few necessary water-holes, or the scattered tequila oases where witty legionnaires of damnation who couldn't understand a word he said, would wave him on, replenished, into that glorious Parián wilderness where man never went thirsty, and where now he was drawn on beautifully by the dissolving mirages past the skeletons like frozen wire and the wandering dreaming lions towards ineluctable personal disaster, always in a delightful way of course, the disaster might even be found at the end to contain a certain element of triumph. Not that the Consul now felt gloomy. Quite the contrary. The outlook had rarely seemed so bright. He became conscious, for the first time, of the extraordinary activity which everywhere surrounded him in his garden : a lizard going up a tree, another kind of lizard coming down another tree, a bottle-green humming-bird exploring a flower, another kind of humming-bird, voraciously at another flower; huge butterflies, whose precise stitched markings reminded one of the blouses in the market, flopping about with indolent gymnastic grace (much as Yvonne had described them greeting her in Acapulco Bay yesterday, a storm of torn-up multicoloured love-letters, tossing to windward past the saloons on the promenade deck); ants with petals or scarlet blossoms tacking hither and thither along the paths; while from above, below, from the sky, and, it might be, from under the earth, came a continual sound of whistling, gnawing, rattling, even trumpeting. Where was his friend the snake now? Hiding up a pear tree probably. A snake that waited to drop rings on you: whore's shoes. From the branches of these pear trees hung carafes full of a glutinous yellow substance for trapping insects still changed religiously every month by the local horticultural college. (How gay were the Mexicans! The horticulturalists made the occasion, as they made every possible occasion, a sort of dance, bringing their womenfolk with them, flitting from tree to tree, gathering up and replacing the carafes as though the whole thing were a movement in a comic ballet, afterwards lolling about in the shade for hours, as if the Consul himself did not exist.) Then the behaviour of Mr Quincey's cat began to fascinate him. The creature had at last caught the insect but instead of devouring it, she was holding its body, still uninjured, delicately between her teeth, while its lovely luminous wings, still beating, for the insect had not stopped flying an instant, protruded from either side of her whiskers, fanning them. The Consul stooped forward to the rescue. But the animal bounded just out of reach. He stooped again, with the same result. In this preposterous fashion, the Consul stooping, the cat dancing just out of reach, the insect still flying furiously in the cat's mouth, he approached his porch. Finally the cat extended a preparate paw for the kill, opening her mouth, and the insect, whose wings had never ceased to beat, suddenly and marvellously, flew out as might indeed the human soul from the jaws of death, flew up, up, up, soaring over the trees: and at that moment he saw them. They were standing on the porch: Yvonne's arms were full of bougainvillea, which she was arranging in a cobalt ceramic vase. ' – but suppose he's absolutely adamant. Suppose he simply won't go ... careful, Hugh, it's got spikes on it, and you have to look at everything carefully to be sure there're no

184

spiders.' 'Hi there, Suchiquetal!' the Consul shouted gaily, waving his hand, as the cat with a frigid look over her shoulder that said plainly, 'I didn't want it anyway; I meant to let it go,' galloped away, humiliated, into the bushes. 'Hi there, Hugh, you old snake in the grass!'

... Why then should he be sitting in the bathroom? Was he asleep? dead? passed out? Was he in the bathroom now or half an hour ago? Was it night? Where were the others? But now he heard some of the others' voices on the porch. Some of the others? It was just Hugh and Yvonne, of course, for the doctor had gone. Yet for a moment he could have sworn the house had been full of people; why, it was still this morning, or barely afternoon, only 12.15 in fact by his watch. At eleven he'd been talking to Mr Quincey. 'Oh ... Oh.' The Consul groaned aloud ... It came to him he was supposed to be getting ready to go to Tomalín. But how had he managed to persuade anyone he was sober enough to go to Tomalín? And why, anyhow, Tomalín?

A procession of thought like little elderly animals filed through the Consul's mind, and in his mind too he was steadily crossing the porch again, as he had done an hour ago, immediately after he'd seen the insect flying away out of the cat's mouth.

He had crossed the porch – which Concepta had swept – smiling soberly to Yvonne and shaking hands with Hugh on his way to the icebox, and unfastening it, he knew not only that they'd been talking about him, but, obscurely, from that bright fragment of overheard conversation, its round meaning, just as had he at that moment glimpsed the new moon with the old one in its arms, he might have been impressed by its complete shape, though the rest were shadowy, illumined only by earthlight.

But what had happened then? 'Oh,' the Consul cried aloud again. 'Oh.' The faces of the last hour hovered before him, the figures of Hugh and Yvonne and Dr Vigil moving quickly and jerkily now like those of an old silent film, their words mute explosions in the brain. Nobody seemed to be doing anything important; yet everything seemed of the utmost hectic importance, for instance Yvonne saying: 'We saw an armadillo': – 'What, no Tarsius spectres!' he had replied, then Hugh opening the freezing bottle of Carta Blanca beer for him, prizing off the fizzing cap on the edge of the parapet and decanting the foam into his glass, the contiguity of which to his strychnine bottle had, it must be admitted now, lost most of its significance . . .

In the bathroom the Consul became aware he still had with him half a glass of slightly flat beer; his hand was fairly steady, but numbed holding the glass, he drank cautiously, carefully postponing the problem soon to be raised by its emptiness.

– 'Nonsense,' he said to Hugh. And he had added with impressive consular authority that Hugh couldn't leave immediately anyway, at least not for Mexico City, that there was only one bus today, the one Hugh'd come on, which had gone back to the City already, and one train that didn't leave till 11.45 p.m. . . .

Then: 'But wasn't it Bougainville, doctor?' Yvonne was asking – and it really was astonishing how sinister and urgent and *inflamed* all these minutiae seemed to him in the bathroom – 'Wasn't it Bougainville who discovered the bougainvillea?' while the doctor bending over her flowers merely looked alert and puzzled, he said nothing save with his eyes which perhaps barely betrayed that he'd stumbled on a 'situation'. – 'Now I come to think of it, I believe it was Bougainville. Hence the name,' Hugh observed fatuously, seating himself on the parapet – '*Sí*: you *can* go to the *botica* and so as not to be misunderstood, say *favor de servir una toma de vino quinado o en su defecto una toma de nuez vómica, pero* –' Dr Vigil was chuckling, talking to Hugh it must have been, Yvonne having slipped into her room a moment, while the Consul, eavesdropping, was at the icebox for another bottle of beer – then; 'Oh, I was so terrible sick this morning I needed to be holding myself to the street windows,' and to the Consul himself as he returned ' – Please forgive my stupid *comport* last night: oh, I have done a lot of stupid things everywhere these last few days, but' – raising his glass of whisky – 'I will never drink more; I will need two full days of sleeping to recover myself' – and then, as Yvonne returned – magnificently giving the whole show away, raising his glass to the Consul again: '*Salud*: I hope you are not as sick as I am. You were so *perfecta*mente *borracho* last night I think you

186

must have killèd yourself with drinking. I think even to send a boy after you this morning to knock your door, and find if drinking have not killed you already,' Dr Vigil had said.

A strange fellow: in the bathroom the Consul sipped his flat beer. A strange, decent, generous-hearted fellow, if slightly deficient in tact save on his own behalf. Why couldn't people hold their liquor? He himself had still managed to be quite considerate of Vigil's position in Quincey's garden. In the final analysis there was no one you could trust to drink with you to the bottom of the bowl. A lonely thought. But of the doctor's generosity there was little doubt. Before long indeed, in spite of the necessary 'two full days of sleeping', he had been inviting them all to come with him to Guanajuato: recklessly he proposed leaving for his holiday by car this evening, after a problematic set of tennis this afternoon with –

The Consul took another sip of beer. 'Oh,' he shuddered. 'Oh.' It had been a mild shock last night to discover that Vigil and Jacques Laruelle were friends, far more than embarrassing to be reminded of it this morning … Anyhow, Hugh had turned down the notion of the two-hundred-mile trip to Guanajuato, since Hugh – and how amazingly well, after all, those cowboy clothes seemed to suit his erect and careless bearing! – was now determined to catch that night train; while the Consul had declined on Yvonne's account.

The Consul saw himself again, hovering over the parapet, gazing down at the swimming-pool below, a little turquoise set in the garden. Thou art the grave where buried love doth live. The inverted reflections of banana trees and birds, caravans of clouds, moved in it. Wisps of new-mown turf floated on the surface. Fresh mountain water trickled into the pool, which was almost overflowing, from the cracked broken hose whose length was a series of small spouting fountains.

Then Yvonne and Hugh, below, were swimming in the pool …

– '*Absolutamente*,' the doctor had said, beside the Consul at the parapet, and attentively lighting a cigarette. 'I have', the Consul was telling him, lifting his face towards the volcanoes and feeling his desolation go out to those heights where even now at mid-morning the howling snow would whip the face, and the ground beneath the feet was dead lava, a soulless petrified residue of extinct plasm in which even the wildest and loneliest trees would never take root; 'I have another enemy round the back you can't see. A sunflower. I know it watches me and I know it hates me.' '*Exactamente,*' Dr Vigil said, 'very posseebly it might be hating you a little less if you would stop from drinking tequila.' 'Yes, but I'm only drinking beer this morning,' the Consul said with conviction, 'as you can see for yourself.' '*Sí, hombre,*' Dr Vigil nodded, who after a few whiskies (from a new bottle) had given up trying to conceal himself from Mr Quincey's house and was standing boldly by the parapet with the Consul. 'There are', the Consul added, 'a thousand aspects of this infernal beauty I was talking about, each with its peculiar tortures, each jealous as a woman of all stimulations save its own.' '*Naturalmente,*' Dr Vigil said. 'But I think if you are very serious about your *progresión a ratos* you may take a longer journey even than this proposèd one.' The Consul placed his glass on the parapet while the doctor continued. 'Me too unless we contain with ourselves never to drink no more. I think, *mi amigo,* sickness is not only in body but in that part used to be call: soul.' 'Soul?' '*Precisamente,*' the doctor said, swiftly clasping and unclasping his fingers. 'But a mesh? Mesh. The nerves are a mesh, like, how do you say it, an eclectic systemë.' 'Ah, very good,' the Consul said, 'you mean an electric system.' 'But after much tequila the eclectic systemë is perhaps *un poco descompuesto, comprenez,* as sometimes in the *cine: claro*?' 'A sort of eclampsia, as it were,' the Consul nodded desperately, removing his glasses, and at this point, the Consul remembered, he had been without a drink nearly ten minutes; the effect of the tequila too had almost gone. He had peered out at the garden, and it was as though bits of his eyelids had broken off and were flittering and jittering before him, turning into nervous shapes and shadows, jumping to the guilty chattering in his mind, not quite voices yet, but they were coming back, they were coming back; a picture of his soul as a town appeared once more before him, but this time a town ravaged and stricken in the black path of his excess and shutting his burning eyes he had thought of the beautiful functioning of the system in those who were truly alive, switches connected, nerves rigid only in real danger, and in nightmareless sleep now calm, not resting, yet poised : a peaceful village. Christ, how it heightened the torture (and meantime there had been every reason to suppose the others imagined he was enjoying himself enormously) to be aware of all this, while at the same time conscious of the whole horrible disintegrating mechanism, the light now on, now off, now on too glaringly, now too dimly, with the glow of a fitful dying battery – then at last to know the whole town plunged into darkness, where communication is lost, motion mere obstruction, bombs threaten, ideas stampede –

The Consul had now finished his glass of flat beer. He sat gazing at the bathroom wall in an attitude like a grotesque parody of an old attitude in meditation. 'I am very much interested in insanes.' That was a strange way to start a conversation with a fellow who'd just stood you a drink. Yet that was precisely how the doctor, in the Bella Vista bar, had started their conversation the previous night. Could it be Vigil considered his practised eye had detected approaching insanity (and this was funny too, recalling his thoughts on the subject earlier, to conceive of it as merely approaching) as some who have watched wind and weather all their lives can prophesy, under a fair sky, the approaching storm, the darkness that will come galloping out of nowhere across the fields of the mind? Not that there could be said to be a very fair sky either in that connexion. Yet how interested would the doctor have been in one who felt himself being shattered by the very forces of the universe? What cataplasms have laid on his soul? What did even the hierophants of science know of the fearful potencies of, for them, unvintageable evil? The Consul wouldn't have needed a practised eye to detect on this wall, or any other, a mene-Tekel-Peres for the world, compared to which mere insanity was a drop in the bucket. Yet who would ever have believed that some obscure man, sitting at the centre of the world in a bathroom, say, thinking solitary miserable thoughts, was authoring their doom, that, even while he was thinking, it was as if behind the scenes certain strings were being pulled, and whole continents burst into flame, and calamity moved nearer – just as now, at this moment perhaps, with a sudden jolt and grind, calamity had moved nearer, and, without the Consul's knowing it, outside the sky had darkened. Or perhaps it was not a man at all, but a child, a little child, innocent as that other Geoffrey had been, who sat up in an organ loft somewhere playing, pulling out all the stops at random, and kingdoms divided and fell, and abominations dropped from the sky – a child innocent as that infant sleeping in the coffin which had slanted past them down the Calle Tierra del Fuego ...

The Consul lifted his glass to his lips, tasted its emptiness again, then set it on the floor, still wet from the feet of the swimmers. The uncontrollable mystery on the bathroom floor. He remembered that the next time he had returned to the porch with a bottle of Carta Blanca, though for some reason this now seemed a terribly long time ago, in the past – it was as if something he could not put his finger on had mysteriously supervened to separate drastically that returning figure from himself sitting in the bathroom (the figure on the porch, for all its damnation, seemed younger, to have more freedom of movement, choice, to have, if only because it held a full glass of beer once more, a better chance of a future) – Yvonne, youthful and pretty-looking in her white satin bathing-suit, had been wandering on tiptoe round the doctor, who was saying:

'Señora Firmin, I am really disappoint though you cannot come me with.'

The Consul and she had exchanged a look of understanding, it almost amounted to, then Yvonne was swimming again, below, and the doctor was saying to the Consul:

'Guanajuato is sited in a beautiful circus of steepy hills.'

'Guanajuato,' the doctor was saying, 'you will not believe me, how she can lie there, like the old golden jewel on the breast of our grandmother.'

'Guanajuato,' Dr Vigil said, 'the streets. How can you resist the names of the streets? Street of Kisses. Street of Singing Frogs. The Street of the Little Head. Is not that revolting?'

'Repellent,' the Consul said. 'Isn't Guanajuato the place they bury everybody standing up?' – ah, and this was where he had remembered about the bullthrowing and, feeling a return of energy, had called down to Hugh, who was sitting thoughtfully by the edge of the pool in the Consul's swimming-trunks. 'Tomalín's quite near Parián, where your pal was going,' he said. 'We might even go on there.' And then to the doctor, 'Perhaps you might come too ... I left my favourite pipe in Parián. Which I might get back, with luck. In the Farolito.' And the doctor had said : '*Wheee, es un infierno,*' while Yvonne, lifting up a corner of her bathing-cap to hear better, said meekly, 'Not a bullfight?' And the Consul : 'No, a bullthrowing. If you're not too tired?'

But the doctor could not of course come to Tomalín with them, though this was never discussed, since just then the conversation was violently interrupted by a sudden terrific detonation, that shook the house and sent birds skimming panic-stricken all over the garden. Target practice in the Sierra Madre. The Consul had been half aware of it in his sleep earlier. Puffs of smoke were drifting high over the rocks below Popo at the end of the valley. Three black vultures came tearing through the trees low over the roof with soft hoarse cries like the cries of love. Driven at unaccustomed speed by their fear they seemed almost to capsize, keeping close together but balancing at different angles to avoid collision. Then they sought another tree to wait in and the echoes of gunfire swept back over the house, soaring higher and higher and growing fainter while somewhere a clock was striking nineteen. Twelve o'clock, and the Consul said to the doctor : 'Ah, that the dream of the dark magician in his visioned cave, even while his hand—that's the bit I like—shakes in its last decay, were the true end of this so lovely world. Jesus. Do you know, *compañero*, I sometimes have the feeling that it's actually sinking, like Atlantis, beneath my feet. Down, down to the frightful "poulps". Meropis of Theopompus ... And the *ignivome* mountains.' And the doctor who was nodding gloomily said : '*Sí,* that is tequila. *Hombre, un poco de cerveza, un poco de vino,* but never no more tequila. Never no more mescal.' And then the doctor was whispering : 'But *hombre,* now that your *esposa* has come back.' (It seemed that Dr Vigil had said this several times, only with a different look on his face : 'But

191

hombre, now that your *esposa* has come back.') And then he was going: 'I did not need to be inquisitive to be knowing you might have wishèd my advice. No *hombre*, as I say last night, I am not so interested in moneys. – *Con permiso*, the plaster he no good.' A little shower of plaster had, indeed, rained down on the doctor's head. Then: *'Hasta la vista' 'Adiós' 'Muchas gracias'* 'Thank you so much' 'Sorry we couldn't come' 'Have a good time,' from the swimming-pool. *'Hasta la vista'* again, then silence.

And now the Consul was in the bathroom getting ready to go to Tomalín. 'Oh ...' he said, 'Oh ...' But, you see, nothing so dire has happened after all. First to wash. Sweating and trembling again, he took off his coat and shirt. He had turned on the water in the basin. Yet for some obscure reason he was standing under the shower, waiting in an agony for the shock of cold water that never came. And he was still wearing his trousers.

The Consul sat helplessly in the bathroom, watching the insects which lay at different angles from one another on the wall, like ships out in the roadstead. A caterpillar started to wriggle toward him, peering this way and that, with interrogatory antennae. A large cricket, with polished fuselage, clung to the curtain, swaying it slightly and cleaning its face like a cat, its eyes on stalks appearing to revolve in its head. He turned, expecting the caterpillar to be much nearer, but it too had turned, just slightly shifting its moorings. Now a scorpion was moving slowly across towards him. Suddenly the Consul rose, trembling in every limb. But it wasn't the scorpion he cared about. It was that, all at once, the thin shadows of isolated nails, the stains of murdered mosquitoes, the very scars and cracks of the wall, had begun to swarm, so that, wherever he looked, another insect was born, wriggling instantly toward his heart. It was as if, and this was what was most appalling, the whole insect world had somehow moved nearer and now was closing, rushing in upon him. For a moment the bottle of tequila at the bottom of the garden gleamed on his soul, then the Consul stumbled into his bedroom.

Here there was no longer that terrible visible swarming, yet – lying now on the bed – it still seemed to persist in his mind, much as the vision of the dead man earlier had persisted, a kind of seething, from which, as from the persistent rolling of drums heard by some great dying monarch, occasionally a half-recognizable voice dissociated itself:

– Stop it, for God's sake, you fool. Watch your step. We can't help you any more.

– I would like the privilege of helping you, of your friendship. I would work you with. I do not care a damn for moneys anyway.

– What, is this you, Geoffrey? Don't you remember me? Your old friend, Abe. What have you done, my boy?

– Ha ha, you're for it now. Straightened out – in a coffin! Yeah.

– My son, my son!

– My lover. Oh come to me again as once in May.

6

—Nel mezzo del bloody *cammin di nostra vita mi ritrovai in* ...
Hugh flung himself down on the porch daybed.

A strong warm gusty wind howled over the garden. Refreshed
by his swim and a lunch of turkey sandwiches, the cigar Geoff
had given him earlier partially shielded by the parapet, he lay
watching the clouds speeding across the Mexican skies. How
fast they went, how far too fast! In the middle of our life, in the
middle of the bloody road of our life ...

Twenty-nine clouds. At twenty-nine a man was in his thirtieth
year. And he was twenty-nine. And now at last, though the feeling had perhaps been growing on him all morning, he knew
what it felt like, the intolerable impact of this knowledge that
might have come at twenty-two, but had not, that ought at least
to have come at twenty-five, but still somehow had not, this
knowledge, hitherto associated only with people tottering on the
brink of the grave and A. E. Housman, that one could not be
young for ever – that indeed, in the twinkling of an eye, one
was not young any longer. For in less than four years, passing
so swiftly today's cigarette seemed smoked yesterday, one would
be thirty-three, in seven more, forty; in forty-seven, eighty. Sixty-
seven years seemed a comfortingly long time but then he would
be a hundred. I am not a prodigy any longer. I have no excuse
any longer to behave in this irresponsible fashion. I am not such
a dashing fellow after all. I am not young. On the other hand : I
am a prodigy. I *am* young. I *am* a dashing fellow. Am I not?
You are a liar, said the trees tossing in the garden. You are a
traitor, rattled the plantain leaves. And a coward too, put in
some fitful sounds of music that might have meant that in the
zócalo the fair was beginning. And they are losing the Battle of
the Ebro. Because of you, said the wind. A traitor even to your
journalist friends you like to run down and who are really
courageous men, admit it – *Ahhh!* Hugh, as if to rid himself of

these thoughts, turned the radio dial back and forth, trying to get San Antonio ('I am none of these things really.' 'I have done nothing to warrant all this guilt.' 'I am no worse than anybody else'...'); but it was no good. All his resolutions of this morning were to no avail. It seemed useless to struggle any further with these thoughts, better to let them have their way. At least they would take his mind from Yvonne for a time, if they only led back to her in the end. Even Juan Cerillo failed him now, as did, at this moment, San Antonio: two Mexican voices on different wavelengths were breaking in. For everything you have done up to now has been dishonest, the first might have been saying. What about the way you treated poor old Bolowski, the music publisher, remember his shabby little shop in Old Compton Street, off the Tottenham Court Road? Even what you persuade yourself is the best thing about you, your passion for helping the Jews, has some basis in a dishonourable action of your own. Small wonder, since he so charitably forgave you, that you forgave him *his* skulduggery, to the point of being prepared to lead the whole Jewish race out of Babylon itself ... No: I am much afraid there is little enough in your past, which will come to your aid against the future. Not even the seagull? said Hugh ...

The seagull – pure scavenger of the empyrean, hunter of edible stars – I rescued that day as a boy when it was caught in a fence on the cliffside and was beating itself to death, blinded by snow, and though it attacked me, I drew it out unharmed, with one hand by its feet, and for one magnificent moment held it up in the sunlight, before it soared away on angelic wings over the freezing estuary?

The artillery started blasting away in the foothills again. A train hooted somewhere, like an approaching steamer; perhaps the very train Hugh'd be taking tonight. From the bottom of the swimming-pool below a reflected small sun blazed and nodded among the inverted papayas. Reflections of vultures a mile deep wheeled upside down and were gone. A bird, quite close really, seemed to be moving in a series of jerks across the glittering summit of Popocatepetl – the wind, in fact, had dropped, which was as well for his cigar. The radio had gone dead too, and Hugh gave it up, settling himself back on the daybed.

Not even the seagull was the answer of course. The seagull had been spoilt already by his dramatizing it. Nor yet the poor little hot-dog man. That bitter December night he had met him trudging down Oxford Street with his new wagon – the first hot-dog wagon in London, and he had been pushing it around for a whole month without selling a single hot dog. Now with a family to support and Christmas approaching he was on his uppers. Shades of Charles Dickens! It was perhaps the *newness* of the wretched wagon he'd been cozened into buying that seemed so awful. But how could he expect, Hugh asked him, as above them the monstrous deceptions twitched on and off, and around them the black soulless buildings stood wrapped in a cold dream of their own destruction (they had halted by a church from whose sooty wall a figure of Christ on the cross had been removed leaving only the scar and the legend: Is it nothing to you all ye who pass by?) how could he expect to sell anything so revolutionary as a hot dog in Oxford Street? He might as well try ice-cream at the South Pole. No, the idea was to camp outside a pub down a back alley, and that not any pub, but the Fitzroy Tavern in Charlotte Street, chock full of starving artists drinking themselves to death simply because their souls pined away, each night between eight and ten, for lack of just such a thing as a hot dog. That was the place to go!

And – not even the hot-dog man was the answer; even though by Christmas time, obviously, he had been doing a roaring trade outside the Fitzroy. Hugh suddenly sat up, scattering cigar-ash everywhere. – And yet is it nothing I am beginning to atone, to atone for my past, so largely negative, selfish, absurd, and dishonest? That I propose to sit on top of a shipload of dynamite bound for the hard-pressed Loyalist armies? Nothing that after all I am willing to give my life for humanity, if not in minute particulars? Nothing to ye that pass by? ... Though what on earth he expected it to be, if none of his friends knew he was going to do it, was not very clear. So far as the Consul was concerned, he probably suspected him of something even more reckless. And it had to be admitted, one was not altogether averse to this, if it had not prevented the Consul from still hinting uncomfortably close to the truth, that the whole stupid beauty of such a decision made by anyone at a time like this, must lie in that it *was* so futile, that it *was* too late, that the Loyalists had already lost, and that should that person emerge safe and sound, no one would be able to say to *him* that he had been carried away by the popular wave of enthusiasm for Spain, when even the Russians had given up, and the Internationals withdrawn. But death and truth could rhyme at a pinch! There was the old dodge too of telling anyone who shook the dust of the City of Destruction from his feet, he was running away from himself and his responsibilities. But the useful thought struck Hugh: I have no responsibilities. And how can I be escaping from myself when I am without a place on earth? No home. A piece of driftwood on the Indian Ocean. Is India my home? Disguise myself as an untouchable, which should not be so difficult, and go to prison on the Andaman Islands for seventy-seven years, until England gives India her freedom? But I will tell you this: you would only by doing so be embarrassing Mahatma Gandhi, secretly the only public figure in the world for whom you have any respect. No, I respect Stalin too, Cárdenas, and Jawaharlal Nehru – all three of whom probably could only be embarrassed by my respect. – Hugh had another shot at San Antonio.

The radio came alive with a vengeance; at the Texan station news of a flood was being delivered with such rapidity one gained the impression the commentator himself was in danger of drowning. Another narrator in a higher voice gabbled bankruptcy, disaster, while yet another told of misery blanketing a threatened capital, people stumbling through debris littering dark streets, hurrying thousands seeking shelter in bomb-torn darkness. How well he knew the jargon. Darkness, disaster! How the world fed on it. In the war to come correspondents would assume unheard of importance, plunging through flame to feed the public its little gobbets of dehydrated excrement. A bawling scream abruptly warned of stocks lower, or irregularly higher, the prices of grain, cotton, metal, munitions. While static rattled on eternally below – poltergeists of the ether, claquers of the idiotic! Hugh inclined his ear to the pulse of this world beating in that latticed throat, whose voice was now pretending to be horrified at the very thing by which it proposed to be engulfed the first moment it could be perfectly certain the engulfing process would last long enough. Impatiently switching the dial around, Hugh thought he heard Joe Venuti's violin suddenly, the joyous little lark of discursive melody soaring in some remote summer of its own above all this abyssal fury, yet furious too, with the wild controlled abandon of that music which still sometimes seemed to him the happiest thing about America. Probably they were rebroadcasting some ancient record, one of those with the poetical names like Little Buttercup or Apple Blossom, and it was curious how much it hurt, as though this music, never outgrown, belonged irretrievably to that which had today at last been lost. Hugh switched the radio off, and lay, cigar between his fingers, staring at the porch ceiling.

Joe Venuti had not been the same, one heard, since Ed Lang died. The latter suggested guitars, and if Hugh ever wrote, as he often threatened to do, his autobiography, though it would have been rather unnecessary, his life being one of those that perhaps lent themselves better to such brief summation in magazines as 'So and so is twenty-nine, has been riveter, song-writer, watcher of manholes, stoker, sailor, riding instructor, variety artist, bandsman, bacon-scrubber, saint, clown, soldier (for five minutes), and usher in a spiritualist church, from which it should not always be assumed that far from having acquired through his experiences a wider view of existence, he has a somewhat narrower notion of it than any bank clerk who has never set foot outside Newcastle-under-Lyme', – but if he ever wrote it, Hugh reflected, he would have to admit that a guitar made a pretty important symbol in his life.

He had not played one, and Hugh could play almost any kind of guitar, for four or five years, and his numerous instruments declined with his books in basements or attics in London or Paris, in Wardour Street night-clubs or behind the bar of the Marquis of Granby or the old Astoria in Greek Street, long since become a convent and his bill still unpaid there, in pawnshops in Tithebarn Street or the Tottenham Court Road, where he imagined them as waiting for a time with all their sounds and echoes for his heavy step, and then, little by little, as they gathered dust, and each successive string broke, giving up hope, each string a hawser to the fading memory of their friend, snapping off, the highest pitched string always first, snapping with sharp gun-like reports, or curious agonized whines, or provocative nocturnal meows, like a nightmare in the soul of George Frederic Watts, till there was nothing but the blank untumultuous face of the songless lyre itself, soundless cave for spiders and steamflies, and delicate fretted neck, just as each breaking string had severed Hugh himself pang by pang from his youth, while the past remained, a tortured shape, dark and palpable and accusing. Or the guitars would have been stolen many times by now, or resold, repawned – inherited by some other master perhaps, as if each were some great thought or doctrine. These sentiments, he was almost diverted to think, were possibly more suited to some exiled dying Segovia than to a mere ex-hot-guitarist. But Hugh, if he could not play quite like Django Reinhardt or Eddie Lang on the one hand or, God help him, Frank Crumit on the other, could not help remembering either that he had once enjoyed the reputation of a tremendous talent. It was in an odd sense spurious, this reputation, like so much else about him, his greatest hits having been made with a tenor guitar tuned as a ukelele and played virtually as a percussion instrument. Yet that in this bizarre manner he had become the magician of commotions mistakable for anything from the Scotch Express to elephants trampling in moonlight, an old Parlophone rhythm classic (entitled, tersely, Juggernaut) testified to this day. At all events, he thought, his guitar had probably been the least fake thing about him. And fake or not one had certainly been behind most of the major decisions of his life. For it was due to a guitar he'd become a journalist, it was due to a guitar he had become a songwriter, it was largely owing to a guitar even – and Hugh felt himself suffused by a slow burning flush of shame – that he had first gone to sea.

Hugh had started writing songs at school and before he was seventeen, at about the same time he lost his innocence, also after several attempts, two numbers of his were accepted by the Jewish firm of Lazarus Bolowski and Sons in New Compton Street, London. His method was each whole holiday to make the rounds of the music publishers with his guitar – and in this respect his early life vaguely recalled that of another frustrated artist, Adolf Hitler – his manuscripts transcribed for piano alone in the guitar case, or another old Gladstone bag of Geoff's. This success in the tin-pan alleys of England overwhelmed him; almost before his aunt knew what was afoot he was leaving school on the strength of it with her permission. At this school, where he sub-edited the magazine, he got on erratically; he told himself that he hated it for the snobbish ideals prevailing there. There was a certain amount of anti-Semitism; and Hugh, whose heart was easily touched, had, though popular for his guitar, chosen Jews as his particular friends and favoured them in his columns. He was already entered at Cambridge for a year or so hence. He had not, however, the slightest intention of going there. The prospect of it, for some reason, he dreaded only less than being stuck meantime at some crammer's. And to prevent this he must act swiftly. As he naïvely saw it, through his songs there was an excellent chance of rendering himself completely independent, which also meant independent in advance of the income that four years later he was to begin receiving from the Public Trustees, independent of everybody, and without the dubious benefit of a degree.

But his success was already beginning to wear off a little. For one thing a premium was required (his aunt had paid the premium) and the songs themselves were not to be published for several months. And it struck him, more than prophetically as it happened, that these songs alone, while both of the requisite thirty-two bars, of an equal banality, and even faintly touched with moronism – Hugh later became so ashamed of their titles that to this day he kept them locked in a secret drawer of his mind – might be insufficient to do the trick. Well, he had other songs, the titles to some of which, *Susquehanna Mammy, Slumbering Wabash, Mississippi Sunset, Dismal Swamp,* etc., were perhaps revelatory, and that of one at least, *I'm Homesick for Being Homesick* (of being homesick for home), Vocal Fox Trot, profound, if not positively Wordsworthian ...

But all this seemed to belong in the future. Bolowski had hinted he might take them if ... And Hugh did not wish to offend him by trying to sell them elsewhere. Not that there were many other publishers left to try! But perhaps, perhaps, if these two songs *did* make a great hit, sold enormously, made Bolowski's fortune, perhaps if some great publicity –

Some great publicity! This was it, this was always it, something sensational was needed, it was the cry of the times, and when that day he had presented himself at the Marine Superintendent's office in Garston – Garston because Hugh's aunt moved from London north to Oswaldtwistle in the spring – to sign on board the s.s. *Philoctetes* he was at least certain something sensational had been found. Oh, Hugh saw, it was a grotesque and pathetic picture enough, that of the youth who imagined himself a cross beween Bix Beiderbecke, whose first records had just appeared in England, the infant Mozart, and the childhood of Raleigh, signing on the dotted line in the office; and perhaps it was true too he had been reading too much Jack London even then, *The Sea Wolf*, and now in 1938 he had advanced to the virile *Valley of the Moon* (his favourite was *The Jacket*), and perhaps after all he did genuinely love the sea, and the nauseous overrated expanse was his only love, the only woman of whom his future wife need be jealous, perhaps all these things were true of that youth, glimpsing probably, too, from afar, beyond the clause Seamen and Firemen mutually to assist each other, the promise of unlimited delight in the brothels of the Orient – an illusion, to say the least: but what unfortunately almost robbed it all of any vestige of the heroic was that in order to gain his ends without, so to say, 'conscience or consideration', Hugh had previously visited every newspaper office within a radius of thirty miles, and most of the big London dailies had branch offices in that part of the north, and *informed* them precisely of his intention to sail on the *Philoctetes*, counting on the prominence of his family, remotely 'news' even in England since the mystery of his father's disappearance, together with his tale of his songs' acceptance – he announced boldly that all were to be published by Bolowski – to make the story, and hence supply the needed publicity, and upon the fear engendered by this that yet *more* publicity and possibly downright ridicule must result for the family should they prevent his sailing, now a public matter, to force their hand. There were other factors too; Hugh had forgotten them. Even at that the newspapers could scarcely have felt his story of much interest had he not faithfully lugged along his bloody little guitar to each newspaper office. Hugh shuddered at the thought. This probably made the reporters, most, in fact, fatherly and decent men who may have seen a private dream being realized, humour the lad so bent on making an ass of himself. Not that anything of the sort occurred to him at the time. Quite the contrary. Hugh was convinced he'd been amazingly clever, and the extraordinary letters of 'congratulation' he received from shipless buccaneers everywhere, who found their lives under a sad curse of futility because they had not sailed with their elder brothers the seas of the last war, whose curious thoughts were merrily brewing the next one, and of whom Hugh himself was perhaps the archtype, served only to strengthen his opinion. He shuddered again, for he *might* not have gone after all, he *might* have been forcibly prevented by certain husky forgotten relatives, never before reckoned with, who'd come as if springing out of the ground to his aunt's aid, had it not been, of all people, for Geoff, who wired back sportingly from Rabat to their father's sister: *Nonsense. Consider Hugh's proposed trip best possible thing for him. Strongly urge you give him every freedom.* – A potent point, one considered; since now his trip had been deprived neatly not only of its heroic aspect but of any possible flavour of rebellion as well. For in spite of the fact that he now was receiving every assistance from the very people he mysteriously imagined himself running away from, even after broadcasting his plans to the world, he still could not bear for one moment to think he was not 'running away to sea'. And for this Hugh had never wholly forgiven the Consul.

Even so, on the very day, Friday the thirteenth of May, that Frankie Trumbauer three thousand miles away made his famous record of *For No Reason at All in C*, to Hugh now a poignant historical coincidence, and pursued by neo-American frivolities from the English Press, which had begun to take up the story with relish, ranging all the way down from 'Schoolboy composer turns seaman', 'Brother of prominent citizen here feels ocean call', 'Will always return Oswaldtwistle, parting words of prodigy', 'Saga of schoolboy crooner recalls old Kashmir mystery', to once, obscurely 'Oh, to be a Conrad', and once, inaccurately, 'Undergraduate song-writer signs on cargo vessel, takes ukelele' – for he was not yet an undergraduate, as an old able seaman was shortly to remind him – to the last, and most terrifying, though under the circumstances bravely inspired 'No silk cushions for Hugh, says Aunt', Hugh himself, not knowing whether he voyaged east or west, nor even what the lowliest hand had at least heard vaguely rumoured, that Philoctetes was a figure in Greek mythology – son of Poeas, friend of Heracles, and whose cross-bow proved almost as proud and unfortunate a possession as Hugh's guitar – set sail for Cathay and the brothels of Palambang. Hugh writhed on the bed to think of all the humiliation his little publicity stunt had really brought down on his head, a humiliation in itself sufficient to send anyone into even more desperate retreat than to sea . . . Meantime it is scarcely an overstatement to say (Jesus, Cock, did you see the bloody paper? We've got a bastard duke on board or something of that) that he was on a false footing with his shipmates. Not that their attitude was at all what might have been expected! Many of them at first seemed kind to him, but it turned out their motives were not entirely altruistic. They suspected, rightly, that he had influence at the office. Some had sexual motives, of obscure origin. Many on the other hand seemed unbelievably spiteful and malignant, though in a petty way never before associated with the sea, and never since with the proletariat. They read his diary behind his back. They stole his money. They even stole his dungarees and made him buy them back again, on credit, since they had already virtually deprived themselves of his purchasing power. They hid chipping hammers in his bunk and in his sea-bag. Then, all at once, when he was cleaning out, say, the petty officer's bathroom, some very young seaman might grow mysteriously obsequious and say something like: 'Do you realize, mate, you're working for us, when we should be working for you?' Hugh, who did not see then he had put his comrades in a false position too, heard this line of talk with disdain. His persecutions, such as they were, he took in good

203

part. For one thing, they vaguely compensated for what was to him one of the most serious deficiencies in his new life.

This was, in a complicated sense, its 'softness'. Not that it was not a nightmare. It was, but of a very special kind he was scarcely old enough to appreciate. Nor that his hands were not worked raw then hard as boards. Or that he did not nearly go crazy with heat and boredom working under winches in the tropics or putting red lead on the decks. Nor that it was not all rather worse than fagging at school, or might have seemed so, had he not carefully been sent to a modern school where there was no fagging. It was, he did, they were; he raised no mental objections. What he objected to were little, inconceivable things.

For instance, that the forecastle was not called the fo'c'sle but the 'men's quarters', and was not forward where it should be, but aft, under the poop. Now everyone knows a forecastle should be forward, and be called the fo'c'sle. But this forecastle was not called the fo'c'sle because in point of fact it was not a fo'c'sle. The deckhead of the poop roofed what all too patently were 'men's quarters', as they were styled, separate cabins just like on the Isle of Man boat, with two bunks in each running along an alleyway broken by the messroom. But Hugh was not grateful for these hard-won 'better' conditions. To him a fo'c'sle – and where else should the crew of a ship live? – meant inescapably a single evil-smelling room forward with bunks around a table, under a swinging kerosene lamp, where men fought, whored, drank, and murdered. On board the *Philoctetes* men neither fought, whored, nor murdered. As for their drinking, Hugh's aunt had said to him at the end, with a truly noble romantic acceptance: 'You know, Hugh, I don't expect you to drink only *coffee* going through the Black Sea.' She was right. Hugh did not go near the Black Sea. On board, nevertheless, he drank mostly coffee: sometimes tea; occasionally water; and, in the tropics, limejuice. Just like all the others. This tea, too, was the subject of another matter that bothered him. Every afternoon, on the stroke of six and eight bells respectively, it was at first Hugh's duty, his mate being sick, to run in from the galley, first to the bosun's mess and afterwards to the crew, what the bosun called, with unction, 'afternoon tea'. With tabnabs. The tabnabs were delicate and delicious little cakes made by the second cook. Hugh ate them with scorn. Imagine the Sea Wolf sitting down to afternoon tea at four o'clock with tabnabs! And this was not the worst. An even more important item was the food itself. The food on board the *Philoctetes*, a common British cargo steamer, contrary to a tradition so strong Hugh had hardly dared contradict it till this moment even in his dreams, was excellent; compared with that of his public school, where he had lived under catering conditions no merchant seaman would tolerate for five minutes, it was a gourmet's fantasy. There were never fewer than five courses for breakfast in the P.O.'s mess, to which at the outset he was more strictly committed; but it proved almost as satisfying in the 'men's quarters'. American dry hash, kippers, poached eggs and bacon, porridge, steaks, rolls, all at one meal, even on one plate; Hugh never remembered having seen so much food in his life. All the more surprising then was it for him to discover it his duty each day to heave vast quantities of this miraculous food over the side. This chow the crew hadn't eaten went into the Indian Ocean, into any ocean, rather, as the saying is, than 'let it go back to the office'. Hugh was not grateful for these hard-won better conditions either. Nor, mysteriously, seemed anyone else to be. For the wretchedness of the food was the great topic of conversation. 'Never mind, chaps, soon we'll be home where a fellow can have some tiddley chow he can eat, instead of all this bloody kind of stuff, bits of paint, I don't know what it is at all.' And Hugh, a loyal soul at bottom, grumbled with the rest. He found his spiritual level with the stewards, however . . .

Yet he felt trapped. The more completely for the realization that in no essential sense had he escaped from his past life. It was all here, though in another form: the same conflicts, faces, same people, he could imagine, as at school, the same spurious popularity with his guitar, the same kind of unpopularity because he made friends with the stewards, or worse, with the Chinese firemen. Even the ship looked like a fantastic mobile football field. Anti-Semitism, it is true, he had left behind, for Jews on the whole had more sense than to go to sea. But if he had expected to leave British snobbery astern with his public school he was sadly mistaken. In fact, the degree of snobbery prevailing on the *Philoctetes* was fantastic, of a kind Hugh had never imagined possible. The chief cook regarded the tireless second cook as a creature of completely inferior station. The bosun despised the carpenter and would not speak to him for three months, though they messed in the same small room, because he was a tradesman, while the carpenter despised the bosun since he, Chips, was the senior petty officer. The chief steward, who affected striped shirts off duty, was clearly contemptuous of the cheerful second, who, refusing to take his calling seriously, was content with a singlet and a sweat-rag. When the youngest apprentice went ashore for a swim with a towel round his neck he was solemnly rebuked by a quartermaster wearing a tie without a collar for being a disgrace to the ship. And the captain himself nearly turned black in the face each time he saw Hugh because, intending a compliment, Hugh had described the *Philoctetes* in an interview as a tramp. Tramp or no, the whole ship rolled and weltered in bourgeois prejudices and taboos the like of which Hugh had not known even existed. Or so it seemed to him. It is wrong, though, to say she rolled. Hugh, far from aspiring to be a Conrad, as the papers suggested, had not then read a word of him. But he was vaguely aware Conrad hinted somewhere that in certain seasons typhoons were to be expected along the China coast. This was such a season; here, eventually, was the China coast. Yet there seemed no typhoons. Or if there were the *Philoctetes* was careful to avoid them. From the time she emerged from the Bitter Lakes till she lay in the roads at Yokohama a dead monotonous calm prevailed. Hugh chipped rust through the bitter watches. Only they were not really bitter; nothing happened. And they were not watches; he was a day worker. Still, he had to pretend to himself, poor fellow, there was something romantic in what he had done. As was there not! He might easily have consoled himself by looking at a map. Unfortunately maps also too vividly suggested school. So that going through the Suez he was not conscious of sphinxes, Ismailia, nor Mt Sinai; nor through the Red Sea, of Hejaz, Asir, Yemen. Because Perim belonged to India while so remote from it, that island had always fascinated him. Yet they stood off the terrible place a whole forenoon without his grasping the fact. An Italian Somaliland stamp with wild herdsmen on it was once his most treasured possession. They passed Guardafui without his realizing this any more than when as a child of three he'd sailed by in the opposite direction. Later he did not think of Cape Comorin, or Nicobar. Nor, in the Gulf of Siam, of Pnom-Penh. Maybe he did not know himself what he thought about; bells struck, the engine thrummed; *videre; videre;* and far above was perhaps another sea, where the soul ploughed its high invisible wake –

Certainly Sokotra only became a symbol to him much later, and that in Karachi homeward bound he might have passed within figurative hailing distance of his birthplace never occurred to him ... Hong Kong, Shanghai; but the opportunities to get ashore were few and far between, the little money there was they could never touch, and after having lain at Yokohama a full month without one shore leave Hugh's cup of bitterness was full. Yet where permission had been granted instead of roaring in bars the men merely sat on board sewing and telling the dirty jokes Hugh had heard at the age of eleven. Or they engaged in loutish neuter compensations. Hugh had not escaped the Pharisaism of his English elders either. There was a good library on board, however, and under the tutelage of the lamp-trimmer Hugh began the education with which an expensive public school had failed to provide him. He read the *Forsyte Saga* and *Peer Gynt*. It was largely owing to the lamp-trimmer too, a kindly quasi-Communist, who normally spent his watch below studying a pamphlet named the Red Hand, that Hugh gave up his notion of dodging Cambridge. 'If I were you I'd go to the poxing place. Get what you bloody can out of the set-up.'

Meanwhile his reputation had followed him relentlessly down the China coast. Though the headlines of the Singapore *Free Press* might read 'Murder of Brother-in-Law's Concubine' it would be surprising if shortly one did not stumble upon some such passage as : 'A curly-headed boy stood on the fo'c's'le head of the *Philoctetes* as she docked in Penang strumming his latest composition on the ukelele.' News which any day now would turn up in Japan. Nevertheless the guitar itself had come to the rescue. And now at least Hugh knew what he was thinking about. It was of England, and the homeward voyage! England, that he had so longed to get away from, now became the sole object of his yearning, the promised land to him; through the monotony of eternally riding at anchor, beyond the Yokohama sunsets like breaks from *Singing the Blues*, he dreamed of her as a lover of his mistress. He certainly didn't think of any other mistresses he might have had at home. His one or two brief affairs, if serious at the time, had been forgotten long ago. A tender smile of Mrs Bolowski's, flashed in dark New Compton Street, had haunted him longer. No: he thought of the double-decker buses in London, the advertisements for music halls up north. Birkenhead Hippodrome: twice nightly 6.30, 8.30. And of green tennis courts, the thud of tennis balls on crisp turf, and their swift passage across the net, the people in deck chairs drinking tea (despite the fact he was well able to emulate them on the *Philoctetes*), the recently acquired taste for good English ale and old cheese ...

But above all there were his songs, which would now be published. What did anything matter when back home at that very Birkenhead Hippodrome perhaps, they were being played and sung, twice nightly, to crowded houses? And what were those people humming to themselves by those tennis courts if not his tunes? Or if not humming them they were talking of him. For fame awaited him in England, not the false kind he had already brought on himself, not cheap notoriety, but real fame, fame he could now feel, having gone through hell, through 'fire' – and Hugh persuaded himself such really was the case – he had earned as his right and reward.

But the time came when Hugh *did* go through fire. One day a poor sister ship of a different century, the *Oedipus Tyrannus*, whose namesake the lamp-trimmer of the *Philoctetes* might have informed him was another Greek in trouble, lay in Yokohama roads, remote, yet too near, for that night the two great ships ceaselessly turning with the tide gradually swung so close together they almost collided, one moment this seemed about to happen, on the *Philoctetes*'s poop all was excitement, then as the vessels barely slid by one another the first mate shouted through a megaphone :

'Give Captain Telson Captain Sanderson's compliments, and tell him he's been given a foul berth!'

The *Oedipus Tyrannus*, which, unlike the *Philoctetes*, carried white firemen, had been away from home the incredible period of fourteen months. For this reason her ill-used skipper was by no means so anxious as Hugh's to deny his ship was a tramp. Twice now the Rock of Gibraltar had loomed on his starboard bow only to presage not Thames, or Mersey, but the Western Ocean, the long trip to New York. And then Vera Cruz and Colón, Vancouver and the long voyage over the Pacific back to the Far East. And now, just as everyone was feeling certain this time at last they were to go home, he had been ordered to New York once more. Her crew, especially the firemen, were weary to death of this state of affairs. The next morning, as the two ships rode again at a gracious distance, a notice appeared in the *Philoctetes*'s after messroom calling for volunteers to replace three seamen and four firemen of the *Oedipus Tyrannus*. These men would thus be enabled to return to England with the *Philoctetes*, which had been at sea only three months, but within the week on leaving Yokohama would be homeward bound.

Now at sea more days are more dollars, however few. And at sea likewise three months is a terribly long while. But fourteen months (Hugh had not yet read Melville either) is an eternity. It was not likely that the *Oedipus Tyrannus* would face more than another six of vagrancy : then one never knew; it might be the idea gradually to transfer her more long-suffering hands to homegoing vessels when she contacted them and keep her wandering two more years. At the end of two days there were only two volunteers, a wireless watcher and an ordinary seaman.

Hugh looked at the *Oedipus Tyrannus* in her new berth, but swinging again rebelliously close, as to the tether of his mind, the old steamer appearing now on one quarter, now on another, one moment near the breakwater, the next running out to sea. She was, unlike the *Philoctetes*, everything in his eyes a ship should be. First she was not in rig a football boat, a mass of low goalposts and trankums. Her masts and derricks were of the lofty coffee-pot variety. These former were black, of iron. Her funnel too was tall, and needed paint. She was foul and rusty, red lead showed along her side. She had a marked list to port, and, who knows, one to starboard as well. The condition of her bridge suggested recent contact – could it be possible? – with a typhoon. If not, she possessed the air of one who would soon attract them. She was battered, ancient, and, happy thought, perhaps even about to sink. And yet there was something youthful and beautiful about her, like an illusion that will never die, but always remains hull-down on the horizon. It was said she was capable of seven knots. And she was going to New York! On the other hand should he sign on her, what became of England? He was not so absurdly sanguine about his songs as to imagine his fame so bright there after two years ... Besides, it would mean a terrible readjustment, starting all over again. Still, there could not be the same stigma attaching to him on board. His name would scarcely have reached Colón. Ah, his brother Geoff, too, knew these seas, these pastures of experience, what would he have done?

But he couldn't do it. Galled as he was lying a month at Yoko-hama without shore leave it was still asking too much. It was as if at school, just as the end of term beautifully came in sight, he had been told there would be no summer holidays, he must go on working as usual through August and September. Save that no one was telling him anything. Some inner self, merely, was urging him to volunteer so that another sea-weary man, home-sick longer than he, might take his place. Hugh signed on board the *Oedipus Tyrannus*.

When he returned to the *Philoctetes* a month later in Singa-pore he was a different man. He had dysentery. The *Oedipus Tyrannus* had not disappointed him. Her food was poor. No refrigeration, simply an icebox. And a chief steward (the dirty 'og) who sat all day in his cabin smoking cigarettes. The fo'c'sle was forward too. He left her against his will however, due to an agential confusion, and with nothing in his mind of Lord Jim, about to pick up pilgrims going to Mecca. New York had been shelved, his shipmates, if not all the pilgrims would probably reach home after all. Alone with his pain off duty Hugh felt a sorry fellow. Yet every now and then he rose on his elbow: my God what a life! No conditions could be too good for the men tough enough to endure it. Not even the ancient Egyptians knew what slavery was. Though what did he know about it? Not much. The bunkers, loaded at Miki – a black coaling port calculated to fulfil any landsman's conception of a sailor's dreams, since every house in it was a brothel, every woman a prostitute, including even an old hag who did tattoos – were soon full: the coal was near the stokehold floor. He had seen only the bright side of a trimmer's job, if it could be said to have one. But was it much better on deck? Not really. No pity there either. To the sailor life at sea was no senseless publicity stunt. It was dead serious. Hugh was horribly ashamed of ever having so exploited it. Years of crashing dullness, of exposure to every kind of obscure peril and disease, your destiny at the mercy of a company interested in your health only because it might have to pay your insurance, your home-life reduced to a hip-bath with your wife on the kitchen mat every eighteen months, that was the sea. That, and a secret longing to be buried in it. And an enormous unquenchable pride. Hugh now thought he realized dimly what the lamp-trimmer had tried to explain, why he had been alternately abused and toadied to on the *Philoctetes*. It was largely because he had foolishly advertised himself as the representative of a heartless system both distrusted and feared. Yet to seamen this system offers far greater inducement than to firemen, who rarely emerge through the hawsehole into the bourgeois upper air. Nevertheless, it remains suspect. Its ways are devious. Its spies are everywhere. It will wheedle to you, who can tell, even on a guitar. For this reason its diary must be read. One must check up, keep abreast of its deviltries. One must, if necessary, flatter it, ape it, seem to collaborate with it. And it, in turn, flatters you. It yields a point here and there, in matters such as food, better living conditions, even though it has first destroyed the peace of mind necessary to benefit by them, libraries. For in this manner it keeps a stranglehold on your soul. And because of this it sometimes happens you grow obsequious and find yourself saying: 'Do you know, you are working for us, when we should be working for you?'. That is right too.

The system is working for you, as you will shortly discover, when the next war comes, bringing jobs for all. 'But don't imagine you can get away with these tricks for ever,' you are repeating all the time in your heart; 'Actually we have you in our grip. Without us in peace or war Christendom must collapse like a heap of ashes!' Hugh saw holes in the logic of this thought. Nevertheless, on board the *Oedipus Tyrannus*, almost without taint of that symbol, Hugh had been neither abused nor toadied to. He had been treated as a comrade. And generously helped, when unequal to his task. Only four weeks. Yet those weeks with the *Oedipus Tyrannus* had reconciled him to the *Philoctetes*. Thus he became bitterly concerned that so long as he stayed sick someone else must do his job. When he turned to again before he was well he still dreamed of England and fame. But he was mainly occupied with finishing his work in style. During these last hard weeks he played his guitar seldom. It seemed he was getting along splendidly. So splendidly that, before docking, his shipmates insisted on packing his bag for him. As it turned out, with stale bread.

They lay at Gravesend waiting for the tide. Around them in the misty dawn sheep were already bleating softly. The Thames, in the half-light, seemed not unlike the Yangtze-Kiang. Then, suddenly, someone knocked out his pipe on a garden wall . . .

Hugh hadn't waited to discover whether the journalist who came aboard at Silvertown liked to play his songs in his spare time. He'd almost thrown him bodily off the ship.

Whatever prompted the ungenerous act did not prevent his somehow finding his way that night to New Compton Street and Bolowski's shabby little shop. Closed now and dark: but Hugh could almost be certain those were his songs in the window. How strange it all was! Almost he fancied he heard familiar chords from above – Mrs Bolowski practising them softly in an upper room. And later, seeking a hotel, that all around him people were humming them. That night too, in the Astoria, this humming persisted in his dreams; he rose at dawn to investigate once more the wonderful window. Neither of his songs was there. Hugh was only disappointed an instant. Probably his songs were so popular no copies could be spared for display.

Nine o'clock brought him again to Bolowski's. The little man was delighted to see him. Yes, indeed, both his songs had been published a considerable time. Bolowski would go and get them. Hugh waited breathlessly. Why was he away so long? After all, Bolowski was his publisher. It could not be, surely, he was having any difficulty *finding* them. At last Bolowski and an assistant returned with two enormous packages. 'Here', he said, 'are your songs. What would you like us to do with them? Would you like to take them? Or would you like us to keep them a while longer?'

And there, indeed, were Hugh's songs. They had been published, a thousand sheets of each, as Bolowski said: that was all. No effort had been made to distribute them. Nobody was humming them. No comedian was singing them at the Birkenhead Hippodrome. No one had ever heard a word more of the songs 'the schoolboy undergraduate' had written. And so far as Bolowski was concerned it was a matter of complete indifference whether anyone heard a word more in the future. He had printed them, thus fulfilling his part of the contract. It had cost him perhaps a third of the premium. The rest was clear profit. If Bolowski published a thousand such songs a year by the unsuspecting half-wits willing to pay why go to the expense of pushing them? The premiums alone were his justification. And after all, Hugh had his songs. Hadn't he known, Bolowski gently explained, there was no market for songs by English composers? That most of the songs published were American? Hugh in spite of himself felt flattered at being initiated into the mysteries of the song-writing business. 'But all the publicity,' he stammered, 'wasn't all that good advertising for you?' And Bolowski gently shook his head. That story had gone dead before the songs were published. 'Yet it would be easy to revive it? – ' Hugh muttered, swallowing all his complicated good intentions as he remembered the reporter he'd kicked off the ship the day before: then, ashamed, he tried another tack … Maybe, after all, one might stand more chance in America as a song-writer? And he thought, remotely of the *Oedipus Tyrannus*. But Bolowski quietly scoffed at one's chances in America; there, where every waiter was a song-writer –

All this while, though, Hugh had been half-hopefully glancing over his songs. At least his name was on the covers. And on one was actually the photograph of a dance-band. Featured with enormous success by Izzy Smigalkin and his orchestra! Taking several copies of each he returned to the Astoria. Izzy Smigalkin was playing at the Elephant and Castle and thither he bent his steps, why he could not have said, since Bolowski had already implied the truth, that even had Izzy Smigalkin been playing at the Kilburn Empire itself he was still not the fellow to prove interested in any songs for which band parts had not been issued, be he featuring them by obscure arrangement through Bolowski with never so much success. Hugh became aware of the world.

He passed his exam to Cambridge but scarcely left his old haunts. Eighteen months must elapse before he went up. The reporter he'd thrown off the *Philoctetes* had said to him, whatever his point: 'You're a fool. You could have every editor in town running after you.' Chastened, Hugh found through this same man a job on a newspaper pasting cuttings in a scrap book. So it had come to this! However he soon acquired some sense of independence – though his board was paid by his aunt. And his rise was rapid. His notoriety had helped, albeit he wrote nothing so far of the sea. At bottom he desired honesty, art, and his story of a brothel burning in Wapping Old Stairs was said to embrace both. But at the back of his mind other fires were smouldering. No longer did he grub around from shady publisher to publisher with his guitar and his manuscripts in Geoff's Gladstone bag. Yet his life once more began to bear a certain resemblance to Adolf Hitler's. He had not lost touch with Bolowski, and in his heart he imagined himself plotting revenge. A form of private anti-Semitism became part of his life. He sweated racial hatred in the night. If it still sometimes struck him that in the stokehold he had fallen down the spout of the capitalist system, that feeling was now inseparable from his loathing of the Jews. It was somehow the fault of the poor old Jews, not merely Bolowski, but all Jews, that he'd found himself down the stokehold in the first place on a wild-goose chase. It was even due to the Jews that such economic excrescences as the British

Mercantile Marine existed. In his day dreams he became the instigator of enormous pogroms – all-inclusive, and hence, bloodless. And daily he moved nearer his design. True, between it and him, from time to time rose up the shadow of the *Philoctetes*'s lamp-trimmer. Or flickered the shadows of the trimmers in the *Oedipus Tyrannus*. Were not Bolowski and his ilk the enemies of their own race and the Jews themselves the cast-out, exploited, and wandering of the earth, even as they, even, once, as he? But what was the brotherhood of man when your brothers put stale bread in your sea-bag? Still, where else to turn for some decent and clear values? Had his father or mother not died perhaps? His aunt? Geoff? But Geoff, like some ghostly other self, was always in Rabat or Timbuctoo. Besides he'd deprived him once already of the dignity of being a rebel. Hugh smiled as he lay on the daybed ... For there had been someone, he now saw, to whose memory at least he might have turned. It reminded him moreover that he'd been an ardent revolutionary for a while at the age of thirteen. And, odd to recall, was it not this same Headmaster of his former prep school, and Scoutmaster, Dr Gotelby, fabulous stalking totem pole of Privilege, the Church, the English gentleman – God save the King and sheet anchor of parents, who'd been responsible for his heresy? Goat old boy ! With admirable independence the fiery old fellow, who preached the virtues each Sunday in Chapel, had illustrated to his goggling history class how the Bolshevists, far from being the child murderers in the *Daily Mail*, followed a way of life only less splendid than that current throughout his own community of Pangbourne Garden City. But Hugh had forgotten his ancient mentor then. Just as he had long since forgotten to do his good turn every day. That a Christian smiles and whistles under all difficulties and that once a scout you were always a Communist. Hugh only remembered to be prepared. So Hugh seduced Bolowski's wife.

This was perhaps a matter of opinion ... But unfortunately it hadn't changed Bolowski's decision to file suit for divorce, naming Hugh as co-respondent. Almost worse was to follow. Bolowski suddenly charged Hugh with attempting to deceive him in other respects, that the songs he'd published were nothing less than plagiarisms of two obscure American numbers. Hugh was staggered. Could this be? Had he been living in a world of illusion so absolute he'd looked forward passionately to the publication of someone else's songs, paid for by himself, or rather by his aunt, that, involvedly, even his disillusionment on their account was false? It was not, it proved, quite so bad as that. Yet there was all too solid ground for the accusation so far as one song was concerned ...

On the daybed Hugh wrestled with his cigar. God almighty. Good God all blistering mighty. He must have known all the time. He knew he had known. On the other hand, caring only for the rendering, it looked as if he could be persuaded by his guitar that almost any song was his. The fact that the American number was infallibly a plagiarism too didn't help the slightest. Hugh was in anguish. At this point he was living in Blackheath and one day, the threat of exposure dogging every footstep, he walked fifteen miles to the city, through the slums of Lewisham, Catford, New Cross, down the Old Kent Road, past, ah, the Elephant and Castle, into the heart of London. His poor songs pursued him in a minor key now, macabre. He wished he could be lost in these poverty-stricken hopeless districts romanticized by Longfellow. He wished the world would swallow him and his disgrace. For disgrace there would be. The publicity he had once evoked on his own behalf assured it. How was his aunt going to feel now? And Geoff? The few people who believed in him? Hugh conceived a last gigantic pogrom; in vain. It seemed, finally, almost a comfort that his mother and father were dead. As for the senior tutor of his college, it wasn't likely he would care to welcome a freshman just dragged through the divorce courts; dread words. The prospect seemed horrible, life at an end, the only hope to sign on another ship immediately it was all over, or if possible, before it all began.

Then, suddenly, a miracle occurred, something fantastic, unimaginable, and for which to this day Hugh could find no logical explanation. All at once Bolowski dropped the whole thing. He forgave his wife. He sent for Hugh and, with the utmost dignity, forgave him. The divorce suit was withdrawn. So were the plagiarism charges. It was all a mistake, Bolowski said. At worst the songs had never been distributed, so what damage had been done? The sooner it was all forgotten the better. Hugh could not believe his ears : nor in memory believe them now, nor that, so soon after everything had seemed so completely lost, and one's life irretrievably ruined, one should, as though nothing had happened, have calmly gone up to –

'Help.'

Geoffrey, his face half covered with lather, was standing in the doorway of his room, beckoning tremulously with a shaving brush and Hugh, throwing his ravaged cigar into the garden, rose and followed him in. He normally had to pass through this interesting room to reach his own (the door of which stood open opposite, revealing the mowing-machine) and at the moment, Yvonne's being occupied, to reach the bathroom. This was a delightful place, and extremely large for the size of the house; its windows, through which sunlight was pouring, looked down the drive towards the Calle Nicaragua. The room was pervaded by some sweet heavy scent of Yvonne's, while the odours of the garden filtered in through Geoff's open bedroom window.

'The shakes are awful, did you never have the shakes?' the Consul was saying, shivering all over : Hugh took the shaving brush from him and began to relather it on a tablet of fragrant asses'-milk soap lying in the basin. 'Yes, you did, I remember. But not the rajah shakes.'

'No – no newspaperman ever had the shakes.' Hugh arranged a towel about the Consul's neck. 'You mean the wheels.'

'The wheels within wheels this is.'

'I deeply sympathize. Now then, we're all set. Stand still.'

'How on earth can I stand still?'

'Perhaps you'd better sit down.'

But the Consul could not sit down either.

'Jesus, Hugh, I'm sorry. I can't stop bouncing about. It's like being in a tank – did I say tank? Christ, I need a drink. What have we here?' The Consul grasped, from the window-sill, an uncorked bottle of bay rum. 'What's this like, do you suppose, eh? For the scalp.' Before Hugh could stop him the Consul took a large drink. 'Not bad. Not at all bad,' he added triumphantly, smacking his lips. 'If slightly underproof ... Like pernod, a little. A charm against galloping cockroaches anyway. And the polygonous proustian stare of imaginary scorpions. Wait a minute, I'm going to be – '

Hugh let the taps run loudly. Next door he heard Yvonne moving about, getting ready to go to Tomalín. But he'd left the radio playing on the porch; probably she could hear no more than the usual bathroom babel.

'Tit for tat,' the Consul, still trembling, commented, when Hugh had assisted him back to his chair. 'I did that for you once.'

'*Sí, hombre.*' Hugh, lathering the brush again on the asses'-milk soap, raised his eyebrows. 'Quite so. Better now, old fellow?'

'When you were an infant,' the Consul's teeth chattered. 'On the P. & O. boat coming back from India . . . The old *Cocanada*.'

Hugh resettled the towel around his brother's neck, then, as if absent-mindedly obeying the other's wordless instructions, went out, humming, through the bedroom back to the porch, where the radio was now stupidly playing Beethoven in the wind, blowing hard again on this side of the house. On his return with the whisky bottle he rightly deduced the Consul to have hidden in the cupboard, his eyes ranged the Consul's books disposed quite neatly – in the tidy room where there was not otherwise the slightest sign its occupant did any work or contemplated any for the future, unless it was the somewhat crumpled bed on which the Consul had evidently been lying – on high shelves around the walls: Dogme et Ritual de la Haute Magie, Serpent and Siva Worship in Central America, there were two long shelves of this, together with the rusty leather bindings and frayed edges of the numerous cabbalistic and alchemical books, though some of them looked fairly new, like the *Goetia of the Lemegaton of Solomon the King*, probably they were treasures, but the rest were a heterogeneous collection: Gogol, the *Maha-bharata*, Blake, Tolstoy, Pontoppidan, the *Upanishads*, a Mermaid Marston, Bishop Berkeley, Duns Scotus, Spinoza, *Vice Versa*, Shakespeare, a complete Taskerson, *All Quiet on the Western Front*, the *Clicking of Cuthbert*, the *Rig Veda* – God knows, *Peter Rabbit*; 'Everything is to be found in *Peter Rabbit*,' the Consul liked to say – Hugh returned, smiling, and with a flourish like a Spanish waiter poured himself a stiff drink into a toothmug.

'Wherever did you find that? – ah! ... You've saved my life!'

'That's nothing. I did the same for Carruthers once.' Hugh now set about shaving the Consul who had become much steadier almost immediately.

'Carruthers – the Old Crow? ... Did what for Carruthers?'

'Held his head.'

'He wasn't tight of course, though.'

'Not tight ... Submerged. In a supervision too.' Hugh flourished the cut-throat razor. 'Try and sit still like that; you're doing fine. He had a great respect for you – he had an enormous number of stories about you, mostly variations on the same one ... however ... The one about your riding into college on a horse – '

'Oh no ... I wouldn't have ridden it in. Anything bigger than a sheep frightens me.'

'Anyway there the horse was, tied up in the buttery. A pretty ferocious horse too. Apparently it took about thirty-seven gyps and the college porter to get it out.'

'Good lord ... But I can't imagine Carruthers ever getting so tight he'd pass out at a supervision. Let me see, he was only praelector in my time. I believe he was really more interested in his first editions than in us. Of course it was at the beginning of the war, a rather trying period ... But he was a wonderful old chap.'

'He was still praelector in mine.'

(In my time? ... But what, exactly, does that mean? What, if anything, did one do at Cambridge, that would show the soul worthy of Siegebert of East Anglia – Or, John Cornford! Did one dodge lectures, cut halls, fail to row for the college, fool one's supervisor, finally, oneself? Read economics, then history, Italian, barely passing one's exams? Climb the gateway against which one had an unseaman-like aversion, to visit Bill Plantagenet in Sherlock Court, and, clutching the wheel of St Catherine, feel, for a moment asleep, like Melville, the world hurling from all havens astern? Ah, the harbour bells of Cambridge! Whose fountains in moonlight and closed courts and cloisters, whose enduring beauty in its virtuous remote self-assurance, seemed part, less of the loud mosaic of one's stupid life there, though maintained perhaps by the countless deceitful memories of such lives, than the strange dream of some old monk, eight hundred years dead, whose forbidding house, reared upon piles and stakes driven into the marshy ground, had once shone like a beacon out of the mysterious silence, and solitude of the fens. A dream jealously guarded: Keep off the Grass. And yet whose unearthly beauty compelled one to say: God forgive me. While oneself lived in a disgusting smell of marmalade and old boots, kept by a cripple, in a hovel near the station yard. Cambridge was the sea reversed; at the same time a horrible regression; in the strictest sense – despite one's avowed popularity, the godsent opportunity – the most appalling of nightmares, as if a grown man should suddenly wake up, like the ill-fated Mr Bultitude in *Vice Versa*, to be confronted, not by the hazards of business, but by the geometry lesson he had failed to prepare thirty years before, and the torments of puberty. Digs and forecastles are where they are in the heart. Yet the heart sickened at running once more full tilt into the past, into its very school-close faces, bloated now like those of the drowned, on gangling overgrown bodies, into everything all over again one had been at such pains to escape from before, but in grossly inflated form. And indeed had it not been so, one must still have been aware of cliques, snobberies, genius thrown into the river, justice declined a recommendation by the appointments board, earnestness debagged – giant oafs in pepper-and-salt, mincing like old women, their only meaning in another war. It was as though that experience of the sea, also, exaggerated by time, had invested one with the profound inner maladjustment of the sailor who can never be happy on land. One had begun, however, to play the guitar more seriously. And once again one's best friends were often Jews, often the same Jews who had been at school with one. It must be admitted they were there first, having been there off and on since A.D. 1106. But now they seemed almost the only people *old* as oneself: only they had any generous, independent sense of beauty. Only a Jew did not deface the monk's dream. And somehow only a Jew, with his rich endowment of premature suffering, could understand one's own suffering, one's isolation, essentially, one's poor music. So that in my time and with my aunt's aid I bought a University weekly. Avoiding college functions, I became a staunch supporter of Zionism. As a leader of a band composed largely of Jews, playing at local dances, and of my own private outfit Three Able Seamen, I amassed a considerable sum. The beautiful Jewish wife of a visiting American lecturer became my mistress. I had seduced her too with my guitar. Like Philoctetes's bow or Oedipus's daughter it was my guide and prop. I played it without bashfulness wherever I went. Nor did it strike me as any less than an unexpected and useful compliment that Phillipson, the artist, should have troubled to represent me, in a rival paper, as an immense guitar, inside which an oddly familiar infant was hiding, curled up, as in a womb –)

'Of course he was always a great connoisseur of wines.'

'He was beginning to get the wines and the first editions slightly mixed up in my day.' Hugh shaved adroitly along the edge of his brother's beard, past the jugular vein and the carotid artery. 'Bring me a bottle of the very best John Donne, will you, Smithers? . . . You know, some of the genuine old 1611.'

'God how funny . . . Or isn't it? The poor Old Crow.'

'He was a marvellous fellow. '

'The best.'

(. . . I have played the guitar before the Prince of Wales, begged in the streets with one for ex-servicemen on Armistice Day, performed at a reception given by the Amundsen society, and to a caucus of the French Chamber of Deputies as they arranged the approaching years. The Three Able Seamen achieved meteoric fame, *Metronome* compared us to Venuti's Blue Four. Once the worst possible thing that could befall me seemed some hand injury. Nevertheless one dreamed frequently of dying, bitten by lions, in the desert, at the last calling for the guitar, strumming to the end . . . Yet I stopped of my own accord. Suddenly, less than a year after going down from Cambridge, stopped, first in bands, then playing it intimately, stopped so completely that Yvonne, despite the tenuous bond of being born in Hawaii, doubtless doesn't know I ever played, so emphatically no one says any longer: Hugh, where's your guitar? Come on and give us a tune –)

'I have', the Consul said, 'a slight confession to make, Hugh ... I cheated a little on the strychnine while you were away.'

'Thalavethiparothiam, is it?' Hugh observed, pleasantly menacing. 'Or strength obtained by decapitation. Now then, don't be careful, as the Mexicans say, I'm going to shave the back of your neck.'

But first Hugh wiped the razor with some tissue paper, glancing absently through the door into the Consul's room. The bedroom windows were wide open; the curtains blew inward very gently. The wind had almost dropped. The scents of the garden were heavy about them. Hugh heard the wind starting to blow again on the other side of the house, the fierce breath of the Atlantic, flavoured with wild Beethoven. But here, on the leeward side, those trees one could see through the bathroom window seemed unaware of it. And the curtains were engaged with their own gentle breeze. Like the crew's washing on board a tramp steamer, strung over number six hatch between sleek derricks lying in grooves, that barely dances in the afternoon sunlight, while abaft the beam not a league away some pitching native craft with violently flapping sails seems wrestling a hurricane, they swayed imperceptibly, as to another control ...

(Why did I stop playing the guitar? Certainly not because, belatedly, one had come to see the point of Phillipson's picture, the cruel truth it contained ... They are losing the Battle of the Ebro – And yet, one might well have seen one's continuing to play as but another form of publicity stunt, a means of keeping oneself in the limelight, as if those weekly articles for the *News of the World* were not limelight enough! Or myself with the thing destined to be some kind of incurable 'love-object', or eternal troubadour, jongleur, interested only in married women – why? – incapable finally of love altogether ... Bloody little man. Who, anyhow, no longer wrote songs. While the guitar as an end in itself at least seemed simply futile; no longer even fun – certainly a childish thing to be put away –)

'Is that right?'

'Is what right?'

'Do you see that poor exiled maple tree outside there,' asked the Consul, 'propped up with those crutches of cedar?'

'No – luckily for you – '

'One of these days, when the wind blows from the other direction, it's going to collapse.' The Consul spoke haltingly while Hugh shaved his neck. 'And do you see that sunflower looking in through the bedroom window? It stares into my room all day.'

'It strolled into your room, do you say?'

'Stares. Fiercely. All day. Like God!'

(The last time I played it ... Strumming in the King of Bohemia, London. Benskin's Fine Ales and Stouts. And waking, after passing out, to find John and the rest singing unaccompanied that song about the balgine run. What, anyhow, is a balgine run? Revolutionary songs; bogus bolshy; – but why had one never heard such songs before? Or, for that matter, in England, seen such rich spontaneous enjoyment in singing? Perhaps because at any given gathering, one had always been singing oneself. Sordid songs: *I Ain't Got Nobody*. Loveless songs: *The One That I Love Loves Me* ... Though John 'and the rest' were not, to one's own experience at least, bogus: no more than who, at sunset walking with the crowd, or receiving bad news, witnessing injustice, once turned and thought, did not believe, turned back and questioned, decided to act ... They are winning the Battle of the Ebro! Not for me, perhaps. Yet no wonder indeed if these friends, some of whom now lie dead on Spanish soil, had, as I then understood, really been bored by my pseudo-American twanging, not even good twanging finally, and had only been listening out of politeness – twanging –)

'Have another drink.' Hugh replenished the toothmug, handed it to the Consul, and picked up for him a copy of *El Universal* lying on the floor. 'I think a little more down the side with that beard, and at the base of the neck.' Hugh stropped the razor thoughtfully.

'A communal drink.' The Consul passed the toothmug over his shoulder. '"Clank of coins irritates at Forth Worth."'

Holding the paper quite steadily the Consul read aloud from the English page: ' "Kink unhappy in exile." I don't believe it myself. "Town counts dogs' noses." I don't believe that either, do you, Hugh? ...

'And – ah – yes!' he went on, ' "Eggs have been in a tree at Klamanth Falls for a hundred years, lumberjacks estimate by rings of wood." Is that the kind of stuff you write nowadays?'

'Almost exactly. Or: Japanese astride all roads from Shanghai. Americans evacuate ... That kind of thing. – Sit still.'

(One had not, however, played it from that day to this ... No, nor been happy from that day to this either ... A little self-knowledge is a dangerous thing. And anyway, without the guitar, was one any less in the limelight, any less interested in married women – so on, and so forth? One immediate result of giving it up was undoubtedly that second trip to sea, that series of articles, the first for the *Globe*, on the British Coasting Trade. Then yet another trip – coming to naught spiritually. I ended a passenger. But the articles were a success. Saltcaked smoke-stacks. Britannia rules the waves. In future my work was looked for with interest ... On the other hand why have I always lacked real ambition as a newspaperman? Apparently I have never overcome that antipathy to journalists, the result of my early ardent courtship of them. Besides it cannot be said I shared with my colleagues the necessity of earning a living. There was always the income. As a roving hand I functioned fairly well, still, up to this day, have done so – yet becoming increasingly conscious of loneliness, isolation – aware too of an odd habit of thrusting myself to the fore, then subsiding – as if one remembered one hadn't the guitar after all ... Maybe I bored people with my guitar. But in a sense – who cares? – it strung me to life –)

'Somebody quoted you in the *Universal*', the Consul was laughing, 'some time ago. I just forget about what, I'm afraid ... Hugh, how would you like, "at a modest sacrifice", an "imported pair embroidered street extra large nearly new fur coat"?'

'Sit still.'

'Or a Cadillac for 500 pesos. Original price 200 ... And what

would this mean, do you suppose? "And a white horse also."
Apply at box seven ... Strange ... Anti-alcoholic fish. Don't
like the sound of that. But here's something for you. "A cen-
tricle apartment suitable for love-nest." Or alternatively, a
"serious, *discrete* – "'

' – ha – '

' – apartment ... Hugh, listen to this. "For a young European lady who must be pretty, acquaintanceship with a cultured
man, not old, with good *positions* – "'

The Consul was shaking with laughter only, it appeared, and
Hugh, laughing too, paused, razor aloft.

'But the remains of Juan Ramírez, the famous singer, Hugh,
are still wandering in a melancholy fashion from place to place
... Hullo, it says here that "grave objections" have been made
to the immodest behaviour of certain police chiefs in Quauhnahuac. "Grave objections to – " what's this? – "performing their
private functions in public" – '

('Climbed the Parson's Nose', one had written, in the visitors'
book at the little Welsh rock-climbing hotel, 'in twenty minutes.
Found the rocks very easy.' 'Came down the Parson's Nose',
some immortal wag had added a day later, 'in twenty seconds.
Found the rocks very hard.' ... So now, as I approach the
second half of my life, unheralded, unsung, and without a guitar,
I am going back to sea again : perhaps these days of waiting are
more like that droll descent, to be survived in order to repeat
the climb. At the top of the Parson's Nose you could walk home
to tea over the hills if you wished, just as the actor in the Passion
Play can get off his cross and go home to his hotel for a Pilsener.
Yet in life ascending or descending you were perpetually involved with the mists, the cold and the overhangs, the treacher-
ous rope and the slippery belay; only, while the rope slipped
there was sometimes time to laugh. None the less, I am afraid ...
As I am also of a simple gate, and climbing windy masts in
port ... Will it be as bad as the first voyage, the harsh reality of
which for some reason suggests Yvonne's farm? One wonders
how she will feel the first time she sees someone stick a pig ...
Afraid; and yet not afraid; I know what the sea is like; can it be
that I am returning to it with my dreams intact, nay, with

dreams that, being without viciousness, are more child-like than before. I love the sea, the pure Norwegian sea. My disillusionment once more is a pose. What am I trying to prove by all this? Accept it; one is a sentimentalist, a muddler, a realist, a dreamer, coward, hypocrite, hero, an Englishman in short, unable to follow out his own metaphors. Tufthunter and pioneer in disguise. Iconoclast and explorer. Undaunted bore undone by trivialities! Why, one asks, instead of feeling stricken in that pub, didn't I set about learning some of those songs, those precious revolutionary songs. What is to prevent one's learning more of such songs now, new songs, different songs, anyhow, if only to recapture some early joy in merely singing, and playing the guitar? What have I got out of my life? Contacts with famous men ... The occasion Einstein asked me the time, for instance. That summer evening, strolling towards the tumultuous kitchen of St John's – who is it that behind me has emerged from the rooms of the Professor living in D4? And who is it also strolling towards the Porter's lodge – where, our orbits crossing, asks me the time? Is this Einstein, up for an honours degree? And who smiles when I say I don't know ... And yet asked me. Yes: the great Jew, who has upset the whole world's notions of time and space, once leaned down over the side of his hammock strung between Aries and the Circlet of the Western Fish, to ask me, befuddled ex-anti-Semite, and ragged freshman huddled in his gown at the first approach of the evening star, the time. And smiled again when I pointed out the clock neither of us had noticed –)

' – better than having them perform their public functions in private anyhow, I should have thought,' Hugh said.

'You might have hit on something there. That is, those birds referred to are not police in the strict sense. As a matter of fact the regular police are – '

'I know, they're on strike.'

'So of course they must be democratic from your point of view ... Just like the army. All right, it's a democratic army ... But meantime these other cads are throwing their weight about a bit. It's a pity you're leaving. It might have been a story right down your alley. Did you ever hear of the Union Militar?'

'You mean the pre-war thingmetight, in Spain?'

'I mean here in this state. It's affiliated to the Military Police, by which they're covered, so to speak, because the Inspector-General, who *is* the Military Police, is a member. So is the Jefe de Jardineros, I believe.'

'I heard they were putting up a new statue to Díaz in Oaxaca.'

' – Just the same,' pursued the Consul, in a slightly lowered tone, as their conversation continued in the next room, 'there is this Union Militar, *sinarquistas*, whatever they're called, if you're interested, I'm not personally – and their headquarters used to be in the policía de Séguridad here, though it isn't any longer, but in Parián somewhere, I heard.'

Finally the Consul was ready. The only further help he had required was with his socks. Wearing a freshly pressed shirt and a pair of tweed trousers with the jacket to them Hugh had borrowed and now brought in from the porch, he stood gazing at himself in the mirror.

It was most surprising, not only did the Consul now appear fresh and lively but to be dispossessed of any air of dissipation whatsoever. True, he had not before the haggard look of a depraved worn-out old man: why should he indeed, when he was only twelve years older than Hugh himself? Yet it was as though fate had fixed his age at some unidentifiable moment in the past, when his persistent objective self, perhaps weary of standing askance and watching his downfall, had at last withdrawn from him altogether, like a ship secretly leaving harbour at night. Sinister stories as well as funny and heroic had been told about his brother, whose own early poetic instincts clearly helped the legend. It occurred to Hugh that the poor old chap might be, finally, helpless, in the grip of something against which all his remarkable defences could avail him little. What use were his talons and fangs to the dying tiger? In the clutches, say, to make matters worse, of a boa-constrictor? But apparently this improbable tiger had no intention of dying just yet. On the contrary, he intended taking a little walk, taking the boa-constrictor with him, even to pretend, for a while, it wasn't there. Indeed, on the face of it, this man of abnormal strength and constitution and obscure ambition, whom Hugh would never know, could never deliver nor make agreement to God for, but in his way loved and desired to help, had triumphantly succeeded in pulling himself together. While what had given rise to all these reflections was doubtless only the photograph on the wall both were now studying, whose presence there at all must surely discount most of those old stories, of a small camouflaged freighter, at which the Consul suddenly gestured with replenished toothmug:

'Everything about the *Samaritan* was a ruse. See those windlasses and bulkheads. That black entrance that looks as though it might be the entrance to the forecastle, that's a shift too – there's an anti-aircraft gun stowed away snugly in there. Over there, that's the way you go down. Those were my quarters ... There's your quartermaster's alley. That galley – it could become a battery, before you could say *Coclogenus paca Mexico* ...

'Curiously enough though,' the Consul peered closer, 'I cut that picture out of a German magazine,' and Hugh too was scrutinizing the Gothic writing beneath the photograph: *Der englische Dampfer tragt Schutzfarben gegen deutsche U-boote.* 'Only on the next page, I recall, was a picture of the *Emden*', the Consul went on, 'with "*So verlies ich der Weltteil unserer Antipoden*", something of that nature, under it. "Our Antipodes".' He gave Hugh a sharp glance that might have meant anything. 'Queer people. But I see you're interested in my old books all of a sudden ... Too bad ... I left my Boehme in Paris.'

'I was just looking.'

At, for God's sake, *A Treatise of Sulphur: written by Michall Sandivogius i.e. anagramatically Divi Leschi Genus Amo; at The Hermetical Triumph or the Victorious Philosophical Stone, a Treatise more compleat and more intelligible than any has been yet, concerning the Hermetical Magistery; at The Secrets Revealed or an Open Entrance to the Sub-Palace of the King, containing the greatest Treasure in Chymistry never yet so plainly discovered, composed by a most famous Englishman styling himself Anonymus or Eyraeneus Philaletha Cosmopolita who by inspiration and reading attained to the Philosopher's Stone at his age of twenty-three years Anno Domini 1645; at The Musaeum Hermeticum, Reformatum et Amplificatum,*

*Omnes Sopho-Spagyricae artis Discipulos fidelissime erudiens,
quo pacto Summa illa vera que Lapidis Philosophici Medicina,
qua res omnes qualemcunque defectum patientes, instaurantur,
inveniri & haberi queat, Continens Tractatus Chimicos xxi Fran-
cofurti, Apud Hermannum à Sande CIƆ IƆC LXXVIII;* at
*Sub-Mundanes, or the Elementaries of the Cabbala, reprinted
from the text of the Abbé de Villars: Physio-Astro-Mystic: with
an Illustrative Appendix from the work Demoniality, wherein
is asserted that there are in existence on earth rational creatures
besides men* ...

'Are there?' Hugh said, holding in his hand this last extraordinary old book – from which emanated a venerable and remote smell – and reflecting: 'Jewish knowledge!' while a sudden absurd vision of Mr Bolowski in another life, in a caftan,
with a long white beard, and skull-cap, and passionate intent
look, standing at a stall in a sort of medieval New Compton
Street, reading a sheet of music in which the notes were Hebrew
letters, was conjured to his mind.

'Erekia, the one who tears asunder; and they who shriek with
a long-drawn cry, Illirikim; Apelki, the misleaders or turners
aside; and those who attack their prey by tremulous motion,
Dresop; ah, and the distressful painbringing ones, Arekesoli;
and one must not forget, either, Burasin, the destroyers by stif-
ling smoky breath; nor Glesi, the one who glistens horribly like
an insect; nor Effrigis, the one who quivers in a horrible manner, you'd like Effrigis ... nor yet the Mames, those who move
by backward motion, nor the movers with a particular creeping
motion, Ramisen ...' the Consul was saying. 'The flesh in-
clothed and the evil questioners. Perhaps you would not call
them precisely rational. But all these at one time or another have
visited my bed.'

They had all of them in a tremendous hurry and the friendliest of humours set off for Tomalín. Hugh, himself somewhat
aware of his drinks, was listening in a dream to the Consul's
voice rambling on – Hitler, he pursued, as they stepped out into
the Calle Nicaragua – which might have been a story right
down his alley, if only he'd shown any interest before – merely
wished to annihilate the Jews in order to obtain just such arcana

as could be found behind them in his bookshelves – when suddenly in the house the telephone rang.

'No, let it ring,' the Consul said as Hugh started back. It went on ringing (for Concepta had gone out), the tintinnabulation beating around the empty rooms like a trapped bird; then it stopped.

As they moved on Yvonne said:

'Why no, Geoff, don't keep bothering about me, I feel quite rested. But if Tomalín's too far for either of you, why don't we go to the zoo?' She looked at them both darkly and directly and beautifully with her candid eyes under the broad brow, eyes with which she did not quite return Hugh's smile, though her mouth suggested one. Perhaps she seriously interpreted Geoff's flow of conversation as a good sign. And perhaps it was! Qualifying it with loyal interest, or at a quick preoccupied tangent with observations upon impersonal change or decay, serapes or carbon or ice, the weather – where was the wind now? they might have a nice calm day after all without too much dust – Yvonne, apparently revived by her swim and taking in everything about her afresh with an objective eye, walked with swiftness and grace and independence, and as though really not tired; yet it struck Hugh she walked by herself. Poor darling Yvonne! Greeting her when she was ready had been like meeting her once again after long absence, but it was also like parting. For Hugh's usefulness was exhausted, their 'plot' subtly lamed by small circumstances, of which not the least was his own continued presence. It would seem impossible now as their old passion to seek without imposture to be alone with her, even with Geoff's interest at heart. Hugh cast a longing glance down the hill, the way they'd gone this morning. Now they were hastening in the opposite direction. This morning might have been already far in the past, like childhood or the days before the last war; the future was beginning to unwind, the euchred stupid bloody terrific guitar-playing future. Unsuitably girded against it, Hugh felt, noted with a reporter's measure, Yvonne, barelegged, was wearing instead of her yellow slacks a white tailored sharkskin suit with one button at the waist, and beneath it a brilliant high-necked blouse, like a detail in a Rousseau; the heels of her red shoes clicking laconically on the broken stones appeared neither flat nor high, and she carried a bright red bag. Passing her one would not have suspected agony. One would not have noticed lack of faith, nor questioned that she knew where she was going, nor wondered if she were walking in her sleep. How happy and pretty she looks, one would say. Probably she is going to meet her lover in the Bella Vista! — Women of medium height, slenderly built, mostly divorced, passionate but envious of the male — angel to him as he is bright or dark, yet unconscious destructive succubus of his ambitions — American women, with that rather graceful swift way of walking, with the clean scrubbed tanned faces of children, the skin finely textured with a satin sheen, their hair clean and shining as though just washed, and looking like that, but carelessly done, the slim brown hands that do not rock the cradle, the slender feet — how many centuries of oppression have produced them? They do not care who is losing the Battle of the Ebro, for it is too soon for them to outsnort Job's warhorse. They see no significance in it, only fools going to death for a —

'One always heard they had a therapeutic quality. They always had zoos in Mexico apparently — Moctezuma, courteous fellow, even showed stout Cortés around a zoo. The poor chap thought he was in the infernal regions.' The Consul had discovered a scorpion on the wall.

'¿Alacrán?' Yvonne produced.

'It looks like a violin.'

'A curious bird is the scorpion. He cares not for priest nor for poor peon ... It's really a beautiful creature. Leave him be. He'll only sting himself to death anyway.' The Consul swung his stick ...

They climbed the Calle Nicaragua, always between the parallel swift streams, past the school with the grey tombstones and the swing like a gallows, past high mysterious walls, and hedges intertwined with crimson flowers, among which marmalade-coloured birds were trapezing, crying raucously. Hugh felt glad of his drinks now, remembering from his boyhood how the last day of the holidays was always worse if you went anywhere, how then time, that one had hoped to bemuse, would at any moment begin to glide after you like a shark following a swimmer. – |Box| said an advertisement. *Arena Tomalín. El Balón vs El Redondillo.* The Balloon vs the Bouncing Ball – was that? Domingo ... But that was for Sunday; while they were only going to a bullthrowing, a purpose in life whose object was not even worth advertising. 666: also said further advertisements for an insecticide, obscure yellow tin plates at the bottom of walls, to the quiet delight of the Consul. Hugh chuckled to himself. So far the Consul was doing superbly. His few 'necessary drinks', reasonable or outrageous, had worked wonders. He was walking magnificently erect, shoulders thrown back, chest out: the best thing about it was his deceitful air of infallibility, of the unquestionable, especially when contrasted with what one must look like oneself in cowboy clothes. In his finely cut tweeds (the coat Hugh had borrowed was not much crumpled, and now Hugh had borrowed another one) and blue and white striped old Chagfordian tie, with the barbering Hugh had given him, his thick fair hair neatly slicked back, his freshly trimmed brownish greying beard, his stick, his dark glasses, who would say that he was not, unmistakably, a figure of complete respectability? And if this respectable figure, the Consul might have been saying, appeared to be undergoing from time to time a slight mutation, what of it? who noticed? It might be – for an Englishman in a foreign country always expects to meet another Englishman – merely of nautical origin. If not, his limp, obviously the result of an elephant hunt or an old brush with Pathans, excused it. The typhoon spun invisibly in the midst of a tumult of broken pavements: who was aware of its existence, let alone what landmarks in the brain it had destroyed? Hugh was laughing.

> 'Plingen, plangen, aufgefangen
> Swingen, swangen at my side,
> Pootle, swootle, off to Bootle,
> Nemesis, a pleasant ride,'

said the Consul mysteriously, and added with heroism, glancing about him:

'It's really an extraordinarily nice day to take a trip.'

No se permite fijar anuncios ...

Yvonne was in fact walking alone now : they climbed in a sort of single file, Yvonne ahead, the Consul and Hugh unevenly behind, and whatever their collective distraught soul might be thinking Hugh was oblivious of it, for he had become involved with a fit of laughing, which the Consul was trying not to find infectious. They walked in this manner because a boy was driving some cows past them down the hill, half running; and, as in a dream of a dying Hindu, steering them by their tails. Now there were some goats. Yvonne turned and smiled at him. But these goats were meek and sweet-looking, jangling little bells. *Father is waiting for you though. Father has not forgotten.* Behind the goats a woman with a black clenched face staggered past them under the weight of a basket loaded with carbon. A peon loped after her down the hill balancing a large barrel of ice-cream on his head and calling apparently for customers, with what hope of success one could not imagine, since he seemed so burdened as to be unable either to look from side to side or to halt.

'It's true that at Cambridge', the Consul was saying, tapping Hugh on the shoulder, 'you may have learned about Guelphs and so on ... But did you know that no angel with six wings is ever transformed?'

'I seem to have learned that no bird ever flew with one – '

'Or that Thomas Burnet, author of the *Telluris Theoria Sacra*, entered Christs in – *Cáscaras! Caracoles! Virgen Santísima! Ave María! Fuego, fuego! Ay, qué me matan!*'

With a shattering and fearful tumult a plane slammed down upon them, skimmed the frightened trees, zooming, narrowly missed a mirador, and was gone the next moment, headed in the direction of the volcanoes, from which rolled again the monotonous sound of artillery.

'*Acabóse,*' sighed the Consul.

Hugh suddenly noticed that a tall man (who must have stepped out of the side-road Yvonne had seemed anxious they should take) with sloping shoulders and handsome, rather swarthy features, though he was obviously a European, doubtless in some state of exile, was confronting them, and it was as though the whole of this man, by some curious fiction, reached up to the crown of his perpendicularly raised Panama hat, for the gap below seemed to Hugh still occupied by something, a sort of halo or spiritual property of his body, or the essence of some guilty secret perhaps that he kept under the hat but which was now momentarily exposed, fluttering and embarrassed. He was confronting them, though smiling, it appeared, at Yvonne alone, his blue, bold protuberant eyes expressing an incredulous dismay, his black eyebrows frozen in a comedian's arch: he hesitated: then this man, who wore his coat open and trousers very high over a stomach they had probably been designed to conceal but merely succeeded in giving the character of an independent tumescence of the lower part of his body, came forward with eyes flashing and mouth under its small black moustache curved in a smile at once false and engaging, yet somehow protective – and somehow, also, increasingly grave – came forward as it were impelled by clockwork, hand out, automatically ingratiating:

'Why Yvonne, what a delightful surprise. Why goodness me, I thought; oh, hullo, old bean – '

'Hugh, this is Jacques Laruelle,' the Consul was saying. 'You've probably heard me speak about him at one time or another. Jacques, my young brother Hugh: ditto ... *Il vient d'arriver* ... or vice versa. How goes it, Jacques? You look as though you needed a drink rather badly.'

'–'

'–'

A minute later M. Laruelle, whose name struck only a very distant chord for Hugh, had taken Yvonne's arm and was walking in the middle of the road with her up the hill. Probably there was no significance in this. But the Consul's introduction had been brusque to say the least. Hugh himself felt half hurt and, whatever the cause, a slight appalling sense of tension as the Consul and he slowly fell behind again. Meantime M. Laruelle was saying:

'Why do we not all drop into my "madhouse"; that would be good fun, don't you think Geoffrey – ah – ah – Hughes?'

'No,' softly remarked the Consul, behind, to Hugh, who on the other hand now felt almost disposed to laugh once more.

For the Consul was also saying something cloacal very quietly to himself over and over again. They were following Yvonne and her friend through the dust which now, chased by a lonely gust of wind, was moving along with them up the road, sizzling in petulant ground-swirls to blow away like rain. When the wind died away the water rushing headlong down the gutters here was like a sudden force in the opposite direction.

M. Laruelle was saying attentively, ahead of them, to Yvonne:

'Yes ... Yes ... But your bus won't leave till two-thirty. You have over an hour.'

– 'But that does sound like an unusual bloody miracle,' Hugh said. 'You mean after all these years – '

'Yeah. It was a great coincidence our meeting here,' the Consul told Hugh in a changed even tone. 'But I really think you two ought to get together, you have something in common. Seriously you might enjoy his house, it's always mildly amusing.'

'Good,' said Hugh.

'Why, here comes the *cartero*,' Yvonne called out ahead, half turning round and disengaging her arm from M. Laruelle's. She was pointing to the corner on the left at the top of the hill where the Calle Nicaragua met the Calle Tierra del Fuego. 'He's simply amazing,' she was saying volubly. 'The funny thing is that all the postmen in Quauhnahuac look exactly alike. Apparently they're all from the same family and have been postmen for positively generations. I think this one's grandfather was a *cartero* at the time of Maximilian. Isn't it delightful to think of the post-office collecting all these grotesque little creatures like so many carrier pigeons to dispatch at their will?'

Why are you so voluble? Hugh wondered: 'How delightful, for the post-office,' he said politely. They were all watching the *cartero*'s approach. Hugh happened not to have observed any of these unique postmen before. He could not have been five feet in height, and from a distance appeared like an unclassifiable but somehow pleasing animal advancing on all fours. He was wearing a colourless dungaree suit and a battered official cap and Hugh now saw he had a tiny goatee beard. Upon his small wizened face as he lunged down the street towards them in his inhuman yet endearing fashion there was the friendliest expression imaginable. Seeing them he stopped, unshouldered the bag and began to unbuckle it.

'There is a letter, a letter, a letter,' he was saying when they came up with him, bowing to Yvonne as if he'd last greeted her yesterday, 'a message *por el señor*, for your horse,' he informed the Consul, withdrawing two packages and smiling roguishly as he undid them.

'What? – nothing for Señor Calígula.'

'Ah.' The *cartero* flicked through another bundle, glancing at them sideways and keeping his elbows close to his sides in order not to drop the bag. 'No.' He put down the bag now altogether, and began to search feverishly; soon letters were spread all over the road. 'It must be. Here. No. This is. Then this one. *Ei ei ei ei ei ei.*'

'Don't bother, my dear fellow,' the Consul said. 'Please.'

But the *cartero* tried again: 'Badrona, Diosdado –'

Hugh too was waiting expectantly, not so much any word from the *Globe*, which would come if at all by cable, but half in hope, a hope which the postman's own appearance rendered delightfully plausible, of another minuscule Oaxaqueñian envelope, covered with bright stamps of archers shooting at the sun, from Juan Cerillo. He listened: somewhere, behind a wall, someone was playing a guitar – badly, he was let down; and a dog barked sharply.

' – Feeshbank, Figueroa, Gómez – no, Quincey, Sandovah, no.'

At last the good little man gathered up his letters and bowing apologetically, disappointedly, lunged off down the street again. They were all looking after him, and just as Hugh was wondering whether the postman's behaviour might not have been part of some enormous inexplicable private joke, if really he'd been laughing at them the whole time, though in the kindliest way, he halted, fumbled once more at one of the packages, turned, and trotting back with little yelps of triumph, handed the Consul what looked like a postal card.

Yvonne, a little ahead again by now, nodded at him over her shoulder, smiling, as to say: 'Good, you've got a letter after all,' and with her buoyant dancing steps walked on slowly beside M. Laruelle, up the dusty hill.

The Consul turned the card over twice, then handed it to Hugh.

'Strange – ' he said.

– It was from Yvonne herself and apparently written at least a year ago. Hugh suddenly realized it must have been posted soon after she'd left the Consul and most probably in ignorance he proposed to remain in Quauhnahuac. Yet curiously it was the card that had wandered far afield : originally addressed to Wells Fargo in Mexico City, it had been forwarded by some error a-broad, gone badly astray in fact, for it was date-stamped from Paris, Gibraltar, and even Algeciras, in Fascist Spain.

'No, read it,' the Consul smiled.

Yvonne's scrawl ran : *Darling, why did I leave? Why did you let me? Expect to arrive in the U.S. tomorrow, California two days later. Hope to find a word from you there waiting. Love Y.*

Hugh turned the card over. There was a picture of the leonine Signal Peak on El Paso with Carlsbad Cavern Highway leading over a white fenced bridge between desert and desert. The road turned a little corner in the distance and vanished.

7

On the side of the drunken madly revolving world hurtling at 1.20 p.m. towards Hercules's Butterfly the house seemed a bad idea, the Consul thought –

There were two towers, Jacques's *zacualis*, one at each end and joined by a catwalk over the roof, which was the glassed-in gable of the studio below. These towers were as if camouflaged (almost like the *Samaritan*, in fact): blue, grey, purple, vermilion, had once been slashed on in zebra stripes. But time and weather had combined to render the effect from a short distance of a uniform dull mauve. Their tops, reached from the catwalk by twin wooden ladders, and from inside by two spiral staircases, made two flimsy crenellated miradors, each scarcely larger than a bartizan, tiny roofless variants of the observation posts which everywhere commanded the valley in Quauhnahuac.

On the battlements of the mirador to their left, as the Consul and Hugh confronted the house, with the Calle Nicaragua stretching downhill to their right, now appeared to them two bilious-looking angels. The angels, carved out of pink stone, knelt facing one another in profile against the sky across the intervening crenels, while behind, upon corresponding merlons at the far side, sat solemnly two nameless objects like marzipan cannonballs, evidently constructed from the same material.

The other mirador was unadorned save by its crenellations and it often struck the Consul that this contrast was somehow obscurely appropriate to Jacques, as indeed was that between the angels and the cannonballs. It was perhaps also significant he should use his bedroom for working whereas the studio itself on the main floor had been turned into a dining-room often no better than a camping-ground for his cook and her relatives.

Coming closer it could be seen that on the left and somewhat larger tower, below that bedroom's two windows – which, as if degenerate machicolations, were built askew, like the separated halves of a chevron – a panel of rough stone, covered with large letters painted in gold leaf, had been slightly set into the wall to give a semblance of bas-relief. These gold letters though very thick were merged together most confusingly. The Consul had noticed visitors to the town staring up at them for half an hour at a time. Sometimes M. Laruelle would come out to explain they really spelt something, that they formed that phrase of Frey Luis de León's the Consul did not at this moment allow himself to recall. Nor did he ask himself why he should have come to be almost more familiar with this extraordinary house than his own as, preceeding M. Laruelle now, who was prodding him cheerfully from behind, he followed Hugh and Yvonne into it, into the studio, empty for once, and up the spiral staircase of its left-hand tower. 'Haven't we overshot the drinks?' he asked, his mood of detachment expiring now he remembered that only a few weeks before he'd sworn never to enter this place again.

'Don't you ever think of anything else?' it seemed Jacques had said.

The Consul made no reply but stepped out into the familiar disorderly room with the askew windows, the degenerate machicolations, now seen from inside, and followed the others obliquely through it to a balcony at the back, into a view of sun-filled valleys and volcanoes, and cloud shadows wheeling across the plain.

M. Laruelle, however, was already nervously going downstairs. 'Not for me!' protested the others. Fools! The Consul took two or three steps after him, a movement apparently without meaning, but it almost constituted a threat: his gaze shifted vaguely up the spiral staircase which continued from the room to the mirador above, then he rejoined Hugh and Yvonne on the balcony.

'Get up on the roof, you people, or stay on the porch, just make yourselves at home,' came from downstairs. 'There's a pair of binoculars on the table there – er – Hughes . . . I won't be a minute.'

'Any objection if I go on the roof?' Hugh asked them.

'Don't forget the binoculars!'

Yvonne and the Consul were alone on the flying balcony.

From where they stood the house seemed situated half-way up a cliff rising steeply from the valley stretched out below them. Leaning round they saw the town itself, built as on top of this cliff, overhanging them. The clubs of flying machines waved silently over the roofs, their motions like gesticulations of pain. But the cries and music of the fair reached them at this moment clearly. Far away the Consul made out a green corner, the golf course, with little figures working their way round the side of the cliff, crawling ... Golfing scorpions. The Consul remembered the card in his pocket, and apparently he had made a movement towards Yvonne, desiring to tell her about it, to say something tender to her concerning it, to turn her towards him, to kiss her. Then he realized that without another drink shame for this morning would prevent his looking in her eyes. 'What do you think, Yvonne,' he said, 'with your astronomical mind – ' Could it be he, talking to her like this, on an occasion like this! Surely not, it was a dream. He was pointing up at the town. ' – With your astronomical mind,' he repeated, but no, he had not said it: 'doesn't all that revolving and plunging up there somehow suggest to you the voyaging of unseen planets, of unknown moons hurtling backwards?' He had said nothing.

'Please Geoffrey – ' Yvonne laid her hand on his arm. 'Please, please believe me, I didn't want to be drawn into this. Let's make some excuse and get away as quickly as possible ... I don't mind how many drinks you have *after*,' she added.

'I wasn't aware I'd said anything about drinks now or after. It's you that have put the thought into my head. Or Jacques, whom I can hear breaking – or should we say, crushing? – the ice down below.'

'Haven't you got any tenderness or love left for me at all?' Yvonne asked suddenly, almost piteously, turning round on him, and he thought: Yes, I do love you, I have all the love in the world left for you, only that love seems so far away from me and so strange too, for it is as though I could almost hear it, a droning or a weeping, but far, far away, and a sad lost sound, it might be either approaching or receding, I can't tell which. 'Don't you think of anything except of how many drinks you're going to have?'

'Yes,' said the Consul (but wasn't it Jacques who'd just asked him this?), 'yes, I do – oh my God, Yvonne!'

'Please, Geoffrey – '

Yet he could not face her. The clubs of the flying machines seen out of the corner of his eye, now seemed as if belabouring him all over. 'Listen,' he said, 'are you asking me to extricate us from all this, or are you starting to exhort me again about drinking?'

'Oh, I'm not exhorting you, really I'm not. I'll never exhort you again. I'll do anything you ask.'

'Then – ' he had begun in anger.

But a look of tenderness came over Yvonne's face and the Consul thought once more of the postcard in his pocket. It ought to have been a good omen. It could be the talisman of their immediate salvation now. Perhaps it would have been a good omen if only it had arrived yesterday or at the house this morning. Unfortunately one could not now conceive of it as having arrived at any other moment. And how could he know whether it was a good omen or not without another drink?

'But I'm back,' she was apparently saying. 'Can't you see it? We're here together again, it's *us*. Can't you see that?' Her lips were trembling, she was almost crying.

Then she was close to him, in his arms, but he was gazing over her head.

'Yes, I can see,' he said, only he couldn't see, only hear, the droning, the weeping, and feel, feel the unreality. 'I do love you. Only – ' 'I can never forgive you deeply enough': was that what was in his mind to add?

– And yet, he was thinking all over again, and all over again as for the first time, how he had suffered, suffered, suffered without her; indeed such desolation, such a desperate sense of abandonment, bereavement, as during this last year without Yvonne, he had never known in his life, unless it was when his mother died. But this present emotion he had never experienced with his mother: this urgent desire to hurt, to provoke, at a time when forgiveness alone could save the day, this, rather, had commenced with his stepmother, so that she would have to cry: 'I

241

can't eat, Geoffrey, the food sticks in my throat!' It was hard to
forgive, hard, hard to forgive. Harder still, not to say how hard
it was, *I hate you*. Even now, of all times. Even though here was
God's moment, the chance to agree, to produce the card, to
change everything; or there was but a moment left ... Too late.
The Consul had controlled his tongue. But he felt his mind
divide and rise, like the two halves of a counterpoised draw-
bridge, ticking, to permit passage of these noisome thoughts.
'Only my heart – ' he said.

'Your heart, darling?' she asked anxiously.

'Nothing – '

'Oh my poor sweetheart, you must be so weary!'

'*Momentito*,' he said, disengaging himself.

He strolled back into Jacques's room, leaving Yvonne on the
porch. Laruelle's voice floated up from downstairs. Was it here
he had been betrayed? This very room, perhaps, had been filled
with her cries of love. Books (among which he did not see his
Elizabethan plays) were strewn all over the floor and on the side
of the studio couch nearest the wall, were stacked, as by some
half-repenting poltergeist, almost to the ceiling. What if Jacques,
approaching his design with Tarquin's ravishing strides, had
disturbed this potential avalanche! Grisly Orozco charcoal drawings, of an unexampled horrendousness, snarled down from the
walls. In one, executed by a hand of indisputable genius, harpies
grappled on a smashed bedstead among broken bottles of tequila,
gnashing their teeth. No wonder; the Consul, peering closer,
sought in vain for a sound bottle. He sought in vain around
Jacques's room too. There were two ruddy Riveras. Expressionless Amazons with feet like legs of mutton testified to the oneness
of the toilers with the earth. Over the chevron-shaped windows,
which looked down the Calle Tierra del Fuego, hung a
terrifying picture he hadn't seen before, and took at first to be a
tapestry. Called *Los Borrachones* – why not *Los Borrachos*? – it
resembled something between a primitive and a prohibitionist
poster, remotely under the influence of Michelangelo. In fact, he
now saw, it really amounted to a prohibitionist poster, though of
a century or so back, half a century, God knows what period.
Down, headlong into hades, selfish and florid-faced, into a

tumult of fire-spangled fiends, Medusae, and belching monstrosities, with swallow-dives or awkwardly, with dread backward leaps, shrieking among falling bottles and emblems of broken hopes, plunged the drunkards; up, up, flying palely, selflessly into the light towards heaven, soaring sublimely in pairs, male sheltering female, shielded themselves by angels with abnegating wings, shot the sober. Not all were in pairs however, the Consul noted. A few lone females on the upgrade were sheltered by angels only. It seemed to him these females were casting half-jealous glances downward after their plummeting husbands, some of whose faces betrayed the most unmistakable relief. The Consul laughed, a trifle shakily. It was ridiculous, but still – had anyone ever given a good reason why good and evil should not be thus simply delimited? Elsewhere in Jacques's room cuneiform stone idols squatted like bulbous infants: on one side of the room there was even a line of them chained together. One part of the Consul continued to laugh, in spite of himself, and all this evidence of lost wild talents, at the thought of Yvonne confronted in the aftermath of her passion by a whole row of fettered babies.

'How are you getting on up there, Hugh?' he called up the staircase.

'I think I've got Parián in pretty good focus.'

Yvonne was reading on the balcony, and the Consul gazed back at *Los Borrachones*. Suddenly he felt something never felt before with such shocking certainty. It was that he was in hell himself. At the same time he became possessed of a curious calm. The inner ferment within him, the squalls and eddies of nervousness, were held again in check. He could hear Jacques moving downstairs and soon he would have another drink. That would help, but it was not the thought which calmed him. Parián – the Farolito! he said to himself. The Lighthouse, the lighthouse that invites the storm, and lights it! After all, some time during the day, when they were at the bullthrowing perhaps, he might break away from the others and go there, if only for five minutes, if only for one drink. That prospect filled him with an almost healing love and at this moment, for it was part of the calm, the greatest longing he had ever known. The Farolito!

243

It was a strange place, a place really of the late night and early dawn, which as a rule, like that one other terrible *cantina* in Oaxaca, did not open till four o'clock in the morning. But today being the holiday for the dead it would not close. At first it had appeared to him tiny. Only after he had grown to know it well had he discovered how far back it ran, that it was really composed of numerous little rooms, each smaller and darker than the last, opening one into another, the last and darkest of all being no larger than a cell. These rooms struck him as spots where diabolical plots must be hatched, atrocious murders planned; here, as when Saturn was in Capricorn, life reached bottom. But here also great wheeling thoughts hovered in the brain; while the potter and the field-labourer alike, early risen, paused a moment in the paling doorway, dreaming ... He saw it all now, the enormous drop on one side of the *cantina* into the *barranca* that suggested Kubla Khan: the proprietor, Ramón Diosdado, known as the Elephant, who was reputed to have murdered his wife to cure her neurasthenia, the beggars, hacked by war and covered with sores, one of whom one night after four drinks from the Consul had taken him for the Christ, and falling down on his knees before him, had pinned swiftly under his coat-lapel two medallions, joined to a tiny worked bleeding heart like a pin-cushion, portraying the Virgin of Guadalupe. 'I ah give you the Saint!' He saw all this, feeling the atmosphere of the *cantina* enclosing him already with its certainty of sorrow and evil, and with its certainty of something else too, that escaped him. But he knew: it was peace. He saw the dawn again, watched with lonely anguish from that open door, in the violet-shaded light, a slow bomb bursting over the Sierra Madre – *Sonnenaufgang!* – the oxen harnessed to their carts with wooden disc wheels patiently waiting outside for their drivers, in the sharp cool pure air of heaven. The Consul's longing was so great his soul was locked with the essence of the place as he stood and he was gripped by thoughts like those of the mariner who, sighting the faint beacon of Start Point after a long voyage, knows that soon he will embrace his wife.

Then they returned to Yvonne abruptly. Had he really forgotten her, he wondered. He looked round the room again. Ah, in how many rooms, upon how many studio couches, among how many books, had they found their own love, their marriage, their life together, a life which, in spite of its many disasters, its total calamity indeed – and in spite too of any slight element of falsehood in its inception on her side, her marriage partly into the past, into her Anglo-Scottish ancestry, into the visioned empty ghost-whistling castles in Sutherland, into an emanation of gaunt lowland uncles chumbling shortbread at six o'clock in the morning – had not been without triumph. Yet for how brief a time. Far too soon it had begun to seem too much of a triumph, it had been too good, too horribly unimaginable to lose, impossible finally to bear : it was as if it had become itself its own foreboding that it could not last, a foreboding that was like a presence too, turning his steps towards the taverns again. And how could one begin all over again, as though the Café Chagrin, the Farolito, had never been? Or without them? Could one be faithful to Yvonne and the Farolito both? – Christ, oh pharos of the world, how, and with what blind faith, could one find one's way back, fight one's way back, now, through the tumultuous horrors of five thousand shattering awakenings, each more frightful than the last, from a place where even love could not penetrate, and save in the thickest flames there was no courage? On the wall the drunks eternally plunged. But one of the little Mayan idols seemed to be weeping . . .

'*Ei ei ei ei,*' M. Laruelle was saying, not unlike the little post-man, coming, stamping up the stairs; cocktails, despicable repast. Unperceived the Consul did an odd thing; he took the postcard he'd just received from Yvonne and slipped it under Jacques's pillow. She emerged from the balcony. 'Hullo, Yvonne, where is Hugh? – sorry I've been so long. Let's get on the roof, shall we?' Jacques continued.

Actually all the Consul's reflections had not occupied seven minutes. Still, Laruelle seemed to have been away longer. He saw, following them, following the drinks up the spiral staircase, that in addition to the cocktail shaker and glasses there were canapés and stuffed olives on the tray. Perhaps despite all his seductive aplomb, Jacques had really gone downstairs frightened by the whole business and completely beside himself. While these elaborate preparations were merely the excuse for his flight. Perhaps also it was quite true, the poor fellow had really loved Yvonne – 'Oh, God,' the Consul said, reaching the mirador, to which Hugh had almost simultaneously ascended, climbing, as they approached, the last rungs of the wooden ladder from the catwalk, 'God, that the dream of dark magician in his visioned cave, even while his hand shakes in its last decay – that's the bit I like – were the true end of this so lousy world ... You shouldn't have gone to all this trouble, Jacques.'

He took the binoculars from Hugh, and now, his drink upon a vacant merlon between the marzipan objects, he gazed steadily over the country. But oddly he had not touched this drink. And the calm mysteriously persisted. It was as if they were standing on a lofty golf-tee somewhere. What a beautiful hole this would make, from here to a green out into those trees on the other side of the *barranca*, that natural hazard which some hundred and fifty yards away could be carried by a good full spoon shot, soaring ... Plock. The Golgotha Hole. High up, an eagle drove downwind in one. It had shown lack of imagination to build the local course back up there, remote from the *barranca*. Golf = gouffre = gulf. Prometheus would retrieve lost balls. And on that other side what strange fairways could be contrived, crossed by lone railway lines, humming with telegraph poles, glistening with crazy lies on embankments, over the hills and far away, like youth, like life itself, the course plotted all over these plains, extending far beyond Tomalín, through the jungle, to the Farolito, the nineteenth hole ... The Case is Altered.

'No, Hugh,' he said, adjusting the lenses but without turning round, 'Jacques means the film he made out of *Alastor* before he went to Hollywood, which he shot in a bathtub, what he could of it, and apparently struck the rest together with sequences of ruins cut out of old travelogues, and a jungle hoiked out of *In dunkelste Afrika*, and a swan out of the end of some old Corinne Griffith – Sarah Bernhardt, she was in it too, I understand, while all the time the poet was standing on the shore, and the orchestra was supposed to be doing its best with the *Sacre du Printemps*. I think I forgot the fog.'

Their laughter somewhat cleared the air.

'But beforehand you do have certain *wisions*, as a German director friend of mine used to say, of what your film should be like,' Jacques was telling them, behind him, over by the angels. 'But afterwards, that is another story ... As for the fog, that is after all the cheapest commodity in any studio.'

'Didn't you make any films in Hollywood?' Hugh asked, who a moment ago had almost drifted into a political argument with M. Laruelle.

'Yes ... But I refuse to see them.'

But what on earth was he, the Consul, the Consul wondered, continuing to look out for there on those plains, in that tumulose landscape, through Jacques's binoculars? Was it for some figment of himself, who had once enjoyed such a simple healthy stupid good thing as golf, as blind holes, for example, driving up into a high wilderness of sand-dunes, yes, once with Jacques himself? To climb, and then to see, from an eminence, the ocean with the smoke on the horizon, then, far below, resting near the pin on the green, his new Silver King, twinkling. Ozone! – The Consul could no longer play golf: his few efforts of recent years had proved disastrous ... I should have become a sort of Donne of the fairways at least. Poet of the unreplaced turf. – Who holds the flag while I hole out in three? Who hunts my Zodiac Zone along the shore? And who, upon that last and final green, though I hole out in four, accepts my ten and three score ... Though I have more. The Consul dropped the glasses at last and turned round. And still he had not touched his drink.

'*Alastor, Alastor,*' Hugh strolled over to him saying. 'Who is, was, why, and/or wrote *Alastor*, anyway?'

'Percy Bysshe Shelley.' The Consul leaned against the mirador beside Hugh. 'Another fellow with ideas ... The story I like about Shelley is the one where he just let himself sink to the bottom of the sea – taking several books with him of course – and just stayed there, rather than admit he couldn't swim.'

'Geoffrey don't you think Hugh ought to see something of the *fiesta*,' suddenly Yvonne was saying from the other side, 'since it's his last day? Especially if there's native dancing?'

So it was Yvonne who was 'extricating them from all this', just when the Consul was proposing to stay. 'I wouldn't know,' he said. 'Won't we get native dancing and things in Tomalín? Would you like to, Hugh?'

'Sure. Of course. Anything you say.' Hugh got down awkwardly from the parapet. 'There's still about an hour before the bus leaves, isn't there?'

'I'm sure Jacques will forgive us if we rush off,' Yvonne was saying almost desperately.

'Let me see you downstairs safely then.' Jacques controlled his voice. 'It's too early for the *fête* to be very much but you ought to see Rivera's murals, Hughes, if you haven't already.'

'Aren't you coming, Geoffrey?' Yvonne turned on the staircase. 'Please come,' her eyes said.

'Well, *fiestas* aren't my strong suit. You run along and I'll meet you at the terminal in time for the bus. I have to talk to Jacques here anyway.'

But they had all gone downstairs and the Consul was alone on the mirador. And yet not alone. For Yvonne had left a drink on the merlon by the angels, poor Jacques's was in one of the crenels, Hugh's was on the side parapet. And the cocktail shaker was not empty. Moreover the Consul had not touched his own drink. And still, now, he did not drink. The Consul felt with his right hand his left bicep under his coat. Strength – of a kind – but how to give oneself courage? That fine droll courage of Shelley's; no, that was pride. And pride bade one go on, either go on and kill oneself, or 'straighten out', as so often before, by oneself, with the aid of thirty bottles of beer and staring at the ceiling. But this time it was different. What if courage here implied admission of total defeat, admission that one couldn't swim, admission indeed (though just for a second the thought was not too bad) into a sanatorium? No, to whatever end, it wasn't merely a matter of being 'got away'. No angels nor Yvonne nor Hugh could help him here. As for the demons, they were inside him as well as outside; quiet at the moment – taking their *siesta* perhaps – he was none the less surrounded by them and occupied; they were in possession. The Consul looked at the sun. But he had lost the sun: it was not his sun. Like the truth, it was well-nigh impossible to face; he did not want to go anywhere near it, least of all, sit in its light, facing it. 'Yet I shall face it.' How? When he not only lied to himself, but himself believed the lie and lied back again to those lying factions, among whom was not even their own honour. There was not even a consistent basis to his self-deceptions. How should there be then to his attempts at honesty? 'Horror,' he said. 'Yet I will not give in.' But who was I, how find that I, where had 'I' gone? 'Whatever I do, it shall be deliberately.' And deliberately, it was true, the Consul still refrained from touching his drink. 'The will of man is unconquerable.' Eat? I should eat. So the Consul ate half a canapé. And when M. Laruelle returned the Consul was still gazing drinklessly – where was he gazing? He didn't know himself. 'Do you remember when we went to Cholula,' he said, 'how much dust there was?'

The two men faced each other in silence. 'I don't want to speak to you at all really,' the Consul added after a moment. 'For that matter I wouldn't mind if this was the last time I ever saw you . . . Did you hear me?'

'Have you gone mad?' M. Laruelle exclaimed at last. 'Am I to understand that your wife has come back to you, something I have seen you praying and howling for under the table – really under the table . . . And that you treat her indifferently as this, and still continue only to care where the next drink's coming from?'

To this unanswerable and staggering injustice the Consul had no word; he reached for his cocktail, he held it, smelt it : but somewhere, where it would do little good, a hawser did not give way : he did not drink; he almost smiled pleasantly at M. Laruelle. You might as well start now as later, refusing the drinks. You might as well start now; as later. Later.

The phone rang out and M. Laruelle ran down the staircase. The Consul sat with his face buried in his hands a while, then, leaving his drink still untouched, leaving, yes, all the drinks untouched, he descended to Jacques's room.

M. Laruelle hung up the phone : 'Well,' he said, 'I didn't know you two were acquainted.' He took off his coat and began to undo his tie. 'That was my doctor, asking about *you*. He wants to know if you are not dead already.'

'Oh . . . Oh, that was Vigil, was it?'

'Arturo Díaz Vigil. *Médico. Cirujano* ... Et cetera!'

'Ah,' the Consul said guardedly, running his finger round the inside of his collar. 'Yes. I met him for the first time last night. As a matter of fact he was along at my house this morning.'

M. Laruelle discarded his shirt thoughtfully, saying: 'We're getting in a set before he goes on his holiday.'

The Consul, sitting down, imagined that weird gusty game of tennis under the hard Mexican sunlight, the tennis balls tossed in a sea of error – hard going for Vigil, but what would he care (and who was Vigil? – the good fellow seemed by now unreal to him as some figure one would forbear to greet for fear he was not your acquaintance of the morning, so much as the living double of the actor seen on the screen that afternoon) while the other prepared to enter a shower which, with that queer architectural disregard for decorum exhibited by a people who value decorum above all else, was built in a little recess spendidly visible from both the balcony and the head of the staircase.

'He wants to know if you have changed your mind, if you and Yvonne will ride with him to Guanajuato after all ... Why don't you?'

'How did he know I was here?' The Consul sat up, shaking a little again, though amazed for an instant at his mastery of the situation, that here it turned out there actually *was* someone named Vigil, who had invited one to come to Guanajuato.

'How? How else ... I told him. It's a pity you didn't meet him long ago. That man might really be of some help to you.'

'You might find ... You can be of some help to him today.' The Consul closed his eyes, hearing the doctor's voice again distinctly: 'But now that your *esposa* has come back. But now that your *esposa* has come back ... I would work you with.' 'What?' He opened his eyes ... But the abominable impact on his whole being at this moment of the fact that that hideously elongated cucumiform bundle of blue nerves and gills below the steaming unselfconscious stomach had sought its pleasure in his wife's body brought him trembling to his feet. How loathsome, how incredibly loathsome was reality. He began to walk around the room, his knees giving way every step with a jerk. Books, too many books. The Consul still didn't see his Elizabethan plays. Yet there

250

was everything else, from *Les Joyeuses Bourgeoises de Windsor* to Agrippa d'Aubigné and Collin d'Harleville, from Shelley to Touchard – Lafosse and Tristan l'Hermite. *Beaucoup de bruit pour rien!* Might a soul bathe there or quench its draught? It might. Yet in none of these books would one find one's own suffering. Nor could they show you how to look at an ox-eye daisy. 'But what could have made you tell Vigil I was here, if you didn't know he knew me?' he asked, almost with a sob.

M. Laruelle, overpowered by steam, explanatory fingers in his ears, hadn't heard : 'What did you find to talk about, you two? Vigil and yourself?'

'Alcohol. Insanity. Medullary compression of the gibbus. Our agreements were more or less bilateral.' The Consul, shaking frankly now, normally, peered out through the open doors of the balcony at the volcanoes over which once more hovered puffs of smoke, accompanied by the rattle of musketry; and once he cast a passionate glance up at the mirador, where his untouched drinks lay. 'Mass reflexes, but only the erections of guns, disseminating death,' he said, noticing too that the sounds of the fair were getting louder.

'What was that?'

'How were you proposing to entertain the others supposing they had stayed,' the Consul almost shrieked soundlessly, for he had himself dreadful memories of showers that slithered all over him like soap slipping from quivering fingers, 'by taking a shower?'

And the observation plane was coming back, or Jesus, yes, here, here, out of nowhere, she came whizzing, straight at the balcony, at the Consul, looking for him perhaps, zooming ... Aaaaaaaah! Berumph.

M. Laruelle shook his head; he hadn't heard a sound, a word. Now he came out of the shower and into another little recess screened by a curtain which he used as a dressing-room :

'Lovely day, isn't it? ... I think we shall have thunder.'

'No.'

The Consul on a sudden went to the telephone, also in a kind of recess (the house seemed fuller of such recesses today than usual), found the telephone book, and now, shaking all over, opened it; not Vigil, no, not Vigil, his nerves gibbered, but Guzmán. A.B.C.G. He was sweating now, terribly; it was suddenly as hot in this little niche as in a telephone booth in New York during a heat wave; his hands trembled frantically; 666, Cafeasperina; Guzmán. Erikson 34. He had the number, had forgotten it: the name Zuzugoitea, Zuzugoitea, then Sanabria, came starting out of the book at him: Erikson 35. Zuzugoitea. He'd already forgotten the number, forgotten the number, 34, 35, 666: he was turning back the leaves, a large drop of sweat splashed on the book – this time he thought he saw Vigil's name. But he'd already taken the receiver off the hook, the receiver off the hook, off the hook, he held it the wrong way up, speaking, splashing into the earhole, the mouth-hole, he could not hear – could they hear? see? – the earhole as before: '¿Qué quieres? Who do you want ... God!' he shouted, hanging up. He would need a drink to do this. He ran for the staircase but half-way up, shuddering, in a frenzy, started down again; I brought the tray down. No, the drinks are still up there. He came on the mirador and drank down all the drinks in sight. He heard music. Suddenly about three hundred head of cattle, dead, frozen stiff in the postures of the living, sprang on the slope before the house, were gone. The Consul finished the contents of the cocktail shaker and came downstairs quietly, picked up a paper-backed book lying on the table, sat down and opened it with a long sigh. It was Jean Cocteau's *La Machine infernale*. '*Oui, mon enfant, mon petit enfant,*' he read, '*les choses qui paraissent abominable aux humains, si tu savais, de l'endroit où j'habite, elles ont peu d'importance.*' 'We might have a drink in the square,' he said, closing the book, then opening it again: sortes Shakespeareanae. 'The gods exist, they are the devil,' Baudelaire informed him.

He had forgotten Guzmán. *Los Borrachones* fell eternally into the flames. M. Laruelle, who hadn't noticed a thing, appeared again, resplendent in white flannels, took his tennis racket from the top of a bookcase; the Consul found his stick and his dark glasses, and they went down the iron spiral staircase together.

'*Absolutamente necesario.*' Outside the Consul paused, turning ...

No se puede vivir sin amar, were the words on the house. In the street there was now not a breath of wind and they walked a while without speaking, listening to the babel of the *fiesta* which grew still louder as they approached the town. Street of the Land of Fire. 666.

– M. Laruelle, possibly because he was walking on the higher part of the banked street, now seemed even taller than he was, and beside him, below, the Consul felt a moment uncomfortably dwarfed, childish. Years before in their boyhood this position had been reversed; then the Consul was the taller. But whereas the Consul had stopped growing when seventeen at five foot eight or nine, M. Laruelle kept on through the years under different skies until now he had grown out of the Consul's reach. Out of reach? Jacques was a boy of whom the Consul could still remember certain things with affection : the way he pronounced 'vocabulary' to rhyme with 'foolery', or 'bible' with 'runcible'. Runcible spoon. And he'd grown into a man who could shave and put on his socks by himself. But out of his reach, hardly. Up there, across the years, at his height of six foot three or four, it did not seem too outlandish to suggest that his influence still reached him strongly. If not, why the English-looking tweed coat similar to the Consul's own, those expensive, expressive English tennis shoes of the kind you could walk in, the English white trousers of twenty-one inches breadth, the English shirt worn English-fashion open at the neck, the extraordinary scarf that suggested M. Laruelle had once won a half-blue at the Sorbonne or something? There was even, in spite of his slight stoutness, an English, almost an ex-consular sort of litheness about his movements. Why should Jacques be playing tennis at all? Have you forgotten it, Jacques, how I myself taught you, that summer long ago, behind the Taskersons', or at the new public courts in Leasowe? On just such afternoons as this. So brief their friendship and yet, the Consul thought, how enormous, how all-permeating, permeating Jacques's whole life, that influence had been, an influence that showed even in his choice of books, his work – why had Jacques come to Quauhnahuac in the first place? Was it not much as though he, the Consul, from afar, had willed it, for obscure purposes of his own? The man he'd met here eighteen months ago seemed, though hurt in his art and destiny, the most completely unequivocal and sincere Frenchman he'd ever known. Nor was the seriousness of M. Laruelle's face, seen now against the sky between houses, compatible with cynical weakness. Was it not almost as though the Consul had tricked him into dishonour and misery, willed, even, his betrayal of him?

'Geoffrey,' M. Laruelle said suddenly, quietly, 'has she really come back?'

'It looks like it, doesn't it?' They both paused, to light their pipes, and the Consul noticed Jacques was wearing a ring he had not seen, a scarab, of simple design, cut into a chalcedony: whether Jacques would remove it to play tennis he didn't know, but the hand that wore it was trembling, while the Consul's was now steady.

'But I mean really come back,' M. Laruelle continued in French as they went forward up the Calle Tierra del Fuego. 'She hasn't merely come down on a visit, or to see you out of curiosity, or on the basis that you'll just be friends, and so on, if you don't mind my asking.'

'As a matter of fact I rather do.'

'Get this straight, Geoffrey, I'm thinking of Yvonne, not you.'

'Get it a little straighter still. You're thinking of yourself.'

'But to*day* – I can see how that's – I suppose you were tight at the ball. I didn't go. But if so why aren't you back home thanking God and trying to rest and sober up instead of making everyone wretched by taking them to Tomalín? Yvonne looks tired out.'

The words drew faint weary furrows across the Consul's mind constantly filling with harmless deliriums. Nevertheless his French was fluent and rapid:

'How do you mean you suppose I was tight when Vigil told you so on the phone? And weren't you suggesting just now I take Yvonne to Guanajuato with him? Perhaps you imagined if you could insinuate yourself into our company on that proposed trip she would miraculously cease to be tired, even though it's fifty times farther than to Tomalín.'

'When I suggested you go it hadn't quite entered my head she'd only arrived this morning.'

'Well – I forget whose idea Tomalín was,' the Consul said. Can it be I discussing Yvonne with Jacques, discussing *us* like this? Though after all they had done it before. 'But I haven't explained just how Hugh fits into the picture, have –'

' – *Eggs!*' had the jovial proprietor of the *abarrotes* called down from the pavement above them to their right.

'*Mescalito!*' had somebody else whizzed past carrying a length of plank, some barfly of his acquaintance; or was that this morning?

– 'And on second thoughts I don't think I'll trouble.'

Soon the town loomed up before them. They had reached the foot of Cortés Palace. Near them children (encouraged by a man also in dark glasses who seemed familiar, and to whom the Consul motioned) were swinging round and round a telegraph pole on an improvised whirligig, a little parody of the Great Carrousel up the hill in the square. Higher, on a terrace of the Palace (because it was also the ayuntamiento), a soldier stood at ease with a rifle; on a still higher terrace dawdled the tourists: vandals in sandals looking at the murals.

The Consul and M. Laruelle had a good view of the Rivera frescoes from where they were. 'You get an impression from here those tourists can't up here,' M. Laruelle said, 'they're too close.' He was pointing with his tennis racket. 'The slow darkening of the murals as you look from right to left. It seems somehow to symbolize the gradual imposition of the Spaniards' conquering will upon the Indians. Do you see what I mean?'

'If you stood at a greater distance still it might seem to symbolize for you the gradual imposition of the Americans' conquering friendship from left to right upon the Mexicans,' the Consul said with a smile, removing his dark glasses, 'upon those who have to look at the frescoes and remember who paid for them.'

The part of the murals he was gazing at portrayed, he knew, the Tlahuicans who had died for this valley in which he lived. The artist had represented them in their battle dress, wearing the masks and skins of wolves and tigers. As he looked it was as though these figures were gathering silently together. Now they had become one figure, one immense, malevolent creature staring back at him. Suddenly this creature appeared to start forward, then make a violent motion. It might have been, indeed unmistakably it was, telling him to go away.

'See, there's Yvonne and Hugues waving at you.' M. Laruelle waved back his tennis racket. Do you know I think they make rather a formidable couple,' he added, with a half pained, half malicious smile.

There they were too, he saw, the formidable couple, up by the frescoes: Hugh with his foot on the rail of the Palace balcony, looking over their heads at the volcanoes perhaps: Yvonne with her back to them now. She was leaning against the rail facing the murals, then she turned sideways towards Hugh to say something. They did not wave again.

M. Laruelle and the Consul decided against the cliff path. They floated along the base of the Palace then, opposite the Banco de Crédito y Ejidal, turned left up the steep narrow road climbing to the square. Toiling, they edged into the Palace wall to let a man on horseback pass, a fine-featured Indian of the poorer class, dressed in soiled white loose clothes. The man was singing gaily to himself. But he nodded to them courteously as if to thank them. He seemed about to speak, reining in his little horse – on either side of which chinked two saddle-bags, and upon whose rump was branded the number seven – to a slow walk beside them, as they ascended the hill. *Jingle jingle little surcingle*. But the man, riding slightly in front, did not speak and at the top he suddenly waved his hand and galloped away, singing.

The Consul felt a pang. Ah, to have a horse, and gallop away, singing, away to someone you loved perhaps, into the heart of all the simplicity and peace in the world; was not that like the opportunity afforded man by life itself? Of course not. Still, just for a moment, it had seemed that it was.

'What is it Goethe says about the horse?' he said. ' "Weary of liberty he suffered himself to be saddled and bridled, and was ridden to death for his pains." '

In the *plaza* the tumult was terrific. Once again they could scarcely hear one another speak. A boy dashed up to them selling papers. *Sangriento Combate en Mora de Ebro. Los Aviones de los Rebeldes Bombardean Barcelona. Es inevitable la muerte del Papa.* The Consul started; this time, an instant, he had thought the headlines referred to himself. But of course it was only the poor Pope whose death was inevitable. As if everyone else's death were not inevitable too! In the middle of the square a man was climbing a slippery flagpole in a complicated manner necessitating ropes and spikes. The huge carrousel, set near the bandstand, was thronged by peculiar long-nosed wooden horses mounted on whorled pipes, dipping majestically as they revolved with a slow piston-like circulation. Boys on roller skates, holding to the stays of the umbrella structure, were being whirled around yelling with joy, while the uncovered machine driving it hammered away like a steam pump : then they were whizzing. 'Barcelona' and 'Valencia' mingled with the crashes and cries against which the Consul's nerves were wooled. Jacques was pointing to the pictures on the panels running entirely around the inner wheel that was set horizontally and attached to the top of the central revolving pillar. A mermaid reclined in the sea combing her hair and singing to the sailors of a five-funnelled battleship. A daub which apparently represented Medea sacrificing her children turned out to be of performing monkeys. Five jovial-looking stags peered, in all their monarchical unlikelihood, out of a Scottish glen at them, then went tearing out of sight. While a fine Pancho Villa with handlebar moustaches galloped for dear life after them all. But stranger than these was a panel showing lovers, a man and a woman reclining by a river. Though childish and crude it had about it a somnambulistic quality and something too of truth, of the pathos of love. The lovers were depicted as awkwardly askance. Yet one felt that really they were wrapped in each other's arms by this river at dusk among gold stars. Yvonne, he thought, with sudden tenderness, where are you, my darling? Darling ... For a moment he had thought her by his side. Then he remembered she was lost; then that no, this feeling belonged to yesterday, to the months of lonely torment behind him. She was not lost at all, she was here all the time, here now, or as good as here. The Consul wanted to raise his head, and shout for joy, like the horseman : she is here! Wake up, she has come back again! Sweetheart, darling, I love you! A desire to find her immediately and take her home (where in the garden still lay the white bottle of Tequila Añejo de Jalisco, unfinished), to put a stop to this senseless trip, to be, above all, alone with her, seized him, and a desire, too, to lead immediately again a normal happy life with her, a life, for instance, in which such innocent happiness as all these good people around him were enjoying, was possible. But had they ever led a normal happy life? Had such a thing as a normal happy life ever been possible for them? It had ... Yet what about that belated postcard, now under Laruelle's pillow? It proved the lonely torment unnecessary, proved, even, he must have wanted it. Would anything really have been *changed* had he received the card at the right time? He doubted it. After all, her other letters – Christ, again, where were they? – had not changed anything. If he had not read them properly, perhaps. But he had not read them properly. And soon he would forget about what had been done with the card. Nevertheless the desire remained – like an echo of Yvonne's own – to find her, to find her now, to reverse their doom, it was a desire amounting almost to a resolution ... Raise your head, Geoffrey Firmin, breathe your prayer of thankfulness, act before it is too late. But the weight of a great hand seemed to be pressing his head down. The desire passed. At the same time, as though a cloud had come over the sun, the aspect of the fair had completely altered for him. The merry grinding of the roller skates, the cheerful if ironic music, the cries of the little children on their goose-necked steeds, the procession of queer pictures – all this had suddenly become transcendentally awful and tragic, distant, transmuted, as it were some final impression on the senses of what the earth was like, carried over into an obscure region of death, a gathering thunder of immedicable sorrow; the Consul needed a drink ...

– 'Tequila,' he said. '*¿Una?*' the boy said sharply, and M. Laruelle called for gaseosa.

'*Sí, señores.*' The boy swept the table. '*Una tequila y una gaseosa.*' He brought immediately a bottle of El Nilo for M. Laruelle together with salt, chile, and a saucer of sliced lemons.

The café, which was in the centre of a little railed-in garden at the edge of the square among trees, was called the Paris. And in fact it was reminiscent of Paris. A simple fountain dripped near. The boy brought them camarones, red shrimps in a saucer, and had to be told again to get the tequila.

At last it arrived.

'Ah – ' the Consul said, though it was the chalcedony ring that had been shaking.

'Do you really like it?' M. Laruelle asked him, and the Consul, sucking a lemon, felt the fire of the tequila run down his spine like lightning striking a tree which thereupon, miraculously, blossoms.

'What are you shaking for?' the Consul asked him.

M. Laruelle stared at him, he gave a nervous glance over his shoulder, he made as if absurdly to twang his tennis racket on his toe, but remembering the press, stood it up against his chair awkwardly.

'What are *you* afraid of – ' the Consul was mocking him.

'I admit, I feel confused . . .' M. Laruelle cast a more protracted glance over his shoulder. 'Here, give me some of your poison.' He leaned forward and took a sip of the Consul's tequila and remained bent over the thimble-shaped glass of terrors, a moment since brimming.

'Like it?'

' – like Oxygénée, and petrol . . . If I ever start to drink that stuff, Geoffrey, you'll know I'm done for.'

'It's mescal with me . . . Tequila, no, that is healthful . . . and delightful. Just like beer. Good for you. But if I ever start to drink mescal again, I'm afraid, yes, that would be the end,' the Consul said dreamily.

'Name of a name of God,' shuddered M. Laruelle.

'You're not afraid of Hugh, are you?' The Consul, mocking, pursued – while it struck him that all the desolation of the months following Yvonne's departure were now mirrored in the *other's* eyes. 'Not jealous of him, by any chance, are you?'

'Why should – '

'But you are thinking, aren't you, that in all this time I have never once told you the truth about my life.' the Consul said, 'isn't that right?'

'No ... For perhaps once or twice, Geoffrey, without knowing it, you have told the truth. No, I truly want to help. But, as usual, you don't give me a chance.'

'I have never told you the truth. I know it, it is worse than terrible. But as Shelley says, the cold world shall not know. And the tequila hasn't cured your trembling.'

'No, I am afraid,' M. Laruelle said.

'But I thought you were never afraid ... *Un otro tequila*,' the Consul told the boy, who came running, repeating sharply, ' – *uno?*'

M. Laruelle glanced round after the boy as if it had been in his mind to say '*dos*' : 'I'm afraid of you,' he said, 'Old Bean.'

The Consul heard, after half the second tequila, every now and then, familiar well-meaning phrases. 'It's hard to say this. As man to man, I don't care who she is. Even if the miracle has occurred. Unless you cut it out altogether.'

The Consul however was looking past M. Laruelle at the flying-boats which were at a little distance : the machine itself was feminine, graceful as a ballet dancer, its iron skirts of gondolas whirling higher and higher. Finally it whizzed round with a tense whipping and whining, then its skirts drooped chastely again when for a time there was stillness, only the breeze stirring them. And how beautiful, beautiful, beautiful –

'For God's sake. Go home to bed ... Or stay here. I'll find the others. And tell them you're not going ...'

'But I am going,' the Consul said, commencing to take one of the shrimps apart. 'Not camarones,' he added. 'Cabrones. That's what the Mexicans call them.' Placing his thumbs at the base of both ears he waggled his fingers. '*Cabrón*. You too, perhaps ... Venus is a horned star.'

'What about the damage you've done, to *her* life ... After all your howling ... If you've got her back ! – If you've got this chance – '

'You are interfering with my great battle,' the Consul said, gazing past M. Laruelle at an advertisement at the foot of the fountain : *Peter Lorre en Las Manos de Orlac, a las 6.30 p.m.* 'I have to have a drink or two now, myself – so long as it isn't mescal of course – else I shall become confused, like yourself.'

' – the truth is, I suppose, that sometimes, when you've calculated the amount exactly, you do see more clearly,' M. Laruelle was admitting a minute later.

'Against death.' The Consul sank back easily in his chair. 'My battle for the survival of the human consciousness.'

'But certainly not the things so important to us despised sober people, on which the balance of any human situation depends. It's precisely your inability to see them, Geoffrey, that turns them into the instruments of the disaster you have created yourself. Your Ben Jonson, for instance, or perhaps it was Christopher Marlowe, your Faust man, saw the Carthaginians fighting on his big toe-nail. That's like the kind of clear seeing you indulge in. Everything seems perfectly clear, because indeed it is perfectly clear, in terms of the toe-nail.'

'Have a devilled scorpion,' invited the Consul, pushing over the camarones with extended arm. 'A bedevilled *cabrón*.'

'I admit the efficacy of your tequila – but do you realize that while you're battling against death, or whatever you imagine you're doing, while what is mystical in you is being released, or whatever it is you imagine is being released, while you're enjoying all this, do you realize what extraordinary allowances are being made for you by the world which has to cope with you, yes, are even now being made by *me*?'

The Consul was gazing upward dreamily at the Ferris wheel near them, huge, but resembling an enormously magnified child's structure of girders and angle brackets, nuts and bolts, in Meccano; tonight it would be lit up, its steel twigs caught in the emerald pathos of the trees; the *wheel of the law, rolling*; and it bore thinking of too that the carnival was not going in earnest now. What a hullabaloo there would be later! His eye fell on another little carrousel, a dazzle-painted wobbling child's toy, and he saw himself as a child making up his mind to go on it, hesitating, missing the next opportunity, and the next, missing all the opportunities finally, until it was too late. What opportunities, precisely, did he mean? A voice on the radio somewhere began to sing a song: *Samaritana mía, alma pía, bebe en tu boca linda,* then went dead. It had sounded like Samaritana.

'And you forget what you exclude from this, shall we say, feeling of omniscience. And at night, I imagine, or between drink and drink, which is a sort of night, what you have excluded, as if it resented that exclusion, returns –'

'I'll say it returns,' the Consul said, listening at this point. 'There are other minor deliriums too, *meteora*, which you can pick out of the air before your eyes, like gnats. And this is what people seem to think is the end ... But d.t.'s are only the beginning, the music round the portal of the Qliphoth, the overture, conducted by the God of Flies ... Why do people see rats? These are the sort of questions that ought to concern the world, Jacques. Consider the word remorse. *Remors. Mordeo, mordere. La Mordida* ! *Agenbite* too ... And why *rongeur*? Why all this biting, all those rodents, in the etymology?'

'*Facilis est descensus Averno* ... It's too easy.'

'You deny the greatness of my battle? Even if I win. And I shall certainly win, if I want to,' the Consul added, aware of a man near them standing on a step-ladder nailing a board to a tree.

'*Je crois que le vautour est doux à Prométhée et que les Ixion se plaisent en Enfers.*'

– *¡Box!*

'To say nothing of what you lose, lose, lose, are losing, man. You fool, you stupid fool ... You've even been insulated from the responsibility of genuine suffering ... Even the suffering you do endure is largely unnecessary. Actually spurious. It lacks the very basis you require of it for its tragic nature. You deceive yourself. For instance that you're drowning your sorrows ... Because of Yvonne and me. But Yvonne knows. And so do I. And so do you. That Yvonne wouldn't have been aware. If you hadn't been so drunk all the time. To know what she was doing. Or care. And what's more. The same thing is bound to happen again you fool it will happen again if you don't pull yourself together. I can see the writing on the wall. Hullo.'

M. Laruelle wasn't there at all; he had been talking to himself. The Consul stood up and finished his tequila. But the writing was there, all right, if not on the wall. The man had nailed his board to the tree.

The Consul realized, leaving the Paris, he was in a state of drunkenness, so to speak, rare with him. His steps teetered to the left, he could not make them incline to the right. He knew in which direction he was going, towards the Bus Terminal, or rather the little dark *cantina* adjacent to it kept by the widow Gregorio, who herself was half English and had lived in Manchester, and to whom he owed fifty centavos he'd suddenly made up his mind to pay back. But simply he could not steer a straight course there ... *Oh we all walk the wibberley wobberley* –

Dies Faustus ... The Consul looked at his watch. Just for one moment, one horrible moment in the Paris, he had thought it night, that it was one of those days the hours slid by like corks bobbing astern, and the morning was carried away by the wings of the angel of night, all in a trice, but tonight quite the reverse seemed to be happening : it was still only five to two. It was already the longest day in his entire experience, a lifetime ; he had not only not missed the bus, he would have plenty of time for more drinks. If only he were not drunk ! The Consul strongly disapproved of this drunkenness.

Children accompanied him, gleefully aware of his plight. Money, money, money, they gibbered. O.K. mistair ! Where har you go ? Their cries grew discouraged, fainter, utterly disappointed as they clung to his trousers leg. He would have liked to give them something. Yet he did not wish to draw more attention to himself. He had caught sight of Hugh and Yvonne, trying their hands at a shooting gallery. Hugh was shooting, Yvonne watched ; *phut, pssst, pffjjng* ; and Hugh brought down a procession of wooden ducks.

The Consul stumbled on without being seen, passing a booth where you could have your photograph taken with your sweetheart against a terrifying thunderous background, lurid and green, with a charging bull, and Popocatepetl in eruption, past, his face averted, the shabby little closed British Consulate, where the lion and the unicorn on the faded blue shield regarded him mournfully. This was shameful. But we are still at your service, in spite of all, they seemed to say. *Dieu et mon droit.* The children had given him up. However he had lost his bearings. He was reaching the edge of the fair. Mysterious tents were shut up here, or lying collapsed, enfolded on themselves. They appeared almost human, the former kind awake, expectant; the latter with the wrinkled crumpled aspect of men asleep, but longing even in unconsciousness to stretch their limbs. Farther on at the final frontiers of the fair, it was the day of the dead indeed. Here the tent booths and galleries seemed not so much asleep as lifeless, beyond hope of revival. Yet there were faint signs of life after all, he saw.

At a point outside the *plaza*'s periphery, half on the pavement, there was another, utterly desolated, 'safe' roundabout. The little chairs circulated beneath a frilled canvas pyramid that twirled slowly for half a minute, then stopped, when it looked just like the hat of the bored Mexican who tended it. Here it was, this little Popocatepetl, nestling far away from the swooping flying-machines, far from the Great Wheel, existing – for whom did it exist, the Consul wondered. Belonging neither to the children nor the adults it stood, untenanted, as one might imagine the whirligig of adolescence as resting deserted, if youth suspected it of offering an excitement so apparently harmless, choosing rather what in the proper square swooned in agonizing ellipses beneath some gigantic canopy.

The Consul walked on a little farther, still unsteadily; he thought he had his bearings again, then stopped:

¡BRAVA ATRACCIÓN!
10 C. MÁQUINA INFERNAL

he read, half struck by some coincidence in this. Wild attraction. The huge looping-the-loop machine, empty, but going full blast over his head in this dead section of the fair, suggested some huge evil spirit, screaming in its lonely hell, its limbs writhing, smiting the air like flails of paddlewheels. Obscured by a tree, he hadn't seen it before. The machine stopped also...

' – Mistair. Money money money.' 'Mistair ! Where har you go?'

The wretched children had spotted him again; and his penalty for avoiding them was to be drawn inexorably, though with as much dignity as possible, into boarding the monster. And now, his ten centavos paid to a Chinese hunchback in a retiform visored tennis cap, he was alone, irrevocably and ridiculously alone, in a little confession box. After a while, with violent bewildering convulsions, the thing started to go. The confession boxes, perched at the end of menacing steel cranks, zoomed upwards and heavily fell. The Consul's own cage hurled up again with a powerful thrusting, hung for a moment upside down at the top, while the other cage, which significantly was empty, was at the bottom, then, before this situation had been grasped, crashed down, paused a moment at the other extremity, only to be lifted upwards again cruelly to the highest point where for an interminable, intolerable period of suspension, it remained motionless. – The Consul, like that poor fool who was bringing light to the world, was hung upside down over it, with only a scrap of woven wire between himself and death. There, above him, poised the world, with its people stretching out down to him, about to fall off the road on to his head, or into the sky. 999. The people hadn't been there before. Doubtless, following the children, they had assembled to watch him. Obliquely he was aware that he was without physical fear of death, as he would have been without fear at this moment of anything else that might sober him up; perhaps this had been his main idea. But he did not like it. This was not amusing. It was doubtless another example of Jacques's – Jacques? – unnecessary suffering. And it was scarcely a dignified position for an ex-representative of His Majesty's government to find himself in, though it was symbolic, of what he could not conceive, but it was undoubtedly symbolic. Jesus. All at once, terribly, the confession boxes had begun to go in reverse : Oh, the Consul said, oh; for the sensation of falling was now as if terribly behind him, unlike anything, beyond experience; certainly this recessive unwinding was not like looping-the-loop in a plane, where the movement was quickly over, the only strange feeling one of increased weight; as a sailor he disapproved of that feeling too, but this – ah, my God ! Everything was falling out of his pockets, was being wrested from him, torn away, a fresh article at each whirling,

sickening, plunging, retreating, unspeakable circuit, his notecase, pipe, keys, his dark glasses he had taken off, his small
change he did not have time to imagine being pounced on by
the children after all, he was being emptied out, returned empty,
his stick, his passport – had that been his passport? He didn't
know if he'd brought it with him. Then he remembered he had
brought it. Or hadn't brought it. It could be difficult even for a
Consul to be without a passport in Mexico. Ex-consul. What did
it matter? Let it go! There was a kind of fierce delight in this
final acceptance. Let everything go! Everything particularly
that provided means of ingress or egress, went bond for, gave
meaning or character, or purpose or identity to that frightful
bloody nightmare he was forced to carry around with him everywhere upon his back, that went by the name of Geoffrey Firmin,
late of His Majesty's Navy, later still of His Majesty's Consular
Service, later still of – Suddenly it struck him that the China-
man was asleep, that the children, the people had gone, that this
would go on for ever; no one could stop the machine . . . It was
over.

And yet not over. On terra firma the world continued to spin
madly round; houses, whirligigs, hotels, cathedrals, *cantinas*,
volcanoes: it was difficult to stand up at all. He was conscious of
people laughing at him but, what was more surprising, of his
possessions being restored to him, one by one. The child who
had his notecase withdrew it from him playfully before returning
it. No: she still had something in her other hand, a crumpled
paper. The Consul thanked her for it firmly. Some telegram of
Hugh's. His stick, his glasses, his pipe, unbroken; yet not his
favourite pipe; and no passport. Well, definitely he could not
have brought it. Putting his other things back in his pockets he
turned a corner, very unsteadily, and slumped down on a bench.
He replaced his dark glasses, set his pipe in his mouth, crossed
his legs, and, as the world gradually slowed down, assumed the
bored expression of an English tourist sitting in the Luxembourg
Gardens.

Children, he thought, how charming they were at heart. The
very same kids who had besieged him for money, had now
brought him back even the smallest of his small change and

then, touched by his embarrassment, had scurried away without waiting for a reward. Now he wished he had given them something. The little girl had gone also. Perhaps this was her exercise book open on the bench. He wished he had not been so brusque with her, that she would come back, so that he could give her the book. Yvonne and he should have had children, would have had children, could have had children, should have . . .

In the exercise book he made out with difficulty :

Escruch is an old man. He lives in London. He lives alone in a large house. Scrooge is a rich man but he never gives to the poor. His is a miser. No one loves Scrooge and Scrooge loves no one. He has no friends. He is alone in the world. The man (*el hombre*): the house (*la casa*): the poor (*los pobres*): he lives (*él vive*): he gives (*él da*): he has no friends (*él no tiene amigos*): he loves (*él ama*): old (*viejo*): large (*grande*): no one (*nadie*): rich (*rico*): Who is Scrooge? Where does he live? Is Scrooge rich or poor? Has he friends? How does he live? Alone. World. On.

At last the earth had stopped spinning with the motion of the Infernal Machine. The last house was still, the last tree rooted again. It was seven minutes past two by his watch. And he was cold stone sober. How horrible was the feeling. The Consul closed the exercise book : bloody old Scrooge; how queer to meet him here!

– Gay-looking soldiers, grimy as sweeps, strolled up and down the avenues with a jaunty unmilitary gait. Their officers, smartly uniformed, sat on benches, leaning forward over their swagger canes as if petrified by remote strategical thoughts. An Indian carrier with a towering load of chairs loped along the Avenida Guerrero. A madman passed, wearing, in the manner of a life-belt, an old bicycle tyre. With a nervous movement he continually shifted the injured tread round his neck. He muttered to the Consul, but waiting neither for reply nor reward, took off the tyre and flung it far ahead of him towards a booth, then followed unsteadily, stuffing something in his mouth from a tin bait jar. Picking up the tyre he flung it far ahead again, repeating this process, to the irreducible logic of which he appeared eternally committed, until out of sight.

The Consul felt a clutch at his heart and half rose. He had caught sight of Hugh and Yvonne again at a booth; she was buying tortilla from an old woman. While the woman plastered the tortilla for her with cheese and tomato sauce, a touchingly dilapidated little policeman, doubtless one on strike, with cap askew, in soiled baggy trousers, leggings, and a coat several sizes too large for him, tore off a piece of lettuce and, with a consummately courteous smile, handed it to her. They were having a splendid time, it was obvious. They ate their tortillas, grinning at each other as the sauce dripped from their fingers; now Hugh had brought out his handkerchief; he was wiping a smear from Yvonne's cheek, while they roared with laughter, in which the policeman joined. What had happened to their plot now, their plot to get him away? Never mind. The clutch at his heart had become a cold iron grip of persecution which had been stayed only by a certain relief; for how, had Jacques communicated his little anxieties to them, would they now be here, laughing? Still, one never knew; and a policeman was a policeman, even if on strike, and friendly, and the Consul was more afraid of the police than death. He placed a small stone upon the child's exercise book, leaving it on the bench, and dodged behind a stall to avoid them. He got a glimpse through the boards of the man still half-way up the slippery pole, neither near enough to the top nor the bottom to be certain of reaching either in comfort, avoided a huge turtle dying in two parallel streams of blood on the pavement outside a sea-food restaurant, and entered El Bosque with a steady gait, as once before, similarly obsessed, at a run : there was no sign of the bus yet; he had twenty minutes, probably more.

The Terminal Cantina El Bosque, however, seemed so dark that even with his glasses off he had to stop dead ... *Mi ritrovai in una bosca oscura* – or *selva*? No matter. The *Cantina* was well named, 'The Boskage'. This darkness, though, was associated in his mind with velvet curtains, and there they were, behind the shadowy bar, velvet or velveteen curtains, too dirty and full of dust to be black, partially screening the entrance to the back room, which one could never be sure was private. For some reason the *fiesta* had not overflowed in here; the place – a

Mexican relative of the English 'Jug and Bottle', chiefly dedicated to those who drank 'off' the premises, in which there was only one spindly iron table and two stools at the bar, and which, facing east, became progressively darker as the sun, to those who noticed such things, climbed higher into the sky – was deserted, as usual at this hour. The Consul groped his way forward. 'Señora Gregorio,' he called softly, yet with an agonized impatient quaver in his voice. It had been difficult to find his voice at all; he now needed another drink badly. The word echoed through the back of the house; Gregorio; there was no answer. He sat down, while gradually the shapes about him became more clearly defined, shapes of barrels behind the bar, of bottles. Ah, the poor turtle ! – The thought struck at a painful tangent. – There were big green barrels of jerez, habanero, catalán, parras, zarzamora, málaga, durazno, membrillo, raw alcohol at a peso a litre, tequila, mescal, rumpope. As he read these names and, as if it were a dreary dawn outside, the *cantina* grew lighter to his eyes, he heard voices in his ears again, a single voice above the muted roar of the fair : 'Geoffrey Firmin, this is what it is like to die, just this and no more, an awakening from a dream in a dark place, in which, as you see, are present the means of escape from yet another nightmare. But the choice is up to you. You are not invited to use those means of escape; it is left up to your judgement; to obtain them it is necessary only to – ' 'Señora Gregorio,' he repeated, and the echo came back : 'Orio.'

In one corner of the bar someone had apparently once begun a small mural, aping the Great Mural in the Palace, two or three figures only, peeling and inchoate Tlahuicans. – There was the sound of slow, dragging footsteps from behind; the widow appeared, a little old woman wearing an unusually long and shabby rustling black dress. Her hair that he recalled as grey seemed to have been recently hennaed, or dyed red, and though it hung untidily in front, it was twisted up at the back into a Psyche knot. Her face, which was beaded with perspiration, evinced the most extraordinary waxen pallor; she looked careworn, wasted with suffering, yet at the sight of the Consul her tired eyes gleamed, kindling her whole expression to one of wry amusement in which there appeared also both a determination and a certain weary expectancy. 'Mescal posseebly,' she said, in a queer, chanting half-bantering tone, 'Mescal imposseebly.' But she made no move to draw the Consul a drink, perhaps because of his debt, an objection he immediately disposed of by laying a tostón on the counter. She smiled almost slyly as she edged towards the mescal barrel.

'*No, tequila, por favor,*' he said.

'*Un obsequio*' – she handed him the tequila. 'Where do you laugh now?'

'I still laugh in the Calle Nicaragua, *cincuenta dos*,' the Consul replied, smiling. 'You mean "live", Señora Gregorio, not "laugh", *con permiso*.'

'Remember,' Señora Gregorio corrected him gently, slowly, 'remember my English. Well, so it is,' she sighed, drawing a small glass of málaga for herself from the barrel chalked with that name. 'Here's to your love. What's my names?' She pushed towards him a saucer filled with salt that was speckled with orange-coloured pepper.

'*Lo mismo.*' The Consul drank the tequila down. 'Geoffrey Firmin.'

Señora Gregorio brought him a second tequila; for a time they regarded one another without speaking. 'So it is,' she repeated at last, sighing once more; and there was pity in her voice for the Consul. 'So it is. You must take it as it come. It can't be helped.'

'No, it can't be helped.'

'If you har your wife you would lose all things in that love,' Señora Gregorio said, and the Consul, understanding that somehow this conversation was being taken up where it had been left off weeks before, probably at the point where Yvonne had abandoned him for the seventh time that evening, found himself not caring to change the basis of shared misery on which their relationship rested – for Gregorio had really abandoned her before he died – by informing her his wife had come back, was indeed, perhaps, not fifty feet away. 'Both minds is occupied in one thing, so you can't lose it,' she continued sadly.

'*Sí,*' said the Consul.

'So it is. If your mind is occupied with all things, then you

270

never lose your mind. Your minds, your life – your everything in it. Once when I was a girl I never used to think I live like I laugh now. I always used to dream about kernice dreams. Nice clothes, nice hairts – "Everything is good for me just now" it was one time, theatres, but everything – now, I don't think of but nothing but trouble, trouble, trouble, trouble; and trouble comes ... So it is.'

'*Sí*, Señora Gregorio.'

'Of course I was a kernice girl from home,' she was saying. 'This – ' she glanced contemptuously round the dark little bar, 'was never in my mind. Life changes, you know, you can never drink of it.'

'Not "drink of it", Señora Gregorio, you mean "think of it".'

'Never drink of it. Oh, well,' she said, pouring out a litre of raw alcohol for a poor noseless peon who had entered silently and was standing in a corner, 'a kernice life among kernice people and now what?'

Señora Gregorio shuffled off into the back room, leaving the Consul alone. He sat with his second large tequila untouched for some minutes. He imagined himself drinking it yet had not the will to stretch out his hand to take it, as if it were something once long and tediously desired but which, an overflowing cup suddenly within reach, had lost all meaning. The *cantina*'s emptiness, and a strange ticking like that of some beetle, within that emptiness, began to get on his nerves; he looked at his watch: only seventeen minutes past two. This was where the tick was coming from. Again he imagined himself taking the drink: again his will failed him. Once the swing door opened, someone glanced round quickly to satisfy himself, went out: was that Hugh, Jacques? Whoever it was had seemed to possess the features of both, alternately. Somebody else entered and, though the next instant the Consul felt this was not the case, went right through into the back room, peering round furtively. A starving pariah dog with the appearance of having lately been skinned had squeezed itself in after the last man; it looked up at the Consul with beady, gentle eyes. Then, thrusting down its poor wrecked dinghy of a chest, from which raw withered breasts drooped, it began to bow and scrape before him. Ah, the ingress of the animal kingdom! Earlier it had been the insects; now these were closing in upon him again, these animals, these people without ideas: '*Dispense usted, por Dios,*' he whispered to the dog, then wanting to say something kind, added, stooping, a phrase read or heard in youth or childhood: 'For God sees how timid and beautiful you really are, and the thoughts of hope that go with you like little white birds –'

The Consul stood up and suddenly declaimed to the dog:

'Yet this day, *pichicho*, shalt thou be with me in –' But the dog hopped away in terror on three legs and slunk under the door.

The Consul finished his tequila in one gulp; he went to the counter. 'Señora Gregorio,' he called; he waited, casting his eyes about the *cantina*, which seemed to have grown very much lighter. And the echo came back: 'Orio.' – Why, the mad pictures of the wolves! He had forgotten they were here. The materialized pictures, six or seven of considerable length, completed, in the defection of the muralist, the decoration of El Bosque. They were precisely the same in every detail. All showed the same sleigh being pursued by the same pack of wolves. The wolves hunted the occupants of the sleigh the entire length of the bar and at intervals right round the room, though neither sleigh nor wolves budged an inch in the process. To what red tartar, oh mysterious beast? Incongruously, the Consul was reminded of Rostov's wolf hunt in *War and Peace* – ah, that incomparable party afterwards at the old uncle's, the sense of youth, the gaiety, the love! At the same time he remembered having been told that wolves never hunted in packs at all. Yes, indeed, how many patterns of life were based on kindred misconceptions, how many wolves do we feel on our heels, while our real enemies go in sheepskin by? 'Señora Gregorio,' he said again, and saw that the widow was returning, dragging her feet, though it was perhaps too late, there would not be time for another tequila.

He held out his hand, then dropped it – Good God, what had come over him? For an instant he'd thought he was looking at his own mother. Now he found himself struggling with his tears, that he wanted to embrace Señora Gregorio, to cry like a child, to hide his face on her bosom. '*Adiós*,' he said, and seeing a tequila on the counter just the same, he drank it rapidly.

Señora Gregorio took his hand and held it. 'Life changes, you know,' she said, gazing at him intently. 'You can never drink of it. I think I see you with your *esposa* again soon. I see you laughing together in some kernice place where you laugh.' She smiled. 'Far away. In some kernice place where all those troubles you har now will har – ' The Consul started : what was Señora Gregorio saying? '*Adiós*,' she added in Spanish, 'I have no house only a shadow. But whenever you are in need of a shadow, my shadow is yours.'

'Thank you.'

'Sank you.'

'Not sank you, Señora Gregorio, thank you.'

'Sank you.'

The coast looked clear : yet when the Consul pushed out cautiously through the jalousie doors he almost fell over Dr Vigil. Fresh and impeccable in his tennis clothes, he was hurrying by, accompanied by Mr Quincey and the local cinema manager, Señor Bustamente. The Consul drew back, fearful now of Vigil, of Quincey, of being seen coming out of the *cantina*, but they appeared not to notice him as they glided past the Tomalín *camión*, which had just arrived, their elbows working like jockeys, chattering unceasingly. He suspected their conversation to be entirely about him; what could be done with him, they were asking, how many drinks had he put away at the Gran Baile last night? Yes, there they were, even going towards the Bella Vista itself, to get a few more 'opinions' about him. They flitted here and there, vanished . . .

Es inevitable la muerte del Papa.

8

DOWNHILL ...

'Let in the clutch, step on the gas,' the driver threw a smile over his shoulder. 'Sure, Mike,' he went on Irish-American for them.

The bus, a 1918 Chevrolet, jerked forward with a noise like startled poultry. It wasn't full, save for the Consul, who spread himself, in a good mood, drunk-sober-uninhibited; Yvonne sat neutral but smiling: they'd started anyhow. No wind; yet a gust lifted the awnings along the street. Soon they were rolling in a heavy sea of chaotic stone. They passed tall hexagonal stands pasted with advertisements for Yvonne's cinema: *Las Manos de Orlac.* Elsewhere posters for the same film showed a murderer's hands laced with blood.

They advanced slowly, past the Baños de la Libertad, the Casa Brandes (La Primera en el Ramo de Electricidad), a hooded hooting intruder through the narrow tilted streets. At the market they stopped for a group of Indian women with baskets of live fowl. The women's strong faces were the colour of dark ceramic ware. There was a massiveness in their movements as they settled themselves. Two or three had cigarette stubs behind their ears, another chewed an old pipe. Their good-humoured faces of old idols were wrinkled with sun but they did not smile.

– 'Look! O.K.,' the driver of the bus invited Hugh and Yvonne, who were changing places, producing, from beneath his shirt where they'd been nestling, little secret ambassadors of peace, of love, two beautiful white tame pigeons. 'My – ah – my aerial pigeons.'

They had to scratch the heads of the birds who, arching their backs proudly, shone as with fresh white paint. (Could he have known, as Hugh, from merely smelling the latest headlines had known, how much nearer even in these moments the Government were to losing the Ebro, that it would now be a matter of days before Modesto withdrew altogether?) The driver replaced the pigeons under his white open shirt: 'To keep them warm. Sure, Mike. Yes, sir,' he told them. '*Vámonos!*'

Someone laughed as the bus lurched off; the faces of the other passengers slowly cracked into mirth, the *camión* was welding the old women into a community. The clock over the market arch, like the one in Rupert Brooke, said ten to three; but it was twenty to. They rambled and bounced into the main highway, the Avenida de la Revolución, past offices whose windows proclaimed, while the Consul nodded his head deprecatingly, Dr Arturo Díaz Vigil, Médico Cirujano y Partero, past the cinema itself. – The old women didn't look as though they knew about the Battle of the Ebro either. Two of them were holding an anxious conversation, in spite of the clatter and squeak of the patient floorboards, about the price of fish. Used to tourists, they took no notice of them. Hugh conveyed to the Consul: 'How are the rajah shakes?'

Inhumaciones: the Consul, laughingly pinching one ear, was pointing for answer at the undertakers' jolting by, where a parrot, head cocked, looked down from its perch suspended in the entrance, above which a sign inquired:

Quo Vadis?

Where they were going immediately was down, at a snail's pace, by a secluded square with great old trees, their delicate leaves like new spring green. In the garden under the trees were doves and a small black goat. *¿Le gusta este jardín, que es suyo? ¡Evite que sus hijos lo destruyan!* Do you like this garden, the notice said, that is yours? See to it that your children do not destroy it!

... There were no children, however, in the garden; just a man sitting alone on a stone bench. This man was apparently the devil himself, with a huge dark red face and horns, fangs, and his tongue hanging out over his chin, and an expression of mingled evil, lechery, and terror. The devil lifted his mask to spit, rose, and shambled through the garden with a dancing, loping step towards a church almost hidden by the trees. There was a sound of clashing machetes. A native dance was going on beyond some awnings by the church, on the steps of which two

Americans, Yvonne and he had seen earlier, were watching on tiptoe, craning their necks.

'Seriously,' Hugh repeated to the Consul, who seemed calmly to have accepted the devil, while Hugh exchanged a look of regret with Yvonne, for they had seen no dancing in the *zócalo*, and it was now too late to get out.

'*Quod semper, quod ubique, quod ab omnibus.*'

They were crossing a bridge at the bottom of the hill, over the ravine. It appeared overtly horrendous here. In the bus one looked straight down, as from the maintruck of a sailing ship, through dense foliage and wide leaves that did not at all conceal the treachery of the drop; its steep banks were thick with refuse, which even hung on the bushes. Turning, Hugh saw a dead dog right at the bottom, nuzzling the refuse; white bones showed through the carcass. But above was the blue sky and Yvonne looked happy when Popocatepetl sprang into view, dominating the landscape for a while as they climbed the hill beyond. Then it dropped out of sight around a corner. It was a long circuitous hill. Half-way up, outside a gaudily decorated tavern, a man in a blue suit and strange headgear, swaying gently and eating half a melon, awaited the bus. From the interior of this tavern, which was called El Amor de los Amores, came a sound of singing. Hugh caught sight of what appeared to be armed policemen drinking at the bar. The *camión* slithered, banking with wheels locked to a stop alongside the sidewalk.

The driver dashed into the tavern, leaving the tilted *camión*, which meanwhile the man with the melon had boarded, throbbing away to itself. The driver emerged; he hurled himself back on to the vehicle, jamming it almost simultaneously into gear. Then, with an amused glance over his shoulder at the man, and a look to his trusting pigeons, he urged his bus up the hill:

'Sure, Mike. Sure. O.K. boy.'

The Consul was pointing back at the El Amor de los Amores:

'*Viva Franco* ... That's one of your Fascist joints, Hugh.'

'So?'

'That hophead's the brother of the proprietor, I believe. I can tell you this much ... He's not an aerial pigeon.'

'A what? ... Oh.'

'You may not think it, but he's a Spaniard.'

The seats ran lengthwise and Hugh looked at the man in the blue suit opposite, who had been talking thickly to himself, who now, drunk, drugged, or both, seemed sunk in stupor. There was no conductor on the bus. Perhaps there would be one later, evidently fares were to be paid the driver on getting off, so none bothered him. Certainly his features, high, prominent nose and firm chin, were of strongly Spanish cast. His hands – in one he still clutched the gnawed half-melon – were huge, capable and rapacious. Hands of the *conquistador*, Hugh thought suddenly. But his general aspect suggested less the *conquistador* than, it was Hugh's perhaps too neat idea, the confusion that tends eventually to overtake *conquistadores*. His blue suit was of quite expensive cut, the open coat, it appeared, shaped at the waist. Hugh had noticed his broad-cuffed trousers draped well over expensive shoes. The shoes however – which had been shined that morning but were soiled with saloon sawdust – were full of holes. He wore no tie. His handsome purple shirt, open at the neck, revealed a gold crucifix. The shirt was torn and in places hung out over his trousers. And for some reason he wore two hats, a kind of cheap Homburg fitting neatly over the broad crown of his *sombrero*.

'How do you mean Spaniard?' Hugh said.

'They came over after the Moroccan war,' the Consul said. 'A *pelado*,' he added, smiling.

The smile referred to an argument about this word he'd had with Hugh, who'd seen it defined somewhere as a shoeless illiterate. According to the Consul, this was only one meaning : pelados were indeed 'peeled ones', the stripped, but also those who did not have to be rich to prey on the really poor. For instance those half-breed petty politicians who will, in order to get into office just for one year, in which year they hope to put by enough to forswear work the rest of their lives, do literally anything whatsoever, from shining shoes, to acting as one who was not an 'aerial pigeon'. Hugh understood this word finally to be pretty ambiguous. A Spaniard, say, could interpret it as Indian, the Indian he despised, used, made drunk. The Indian, however, might mean Spaniard by it. Either might mean by it anyone who made a show of himself. It was perhaps one of those words that had actually been distilled out of conquest, suggesting, as it did, on the one hand thief, on the other exploiter. Interchangeable ever were the terms of abuse with which the aggressor discredits those about to be ravaged !

The hill behind them, the bus was stopping opposite the foot of an avenue, with fountains, leading to a hotel : the Casino de la Selva. Hugh made out tennis courts, and white figures moving, the Consul's eyes pointed – there were Dr Vigil and M. Laruelle. M. Laruelle, if it was he, tossed a ball high into the blue, smacked it down, but Vigil walked right past it, crossing to the other side.

Here the American highway really began; and they enjoyed a brief stretch of good road. The *camión* reached the railway station, sleepy, signals up, points locked in somnolence. It was closed like a book. Unusual pullmans snored along a siding. On the embankment Pearce oiltanks were pillowed. Their burnished silver lightning alone was awake, playing hide-and-seek among the trees. And on that lonely platform tonight he himself would stand, with his pilgrim's bundle.

QUAUHNAHUAC

'How are you?' (meaning how much more!) Hugh smiled, leaning over to Yvonne.

'This is *such* fun – '

Like a child Hugh wanted everyone to be happy on a trip. Even had they been going to the cemetery he would have wanted them to be happy. But Hugh felt more as if, fortified by a pint of bitter, he were going to play in some important 'away' match for a school fifteen in which he'd been included at the last minute : when the dread, hard as nails and boots, of the foreign twenty-five line, of the whiter, taller goalposts, expressed itself in a strange exaltation, an urgent desire to chatter. The noonday languor had passed him by : yet the naked realities of the situation, like the spokes of a wheel, were blurred in motion towards unreal high events. This trip now seemed to him the best of all possible ideas. Even the Consul seemed still in a good mood. But communication between them all soon became again virtually impossible; the American highway rolled away into the distance.

They left it abruptly, rough stone walls shut out the view. Now they were rattling between leafy hedges full of wild flowers with deep royal bluebells. Possibly, another kind of convolvulus. Green and white clothing hung on the cornstalks outside the low grass-roofed houses. Here the bright blue flowers climbed right up into the trees that were already snowy with blooms.

To their right, beyond a wall that suddenly became much higher, now lay their grove of the morning. And here, announced by its smell of beer, was the Cervecería Quauhnahuac itself. Yvonne and Hugh, around the Consul, exchanged a look of encouragement and friendship. The massive gate was still open. How swiftly they clattered past! Yet not before Hugh had seen again the blackened and leaf-covered tables and, in the distance, the fountain choked with leaves. The little girl with the armadillo had gone, but the visored man resembling a gamekeeper was standing alone in the courtyard, his hands behind his back, watching them. Along the wall the cypresses stirred gently together, enduring their dust.

Beyond the level-crossing the Tomalín road became smoother for a time. A cool breeze blew gratefully through the windows into the hot *camión*. Over the plains to their right wound now the interminable narrow-gauge railway, where – though there were twenty-one other paths they might have taken ! – they had ridden home abreast. And there were the telegraph poles refusing, for ever, that final curve to the left, and striding straight ahead ... In the square too they'd talked of nothing but the Consul. What a relief, and what a joyful relief for Yvonne, when he'd turned up at the Terminal after all ! – But the road was rapidly growing much worse again, it was now well-nigh impossible to think, let alone talk –

They jogged on into ever rougher and rougher country. Popocatepetl came in view, an apparition already circling away, that beckoned them forward. The ravine appeared once more on the scene, patiently creeping after them in the distance. The *camión* crashed down a pothole with a deafening jolt that threw Hugh's soul between his teeth. And then crashed into, and over, a second series of deeper potholes :

'This is like driving *over* the moon,' he tried to say to Yvonne.

She couldn't hear ... He noticed new fine lines about her mouth, a weariness that had not been there in Paris. Poor Yvonne! May she be happy. May everything come, somehow, right. May we all be happy. God bless us. Hugh now wondered if he should produce, from his inside pocket, a very small pinch bottle of habanero he had acquired, against emergency, in the square, and frankly offer the Consul a drink. But he obviously didn't need it yet. A faint calm smile played about the Consul's lips which from time to time moved slightly, as if, in spite of the racket, the swaying and jolting, and their continually being sent sprawling against one another, he were solving a chess problem, or reciting something to himself.

Then they were hissing along a good stretch of oiled road through flat wooded country with neither volcano nor ravine in sight. Yvonne had turned sideways and her clear profile sailed along reflected in the window. The more even sounds of the bus wove into Hugh's brain an idiotic syllogism : I am losing the Battle of the Ebro, I am also losing Yvonne, therefore Yvonne is ...

The *camión* was now somewhat fuller. In addition to the *pelado* and the old women there were men dressed in their Sunday best, white trousers and purple shirts, and one or two younger women in mourning, probably going to the cemeteries. The poultry were a sad sight. All alike had submitted to their fate; hens, cocks, and turkeys, whether in their baskets, or still loose. With only an occasional flutter to show they were alive they crouched passively under the long seats, their emphatic spindly claws bound with cord. Two pullets lay, frightened and quivering, between the hand brake and the clutch, their wings linked with the levers. Poor things, they had signed their Munich agreement too. One of the turkeys even looked remarkably like Neville Chamberlain. *Su salud estará a salvo no escupiendo en el interior de este vehículo* : these words, over the windscreen, ran the entire breadth of the bus. Hugh concentrated upon different objects in the *camión*; the driver's small mirror with the legend running round it – *Cooperación de la Cruz Roja*, the three picture postcards of the Virgin Mary pinned beside it, the two slim vases of marguerites over the dashboard, the gangrened fire extinguisher, the dungaree jacket and whiskbroom under the seat where the *pelado* was sitting – he watched him as they hit another bad stretch of road.

Swaying from side to side with his eyes shut, the man was trying to tuck in his shirt. Now he was methodically buttoning his coat on the wrong buttons. But it struck Hugh all this was merely preparatory, a sort of grotesque toilet. For, still without opening his eyes, he had now somehow found room to lie full length on the seat. It was extraordinary, too, how, stretched out, a corpse, he yet preserved the appearance of knowing everything that was going on. Despite his stupor, he was a man on guard. The half-melon jumped from his hand, the chawed fragment full of seeds like raisins rolled on the seat; those closed eyes saw it. His crucifix was slipping off; he was conscious of it. The Homburg fell from his *sombrero*, slid to the floor, he knew all about it, though he made no effort to pick the hat up. He was guarding himself against theft, while at the same time gathering strength for more debauchery. In order to get into another *cantina* not his brother's he might have to walk straight. Such prescience was worthy of admiration.

Nothing but pines, fircones, stones, black earth. Yet that earth looked parched, those stones, unmistakably, volcanic. Everywhere, quite as Prescott informed one, were attestations to Popocatepetl's presence and antiquity. And here the damned thing was again! Why were there volcanic eruptions? People pretended not to know. Because, they might suggest tentatively, under the rocks beneath the surface of the earth, steam, its pressure constantly rising, was generated; because the rocks and the water, decomposing, formed gases, which combined with the molten material from below; because the watery rocks near the surface were unable to restrain the growing complex of pressures, and the whole mass exploded; the lava flooded out, the gases escaped, and there was your eruption. – But not your explanation. No, the whole thing was a complete mystery still. In movies of eruptions people were always seen standing in the midst of the encroaching flood, delighted by it. Walls fell over, churches collapsed, whole families moved away their possessions in a panic, but there were always these people, jumping about between the streams of molten lava, smoking cigarettes ...

Christ! He hadn't realized how fast they were going, in spite of the road and their being in a 1918 Chevrolet, and it seemed to him that because of this a quite different atmosphere now pervaded the little bus; the men were smiling, the old women gossiping knowingly and chuckling, two boys, newcomers hanging on by their eyebrows at the back, were whistling cheerfully – the bright shirts, the brighter serpentine confetti of tickets, red, yellow, green, blue, dangling from a loop on the ceiling, all contributed to a sense of gaiety, a feeling, almost, of the *fiesta* itself again, that hadn't been there before.

But the boys were dropping off, one by one, and the gaiety, short-lived as a burst of sunlight, departed. Brutal-looking candelabra cactus swung past, a ruined church, full of pumpkins, windows bearded with grass. Burned, perhaps, in the revolution, its exterior was blackened with fire, and it had an air of being damned.

– The time has come for you to join your comrades, to aid the workers, he told Christ, who agreed. It had been His idea all the while, only until Hugh had rescued Him those hypocrites had kept him shut up inside the burning church where He couldn't breathe. Hugh made a speech. Stalin gave him a medal and listened sympathetically while he explained what was on his mind. 'True ... I wasn't in time to save the Ebro, but I did strike my blow – ' He went off, the star of Lenin on his lapel; in his pocket a certificate; Hero of the Soviet Republic, and the True Church, pride and love in his heart –

Hugh looked out of the window. Well, after all. Silly bastard. But the queer thing was, that love was real. Christ, why can't we be simple, Christ Jesus why may we not be simple, why may we not all be brothers?

Buses with odd names on them, a procession out of a side-road, were bobbing past in the opposite direction : buses to Tetecala, to Jujuta, to Xuitepec : buses to Xochitepec, to Xoxitepec –

Popocatepetl loomed, pyramidal, to their right, one side beautifully curved as a woman's breast, the other precipitous, jagged, ferocious. Cloud drifts were massing again, high-piled, behind it. Ixtaccihuatl appeared . . .

– *Xiutepecanochtitlantehuantepec, Quintanarooroo, Tlacolula, Moctezuma, Juarez, Puebla, Tlampam* – bong! suddenly snarled the bus. They thundered on, passing little pigs trotting along the road, an Indian screening sand, a bald boy, with ear-rings, sleepily scratching his stomach and swinging madly on a hammock. Advertisements on ruined walls swam by. *¡Atchis! ¡Instante! Resfriados, Dolores, Cafeasperina. Rechace Imitaciones. Las Manos de Orlac. Con Peter Lorre.*

When there was a bad patch the bus rattled and sideslipped ominously, once it altogether ran off the road, but its determination outweighed these waverings, one was pleased at last to have transferred one's responsibilities to it, lulled into a state from which it would be pain to waken.

Hedges, with low steep banks, in which grew dusty trees, were hemming them in on either side. Without decreasing pace they were running into a narrow, sunken section of road, winding, and so reminiscent of England one expected at any point to see a sign : Public Footpath to Lostwithiel.

¡Desviación! ¡Hombres Trabajando!

With a yelping of tyres and brakes they made the detour leftward too quickly. But Hugh had seen a man, whom they'd narrowly missed, apparently lying fast asleep under the hedge on the right side of the road.

Neither Geoffrey nor Yvonne, staring sleepily out of the opposite window, had seen him. Nor did anyone else, were they aware of it, seem to think it peculiar a man should choose to sleep, however perilous his position, in the sun on the main road.

Hugh leaned forward to call out, hesitated, then tapped the driver on the shoulder; almost at the same moment the bus leaped to a standstill.

Guiding the whining vehicle swiftly, steering an erratic course with one hand, the driver, craning out of his seat to watch the corners behind and before, reversed out of the detour back into the narrow highway.

The friendly harsh smell of exhaust gases was tempered with the hot tar smell from the repairs, ahead of them now, where the road was broader with a wide grass margin between it and the hedge, though nobody was working there, everyone knocked off for the day possibly hours before, and there was nothing to be seen, just the soft, indigo carpet sparkling and sweating away to itself.

There appeared now, standing alone in a sort of rubbish heap where this grass margin stopped, opposite the detour, a stone wayside cross. Beneath it lay a milk bottle, a funnel, a sock, and part of an old suitcase.

And now, farther back still, in the road, Hugh saw the man again. His face covered by a wide hat, he was lying peacefully on his back with his arms stretched out towards this wayside cross, in whose shadow, twenty feet away, he might have found a grassy bed. Nearby stood a horse meekly cropping the hedge.

As the bus jerked to another stop the *pelado*, who was still lying down, almost slid from the seat to the floor. Managing to recover himself though, he not only reached his feet and an equilibrium he contrived remarkably to maintain but had, with one strong counter-movement, arrived half-way to the exit, crucifix fallen safely in place around his neck, hats in one hand, what remained of the melon in the other. With a look that might have withered at its inception any thought of stealing them, he placed the hats carefully on a vacant seat near the door, then, with exaggerated care, let himself down to the road. His eyes were still only half open, and they preserved a dead glaze. Yet there could be no doubt he had already taken in the whole situation. Throwing away the melon he started over towards the man, stepping tentatively, as over imaginary obstacles. But his course was straight, he held himself erect.

Hugh, Yvonne, the Consul, and two of the male passengers got out and followed him. None of the old women moved.

It was stiflingly hot in the sunken deserted road. Yvonne gave a nervous cry and turned on her heel; Hugh caught her arm.

'Don't mind me. It's just that I can't stand the sight of blood, damn it.'

She was climbing back into the *camión* as Hugh came up with the Consul and the two passengers.

The *pelado* was swaying gently over the recumbent man who was dressed in the usual loose white garments of the Indian.

There was not, however, much blood in sight, save on one side of his hat.

But the man was certainly not sleeping peacefully. His chest heaved like a spent swimmer's, his stomach contracted and dilated rapidly, one fist clenched and unclenched in the dust ...

Hugh and the Consul stood helplessly, each, he thought, waiting for the other to remove the Indian's hat, to expose the wound each felt must be there, checked from such action by a common reluctance, perhaps an obscure courtesy. For each knew the other was also thinking it would be better still should one of the passengers, even the *pelado*, examine the man.

As nobody made any move at all Hugh grew impatient. He shifted from foot to foot. He looked at the Consul expectantly: he'd been in this country long enough to know what should be done, moreover he was the one among them most nearly representing authority. Yet the Consul seemed lost in reflection. Suddenly Hugh stepped forward impulsively and bent over the Indian – one of the passengers plucked his sleeve.

'Har you throw your cigarette?'

'Throw it away.' The Consul woke up. 'Forest fires.'

'*Sí*, they have prohibidated it.'

Hugh stamped his cigarette out and was about to bend over the man once more when the passenger again plucked his sleeve :

'No, no,' he said, tapping his nose, 'they har prohibidated that, *también*.'

'You can't touch him – it's the law,' said the Consul sharply, who looked now as though he would like to get as far from this scene as possible, if necessary even by means of the Indian's horse. 'For his protection. Actually it's a sensible law. Otherwise you might become an accessory after the fact.'

The Indian's breathing sounded like the sea dragging itself down a stone beach.

A single bird flew, high.

'But the man may be dy –' Hugh muttered to Geoffrey.

'God, I feel terrible,' the Consul replied, though it was a fact he was about to take some action, when the *pelado* anticipated him : he went down on one knee and, quick as lightning, whipped off the Indian's hat.

They all peered over, seeing the cruel wound on the side of his head, where the blood had almost coagulated, the flushed moustachioed face turned aside, and before they stood back Hugh caught a glimpse of a sum of money, four or five silver pesos and a handful of centavos, that had been placed neatly under the loose collar to the man's blouse, which partly concealed it. The *pelado* replaced the hat and, straightening himself, made a hopeless gesture with hands now blotched with half-dried blood.

How long had he been here, lying in the road?

Hugh gazed after the *pelado* on his way back to the *camión*, and then, once more, at the Indian, whose life, as they talked, seemed gasping away from them all. '*Diantre! ¿Dónde buscamos un médico?*' he asked stupidly.

This time from the *camión*, the *pelado* made again that gesture of hopelessness, which was also like a gesture of sympathy : what could they do, he appeared trying to convey to them through the window, how could they have known, when they got out, that they could do nothing?

'Move his hat farther down though so that he can get some air,' the Consul said, in a voice that betrayed a trembling tongue; Hugh did this and, so swiftly he did not have time to see the money again, also placed the Consul's handkerchief over the wound, leaving it held in place by the balanced *sombrero*.

The driver now came for a look, tall, in his white shirt sleeves, and soiled whipcord breeches like bellows, inside high-laced, dirty boots. With his bare tousled head, laughing dissipated intelligent face, shambling yet athletic gait, there was something lonely and likeable about this man whom Hugh had seen twice before walking by himself in the town.

Instinctively you trusted him. Yet here, his indifference seemed remarkable; still, he had the responsibility of the bus, and what could he do, with his pigeons?

From somewhere above the clouds a lone plane let down a single sheaf of sound.

– '*Pobrecito.*'

– '*Chingar.*'

Hugh was aware that gradually these remarks had been taken up as a kind of refrain around him – for their presence, together with the *camión* having stopped at all, had ratified approach at least to the extent that another male passenger, and two peasants hitherto unnoticed, and who knew nothing, had joined the group about the stricken man whom nobody touched again – a quiet rustling of futility, a rustling of whispers, in which the dust, the heat, the bus itself with its load of immobile old women and doomed poultry, might have been conspiring, while only these two words, the one of compassion, the other of obscene contempt, were audible above the Indian's breathing.

The driver, having returned to his *camión*, evidently satisfied all was as it should be save he had stopped on the wrong side of the road, now began to blow his horn, yet far from this producing the desired effect, the rustling punctuated by a heckling accompaniment of indifferent blasts, turned into a general argument.

Was it robbery, attempted murder, or both? The Indian had probably ridden from market, where he'd sold his wares, with much more than that four or five pesos hidden by the hat, with *mucho dinero*, so that a good way to avoid suspicion of theft was to leave a little of the money, as had been done. Perhaps it wasn't robbery at all, he had only been thrown from his horse? Posseebly. Imposseebly.

Sí, hombre, but hadn't the police been called? But clearly somebody was already going for help. *Chingar.* One of them now should go for help, for the police. An ambulance – the Cruz Roja – where was the nearest phone?

But it was absurd to suppose the police were not on their way. How could the chingados be on their way when half of them were on strike? No it was only a quarter of them that were on strike. They would be on their way, all right though. A taxi? *No, hombre,* there was a strike there too. – But was there any truth, someone chimed in, in the rumour that the Servicio de

Ambulancia had been suspended? It was not a red, but a green cross anyhow, and their business began only when they were informed. Get Dr Figueroa. *Un hombre noble*. But there was no phone. Oh, there was a phone once, in Tomalín, but it had decomposed. No, Dr Figueroa had a nice new phone. Pedro, the son of Pepe, whose mother-in-law was Josefina, who also knew, it was said, Vincente González, had carried it through the streets himself.

Hugh (who had wildly thought of Vigil playing tennis, of Guzmán, wildly of the *habanero* in his pocket) and the Consul also had their personal argument. For the fact remained, whoever had placed the Indian by the roadside – though in that case why not on the grass, by the cross? – who had slipped the money for safety in his collar – but perhaps it slipped there of its own accord – who had providently tied his horse to the tree in the hedge it was now cropping – yet was it necessarily his horse? – probably was, whoever he was, wherever he was – or they were, who acted with such wisdom and compassion – even now getting help.

There was no limit to their ingenuity. Though the most potent and final obstacle to doing anything about the Indian was this discovery that it wasn't one's own business, but someone else's. And looking round him, Hugh saw that this too was just what everyone else was arguing. It is not my business, but, as it were, yours, they all said, as they shook their heads, and no, not yours either, but someone else's, their objections becoming more and more involved, more and more theoretical, till at last the discussion began to take a political turn.

This turn, as it happened, made no sense to Hugh, who was thinking that had Joshua appeared at this moment to make the sun stand still, a more absolute dislocation of time could not have been created.

Yet it was not that time stood still. Rather was it time was moving at different speeds, the speed at which the man seemed dying contrasting oddly with the speed at which everybody was finding it impossible to make up their minds.

However the driver had given up blowing his horn, he was about to tinker with the engine, and leaving the unconscious man the Consul and Hugh walked over to the horse, which, with its cord reins, empty bucket saddle, and jangling heavy iron sheaths for stirrups, was calmly chewing the convolvulus in the hedge, looking innocent as only one of its species can when under mortal suspicion. Its eyes, that had shut blandly at their approach, now opened, wicked and plausible. There was a sore on its hipbone and on the beast's rump a branded number seven.

'Why – good God – this must be the horse Yvonne and I saw this morning!'

'You did, eh? Well.' The Consul made to feel, though did not touch, the horse's surcingle. 'That's funny ... So did I. That is, I think I saw it.' He glanced over at the Indian in the road as though trying to tear something out of his memory. 'Did you notice if it had any saddlebags on when you saw it? It had when I think I saw it.'

'It must be the same fellow.'

'I don't suppose if the horse kicked the man to death it would have sufficient intelligence to kick its saddlebags off too, and hide them somewhere, do you – '

But the bus, with a terrific hooting, was going off without them.

It came at them a little, then stopped, in a wider part of the road, to let through two querulous expensive cars that had been held up behind. Hugh shouted at them to halt, the Consul half waved to someone who perhaps half recognized him, while the cars, that both bore upon their rear number-plates the sign 'Diplomático', surged on past, bouncing on their springs, and brushing the hedges, to disappear ahead in a cloud of dust. From the second car's rear seat a Scotch terrier barked at them merrily.

'The diplomatic thing, doubtless.'

The Consul went to see to Yvonne; the other passengers, shielding their faces against the dust, climbed on board the bus which had continued to the detour where, stalled, it waited still as death, as a hearse. Hugh ran to the Indian. His breathing sounded fainter, and yet more laboured. An uncontrollable desire to see his face again seized Hugh and he stooped over him. Simultaneously the Indian's right hand raised itself in a blind groping gesture, the hat was partially pushed away, a voice muttered or groaned one word:

'*Compañero.*'

– 'The hell they won't,' Hugh was saying, why he scarcely knew, a moment later to the Consul. But he'd detained the *camión*, whose engine had started once more, a little longer, and he watched the three smiling vigilantes approach, tramping through the dust, with their holsters slapping their thighs.

'Come on, Hugh, they won't let you on the bus with him, and you'll only get hauled into jail and entangled in red tape for Christ knows how long,' the Consul was saying. 'They're not the pukka police anyhow, only those birds I told you about ... Hugh –'

'*Momentito* – ' Hugh was almost immediately expostulating with one of the vigilantes – the other two had gone over to the Indian – while the driver, wearily, patiently, honked. Then the policeman pushed Hugh towards the bus: Hugh pushed back. The policeman dropped his hand and began to fumble with his holster: it was a manoeuvre, not to be taken seriously. With his other hand he gave Hugh a further shove, so that, to maintain balance, Hugh was forced to ascend the rear step of the bus which, at that instant suddenly, violently, moved away with them. Hugh would have jumped down only the Consul, exerting his strength, held him pinned to a stanchion.

'Never mind, old boy, it would have been worse than the windmills.' – 'What windmills?'

Dust obliterated the scene ...

The bus thundered on, reeling, cannonading, drunk. Hugh sat staring at the quaking, shaking floor.

– Something like a tree stump with a tourniquet on it, a severed leg in an army boot that someone picked up, tried to unlace, and then put down, in a sickening smell of petrol and blood, half reverently on the road; a face that gasped for a cigarette, turned grey, and was cancelled; headless things, that sat, with protruding windpipes, fallen scalps, bolt upright in motor cars; children piled up, many hundreds; screaming burning things; like the creatures, perhaps, in Geoff's dreams: among the stupid props of war's senseless Titus Andronicus, the horrors that could not even make a good story, but which had been, in a flash, evoked by Yvonne when they got out, Hugh moderately case-hardened, could have acquitted himself, have done something, have not done nothing ...

Keep the patient absolutely quiet in a darkened room. Brandy may sometimes be given to the dying.

Hugh guiltily caught the eye of an old woman. Her face was completely expressionless ... Ah, how sensible were these old women, who at least knew their own mind, who had made a silent communal decision to have nothing to do with the whole affair. No hesitation, no fluster, no fuss. With what solidarity, sensing danger, they had clutched their baskets of poultry to them, when they stopped, or peered round to identify their property, then had sat, as now, motionless. Perhaps they remembered the days of revolution in the valley, the blackened buildings, the communications cut off, those crucified and gored in the bull-ring, the pariah dogs barbecued in the market place. There was no callousness in their faces, no cruelty. Death they knew, better than the law, and their memories were long. They sat ranked now, motionless, frozen, discussing nothing, without a word, turned to stone. It was natural to have left the matter to the men. And yet, in these old women it was as if, through the various tragedies of Mexican history, pity, the impulse to approach, and terror, the impulse to escape (as one had learned at college), having replaced it, had finally been reconciled by prudence, the conviction it is better to stay where you are.

And what of the other passengers, the younger women in mourning – there were no women in mourning; they'd all got out, apparently, and walked; since death, by the roadside, must not be allowed to interfere with one's plans for resurrection, in the cemetery. And the men in the purple shirts, who'd had a good look at what was going on, yet hadn't stirred from the bus? Mystery. No one could be more courageous than a Mexican. But this was not clearly a situation demanding courage. *Frijoles* for all : *Tierra, Libertad, Justicia y Ley*. Did all that mean anything? *¿Quién sabe?* They weren't sure of anything save that it was foolish to get mixed up with the police, especially if they weren't proper police; and this went equally for the man who'd plucked Hugh's sleeve, and the two other passengers who'd joined in the argument around the Indian, now all dropping off the bus going full speed, in their graceful, devil-may-care fashion.

While as for him, the hero of the Soviet Republic and the True Church, what of him, old *camarado*, had he been found wanting? Not a bit of it. With the unerring instinct of all war correspondents with any first-aid training he had been only too ready to produce the wet blue bag, the lunar caustic, the camel's-hair brush.

He had remembered instantly that the word shelter must be understood as including an extra wrap or umbrella or temporary protection against the rays of the sun. He had been on the lookout immediately for possible clues to diagnosis such as broken ladders, stains of blood, moving machinery, and restive horses. He had, but it hadn't done any good, unfortunately.

And the truth was, it was perhaps one of those occasions when nothing *would* have done any good. Which only made it worse than ever. Hugh raised his head and half looked at Yvonne. The Consul had taken her hand and she was holding his hand tightly.

The *camión*, hastening towards Tomalín, rolled and swayed as before. Some more boys had jumped on the rear, and were whistling. The bright tickets winked with the bright colours. There were more passengers, they came running across the fields, and the men looked at each other with an air of agreement, the bus was out-doing itself, it had never before gone so fast, which must be because it too knew today was a holiday.

An acquaintance of the driver's, perhaps the driver for the return journey, had by now added himself to the vehicle. He dodged round the outside of the bus with native skill, taking the fares through the open windows. Once, when they were breasting an incline, he even dropped off to the road on the left, swerved round behind the *camión* at a run, to appear again on the right, grinning in at them clownishly.

A friend of his sprang on the bus. They crouched, one on either side of the bonnet, by the two front mudguards, every so often joining hands over the radiator cap, while the first man, leaning dangerously outwards, looked back to see if one of the rear tyres, which had acquired a slow puncture, was holding. Then he went on taking fares.

Dust, dust, dust – it filtered in through the windows, a soft invasion of dissolution, filling the vehicle.

Suddenly the Consul was nudging Hugh, inclining his head towards the *pelado*, whom Hugh had not forgotten however: he had been sitting bolt upright all this time, fidgeting with something in his lap, coat buttoned, both hats on, crucifix adjusted, and wearing much the same expression as before, though after his oddly exemplary behaviour in the road, he seemed much refreshed and sobered.

Hugh nodded, smiling, lost interest; the Consul nudged him again:

'Do you see what I see?'

'What is it?'

Hugh shook his head, looked obediently towards the *pelado*, could see nothing, then saw, at first without comprehending.

The *pelado*'s smeared *conquistador*'s hands, that had clutched the melon, now clutched a sad bloodstained pile of silver pesos and centavos.

The *pelado* had stolen the dying Indian's money.

Moreover, surprised at this point by the conductor grinning in the window, he carefully selected some coppers from this little pile, smiled round at the preoccupied passengers as though he almost expected some comment to be made upon his cleverness, and paid his fare with them.

But no comment was made, for the good reason none save the Consul and Hugh seemed aware quite how clever he was.

Hugh now produced the small pinch bottle of *habanero*, handing it to Geoff, who passed it to Yvonne. She choked, had still noticed nothing; and it was as simple as that; they all took a short drink.

– What was so astonishing on second thoughts was not that on an impulse the *pelado* should have stolen the money, but that he was making now only this half-hearted effort to conceal it, that he should be continually opening and closing his palm with the bloody silver and copper coins for anyone to see who wished.

It occurrred to Hugh he was not trying to conceal it at all, that he was perhaps attempting to persuade the passengers, even though they knew nothing about it, that he had acted from motives explicable as just, that he had taken the money merely to keep it safe which, as had just been shown by his own action, no money could reasonably be called in a dying man's collar on the Tomalín road, in the shadow of the Sierra Madre.

And further, suppose he were suspected of being a thief, his eyes, that were now fully open, almost alert, and full of mischief, said to them, and were arrested, what chance then would the Indian should he survive have of seeing his money again? Of course, none, as everyone well knew. The real police might be honourable, of the people. But were he arrested by these deputies, these other fellows, they would simply steal it from him, that much was certain, as they would even now be stealing it from the Indian, but for his kindly action.

Nobody, therefore, who was genuinely concerned about the Indian's money, must suspect anything of the sort, or at any rate, must not think too clearly about it; even if now, in the *camión*, he should choose to stop juggling the money from hand to hand, like that, or slip part of it into his pocket, like that, or even supposing what remained happened to slip accidentally into his other pocket, like that – and this performance was undoubtedly rather for their own benefit, as witnesses and foreigners – no significance attached to it, none of these gestures meant that he had been a thief, or that, in spite of excellent intentions, he had decided to steal the money after all, and become a thief.

And this remained true, whatever happened to the money, since his possession of it was open and above board, for all the world to know about. It was a recognized thing, like Abyssinia.

The conductor went on taking the remaining fares and now, concluded, gave them to the driver. The bus trampled on faster; the road narrowed again, becoming dangerous.

Downhill ... The driver kept his hand on the screaming emergency brake as they circled down into Tomalín. On the right was a sheer unguarded drop, a huge scrub-covered dusty hill leaned from the hollow below, with trees jutting out sideways –

Ixtaccihuatl had slipped out of sight but as, descending,

they circled round and round, Popocatepetl slid in and out of view continually, never appearing the same twice, now far away, then vastly near at hand, incalculably distant at one moment, at the next looming round the corner with its splendid thickness of sloping fields, valleys, timber, its summit swept by clouds, slashed by hail and snow ...

Then a white church, and they were in a town once more, a town of one long street, a cul-de-sac, and many paths, that converged upon a small lake or reservoir ahead, in which people were swimming, beyond which lay the forest. By this lake was the bus stop.

The three of them stood again in the dust, dazzled by the whiteness, the blaze of the afternoon. The old women and the other passengers had gone. From a doorway came the plangent chords of a guitar, and at hand was the refreshing sound of rushing water, of a falls. Geoff pointed the way and they set off in the direction of the Arena Tomalín.

But the driver and his acquaintance were going into a *pulquería*. They were followed by the *pelado*. He walked very straight, stepping high, and holding his hats on, as though the wind were blowing, on his face a fatuous smile, not of triumph, almost of entreaty.

He would join them; some arrangement would be made. *¿Quién sabe?*

They stared after them as the twin doors of the tavern swung to : – it had a pretty name, the Todos Contentos y Yo También. The Consul said nobly :

'Everybody happy, including me.'

And including those, Hugh thought, who effortlessly, beautifully, in the blue sky above them, floated, the vultures – xopilotes, who wait only for the ratification of death.

9

Arena Tomalín . . .

– What a wonderful time everybody was having, how happy they were, how happy everyone was! How merrily Mexico laughed away its tragic history, the past, the underlying death!

It was as though she had never left Geoffrey, never gone to America, never suffered the anguish of the last year, as though even, Yvonne felt a moment, they were in Mexico again for the first time; there was that same warm poignant happy sense, indefinable, illogically, of sorrow that would be overcome, of hope – for had not Geoffrey met her at the Bus Terminal? – above all of hope, of the future –

A smiling, bearded giant, a white serape decorated with cobalt dragons flung over his shoulder, proclaimed it. He was stalking importantly around the arena, where the boxing would be on Sunday, propelling through the dust – the 'Rocket' it might have been, the first locomotive.

It was a marvellous peanut wagon. She could see its little donkey engine toiling away minutely inside, furiously grinding the peanuts. How delicious, how good, to feel oneself, in spite of all the strain and stress of the day, the journey, the bus, and now the crowded rickety grandstand, part of the brilliantly coloured serape of existence, part of the sun, the smells, the laughter!

From time to time the peanut wagon's siren jerked, its fluted smokestack belched, its polished whistle shrieked. Apparently the giant didn't want to sell any peanuts. Simply, he couldn't resist showing off this engine to everyone : see, this is my possession, my joy, my faith, perhaps even (he would like it to be imagined) my invention! And everyone loved him.

He was pushing the wagon, all of a final triumphant belch and squeal, from the arena just as the bull shot out of a gate on the opposite side.

A merry bull at heart too – obviously. ¿Por qué no? It knew it wasn't going to be killed, merely to play, to participate in the gaiety. But the bull's merriment was controlled as yet; after its explosive entrance it began to cruise round the edge of the ring slowly, thoughtfully, though raising much dust. It was prepared to enjoy the game as much as anyone, at its own expense if need be, only its dignity must receive proper recognition first.

Nevertheless some people sitting on the rude fence that enclosed the ring scarcely bothered to draw their legs up at its approach, while others lying prone on the ground just outside, with their heads as if thrust through luxurious stocks, did not withdraw an inch.

On the other hand some responsive *borrachos* straying into the ring prematurely essayed to ride the bull. This was not playing the game : the bull must be caught in a special way, fair play was in order, and they were escorted off, tottering, weak-kneed, protesting, yet always gay ...

The crowd, in general more pleased with the bull even than with the peanut vendor, started to cheer. Newcomers gracefully swung up on to fences, to appear standing there, marvellously balanced, on the top railings. Muscular hawkers lifted aloft, in one sinewy stretch of the forearm, heavy trays brimmed with multi-coloured fruits. A boy stood high upon the crotch of a tree, shading his eyes as he gazed over the jungle at the volcanoes. He was looking for an airplane in the wrong direction ; she made it out herself, a droning hyphen in abyssal blue. Thunder was in the air though, at her back somewhere, a tingle of electricity.

The bull repeated his tour of the ring at a slightly increased though still steadily measured gait, deviating only once when a smart little dog snapping at his heels made him forget where he was going.

Yvonne straightened her back, pulled down her hat, and began to powder her nose, peering into the traitorous mirror of the bright enamel compact. It reminded her that only five minutes ago she had been crying and imaged too, nearer, looking over her shoulder, Popocatepetl.

The volcanoes! How sentimental one could become about

them! It was 'volcano' now; however she moved the mirror she couldn't get poor Ixta in, who, quite eclipsed, fell away sharply into invisibility, while Popocatepetl seemed even more beautiful for being reflected, its summit brilliant against pitch-massed cloud banks. Yvonne ran one finger down her cheek, drew down an eyelid. It was stupid to have cried, in front of the little man at the door of Las Novedades too, who'd told them it 'was half past three by the cock', then that it was 'imposseebly' to phone because Dr Figueroa had gone to Xiutepec . . .

' – Forward to the bloody arena then,' the Consul had said savagely, and she had cried. Which was almost as stupid as to have turned back this afternoon, not at the sight, but at the mere suspicion of blood. That was her weakness though, and she remembered the dog that was dying on the street in Honolulu, rivulets of blood streaked the deserted pavement, and she had wanted to help, but fainted instead, just for a minute, and then was so dismayed to find herself lying there alone on the kerb – what if anyone had seen her ? – she hurried away without a word, only to be haunted by the memory of the wretched abandoned creature so that once – but what was the good thinking of that? Besides, hadn't everything possible been done? It wasn't as if they'd come to the bullthrowing without first making sure there was no phone. And even had there been one ! So far as she could make out, the poor Indian was obviously being taken care of when they left, so now she seriously thought of it, she couldn't understand why – She gave her hat a final pat before the mirror, then blinked. Her eyes were tired and playing tricks. For a second she'd had the awful sensation that, not Popocatepetl, but the old woman with the dominoes that morning, was looking over her shoulder. She closed the compact with a snap, and turned to the others smiling.

Both the Consul and Hugh were staring gloomily at the arena. From the grandstand around her came a few groans, a few belches, a few half-hearted *olés*, as now the bull, with two shuffling broom-like sweeps of the head along the ground, drove away the dog again and resumed his circuit of the ring. But no gaiety, no applause. Some of the rail sitters actually nodded with slumber. Someone else was tearing a *sombrero* to pieces while another spectator was trying unsuccessfully to skim, like a boomerang, a straw hat at a friend. Mexico was not laughing away her tragic history; Mexico was bored. The bull was bored. Everyone was bored, perhaps had been all the time. All that had happened was that Yvonne's drink in the bus had taken effect and was now wearing off. As amid boredom the bull circled the arena and, boredom, he now finally sat down in a corner of it.

'Just like Ferdinand – ' Yvonne began, still almost hopefully.

'Nandi,' the Consul (and ah, had he not taken her hand in the bus?) muttered, peering sideways with one eye through cigarette smoke at the ring, 'the bull, I christen him Nandi, vehicle of Siva, from whose hair the River Ganges flows, and who has also been identified with the Vedic storm-god Vindra – known to the ancient Mexicans as Huracán.'

'For Jesus' sake, papa,' Hugh said, 'thank you.'

Yvonne sighed; it was a tiresome and odious spectacle, really. The only people happy were the drunks. Gripping tequila or mescal bottles they tottered into the ring, approached the recumbent Nandi, and sliding and tripping over each other were chased out again by several *charros*, who now attempted to drag the miserable bull to its feet.

But the bull would not be dragged. At last a small boy no one had seen before appeared to nip its tail with his teeth, and as the boy ran away, the animal clambered up convulsively. Instantly it was lassoed by a cowboy mounted on a malicious-looking horse. The bull soon kicked itself free : it had been roped only around one foot, and walked from the scene shaking its head, then catching sight of the dog once more, wheeled, and pursued it a short distance ...

There was suddenly more activity in the arena. Presently everyone there, whether on horseback, pompously, or on foot – running or standing still, or swaying with an old serape or rug or even a rag held out – was trying to attract the bull.

The poor old creature seemed now indeed like someone being drawn, lured, into events of which he has no real comprehension, by people with whom he wishes to be friendly, even to play, who entice him by encouraging that wish and by whom, because they really despise and desire to humiliate him, he is finally entangled.

... Yvonne's father made his way towards her, through the seats, hovering, responding eagerly as a child to anyone who held out a friendly hand, her father, whose laughter in memory still sounded so warmly rich and generous, and whom the small sepia photograph she still carried with her depicted as a young captain in the uniform of the Spanish-American war, with earnest candid eyes beneath a high fine brow, a full-lipped sensitive mouth beneath the dark silky moustache, and a cleft chin – her father, with his fatal craze for invention, who had once so confidently set out for Hawaii to make his fortune by raising pineapples. In this he had not succeeded. Missing army life, and abetted by his friends, he wasted time tinkering over elaborate projects. Yvonne had heard that he'd tried to make synthetic hemp from the pineapple tops and even attempted to harness the volcano behind their estate to run the hemp machine. He sat on the *lanai* sipping okoolihao and singing plaintive Hawaiian songs, while the pineapples rotted in the fields, and the native help gathered round to sing with him, or slept through the cutting season, while the plantation ran into weeds and ruin, and the whole place hopelessly into debt. That was the picture; Yvonne remembered little of the period save her mother's death. Yvonne was then six. The World War, together with the final foreclosure, was approaching, and with it the figure of her Uncle Macintyre, her mother's brother, a wealthy Scotchman with financial interests in South America, who had long prophesied his brother-in-law's failure, and yet to whose large influence it was undoubtedly due that, all at once and to everyone's surprise, Captain Constable became American consul to Iquique.

– Consul to Iquique ! ... Or Quauhnahuac ! How many times in the misery of the last year had Yvonne not tried to free herself of her love for Geoffrey by rationalizing it away, by analysing it away, by telling herself – Christ, after she'd waited, and written at first hopefully, with all her heart, then urgently, frantically, at last despairingly, waited and watched every day for the letter – ah, that daily crucifixion of the post !

She looked at the Consul, whose face for a moment seemed to have assumed that brooding expression of her father's she

remembered so well during those long war years in Chile. Chile!
It was as if that republic of stupendous coastline yet narrow
girth, where all thoughts bring up at Cape Horn, or in the
nitrate country, had had a certain attenuating influence on his
mind. For what, precisely, was her father brooding about all that
time, more spiritually isolated in the land of Bernardo O'Hig-
gins than was once Robinson Crusoe, only a few hundred miles
from the same shores? Was it of the outcome of the war itself,
or of obscure trade agreements he perhaps initiated, or the lot
of American sailors stranded in the Tropic of Capricorn? No,
it was upon a single notion that had not, however, reached its
fruition till after the Armistice. Her father had invented a new
kind of pipe, insanely complicated, that one took to pieces for
purposes of cleanliness. The pipes came into something like
seventeen pieces, came, and thus remained, since apparently
none save her father knew how to put them together again. It
was a fact that the Captain did not smoke a pipe himself. Nevertheless, as usual, he had been led on and encouraged ... When
his factory in Hilo burned down within six weeks of its com-
pletion he had returned to Ohio where he was born and for a
time worked in a wire-fence company.

And there, it had happened. The bull was hopelessly entangled. Now one, two, three, four more lassoes, each launched with a
new marked lack of friendliness, caught him. The spectators
stamped on the wooden scaffolding, clapping rhythmically, without enthusiasm. – Yes, it struck her now that this whole business
of the bull was like a life; the important birth, the fair chance,
the tentative, then assured, then half-despairing circulations of
the ring, an obstacle negotiated – a feat improperly recognized –
boredom, resignation, collapse: then another, more convulsive
birth, a new start; the circumspect endeavours to obtain one's
bearings in a world now frankly hostile, the apparent but deceptive encouragement of one's judges, half of whom were
asleep, the swervings into the beginnings of disaster because of
that same negligible obstacle one had surely taken before at a
stride, the final enmeshment in the toils of enemies one was
never quite certain weren't friends more clumsy than actively
ill-disposed, followed by disaster, capitulation, disintegration –

– The failure of a wire-fence company, the failure, rather less emphatic and final, of one's father's mind, what were these things in the face of God or destiny? Captain Constable's besetting illusion was that he'd been cashiered from the army; and everything started up to this imagined disgrace. He set out on his way back yet once more to Hawaii, the dementia that arrested him in Los Angeles however, where he discovered he was penniless, being strictly alcoholic in character.

Yvonne glanced again at the Consul who was sitting meditative with pursed lips apparently intent on the arena. How little he knew of this period of her life, of that terror, the terror, terror that still could wake her in the night from that recurrent nightmare of things collapsing; the terror that was like that she had been supposed to portray in the white-slave-traffic film, the hand clutching her shoulder through the dark doorway; or the real terror she'd felt when she actually had been caught in a ravine with two hundred stampeding horses; no, like Captain Constable himself, Geoffrey had been almost bored, perhaps ashamed, by all this: that she had, starting when she was only thirteen, supported her father for five years as an actress in 'serials' and 'westerns'; Geoffrey might have nightmares, like her father in this too, be the only person in the world who ever had such nightmares, but that *she* should have them ... Nor did Geoffrey know much more of the false real excitement, or the false flat bright enchantment of the studios, or the childish adult pride, as harsh as it was pathetic, and justifiable, in having, somehow, at that age, earned a living.

Beside the Consul Hugh took out a cigarette, tapped it on his thumbnail, noted it was the last in the package, and placed it between his lips. He put his feet up on the back of the seat beneath him and leaned forward, resting his elbows on his knees, frowning down into the arena. Then, fidgeting still, he struck a match, drawing his thumbnail across it with a crackle like a small cap-pistol, and held it to the cigarette, cupping his quite beautiful hands, his head bent ... Hugh was coming towards her this morning, in the garden, through the sunlight. With his rolling swagger, his Stetson hat on the back of his head, his holster, his pistol, his bandolier, his tight trousers tucked inside the elaborately stitched and decorated boots, she'd thought, just for an instant, that he was – actually! – Bill Hodson, the cowboy star, whose leading lady she'd been in three pictures when she was fifteen. Christ, how absurd! How marvellously absurd! *The Hawaiian Islands gave us this real outdoor girl who is fond of swimming, golf, dancing, and is also an expert horsewoman! She . . .* Hugh hadn't said one word this morning about how well she rode, though he'd afforded her not a little secret amusement by explaining that her horse – miraculously – didn't want to drink. Such areas there are in one another we leave, perhaps for ever, unexplored! – She'd never told him a word about her movie career, no, not even that day in Robinson . . . But it was a pity Hugh himself hadn't been old enough to interview her, if not the first time, that second awful time after Uncle Macintyre sent her to college, and after her first marriage, and the death of her child, when she had gone back once more to Hollywood. *Yvonne the Terrible! Look out, you sarong sirens and glamour girls, Yvonne Constable, the 'Boomp Girl', is back in Hollywood! Yes, Yvonne is back, determined to conquer Hollywood for the second time. But she's twenty-four now, and the 'Boomp Girl' has become a poised exciting woman who wears diamonds and white orchids and ermine – and a woman who has known the meaning of love and tragedy, who has lived a lifetime since she left Hollywood a few short years ago. I found her the other day at her beach home, a honey-tanned Venus just emerging from the surf. As we talked she gazed out over the water with her slumbrous dark eyes and the Pacific breezes played with her thick dark hair. Gazing at her for a moment it was hard to associate the Yvonne Constable of today with the rough-riding serial queen of yesteryear, but the torso's still terrific, and the energy is still absolutely unparalleled! The Honolulu Hellion, who at twelve was a war-whooping tomboy, crazy about baseball, disobeying everyone but her adored Dad, who she called 'The Boss-Boss', became at fourteen a child actress, and at fifteen, leading lady to Bill Hodson. And she was a powerhouse even then. Tall for her age, she had a lithe strength that came from a childhood of swimming and surfboarding in the Hawaiian breakers. Yes, though you may not think it now, Yvonne has* been submerged in burning lakes, suspended over precipices, ridden horses down ravines, and she's an expert at 'double pick-offs'. Yvonne laughs merrily today when she remembers the frightened determined girl who declared she could ride very well indeed, and then, the picture in progress, the company on location, tried to mount her horse from the wrong side! A year later she could do a 'flying mount' without turning a hair. 'But about that time I was rescued from Hollywood,' as she smilingly puts it, 'and very unwillingly too, by my Uncle Macintyre, who literally swooped down, after my father died, and sailed me back to Honolulu!' But when you've been a 'Boomp Girl' and are well on your way to being an 'Oomph Girl!' at eighteen, and when you've just lost your beloved 'Boss-Boss', it's hard to settle down in a strict loveless atmosphere. 'Uncle Macintyre', Yvonne admits, 'never conceded a jot or tittle to the tropics. Oh, the mutton broth and oatmeal and hot tea!' But Uncle Macintyre knew his duty and, after Yvonne had studied with a tutor, he sent her to the University of Hawaii. There – perhaps, she says, 'because the word "star" had undergone some mysterious trans-formation in my mind' – she took a course in astronomy! Try-ing to forget the ache in her heart and its emptiness, she forced an interest in her studies and even dreamed briefly of becoming the 'Madame Curie' of astronomy! And there too, before long, she met the millionaire playboy, Cliff Wright. He came into Yvonne's life at a moment when she was discouraged in her University work, restless under Uncle Macintyre's strict régime, lonely, and longing for love and companionship. And Cliff was young and gay, his rating as an eligible bachelor was absolutely blue ribbon. It's easy to see how he was able to persuade her, beneath the Hawaiian moon, that she loved him, and that she should leave college and marry him. ('Don't tell me for Christ sake about this Cliff,' the Consul wrote in one of his rare early let-ters, 'I can see him and I hate the bastard already : short-sighted and promiscuous, six foot three of gristle and bristle and pathos, of deep-voiced charm and casuistry.' The Consul had seen him with some astuteness as a matter of fact – poor Cliff! – one sel-dom thought of him now and one tried not to think of the self-righteous girl whose pride had been outraged by his infidelities –

'businesslike, inept and unintelligent, strong and infantile, like most American men, quick to wield chairs in a fight, vain, and who, at thirty still ten, turns the act of love into a kind of dysentery ...') *Yvonne has already been a victim of 'bad Press' about her marriage and in the inevitable divorce that followed, what she said was misconstrued, and when she didn't say anything, her silence was misinterpreted. And it wasn't only the Press who misunderstood:* 'Uncle Macintyre', she says ruefully, 'simply washed his hands of me.' (Poor Uncle Macintyre. It was fantastic, it was almost funny – it was screamingly funny, in a way, as one related it to one's friends. She was a Constable through and through, and no child of her mother's people ! Let her go the way of the Constables ! God knows how many of them had been caught up in, or invited, the same kind of meaningless tragedy, or half-tragedy, as herself and her father. They rotted in asylums in Ohio or dozed in dilapidated drawing-rooms in Long Island with chickens pecking among the family silver and broken teapots that would be found to contain diamond necklaces. The Constables, a mistake on the part of nature, were dying out. In fact, nature meant to wipe them out, having no further use for what was not self-evolving. The secret of their meaning, if any, had been lost.) *So Yvonne left Hawaii with her head high and a smile on her lips, even if her heart was more achingly empty than ever before. And now she's back in Hollywood and people who know her best say she has no time in her life now for love, she thinks of nothing but her work. And at the studio they're saying the tests she's been making recently are nothing short of sensational. The 'Boomp Girl' has become Hollywood's greatest dramatic actress! So Yvonne Constable, at twenty-four, is well on the way for the second time to becoming a star.*

– But Yvonne Constable had not become a star for the second time. Yvonne Constable had not even been on her way to becoming a star. She had acquired an agent who managed to execute some excellent publicity – excellent in spite of the fact that publicity of any kind, she persuaded herself, was one of her greatest secret fears – on the strength of her earlier rough-riding successes; she received promises, and that was all. In the end she walked alone down Virgil Avenue or Mariposa beneath the dusty dead shallow-planted palms of the dark and accursed City of the Angels without even the consolation that her tragedy was no less valid for being so stale. For her ambitions as an actress had always been somewhat spurious : they suffered in some sense from the dislocations of the functions – she saw this – of woman-hood itself. She saw it, and at the same time, now it was all quite hopeless (and now that she had, after everything, *outgrown* Hollywood), saw that she might under other conditions have become a really first-rate, even a great artist. For that matter what was she if not that now (if greatly directed) as she walked or drove furiously through her anguish and all the red lights, seeing, as might the Consul, the sign in the Town House window 'Informal Dancing in the Zebra Room' turn 'Infernal' – or 'Notice to Destroy Weeds' become 'Notice to Newlyweds'. While on the hoarding – 'Man's public inquiry of the hour' – the great pendulum on the giant blue clock swung ceaselessly. Too late ! And it was this, it was all this that had perhaps helped to make meeting Jacques Laruelle in Quauhnahuac such a shat-tering and ominous thing in her life. It was not merely that they had the Consul in common, so that through Jacques she had been mysteriously able to reach, in a sense to avail herself of, what she had never known, the Consul's innocence ; it was only to him that she'd been able to talk of Hollywood (not always honestly, yet with the enthusiasm with which close relatives may speak of a hated parent and with what relief !) on the mutual grounds of contempt and half-admitted failure. More-over they discovered that they were both there in the same year, in 1932, had been once, in fact, at the same party, outdoor-barbe-cue-swimming-pool-and-bar ; and to Jacques she had shown also, what she had kept hidden from the Consul, the old photo-graphs of Yvonne the Terrible dressed in fringed leather shirts and riding-breeches and high-heeled boots, and wearing a ten-gallon hat, so that in his amazed and bewildered recognition of her this horrible morning, she had wondered was there not just an instant's faltering – for surely Hugh and Yvonne were in some grotesque fashion transposed ! ... And once too in his studio, where the Consul was so obviously not going to arrive,

M. Laruelle had shown her some stills of his old French films, one of which it turned out – good heavens! – she'd seen in New York soon after going east again. And in New York she'd stood once more (still in Jacques's studio) on that freezing winter night in Times Square – she was staying at the Astor – watching the illuminated news aloft travelling around the Times Building, news of disaster, of suicide, of banks failing, of approaching war, of nothing at all, which, as she gazed upward with the crowd, broke off abruptly, snapped off into darkness, into the end of the world, she had felt, when there was no more news. Or was it – Golgotha? A bereaved and dispossessed orphan, a failure, yet rich, yet beautiful, walking, but not back to her hotel, in the rich fur trappings of alimony, afraid to enter the bars alone whose warmth she longed for then, Yvonne had felt far more desolate than a streetwalker; walking – and being followed, always followed – through the numb brlliant jittering city – *the best for less*, she kept seeing, or *Dead End*, or *Romeo and Juliet*, and then again, *the best for less* – that awful darkness had persisted in her mind, blackening still further her false wealthy loneliness, her guilty divorced dead helplessness. The electric arrows thrust at her heart – yet they were cheating: she knew, increasingly frightened by it, that darkness to be still there, in them, of them. The cripples jerked themselves slowly past. Men muttered by in whose faces all hope seemed to have died. Hoodlums with wide purple trousers waited where the icy gale streamed into open parlours. And everywhere, that darkness, the darkness of a world without meaning, a world without aim – *the best for less* – but where everyone save herself, it seemed to her, however hypocritically, however churlish, lonely, crippled, hopeless, was capable, if only in a mechanical crane, a cigarette butt plucked from the street, if only in a bar, if only in accosting Yvonne herself, of finding some faith ... *Le Destin de Yvonne Griffaton* ... And there she was – and she was still being followed – standing outside the little cinema in Fourteenth Street which showed revivals and foreign films. And there, upon the stills, who could it be, that solitary figure, but herself, walking down the same dark streets, even wearing the same fur coat, only the signs above her and around her said: *Dubonnet, Amer*

Picon, Les 10 Frattelinis, Moulin Rouge. And 'Yvonne, Yvonne!' a voice was saying at her entrance, and a shadowy horse, gigantic, filling the whole screen, seemed leaping out of it at her: it was a statue that the figure had passed, and the voice, an imaginary voice, which pursued Yvonne Griffaton down the dark streets, and Yvonne herself too, as if she had walked straight out of that world outside into this dark world on the screen, without taking breath. It was one of those pictures that, even though you have arrived in the middle, grip you with the instant conviction that it is the best film you have ever seen in your life; so extraordinarily complete is its realism, that what the story is all about, who the protagonist may be, seems of small account beside the explosion of the particular moment, beside the immediate threat, the identification with the one hunted, the one haunted, in this case Yvonne Griffaton – or Yvonne Constable! But if Yvonne Griffaton was being followed, was being hunted – the film apparently concerned the downfall of a Frenchwoman of rich family and aristocratic birth – she in turn was also the hunter, was searching, was groping for something, Yvonne couldn't understand what at first, in this shadowy world. Strange figures froze to the walls, or into alleyways, at her approach: they were the figures of her past evidently, her lovers, her one true love who had committed suicide, her father – and as if seeking sanctuary from them, she had entered a church. Yvonne Griffaton was praying, but the shadow of one follower fell on the chancel steps: it was her first lover and at the next moment she was laughing hysterically, she was at the Folies Bergères, she was at the Opéra, the orchestra was playing Leoncavallo's *Zaza*; then she was gambling, the roulette wheel spun crazily, she was back in her room; and the film turned to satire, to satire, almost, of itself: her ancestors appeared before her in swift succession, static dead symbols of selfishness and disaster, but in her mind romanticized, so it seemed, heroic, standing weary with their backs to the walls of prisons, standing upright in tumbrils in wooden gesticulation, shot by the Commune, shot by the Prussians, standing upright in battle, standing upright in death. And now Yvonne Griffaton's father, who had been implicated in the Dreyfus case, came to mock and mow at her. The sophisticated audience laughed, or coughed, or murmured, but most of them presumably knew what Yvonne never as it happened ever found out later, how these characters and the events in which they had participated, contributed to Yvonne Griffaton's present estate. All this was buried back in the earlier episodes of the film. Yvonne would have first to endure the newsreel, the animated cartoon, a piece entitled *The Life of the African Lungfish* and a revival of *Scarface*, in order to see, just as so much that conceivably lent some meaning (though she doubted even this) to her own destiny was buried in the distant past, and might for all she knew repeat itself in the future. But what Yvonne Griffaton was asking herself was now clear. Indeed the English sub-titles made it all too clear. What could she do under the weight of such a heritage? How could she rid herself of this old man of the sea? Was she doomed to an endless succession of tragedies that Yvonne Griffaton could not believe either formed part of any mysterious expiation for the obscure sins of others long since dead and damned, but were just frankly meaningless? Yes, how? Yvonne wondered herself. Meaningless – and yet, *was* one doomed? Of course one could always romanticize the unhappy Constables : one could see oneself, or pretend to, as a small lone figure carrying the burden of those ancestors, their weakness and wildness (which could be invented where it was lacking) in one's blood, a victim of dark forces – everybody was, it was inescapable! – misunderstood and tragic, yet at least with a will of your own! But what was the use of a will if you had no faith? This indeed, she saw now, was also Yvonne Griffaton's problem. This was what she too was seeking, and had been all the time, in the face of everything, for some faith – as if one could find it like a new hat or a house for rent ! – yes, even what she was now on the point of finding, and losing, a faith in a cause, was better than none. Yvonne felt she had to have a cigarette and when she returned it looked much as though Yvonne Griffaton had at last succeeded in her quest. Yvonne Griffaton was finding her faith in life itself, in travel, in another love, in the music of Ravel. The chords of *Bolero* strutted out redundantly, snapping and clicking their heels, and Yvonne Griffaton was in Spain, in Italy; the sea was seen, Algiers,

Cyprus, the desert with its mirages, the Sphinx. What did all this mean? Europe, Yvonne thought. Yes, for her, inevitably Europe, the Grand Tour, the Tour Eiffel, as she had known all along. – But why was it, richly endowed in a capacity for living as she was, *she* had never found a faith merely in 'life' sufficient? If that were *all*! ... In unselfish love – in the stars! Perhaps it should be enough. And yet, and yet, it was entirely true, that one had never given up, or ceased to hope, or to try, gropingly, to find a meaning, a pattern, an answer –

The bull pulled against the opposing forces of ropes a while longer, then subsided gloomily, swinging his head from side to side with those shuffling sweeps along the ground, into the dust where, temporarily defeated but watchful, he resembled some fantastic insect trapped at the centre of a huge vibrating web ... Death, or a sort of death, just as it so often was in life; and now, once more, resurrection. The *charros*, making strange knotty passes at the bull with their lariats, were rigging him for his eventual rider, wherever, and whoever, he might be.

– 'Thank you.' Hugh had passed her the pinch bottle of habanero also absently. She took a sip and gave it to the Consul who sat holding the bottle gloomily in his hands without drinking. And had he not, too, met her at the Bus Terminal?

Yvonne glanced around the grandstand : there was not, so far as she could see, in this whole gathering one other woman save a gnarled old Mexican selling pulque. No, she was wrong. An American couple had just climbed up the scaffolding farther down, a woman in a dove-grey suit, and a man with horn-rimmed spectacles, a slight stoop, and hair worn long at the back, who looked like an orchestra conductor; it was the couple Hugh and she had seen before in the *zócalo*, at a corner Novedades buying *huaraches* and strange rattles and masks, and then later, from the bus, on the church steps, watching the natives dancing. How happy they seemed in one another; lovers they were, or on their honeymoon. Their future would stretch out before them pure and untrammelled as a blue and peaceful lake, and thinking of this Yvonne's heart felt suddenly light as that of a boy on his summer holidays, who rises in the morning and disappears into the sun.

Instantly Hugh's shack began to take form in her mind. But it was not a shack – it was a home! It stood, on wide-girthed strong legs of pine, between the forest of pine and high, high waving alders and tall slim birches, and the sea. There was the narrow path that wound down through the forest from the store, with salmonberries and thimbleberries and wild blackberry bushes that on bright winter nights of frost reflected a million moons; behind the house was a dogwood tree that bloomed twice in the year with white stars. Daffodils and snowdrops grew in the little garden. There was a wide porch where they sat on spring mornings, and a pier going right out into the water. They would build this pier themselves when the tide was out, sinking the posts one by one down the steep slanting beach. Post by post they'd build it until one day they could dive from the end into the sea. The sea was blue and cold and they would swim every day, and every day climb back up a ladder on to their pier, and run straight along it into their house. She saw the house plainly now; it was small and made of silvery weathered shingles, it had a red door, and casement windows, open to the sun. She saw the curtains she had made herself, the Consul's desk, his favourite old chair, the bed, covered with brilliant Indian blankets, the yellow light of the lamps against the strange blue of long June evenings, the crab-apple tree that half supported the open sunny platform where the Consul would work in summer, the wind in the dark trees above and the surf beating along the shore on stormy autumn nights; and then the mill-wheel reflections of sunlight on water, as Hugh described those on the Cervecería Quauhnahuac, only sliding down the front of their house, sliding, sliding, over the windows, the walls, the reflections that, above and behind the house, turned the pine boughs into green chenille: and at night they stood on their pier and watched the constellations, Scorpio and Triangulum, Bootes and the Great Bear, and then the millwheel reflections would be of moonlight on water ceaselessly sliding down the wooden walls of silver overlapping shingles, the moonlight that on the water also embroidered their waving windows –

And it was possible. It was possible! It was all there, waiting for them. If only she were alone with Geoffrey so she could tell him of it! Hugh, his cowboy hat on the back of his head, his feet in their high-heeled boots on the seat in front, seemed now an interloper, a stranger, part of the scene below. He was watching the rigging of the bull with intense interest, but becoming conscious of her gaze, his eyelids drooped nervously and he sought and found his cigarette package, corroborating its emptiness more with his fingers than his eyes.

Down in the arena a bottle was passed among the men on horseback who handed it to the others working on the bull. Two of the horsemen galloped about the ring aimlessly. The spectators bought lemonade, fruit, potato chips, pulque. The Consul himself made as if to buy some pulque but changed his mind, fingering the habanero bottle.

More drunks interfered, wanting to ride the bull again; they lost interest, became sudden horse fanciers, lost that concern too, and were chased out, careening.

The giant returned with the belching squealing Rocket, vanished, was sucked away by it. The crowd grew silent, so silent she could almost make out some sounds that might have been the fair again, in Quauhnahuac.

Silence was as infectious as mirth, she thought, an awkward silence in one group begetting a loutish silence in another, which in turn induced a more general, meaningless silence in a third, until it had spread everywhere. Nothing in the world is more powerful than one of these sudden strange silences –

– the house, dappled with misty light that fell softly through the small new leaves, and then the mist rolling away across the water, and the mountains, still white with snow appearing sharp and clear against the blue sky, and blue wood-smoke from the driftwood fire curling out of the chimney; the sloping shingled woodshed on whose roof the dogwood blossoms fell, the wood packed with beauty inside; the axe, the trowels, the rake, the spade, the deep, cool well with its guardian figure, a flotsam, a wooden sculpture of the sea, fixed above it; the old kettle, the new kettle, the teapot, the coffee pot, the double boilers, the saucepans, the cupboard. Geoffrey worked outside, longhand, as he liked to do, and she sat typing at a desk by the window – for she would learn to type, and transcribe all his manuscripts from the slanting script with its queer familiar Greek e's and odd t's into neat clean pages – and as she worked she would see a seal rise out of the water, peer round, and sink soundlessly. Or a heron, that seemed made of cardboard and string, would flap past heavily, to alight majestically on a rock and stand there, tall and motionless. Kingfishers and swallows flitted past the eaves or perched on their pier. Or a seagull would glide past perched on a piece of floating driftwood, his head in his wing, rocking, rocking with the motion of the sea ... They would buy all their food, just as Hugh said, from a store beyond the woods, and see nobody, save a few fishermen, whose white boats in winter they would see pitching at anchor in the bay. She would cook and clean and Geoffrey would chop the wood and bring the water from the well. And they would work and work on this book of Geoffrey's, which would bring him world fame. But absurdly they would not care about this; they would continue to live, in simplicity and love, in their home between the forest and the sea. And at half-tide they would look down from their pier and see, in the shallow lucid water, turquoise and vermilion and purple starfish, and small brown velvet crabs sidling among barnacled stones brocaded like heart-shaped pin-cushions. While at week-ends, out on the inlet, every little while, ferry-boats would pass ferrying song upstream –

The spectators sighed with relief, there was a leafy rustling among them, something, Yvonne couldn't see what, had been accomplished down below. Voices began to buzz, the air to tingle once more with suggestions, eloquent insults, repartee.

The bull was clambering to its feet with its rider, a fat tousle-headed Mexican, who seemed rather impatient and irritated with the whole business. The bull too looked irritated and now stood quite still.

A string band in the grandstand opposite struck up *Guadala-jara* out of tune. Guadalajara, Guadalajara, half the band was singing ...

'*Guadalajara*,' Hugh slowly pronounced each syllable.

Down up, down down up, down down up, banged the guitars, while the rider glowered at them, then, with a furious look, took a firmer grip of the rope round the bull's neck, jerked it, and for a moment the animal actually did what was apparently expected of it, convulsing itself violently, like a rocking-machine, and giving little leaps into the air with all four feet. But presently it relapsed into its old, cruising gait. Ceasing to participate altogether, it was no longer difficult to ride, and after one ponderous circuit of the arena, headed straight back for its pen which, opened by the pressure of the crowd on the fences, it'd doubtless been secretly longing for all the time, trotting back into it with suddenly positive, twinkling innocent hooves.

Everyone laughed as at a poor joke: it was laughter keyed to and somewhat increased by a further misfortune, the premature appearance of another bull, who, driven at a near gallop from the open pen by the cruel thrusts and pokes and blows intended to arrest him, on reaching the ring stumbled, and fell headlong into the dust.

The first bull's rider, glum and discredited, had dismounted in the pen: and it was difficult not to feel sorry for him too, as he stood by the fence scratching his head, explaining his failure to one of the boys standing, marvellously balanced, on the top railing –

– and perhaps even this month, if there had been a late Indian summer, she would stand on their porch looking down over Geoffrey's work, over his shoulder into the water and see an archipelago, islands of opalescent foam and branches of dead bracken – yet beautiful, beautiful – and the reflected alder trees, almost bare now, casting their sparse shadows over the brocaded stones like pincushions, over which the brocaded crabs scuttled among a few drowned leaves –

The second bull made two feeble attempts to get up, and lay down again; a lone horseman galloped across the ring swinging a rope and shouting at it in a husky tone: *'Booa, shooa, booa'* – other *charros* appeared with more ropes; the little dog came scampering up from nowhere, scuttling about in circles; but it did no good. Nothing definite happened and nothing seemed likely to budge the second bull who was roped casually where it lay.

Everybody became resigned to another long wait, another

long silence, while below, and with a bad conscience, they half-heartedly set about rigging the second bull.

'See the old unhappy bull', the Consul was saying, 'in the *plaza* beautiful. Do you mind if I have a very small drink, darling, a poquitín ... No? Thank you. Waiting with a wild surmise for the ropes that tantalize – '

– and gold leaves too, on the surface, and scarlet, one green, waltzing downstream with her cigarette, while a fierce autumn sun glared up from beneath the stones –

'Or waiting with seven – why not? – wild surmises, for the rope which tantalizes. Stout Cortés ought to come into the next bit, gazing at the horrific, who was the least pacific of all men ... Silent on a peak in Quauhnahuac. Christ, what a disgusting performance – '

'Isn't it?' Yvonne said, and turning away thought she saw standing opposite below the band, the man in dark glasses who'd been outside the Bella Vista this morning and then later – or had she imagined it? – standing up beside Cortez Palace. 'Geoffrey, who's that man?'

'Strange about the bull,' the Consul said. 'He's so elusive. – There's your enemy, but he doesn't want to play ball today. He lies down ... Or just falls down; see, he's quite forgotten he's your enemy now, so *you* think, and pat him ... Actually ... Next time you meet him you might not recognize him as an enemy at all.'

'*Es ist vielleicht* an ox,' Hugh muttered.

'An oxymoron ... Wisely foolish.'

The animal lay supine as before, but momentarily abandoned. People were huddled down below in argumentative groups. Horsemen also arguing continued to whoop about the ring. Yet there was no definite action, still less any indication that such was forthcoming. Who was going to ride the second bull? seemed the main question in the air. But then what of the first bull, who was raising Cain in the pen and was even with difficulty being restrained from taking the field again. Meanwhile the remarks around her echoed the contention in the arena. The first rider hadn't been given a fair chance, *verdad? No hombre,* he shouldn't even have been given that chance. *No hombre,* he should be given another. Imposseebly, another rider was scheduled. *Vero*, he wasn't present, or couldn't come, or was present but wasn't going to ride, or wasn't present but was trying hard to get here, *verdad*? – still, that didn't change the arrangement or give the first rider his opportunity to try again.

Drunks were as anxious as ever to deputize; one was mounted on the bull now, pretending to ride it already, though it hadn't moved a fraction. He was dissuaded by the first rider, who looked very sulky: just in time: at that moment the bull woke up and rolled over.

The first rider was on the point now, in spite of all comments, of trying again when – no; he had been too bitterly insulted, and wasn't going to ride on any account. He walked away over towards the fence, to do some more explaining to the boy still balanced on top.

A man down below wearing an enormous *sombrero* had shouted for silence and paddling his arms was addressing them from the ring. They were being appealed to, either for their continued patience, or for a rider to volunteer.

Yvonne never found out which. For something extraordinary had happened, something ridiculous, yet with earth-shattering abruptness –

It was Hugh. Leaving his coat behind he had jumped from the scaffolding into the arena and was now running in the direction of the bull from which, perhaps in jest, or because they mistook him for the scheduled rider, the ropes were being whipped as by magic. Yvonne stood up : the Consul came to his feet beside her.

'Good Christ, the bloody fool!'

The second bull, not indifferent as might have been supposed to the removal of the ropes, and perplexed by the confused uproar that greeted his rider's arrival, had clambered up bellowing; Hugh was astride him and already cake-walking crazily in the middle of the ring.

'God damn the stupid ass!' the Consul said.

Hugh was holding the rigging tightly with one hand and beating the brute's flanks with the other, and doing this with an expertness Yvonne was astonished to find she was still almost competent to judge. Yvonne and the Consul sat down again.

The bull jumped to the left, then to the right with both fore-legs simultaneously, as though they were strung together. Then it sank to its knees. It clambered up, angry; Yvonne was aware of the Consul beside her drinking habanero and then of him corking the bottle.

'Christ ... Jesus.'

'It's all right, Geoff. Hugh knows what he's doing.'

'The bloody fool ...'

'Hugh'll be all right – Wherever he learnt it.'

'The pimp ... the poxbox.'

It was true that the bull had really waked up and was doing its best to unseat him. It pawed the earth, galvanized itself like a frog, even crawled on its belly. Hugh held on fast. The spectators laughed and cheered, though Hugh, really indistinguishable from a Mexican now, looked serious, even grim. He leaned back, holding on determinedly, with feet splayed, heels knocking the sweaty flanks. The *charros* galloped across the arena.

'I don't think he means to show off,' Yvonne smiled. No, he was simply submitting to that absurd necessity he felt for action, so wildly exacerbated by the dawdling inhuman day. All his thoughts now were bringing that miserable bull to its knees. 'This is the way you like to play? This is the way I like to play. You don't like the bull for some reason? Very well, I don't like the bull either.' She felt these sentiments helping to smite Hugh's mind rigid with concentration upon the defeat of the bull. And somehow one had little anxiety watching him. One trusted him implicitly in this situation, just as one trusted in a trick diver, a tightrope walker, a steeplejack. One felt, even, half ironically, that this was the kind of thing Hugh might be best fitted to do and Yvonne was surprised to recall her instant's panic this morning when he had jumped on the parapet of the bridge over the *barranca*.

'The risk ... the fool,' the Consul said, drinking habanero.

Hugh's troubles, in fact, were only beginning. The *charros*, the man in the *sombrero*, the child who'd bitten the first bull's tail, the *serape* and rag *hombres*, even the little dog who came sneaking in again under the fence, were all closing in to increase them; all had their part.

Yvonne was abruptly aware that there were black clouds climbing the sky from the north-east, a temporary ominous darkness that lent a sense of evening, thunder sounded in the mountains, a single grumble, metallic, and a gust of wind raced through the trees, bending them : the scene itself possessed a remote strange beauty; the white trousers and bright *serapes* of the men enticing the bull shining against the dark trees and lowering sky, the horses, transformed instantly into clouds of dust by their riders with their scorpion-tailed whips, who leaned far out of their bucket saddles to throw wildly, ropes anywhere, everywhere. Hugh's impossible yet somehow splendid performance in the midst of it all, the boy, whose hair was blowing madly over his face, high up in the tree.

The band struck up *Guadalajara* again in the wind, and the bull bellowed, his horns caught in the railings through which, helpless, he was being poked with sticks in what remained of his testicles, tickled with switches, a machete, and, after getting clear and re-entangled, a garden rake; dust too and dung was thrown in his red eyes; and now there seemed no end to this childish cruelty.

'Darling,' Yvonne whispered suddenly, 'Geoffrey – look at me. Listen to me, I've been ... there isn't anything to keep us here any longer ... Geoffrey ...'

The Consul, pale, without his dark glasses, was looking at her piteously; he was sweating, his whole frame was trembling. 'No,' he said. 'No ... *No*,' he added, almost hysterically.

'Geoffrey darling ... don't tremble ... what are you afraid of? Why don't we go away, now, tomorrow, today ... what's to stop us?'

'No ...'

'Ah, how good you've been – '

The Consul put his arm around her shoulders, leaning his damp head against her hair like a child, and for a moment it was as if a spirit of intercession and tenderness hovered over them, guarding, watching. He said wearily :

'Why not. Let's for Jesus Christ's sweet sake get away. A thousand, a million miles away, Yvonne, anywhere, so long as it's away. Just away. Away from all this. Christ, from this.'

– into a wild sky full of stars at rising, and Venus and the golden moon at sunrise, and at noon blue mountains with snow and blue cold rough water – 'Do you *mean* it?'

'Do I mean it!'

'Darling ...' It ran in Yvonne's mind that all at once they were talking – agreeing hastily – like prisoners who do not have much time to talk; the Consul took her hand. They sat closely, hands clasped, with their shoulders touching. In the arena Hugh tugged; the bull tugged, was free, but furious now, throwing himself at any place on the fence that reminded him of the pen he'd so prematurely left, and now, tired, persecuted beyond measure, finding it, hurling himself at the gate time after time with an incensed, regressive bitterness until, the little dog barking at his heels, he'd lost it again ... Hugh rode the tiring bull round and round the ring.

'This isn't just escaping, I mean, let's start again *really*, Geoffrey, really and cleanly somewhere. It could be like a rebirth.'

'Yes. Yes it could.'

'I think I know, I've got it all clear in my mind at last. Oh Geoffrey, at last I think I have.'

'Yes, I think I know too.'

Below them, the bull's horns again involved the fence.

'Darling ...' They would arrive at their destination by train, a train that wandered through an evening land of fields beside water, an arm of the Pacific –

'Yvonne?'

'Yes, darling?'

'I've fallen down, you know ... Somewhat.'

'Never mind, darling.'

'... Yvonne?'

'Yes?'

'I love you ... Yvonne?'

'Oh, I love you too!'

'My dear one ... My sweetheart.'

'Oh, Geoffrey. We *could* be happy, we *could* – '

'Yes ... We could.'

– and far across the water, the little house, waiting –

There was a sudden roar of applause followed by the accelerated clangour of guitars deploying downwind; the bull had pulled away from the fence and once more the scene was becoming animated: Hugh and the bull tussled for a moment in the centre of a small fixed circle the others created by their exclusion from it within the arena; then the whole was veiled in dust; the pen gate to their left had broken open again, freeing all the other bulls, including the first one, who was probably responsible; they were charging out amid cheers, snorting, scattering in every direction.

Hugh was eclipsed for a while, wrestling with his bull in a far corner: suddenly someone on that side screamed. Yvonne pulled herself from the Consul and stood up.

'Hugh ... Something's happened.'

The Consul stood up unsteadily. He was drinking from the habanero bottle, drinking, till he almost finished it. Then he said:

'I can't see. But I think it's the bull.'

It was still impossible to make out what was happening on the far side in the dusty confusion of horsemen, bulls, and ropes. Then Yvonne saw yes it was the bull, which, played out, was lying in the dust again. Hugh calmly walked off it, bowed to the cheering spectators, and, dodging other bulls, vaulted over the distant fence. Someone restored his hat to him.

'Geoffrey – ' Yvonne began hurriedly, 'I don't expect you to – I mean – I know it's going to be – '

But the Consul was finishing the habanero. He left a little for Hugh, however.

... The sky was blue again overhead as they went down into Tomalín; dark clouds still gathered behind Popocatepetl, their purple masses shot through with the bright late sunlight, that fell too on another little silver lake glittering cool, fresh, and inviting before them, Yvonne had neither seen on the way, nor remembered.

'The Bishop of Tasmania,' the Consul was saying, 'or somebody dying of thirst in the Tasmanian desert, had a similar experience. The distant prospect of Cradle Mountain had consoled him a while, and then he saw this water ... Unfortunately it turned out to be sunlight blazing on myriads of broken bottles.'

The lake was a broken greenhouse roof belonging to El Jardín Xicotancatl : only weeds lived in the greenhouse.

But their house was in her mind now as she walked : their home was real : Yvonne saw it at sunrise, in the long afternoons of south-west winds, and at nightfall she saw it in starlight and moonlight, covered with snow : she saw it from above, in the forest, with the chimney and the roof below her, and the fore-shortened pier : she saw it from the beach rising above her, and she saw it, tiny, in the distance, a haven and a beacon against the trees, from the sea. It was only that the little boat of their conversation had been moored precariously; she could hear it banging against the rocks; later she would drag it up farther, where it was safe. – Why was it though, that right in the centre of her brain, there should be a figure of a woman having hysterics, jerking like a puppet and banging her fists upon the ground?

'Forward to the Salón Ofelia,' cried the Consul.

A hot thundery wind launched itself at them, spent itself, and somewhere a bell beat out wild tripthongs.

Their shadows crawled before them in the dust, slid down white thirsty walls of houses, were caught violently for a moment in an elliptical shade, the turning wrenched wheel of a boy's bicycle.

The spoked shadow of the wheel, enormous, insolent, swept away.

Now their own shadows fell full across the square to the raised twin doors of the tavern, Todos Contentos y Yo También: under the doors they noticed what looked like the bottom of a crutch, someone leaving. The crutch didn't move; its owner was having an argument at the door, a last drink perhaps. Then it disappeared : one door of the *cantina* was propped back, something emerged.

Bent double, groaning with the weight, an old lame Indian was carrying on his back, by means of a strap looped over his forehead, another poor Indian, yet older and more decrepit than himself. He carried the older man and his crutches, trembling in every limb under this weight of the past, he carried both their burdens.

They all stood watching the Indian as he disappeared with the old man round a bend of the road, into the evening, shuffling through the grey white dust in his poor sandals . . .

10

'MESCAL,' the Consul said, almost absent-mindedly. What had he said? Never mind. Nothing less than mescal would do. But it musn't be a serious mescal, he persuaded himself. '*No, Señor Cervantes,*' he whispered, '*mescal, poquito.*'

Nevertheless, the Consul thought, it was not merely that he shouldn't have, not merely that, no, it was more as if he had lost or missed something, or rather, not precisely lost, not necessarily missed. – It was as if, more, he were waiting for something, and then again, not waiting. – It was as if, almost, he stood (instead of upon the threshold of the Salón Ofélia, gazing at the calm pool where Yvonne and Hugh were about to swim) once more upon that black open station platform, with the cornflowers and meadowsweet growing on the far side, where after drinking all night he had gone to meet Lee Maitland returning from Virginia at 7.40 in the morning, gone, light-headed, light-footed, and in that state of being where Baudelaire's angel indeed wakes, desiring to meet trains perhaps, but to meet no trains that stop, for in the angel's mind are no trains that stop, and from such trains none descends, not even another angel, not even a fair-haired one, like Lee Maitland. – Was the train late? Why was he pacing the platform? Was it the second or third train from Suspension Bridge – *Suspension!* – the Station Master had said would be her train? What had the porter said? Could she be on this train? Who was she? It was impossible that Lee Maitland could be on any such train. And besides, all these trains were expresses. The railway lines went into the far distance uphill. A lone bird flapped across the lines far away. To the right of the level-crossing, at a little distance, stood a tree like a green exploding sea-mine, frozen. The dehydrated onion factory by the sidings awoke, then the coal companies. *It's a black business but we use you white: Daemon's Coal* ... A delicious smell of onion soup in side-streets of Vavin impregnated the early morning. Grimed

sweeps at hand trundled barrows, or were screening coal. Rows of
dead lamps like erect snakes poised to strike along the platform.
On the other side were cornflowers, dandelions, a garbage-can
like a brazier blazing furiously all by itself among meadowsweet. The morning grew hot. And now, one after one, the terrible trains appeared on top of the raised horizon, shimmering
now, in mirage : first the distant wail, then, the frightful spouting and spindling of black smoke, a sourceless towering pillar,
motionless, then a round hull, as if not on the lines, as if going
the other way, or as if stopping, as if not stopping, or as if slipping away over the fields, as if stopping; oh God, not stopping;
downhill : *clipperty-one* clipperty-one : *clipperty-two* clipperty-
two : *clipperty-three* clipperty-three : *clipperty-four clipperty-
four* : alas, thank God, not stopping, and the lines shaking, the
station flying, the coal dust, black bituminous : *lickety-cut
lickety-cut lickety-cut* : and then another train, *clipperty-one
clipperty-one*, coming in the other direction, swaying, whizzing,
two feet above the lines, flying, *clipperty-two*, with one light
burning against the morning, *clipperty-three* clipperty-three, a
single useless strange eye, red-gold : trains, trains, trains, each
driven by a banshee playing a shrieking nose-organ in D minor;
lickety-cut lickety-cut lickety-cut. But not his train; and not her
train. Still, the train would come doubtless—had the Station Master said the third or fourth train from which way? Which was
north, west? And anyhow, whose north, whose west? ... And he
must pick flowers to greet the angel, the fair Virginian descending
from the train. But the embankment flowers would not pick, spur-
ting sap, sticky, the flowers were on the wrong end of the stalks
(and he on the wrong side of the tracks), he nearly fell into the
brazier, the cornflowers grew in the middle of their stalks, the
stalks of meadowsweet – or was it queen's lace? – were too long,
his bouquet was a failure. And how to get back across the tracks
– here was a train now coming in the wrong direction again,
clipperty-one clipperty-one, the lines unreal, not there, walking
on air; or rails that did lead somewhere, to unreal life, or, perhaps, Hamilton, Ontario. – Fool, he was trying to walk along a
single line, like a boy on the kerb : *clipperty-two* clipperty-two :
clipperty-three clipperty-three : *clipperty-four clipperty-four* :

clipperty-five clipperty-five : clipperty-six clipperty-six : clipperty-seven; clipperty seven – trains, trains, trains, trains, converging upon him from all sides of the horizon, each wailing for its demon lover. Life had no time to waste. Why, then, should it waste so much of everything else? With the dead cornflowers before him, at evening – the next moment – the Consul sat in the station tavern with a man who'd just tried to sell him three loose teeth. Was it tomorrow he was supposed to meet the train? What had the Station Master said? Had that been Lee Maitland herself waving at him frantically from the express? And who had flung the soiled bundle of tissue papers out of the window? What had he lost? Why was that idiot sitting there, in a dirty grey suit, and trousers baggy at the knees, with one bicycle clip, in his long, long baggy grey jacket, and grey cloth cap, and brown boots, with his thick fleshy grey face, from which three upper teeth, perhaps the *very* three teeth, were missing, all on one side, and thick neck, saying, every few minutes to anyone who came in : 'I'm watching you.' 'I can see you ...' 'You won't escape me.' – 'If you only kept quiet, Claus, no one'd know you were crazy.' ... That was the time too, in the storm country, when 'the lightning is peeling the poles, Mr Firmin, and biting the wires, sir – you can taste it afterwards too, in the water, pure sulphur,' – that at four o'clock each afternoon, preceded, out of the adjacent cemetery, by the gravedigger – sweating, heavy-footed, bowed, long-jawed and trembling, and carrying his special tools of death – he would come to this same tavern to meet Mr Quattras, the Negro bookie from Codrington, in the Barbados. 'I'm a race-track man and I was brought up with whites, so the blacks don't like me.' Mr. Quattras, grinning and sad, feared deportation ... But that battle against death had been won. And he had saved Mr Quattras. That very night, had it been? – with a heart like a cold brazier standing by a railway platform among meadowsweet wet with dew : they are beautiful and terrifying, these shadows of cars that sweep down fences, and sweep zebra-like across the grass path in the avenue of dark oaks under the moon : a single shadow, like an umbrella on rails, travelling down a picket fence; portents of doom, of the heart failing ... Gone. Eaten up in reverse by night. And the moon gone. *C'était pendant l'horreur d'une profonde nuit.* And the deserted cemetery in the starlight, forsaken by the grave-digger, drunk now, wandering home across the fields – 'I can dig a grave in three hours if they'll let me,' – the cemetery in the dappled moonlight of a single street lamp, the deep thick grass, the towering obelisk lost in the Milky Way. *Jull*, it said on the monument. What had th Station Master said? The dead. Do they sleep? Why should they, when we cannot? *Mais tout dort, et l'armée, et les vents, et Neptune.* And he had placed the poor ragged cornflowers reverently on a neglected grave … That was Oakville. – But Oaxaca or Oakville, what difference? Or be-'tween a tavern that opened at four o'clock in the afternoon, and one that opened (save on holidays) at four o'clock in the morning? … *'I ain't telling you the word of a lie but once I had a whole vault dug up for $100 and sent to Cleveland!'*

A corpse will be transported by express …

Oozing alcohol from every pore, the Consul stood at the open door of the Salón Ofelia. How sensible to have had a mescal. How sensible! For it was the right, the sole drink to have under the circumstances. Moreover he had not only proved to himself he was not afraid of it, he was now fully awake, fully sober again, and well able to cope with anything that might come his way. But for this slight continual twitching and hopping within his field of vision, as of innumerable sand fleas, he might have told himself he hadn't had a drink for months. The only thing wrong with him, he was too hot.

A natural waterfall crashing down into a sort of reservoir built on two levels – he found the sight less cooling than grotesquely suggestive of some organized ultimate sweat; the lower level made a pool where Hugh and Yvonne were still not yet swimming. The water on the turbulent upper level raced over an artificial falls beyond which, becoming a swift stream, it wound through thick jungle to spill down a much larger natural *cascada* out of sight. After that it dispersed, he recalled, lost its identity, dribbled, at various places, into the *barranca*. A path followed the stream through the jungle and at one place another path branched off to the right which went to Parián : and the Farolito. Though the first path led you to rich *cantina* country too. God knows why. Once, perhaps, in *hacienda* days, Tomalín had held some irrigational importance. Then, after the burning of the sugar plantations, schemes, cleavable and lustrous, evolved for a spa, were abandoned sulphurously. Later, vague dreams of hydro-elecric power hovered in the air, though nothing had been done about them. Parián was an even greater mystery. Originally settled by a scattering of those fierce forebears of Cervantes who had succeeded in making Mexico great even in her betrayal, the traitorous Tlaxcalans, the nominal capital of the state had been quite eclipsed by Quauhnahuac since the revolution, and while still an obscure administrative centre, no one had ever adequately explained its continued existence to him. One met people going there; few, now he thought about it, ever coming back. Of course they'd come back, he had himself: there was an explanation. But why didn't a bus run there, or only grudgingly, and by a strange route? The Consul started.

Near him lurked some hooded photographers. They were waiting by their tattered machines for the bathers to leave their boxes. Now two girls were squealing as they came down to the water in their ancient, hired costumes. Their escorts swaggered along a grey parapet dividing the pool from the rapids above, obviously deciding not to dive in, pointing for excuse up at a ladderless springboard, derelict, like some forgotten victim of tidal catastrophe, in a weeping pepper tree. After a time they rushed howling down a concrete incline into the pool. The girls bridled, but waded in after, tittering. Nervous gusts agitated the surface of the baths. Magenta clouds piled higher against the horizon, though overhead the sky remained clear.

Hugh and Yvonne appeared, grotesquely costumed. They stood laughing on the brink of the pool – shivering, though the horizontal rays of the sun lay on them all with solid heat.

The photographers took photographs.

'Why,' Yvonne called out, 'this is like the Horseshoe Falls in Wales.'

'Or Niagara', observed the Consul, '*circa* 1900. What about a trip on the *Maid of the Mist*, seventy-five cents with oilskins.'

Hugh turned round gingerly, hands on knees.

'Yeah. To where the rainbow ends.'

'The Cave of the Winds. The Cascada Sagrada.'

There were, in fact, rainbows. Though without them the mescal (which Yvonne couldn't of course have noticed) would have already invested the place with a magic. The magic was of Niagara Falls itself, not its elemental majesty, the honeymoon town; in a sweet, tawdry, even hoydenish sense of love that haunted this nostalgic spray-blown spot. But now the mescal struck a discord, then a succession of plaintive discords to which the drifting mists all seemed to be dancing, through the elusive subtleties of ribboned light, among the detached shreds of rainbows floating. It was a phantom dance of souls, baffled by these deceptive blends, yet still seeking permanence in the midst of what was only perpetually evanescent, or eternally lost. Or it was a dance of the seeker and his goal, here pursuing still the gay colours he did not know he had assumed, there striving to identify the finer scene of which he might never realize he was already a part ...

Dark coils of shadows lay in the deserted bar-room. They sprang at him. '*Otro mescalito. Un poquito.*' The voice seemed to come from above the counter where two wild yellow eyes pierced the gloom. The scarlet comb, the wattles, then the bronze green metallic feathers of some fowl standing on the bar, materialized, and Cervantes, rising playfully from behind it, greeted him with Tlaxcaltecan pleasure: '*Muy fuerte. Muy* terreebly,' he cackled.

Was this the face that launched five hundred ships, and betrayed Christ into being in the Western Hemisphere? But the bird appeared tame enough. Half past tree by the cock, that other fellow had said. And here was the cock. It was a fighting cock. Cervantes was training it for a fight in Tlaxcala, but the Consul couldn't be interested. Cervantes's cockerels always lost – he'd attended drunkenly one session in Cuautla; the vicious little man-made battles, cruel and destructive, yet somehow bedraggledly inconclusive, each brief as some hideously mismanaged act of intercourse, disgusted and bored him. Cervantes took the cock away. '*Un bruto,*' he added.

The subdued roar of the falls filled the room like a ship's engine ... Eternity ... The Consul, cooler, leaned on the bar, staring into his second glass of the colourless ether-smelling liquid. To drink or not to drink. – But without mescal, he imagined, he had forgotten eternity, forgotten their world's voyage, that the earth was a ship, lashed by the Horn's tail, doomed never to make her Valparaiso. Or that it was like a golf ball, launched at Hercules's Butterfly, wildly hooked by a giant out of an asylum window in hell. Or that it was a bus, making its erratic journey to Tomalín and nothing. Or that it was like – whatever it would be shortly, after the next mescal.

Still, there had not yet been a 'next' mescal. The Consul stood, his hand as if part of the glass, listening, remembering ... Suddenly he heard, above the roar, the clear sweet voices of the young Mexicans outside: the voice of Yvonne too, dear, intolerable – and different, after the first mescal – shortly to be lost.

Why lost? ... The voices were as if confused now with the blinding torrent of sunlight which poured across the open doorway, turning the scarlet flowers along the path into flaming swords. Even almost bad poetry is better than life, the muddle of voices might have been saying, as, now, he drank half his drink.

The Consul was aware of another roaring, though it came from inside his head: *clipperty-one*: the American Express, swaying, bears the corpse through the green meadows. What is man but a little soul holding up a corpse? The soul! Ah, and did she not too have her savage and traitorous Tlaxcalans, her Cortés and her *noches tristes*, and, sitting within her innermost citadel in chains, drinking chocolate, her pale Moctezuma?

The roaring rose, died away, rose again; guitar chords mingled with the shouting of many voices, calling, chanting, like native women in Kashmir, pleading, above the noise of the maelstrom: '*Borrrrraaacho,*' they wailed. And the dark room with its flashing doorway rocked under his feet.

' – what do you think, Yvonne, if sometime we climb that baby, Popo I mean – '

'Good heavens why! Haven't you had enough exercise for one – '

' – might be a good idea to harden your muscles first, try a few small peaks.'

329

They were joking. But the Consul was not joking. His second mescal had become serious. He left it still unfinished on the counter, Señor Cervantes was beckoning from a far corner.

A shabby little man with a black shade over one eye, wearing a black coat, but a beautiful *sombrero* with long gay tassels down the back, he seemed, however savage at heart, in almost as highly nervous a state as himself. What magnetism drew these quaking ruined creatures into his orbit? Cervantes led the way behind the bar, ascended two steps, and pulled a curtain aside. Poor lonely fellow, he wanted to show him round his house again. The Consul made the steps with difficulty. One small room occupied by a huge brass bedstead. Rusty rifles in a rack on the wall. In one corner, before a tiny porcelain Virgin, burned a little lamp. Really a sacramental candle, it diffused a ruby shimmer through its glass into the room, and cast a broad yellow flickering cone on the ceiling : the wick was burning low. 'Mistair,' Cervantes tremulously pointed to it. '*Señor*. My grandfather tell me never to let her go out.' Mescal tears came to the Consul's eyes, and he remembered sometime during last night's debauch going with Dr Vigil to a church in Quauhnahuac he didn't know, with sombre tapestries, and strange votive pictures, a compassionate Virgin floating in the gloom, to whom he prayed, with muddily beating heart, he might have Yvonne again. Dark figures, tragic and isolated, stood about the church, or were kneeling – only the bereaved and lonely went there. 'She is the Virgin for those who have nobody with,' the doctor told him, inclining his head towards the image. 'And for mariners on the sea.' Then he knelt in the dirt and placing his pistol – for Dr Vigil always went armed to Red Cross Balls – on the floor beside him, said sadly, 'Nobody come here, only those who have nobody them with.' Now the Consul made this Virgin the other who had answered his prayer and as they stood in silence before her, prayed again. 'Nothing is altered and in spite of God's mercy I am still alone. Though my suffering seems senseless I am still in agony. There is no explanation of my life.' Indeed there was not, nor was this what he'd meant to convey. 'Please let Yvonne have her dream – dream? – of a new life with me – please let me believe that all that is not an abominable self-deception,' he tried . . . 'Please let me make her happy, deliver me from this dreadful tyranny of self. I have sunk low. Let me sink lower still, that I may know the truth. Teach me to love again, to love life.' That wouldn't do either . . . 'Where is love? Let me truly suffer. Give me back my purity, the knowledge of the Mysteries, that I have betrayed and lost. – Let me be truly lonely, that I may honestly pray. Let us be happy again somewhere, if it's only together, if it's only out of this terrible world. Destroy the world!' he cried in his heart. The Virgin's eyes were turned down in benediction, but perhaps she hadn't heard. – The Consul had scarcely noticed that Cervantes had picked up one of the rifles. 'I love hunting.' After replacing it he opened the bottom drawer of a wardrobe which was squeezed in another corner. The drawer was chock full of books, including the *History of Tlaxcala*, in ten volumes. He shut it immediately. 'I am an insignificant man, and I do not read these books to prove my insignificance,' he said proudly. '*Sí hombre*,' he went on, as they descended to the bar again, 'as I told you, I obey my grandfather. He tell me to marry my wife. So I call my wife my mother.' He produced a photograph of a child lying in a coffin and laid it on the counter. 'I drank all day.'

' – snow goggles and an alpenstock. You'd look awfully nice with – '

' – and my face all covered with grease. And a woollen cap pulled right down over my eyes – '

Hugh's voice came again, then Yvonne's, they were dressing, and conversing loudly over the tops of their bathing boxes, not six feet away, beyond the wall :

' – hungry now, aren't you?'

' – a couple of raisins and half a prune!'

' – not forgetting the limes – '

The Consul finished his mescal : all a pathetic joke, of course, still, this plan to climb Popo, if just the kind of thing Hugh would have found out about before arriving, while neglecting so much else : yet could it be that the notion of climbing the volcano had somehow struck them as having the significance of a lifetime together? Yes, there it rose up before them, with all its hidden dangers, pitfalls, ambiguities, deceptions, portentous as

331

what they could imagine for the poor brief self-deceived space of a cigarette was their own destiny – or was Yvonne simply, alas, happy?

' – where is it we start from, Amecameca –'

'To prevent mountain sickness.'

' – though quite a pilgrimage at that, I gather! Geoff and I thought of doing it, years ago. You go on horseback first, to Tlamancas –'

' – at midnight, at the Hotel Fausto!'

'What would you all prefer? Cauliflowers or pootootsies,' the Consul, innocent, drinkless in a booth, greeted them, frowning; the supper at Emmaus, he felt, trying to disguise his distant mescal voice as he studied the bill of fare provided him by Cervantes. 'Or extramapee syrup. Onans in garlic soup on egg . . .

'Pep with milk? Or what about a nice Filete de Huachinango *rebozado tartar con* German friends?'

Cervantes had handed Yvonne and Hugh each a menu but they were sharing hers: 'Dr Moise von Schmidthaus's special soup,' Yvonne pronounced the words with gusto.

'I think a pepped petroot would be about my mark,' said the Consul, 'after those onans.'

'Just one,' the Consul went on, anxious, since Hugh was laughing so loudly, for Cervantes's feelings, 'but please note the German friends. They even get into the filet.'

'What about the tartar?' Hugh inquired.

'Tlaxcala!' Cervantes, smiling, debated between them with trembling pencil. '*Sí*, I am Tlaxcaltecan . . . You like eggs, *señora*. Stepped on eggs. *Muy sabrosos*. Divorced eggs? For fish, sliced of filet with peas. Vol-au-vent à la reine. Somersaults for the queen. Or you like poxy eggs, poxy in toast. Or veal liver tavernman? Pimesan chike chup? Or spectral chicken of the house? Youn' pigeon. Red snappers with a fried tartar, you like?'

'Ha, the ubiquitous tartar,' Hugh exclaimed.

'I think the spectral chicken of the house would be even more terrific, don't you?' Yvonne was laughing, the foregoing bawdry mostly over her head however, the Consul felt, and still she hadn't noticed anything.

'Probably served in its own ectoplasm.'

'*Sí*, you like sea-sleeves in his ink? Or tunny fish? Or an exquisite mole? Maybe you like fashion melon to start? Fig mermelade? Brambleberry *con* crappe Gran Duc? Omele he sourpusse, you like? You like to drink first a gin fish? Nice gin fish? Silver fish? Sparkenwein?'

'*Madre?*' the Consul asked, 'What's this *madre* here? – You like to eat your mother, Yvonne?'

'*Badre, señor.* Fish *también.* Yautepec fish. *Muy sabroso.* You like?'

'What about it, Hugh – do you want to wait for the fish that dies?'

'I'd like a beer.'

'*Cerveza, sí, Moctezuma? Dos Equis? Carta Blanca?*'

At last they all decided on clam chowder, scrambled eggs, the spectral chicken of the house, beans, and beer. The Consul at first had ordered only shrimps and a hamburger sandwich but yielded to Yvonne's: 'Darling, won't you eat more than that, I could eat a youn' horse,' and their hands met across the table.

And then, for the second time that day, their eyes, in a long look, a long look of longing. Behind her eyes, beyond her, the Consul, an instant, saw Granada, and the train waltzing from Algeciras over the plains of Andalusia, *chufferty pupperty*, *chufferty pupperty*, the low dusty road from the station past the old bull-ring and the Hollywood bar and into the town, past the British Consulate and convent of Los Angeles up past the Washington Irving Hotel (You can't escape me, I can see you, England must return again to New England for her values!), the old number seven train running there: evening, and the stately horse cabs clamber up through the gardens slowly, plod through the arches, mounting past where the eternal beggar is playing on a guitar with three strings, through the gardens, gardens, gardens everywhere, up, up, to the marvellous traceries of the Alhambra (which bored him) past the well where they had met, to the América Pensión; and up, up, now they were climbing themselves, up to the Generalife Gardens, and now from the Generalife Gardens to the Moorish tomb on the extreme summit of the hill; here they plighted their troth . . .

The Consul dropped his eyes at last. How many bottles since then? In how many glasses, how many bottles had he hidden himself, since then alone? Suddenly he saw them, the bottles of aguardiente, of anís, of jerez, of Highland Queen, the glasses, a babel of glasses – towering, like the smoke from the train that day – built to the sky, then falling, the glasses toppling and crashing, falling downhill from the Generalife Gardens, the bottles breaking, bottles of Oporto, tinto, blanco, bottles of Pernod, Oxygénée, absinthe, bottles smashing, bottles cast aside, falling with a thud on the ground in parks, under benches, beds, cinema seats, hidden in drawers at Consulates, bottles of Calvados dropped and broken, or bursting into smithereens, tossed into garbage heaps, flung into the sea, the Mediterranean, the Caspian, the Caribbean, bottles floating in the ocean, dead Scotchmen on the Atlantic highlands – and now he saw them, smelt them, all, from the very beginning–bottles, bottles, bottles, and glasses, glasses, glasses, of bitter, of Dubonnet, of Falstaff, Rye, Johnny Walker, Vieux Whisky, *blanc* Canadien, the apéritifs, the digestifs, the demis, the dobles, the *noch ein* Herr Obers, the *et glas* Araks, the *tusen taks*, the bottles, the bottles, the beautiful bottles of tequila, and the gourds, gourds, gourds, the millions of gourds of beautiful mescal ... The Consul sat very still. His conscience sounded muffled with the roar of water. It whacked and whined round the wooden frame-house with the spasmodic breeze, massed, with the thunderclouds over the trees, seen through the windows, its factions. How indeed could he hope to find himself to begin again when, somewhere, perhaps, in one of those lost or broken bottles, in one of those glasses, lay, for ever, the solitary clue to his identity? How could he go back and look now, scrabble among the broken glass, under the eternal bars, under the oceans?

Stop! Look! Listen! How drunk, or how drunkly sober undrunk, can you calculate you are *now*, at any rate? There had been those drinks at Señora Gregorio's, no more than two certainly. And before? Ah, before! But later, in the bus, he'd only had that sip of Hugh's habanero, then, at the bullthrowing, almost finished it. It was this that made him tight again, but tight in a way he didn't like, in a worse way than in the square

334

even, the tightness of impending unconsciousness, of seasickness, and it was from this sort of tightness – was it? – he'd tried to sober up by taking those *mescalitos* on the sly. But the mescal, the Consul realized, had succeeded in a manner somewhat outside his calculations. The strange truth was, he had another hangover. There was something in fact almost beautiful about the frightful extremity of that condition the Consul now found himself in. It was a hangover like a great dark ocean swell finally rolled up against a foundering steamer, by countless gales to windward that have long since blown themselves out. And from all this it was not so much necessary to sober up again, as once more to wake, yes, as to wake, so much as to –

'Do you remember this morning, Yvonne, when we were crossing the river, there was a *pulquería* on the other side, called La Sepultura or something, and there was an Indian sitting with his back against the wall, with his hat over his face, and his horse tethered to a tree, and there was a number seven branded on the horse's hipbone –'

'– saddlebags –'

... Cave of the Winds, seat of all great decisions, little Cythère of childhood, eternal library, sanctuary bought for a penny or nothing, where else could man absorb and divest himself of so much at the same time? The Consul was awake all right, but he was not, at the moment apparently, having dinner with the others, though their voices came plainly enough. The toilet was all of grey stone, and looked like a tomb – even the seat was cold stone. 'It is what I deserve ... It is what I am,' thought the Consul. 'Cervantes,' he called, and Cervantes, surprisingly, appeared, half round the corner – there was no door to the stone tomb – with the fighting cock, pretending to struggle, under his arm, chuckling:

'– Tlaxcala!'

'– or perhaps it was on his rump –'

After a moment, comprehending the Consul's plight, Cervantes advised:

'A stone, hombre, I bring you a stone.'

'Cervantes!'

335

' – *branded* –'

'... clean yourself on a stone, *señor*.'

– The meal had started well too, he remembered now, a minute or so since, despite everything, and : 'Dangerous Clam Magoo,' he had remarked at the onset of the chowder. 'And our poor spoiling brains and eggs at home!' had he not commiserated, at the apparition, swimming in exquisite mole, of the spectral chicken of the house? They had been discussing the man by the roadside and the thief in the bus, then : '*Excusado.*' And this, this grey final Consulate, this Franklin Island of the soul, was the *excusado.* Set apart from the bathing places, convenient yet hidden from view, it was doubtless a purely Tlaxcaltecan fantasy, Cervantes's own work, built to remind him of some cold mountain village in a mist. The Consul sat, fully dressed however, not moving a muscle. Why was he here? Why was he always more or less, here? He would have been glad of a mirror, to ask himself that question. But there was no mirror. Nothing but stone. Perhaps there was no time either, in this stone retreat. Perhaps this was the eternity that he'd been making so much fuss about, eternity already, of the Svidrigailov variety, only instead of a bath-house in the country full of spiders, here it turned out to be a stone monastic cell wherein sat – strange! – who but himself?

' – *Pulquería* –'

' – and then there was this Indian – '

SEAT OF THE HISTORY OF THE CONQUEST
VISIT TLAXCALA!

read the Consul. (And how was it that, beside him, was standing a lemonade bottle half full of mescal, how had he obtained it so quickly, or Cervantes, repenting, thank God, of the stone, together with the tourist folder, to which was affixed a railway and bus time-table, brought it – or had he purchased it before, and if so, when?)

|VISITE VD. TLAXCALA!

Sus Monumentos, Sitios Históricos y De Bellezas Naturales. Lugar De Descanso, El Mejor Clima. El Aire Más Puro. El Cielo Más Azul.

' – this morning, Yvonne, when we were crossing the river there was this *pulquería* on the other side – '

' ... La Sepultura?'

' – Indian sitting with his back against the wall – '

GEOGRAPHIC SITUATION

The State is located between 19° 06' 10" and 19° 44' 00" North latitude and between 0° 23' 38" and 1° 30' 34" Eastern longitude from Mexico's meridian. Being its boundaries to the North-West and South with Puebla State, to the West with Mexico State and to the North-West with Hidalgo State. Its territorial extension is of 4.132 square kilometres. Its population is about 220,000 inhibitants, giving a density of 53 inhibitants to the square kilometre. It is situated in a valley surrounded by mountains, among them are those called Matlalcueyatl and Ixtaccihuatl.

' – Surely you remember, Yvonne, there was this *pulquería* – '

' – What a glorious morning it was! – '

CLIMATE

Intertropical and proper of highlands, regular and healthy. The malarial sickness is unknown.

' – well, Geoff said he was a Spaniard, for one thing – '

' – but what difference – '

'So that the man beside the road may be an Indian, of course,' the Consul suddenly called from his stone retreat, though it was strange, nobody seemed to have heard him. 'And why an Indian? So that the incident may have some social significance to him, so that it should appear a kind of latter-day repercussion of the Conquest, and a repercussion of the Conquest, if you please, so that that may in turn seem a repercussion of – '

' – crossing the river, a windmill – '

'Cervantes!'

'A stone ... You want a stone, *señor*?'

HYDROGRAPHY

Zahuapan River – Streaming from Atoyac river and bordering the City of Tlaxcala, it supplies a great quantity of power to several factories; among the lagoons, the Acuitlapilco is the most notable and is lying two kilometres South from Tlaxcala City ... Plenty of web-footed fowl is found in the first lagoon.

' – Geoff said the pub he came out of was a Fascist joint. The El Amor de los Amores. What I gathered was he used to be the owner of it, though I think he's come down in the world and he just works there now ... Have another bottle of beer ?'

'Why not? Let's do.'

'What if this man by the roadside had been a Fascist and your Spaniard a Communist? – In his stone retreat the Consul took a sip of mescal. – 'Never mind, I think your thief is a Fascist, though of some ignominious sort, probably a spy on other spies or – '

'The way I feel, Hugh, I thought he must be just some poor man riding from market who'd taken too much pulque, and fell off his horse, and was being taken care of, but then we arrived, and he was robbed ... Though do you know, I didn't notice a thing ... I'm ashamed of myself.'

'Move his hat farther down though, so he can get some air.'

' – outside La Sepultura.'

CITY OF TLAXCALA

The Capital of the State, said to be like Granada, *the Capital of the State, said to be like Granada, said to be like Granada, Granada, the Capital of the State said to be like Granada*, is of a pleasant appearances, straight streets, archaic buildings, neat fine climate, efficient public electric light, and up-to-date Hotel for tourists. It has a beautiful Central Park named 'Francisco I Madero' covered by stricken in years trees, ash-trees being the majority, a garden clothed by many beautiful flowers; seats all over, *four clean, seats all over*, four clean and well-arranged lateral avenues. During the days the birds are singing melodiously among the foliage of the trees. Its whole gives a sight of emotional majesty, *emotional majesty* without losing the tranquillity and rest appearance. The Zahuapan River causeway with an extension of 200 metres long, has on both sides corpulent ash-trees along the river, in some parts there are built ramparts, giving the impression of dikes, in the middle part of the causeway is a wood where there are found 'Senadores' (pic-nic-eaters) in order to make easier the rest days to walkers. From this causeway one can admire the suggestive sceneries showing the Popocatepetl and Ixtaccihuatl.

338

' – or he didn't pay for his pulque at the El Amor de los Amores and the pubkeeper's brother followed him and claimed the reckoning. I see the extraordinary likelihood of that.'

'... What *is* the Ejidal, Hugh?'

' – a bank that advances money to finance collective effort in the villages ... These messengers have a dangerous job. I have that friend in Oaxaca ... Sometimes they travel disguised as, well, peons ... From something Geoff said ... Putting two and two together ... I thought the poor man might have been a bank messenger ... But he was the same chap we saw this morning, at any rate, it was the same horse, do you remember if it had any saddlebags on it, when we saw it?'

'That is, I think I saw it ... It had when I think I saw it.'

' – Why, I think there's a bank like that in Quauhnahuac, Hugh, just by Cortez Palace.'

' – lots of people who don't like the Credit Banks and don't like Cárdenas either, as you know, or have any use for his agrarian reform laws – '

SAN FRANCISCO CONVENT

Within the city limits of Tlaxcala is one of the oldest churches of the New World. This place was the residence of the first Apostolical See, named 'Carolence' in honour of the Spanish King Carlos V, being the first Bishop Don Fray Julián Garcés, on the year 1526. In said Convent, according to tradition, were baptized the four Senators of the Tlaxcaltecan Republic, existing still on the right side of the Church the Baptismal Font, being their God-Fathers the conqueror Hernán Cortés and several of his Captains. The main entrance of the Convent offers a magnificent series of arches and in the inside there is a secret passage, *secret passage*. On the right side of the entrance is erected a majestic tower, which is rated as the only one through America. The Convent's altars are of a churrigueresque (overloaded) style and they are decorated with paintings drew by the most celebrated Artists, such as Cabrera, Echave, Juaréz, etc. In the chapel of the right side there is still the famous pulpit from where was preached in the New World, for first time, the Gospel. The ceiling of the Convent's Church shows magnificent carved cedar panels and decorations forming golden stars. The ceiling is the only one in the whole Spanish America.

' – in spite of what I've been working on and my friend Weber, and what Geoff said about the Unión Militar, I still don't think the Fascists have any hold here to speak of.'

'Oh Hugh, for heaven's sake – '

THE CITY PARISH

The church is erected in the same place where the Spaniards built the first Hermitage consecrated to Virgin Mary. Some of the altars are decorated with overloaded art work. The portico of the church is of beautiful and severe appearance.

'*Ha ha ha!*'
'*Ha ha ha!*'
'I am very sorry you cannot come me with.'
'For she is the Virgin for those who have nobody with.'
'Nobody come here, only those who have nobody them with.'
' – who have nobody with – '
' – who have nobody them with – '

TLAXCALA ROYAL CHAPEL

Opposite to Francisco I Madero Park could be seen the ruins of the Royal Chapel, where the Tlaxcaltecan Senators, for first time, prayed to the Conqueror's God. It has been left only the portico, showing the Pope's shield, as well as those of the Mexican Pontificate and King Carlos V. History relates that the construction of the Royal Chapel was built at a cost amounting to $200,000.00 –

'A Nazi may not be a Fascist, but there're certainly plenty of them around, Yvonne. Beekeepers, miners, chemists. And keepers of pubs. The pubs themselves of course make ideal headquarters. In the Pilsener Kindl, for instance, in Mexico City – '

'Not to mention in Parián, Hugh,' said the Consul, sipping mescal, though nobody seemed to have heard him save a humming-bird, who at this moment snored into his stone retreat, whirred, jittering, in the entrance, and bounced out almost into the face of the godson of the Conqueror himself, Cervantes, who came gliding past again, carrying his fighting cock. 'In the Farolito – '

340

It is a Sanctuary whose white and embellished steeples 38.7 metres high, of an overloading style, gives an imposing and majestic impression. The frontage trimmed with sacred Archangels, St Francis and the epithet of Virgin Mary statues. Its construcción is made out of carved work in perfect dimensions decorated with allegorical symbols and flowers. It was constructed on the colonial epoch. Its central altar is of an overloaded and embellished style. The most admirable is the vestry, arched, decorated with graceful carved works, prevailing the green, red, and golden colours. In the highest part inside of the cúpula are carved the twelve apostles. The whole is of a singular beauty, not found in any church of the Republic.

' – I don't agree with you, Hugh. We go back a few years – '

' – forgetting, of course, the Miztecs, the Toltecs, Quetzelcoatl – '

' – not necessarily – '

' – oh yes you do! And you say first, Spaniard exploits Indian, then, when he had children, he exploited the half-breed, then the pure-blooded Mexican Spaniard, the *criollo*, then the *mestizo* exploits everybody, foreigners, Indians, and all. Then the Germans and Americans exploited him : now the final chapter, the exploitation of everybody by everybody else – '

Historic Places – SAN BUENAVENTURA ATEMPAM

In this town was built and tried in a dike the ships used for the conquerors in the attack to Tenochtitlán the great capital of the Moctezuma's Empire.

'*Mar Cantábrico.*'

'All right, I heard you, the Conquest took place in an organized community in which naturally there was exploitation already.'

'Well – '

' . . . no, the point is, Yvonne, that the Conquest took place in a civilization which was as good if not better than that of the conquerors, a deep-rooted structure. The people weren't all savages or nomadic tribes, footloose and wandering – '

' – suggesting that had they been footloose and wandering there would never have been any exploitation?'

'Have another bottle of beer . . . Carta Blanca?'

'Moctezuma . . . Dos Equis.'

'Or is it Montezuma?'

'Moctezuma on the bottle.'

'That's all he is now –'

TIZATLÁN

In this town, very near to Tlaxcala City, are still erected the ruins of the Palace, residence of Senator Xicohtencatl, father of the warrior by the same name. In said ruins could be still appreciated the stone blocks where were offered the sacrifices to their Gods . . . In the same town, a long time ago, were the headquarters of the Tlaxcaltecan warriors . . .

'I'm watching you . . . You can't escape me.'

' – this is not just escaping. I mean, let's start again, really and cleanly.'

'I think I know the place.'

'I can see you.'

' – where are the letters, Geoffrey Firmin, the letters she wrote till her heart broke –'

'But in Newcastle, Delaware, now that's another thing again!'

' – the letters you not only have never answered you didn't you did you didn't you did then where is your reply –'

' – but oh my God, this city – the noise! the chaos! If I could only get out! If I only knew where you could get to!'

OCOTELULCO

In this town near Tlaxcala existed, long back, the Maxixcatzin Palace. In that place, according to tradition took place the baptism of the first Christian Indian.

'It will be like a rebirth.'

'I'm thinking of becoming a Mexican subject, of going to live among the Indians, like William Blackstone.'

'Napoleon's leg twitched.'

' – might have run over you, there must be something wrong, what? No, going to –'

'Guanajuato – the streets – how can you resist the names of the streets – the Street of Kisses –'

342

This mountain are still the ruins of the shrine dedicated to the God of Waters, Tlaloc, which vestiges are almost lost, therefore, are no longer visited by tourists, and it is referred that on this place, young Xicohtencatl harangued his soldiers, telling them to fight the conquerors to the limit, dying if necessary.

    ' ... no pasarán.'
    'Madrid.'
    'They plugged 'em too. They shoot first and ask questions later.'
    'I can see you.'
    'I'm watching you.'
    'You can't escape me.'
    'Guzmán ... Erikson 43.'
    'A corpse will be transported by – '

RAILROAD AND BUS SERVICE
(MEXICO–TLAXCALA)

Lines	MEXICO	TLAXCALA		Rates
Mexico–Vera Cruz Railroad	Lv 7.30	Ar 18.50	Ar 12.00	$7.50
Mexico–Puebla Railroad	Lv 16.05	Ar 11.05	Ar 20.00	7.75

Transfer in Santa Ana Chiautempan in both ways.
Buses Flecha Roja. Leaving every hour from 5 to 19 hours.
Pullmans Estrella de Oro leaving every hour from 7 to 22.
Transfer in San Martín Texmelucán in both ways.

... And now, once more, their eyes met across the table. But this time there was, as it were, a mist between them, and through the mist the Consul seemed to see not Granada but Tlaxcala. It was a white beautiful cathedral city toward which the Consul's soul yearned and which indeed in many respects was like Granada; only it appeared to him, just as in the photographs in the folder, perfectly empty. That was the queerest thing about it, and at the same time the most beautiful; there was nobody there, no one – and in this it also somewhat resembled Tortu – to interfere with the business of drinking, not even Yvonne, who, so far as she was in evidence at all, was drinking with him.

The white sanctuary of the church in Ocotlán, of an overloaded style, rose up before them : white towers with a white clock and no one there. While the clock itself was timeless. They walked, carrying white bottles, twirling walk canes and ash plants, in the neat fine better climate, the purer air, among the corpulent ash-trees, the stricken in years trees, through the deserted park. They walked, happy as toads in a thunderstorm, arm-in-arm down the four clean and well-arranged lateral avenues. They stood, drunk as larks, in the deserted convent of San Francisco before the empty chapel where was preached, for the first time in the New World, the Gospel. At night they slept in cold white sheets among the white bottles at the Hotel Tlaxcala. And in the town too were innumerable white *cantinas*, where one could drink for ever on credit, with the door open and the wind blowing. 'We could go straight there,' he was saying, 'straight to Tlaxcala. Or we could all spend the night in Santa Ana Chiautempan, transferring in both ways of course, and go to Vera Cruz in the morning. Of course that means going – ' he looked at his watch ' – straight back now ... We could catch the next bus ... We'll have time for a few drinks,' he added consularly.

The mist had cleared, but Yvonne's eyes were full of tears, and she was pale.

Something was wrong, was very wrong. For one thing both Hugh and Yvonne seemed quite surprisingly tight.

'What's that, don't you want to go back now, to Tlaxcala?' said the Consul, perhaps too thickly.

'That's not it, Geoffrey.'

Fortunately, Cervantes arrived at this moment with a saucer full of live shellfish and toothpicks. The Consul drank some beer that had been waiting for him. The drink situation was now this, was this : there had been one drink waiting for him and this drink of beer he had not yet quite drunk. On the other hand there had been until recently several drinks of mescal (why not? – the word did not intimidate him, eh?) waiting for him outside in a lemonade bottle and all these he both had and had not drunk : had drunk in fact, had not drunk so far as the others were concerned. And before that there had been two mescals that he both should and should not have drunk. Did they suspect? He had adjured Cervantes to silence; had the Tlaxcaltecan, unable to resist it, betrayed him? What had they really been talking about while he was outside? The Consul glanced up from his shellfish at Hugh; Hugh, like Yvonne, as well as quite tight, appeared angry and hurt. What were they up to? The Consul had not been away very long (he thought), no more than seven minutes all told, had reappeared washed and combed – who knows how? – his chicken was scarcely cold, while the others were only just finishing theirs ... *Et tu Brute!* The Consul could feel his glance at Hugh becoming a cold look of hatred. Keeping his eyes fixed gimlet-like upon him he saw him as he had appeared that morning, smiling, the razor edge keen in sunlight. But now he was advancing as if to decapitate him. Then the vision darkened and Hugh was still advancing, but not upon him. Instead, back in the ring, he was bearing down upon an ox : now he had exchanged his razor for a sword. He thrust forward the sword to bring the ox to its knees ... The Consul was fighting off an all but irresistible, senseless onrush of wild rage. Trembling, he felt, from nothing but this effort – the constructive effort too, for which no one would give him credit, to change the subject – he impaled one of the shellfish on a toothpick and held it up, almost hissing through his teeth :

'Now you see what sort of creatures we are, Hugh. Eating things alive. That's what we do. How can you have much respect for mankind, or any belief in the social struggle?'

Despite this, Hugh was apparently saying, remotely, calmly, after a while : 'I once saw a Russian film about a revolt of some fishermen ... A shark was netted with a shoal of other fish and killed ... This struck me as a pretty good symbol of the Nazi system which, even though dead, continues to go on swallowing live struggling men and women!'

'It would do just as well for any other system ... Including the Communist system.'

'See here, Geoffrey –'

'See here, old bean,' the Consul heard himself saying, 'to have against you Franco, or Hitler, is one thing, but to have

Actinium, Argon, Beryllium, Dysprosium, Nobium, Palladium, Praseodymium – '

'Look here, Geoff – '

' – Ruthenium, Samarium, Silicon, Tantalum, Tellurium, Terbium, Thorium – '

'See here – '

' – Thulium, Titanium, Uranium, Vanadium, Virginium, Xenon, Ytterbium, Yttrium, Zirconium, to say nothing of Europium and Germanium – ahip ! – and Columbium ! – against you, and all the others, is another.' The Consul finished his beer.

Thunder suddenly sprang again outside with a clap and bang, slithering.

Despite which Hugh seemed to be saying, calmly, remotely, 'See here, Geoffrey. Let's get this straight once and for all. Communism to me is not, essentially, whatever its present phase, a system at all. It is simply a new spirit, something which one day may or may not seem as natural as the air we breathe. I seem to have heard that phrase before. What I have to say isn't original either. In fact were I to say it five years from now it would probably be downright banal. But to the best of my knowledge, no one has yet called in Matthew Arnold to the support of their argument. So I am going to quote Matthew Arnold for you, partly because you don't think I am capable of quoting Matthew Arnold. But that's where you're quite wrong. My notion of what we call – '

'Cervantes !'

' – is a spirit in the modern world playing a part analogous to that of Christianity in the old. Matthew Arnold says, in his essay on Marcus Aurelius – '

'Cervantes, *por* Christ sake – '

' "Far from this, the Christianity which those emperors aimed at repressing was, in their conception of it, something philosophically contemptible, politically subversive, and morally abominable. As men they sincerely regarded it much as well-conditioned people, with us, regard Mormonism : as rulers, they regarded it much as liberal statesmen, with us, regard the Jesuits. A kind of Mormonism – " '

' — '

' " – constituted as a vast secret society, with obscure aims of political and social subversion, was what Antoninus Pius – " '

'*Cervantes!*'

' "The inner and moving cause of the representation lay, no doubt, in this, that Christianity was a new spirit in the Roman world, destined to act in that world as its dissolvent; and it was inevitable that Christianity – " '

'Cervantes,' the Consul interrupted, 'you are Oaxaqueñian?'

'*No, señor.* I am Tlaxcalan, Tlaxcala.'

'You are,' said the Consul. 'Well, *hombre*, and are there not stricken in years trees in Tlaxcala?'

'*Sí, sí, hombre.* Stricken in years trees. Many trees.'

'And Ocotlán. Santuario de Ocotlán. Is not that in Tlaxcala?'

'*Sí, sí, señor, sí*, Santuario de Ocotlán,' said Cervantes, moving back toward the counter.

'And Matlalcuayatl.'

'*Sí, hombre.* Matlalcuayatl ... Tlaxcala.'

'And lagoons?'

'*Sí* ... many lagoons.'

'And are there not many web-footed fowl in these lagoons?'

'*Sí, señor. Muy fuerte* ... In Tlaxcala.'

'Well then,' said the Consul, turning round on the others, 'what's wrong with my plan? What's wrong with all you people? Aren't you going to Vera Cruz after all, Hugh?'

Suddenly a man started to play the guitar in the doorway angrily, and once again Cervantes came forward: 'Black Flowers is the name of that song.' Cervantes was about to beckon the man to come in. 'It say: I suffer, because your lips say only lies and they have death in a kiss.'

'Tell him to go away,' the Consul said. 'Hugh – *cuántos trenes hay el día para Vera Cruz?*'

The guitar player changed his tune:

'This is a farmer's song,' said Cervantes, 'for oxen.'

'Oxen, we've had enough oxen for one day. Tell him to go far away, *por favor*,' said the Consul. 'My God, what's wrong with you people? Yvonne, Hugh ... It's a perfectly good idea, a most practical idea. Don't you see it'll kill two birds with one

347

stone – a stone, Cervantes! ... Tlaxcala is on the way to Vera Cruz, Hugh, the true cross ... This is the last time we'll be seeing you, old fellow. For all I know ... We could have a celebration. Come on now, you can't lie to me, I'm watching you ... Change at San Martín Texmelucán in both ways ...'

Thunder, single, exploded in mid-air just outside the door and Cervantes came hurrying forward with the coffee: he struck matches for their cigarettes: '*La superstición dice', he smiled, striking a fresh one for the Consul, '*que cuando tres amigos prenden su cigarro con la misma cerilla, el último muere antes que los otros dos.*'

'You have that superstition in Mexico?' Hugh asked.

'*Sí, señor,*' Cervantes nodded, 'the fantasy is that when three friends take fire with the same match, the last die before the other two. But in war it is impossible because many soldiers have only one match.'

'*Feurstick,*' said Hugh, shielding yet another light for the Consul. 'The Norwegians have a better name for matches.'

– It was growing darker, the guitar player, it seemed, was sitting in the corner, wearing dark glasses, they had missed this bus back, if they'd meant to take it, the bus that was going to take them home to Tlaxcala, but it seemed to the Consul that, over the coffee, he had, all at once, begun to talk soberly, brilliantly, and fluently again, that he was, indeed, in top form, a fact he was sure was making Yvonne, opposite him, happy once more. *Feurstick*, Hugh's Norwegian word, was still in his head. And the Consul was taking about the Indo-Aryans, the Iranians and the sacred fire, Agni, called down from heaven, with his firesticks, by the priest. He was talking of *soma*, Amrita, the nectar of immortality, praised in one whole book of the Rig Veda – *bhang*, which was, perhaps, much the same thing as mescal itself, and, changing the subject here, delicately, he was talking of Norwegian architecture, or rather how much architecture, in Kashmir, was almost, so to speak, Norwegian, the Hamadan mosque for instance, wooden, with its tall tapering spires, and ornaments pendulous from the eaves. He was talking of the Borda gardens in Quauhnahuac, opposite Bustamente's cinema, and how much they, for some reason, always reminded him of the terrace of the Nishat Bagh. The Consul was talking about the Vedic Gods, who were not properly anthropomorphized, whereas Popocatepetl and Ixtaccihuatl ... Or were they not? In any event the Consul, once more, was talking about the sacred fire, the sacrificial fire, of the stone *soma* press, the sacrifices of cakes and oxen and horses, the priest chanting from the Veda, how the drinking rites, simple at first, became more and more complicated as time went on, the ritual having to be carried out with meticulous care, since one slip – *tee hee!* – would render the sacrifice invalid. *Soma*, *bhang*, mescal, ah yes, mescal, he was back upon that subject again, and now from it, had departed almost as cunningly as before. He was talking of the immolation of wives, and the fact that, at the time he was referring to, in Taxila, at the mouth of the Khyber Pass, the widow of a childless man might contract a Levirate marriage with her brother-in-law. The Consul found himself claiming to see an obscure relation, apart from any purely verbal one, between Taxila and Tlaxcala itself : for when that great pupil of Aristotle's – Yvonne – Alexander, arrived in Taxila, had he not Cortez-like already been in communication with Ambhi, Taxila's king, who likewise had seen in an alliance with a foreign conqueror, an excellent chance of undoing a rival, in this case not Moctezuma but the Paurave monarch, who ruled the country between the Jhelma and the Chenab? Tlaxcala ... The Consul was talking, like Sir Thomas Browne, of Archimedes, Moses, Achilles, Methuselah, Charles V, and Pontius Pilate. The Consul was talking furthermore of Jesus Christ, or rather of Yus Asaf who, according to the Kashmiri legend, *was* Christ – Christ, who had, after being taken down from the cross, wandered to Kashmir in search of the lost tribes of Israel, and died there, in Srinagar –

But there was a slight mistake. The Consul was not talking. Apparently not. The Consul had not uttered a single word. It was all an illusion, a whirling cerebral chaos, out of which, at last, at long last, at this very instant, emerged, rounded and complete, order :

'The act of a madman or a drunkard, old bean,' he said, 'or of a man labouring under violent excitement seems less free and more inevitable to the one who knows the mental condition of

349

the man who performed the action, and more free and less inevitable to the one who does not know it.'

It was like a piece on a piano, it was like that little bit in seven flats, on the black keys – it was what, more or less, he now remembered, he'd gone to the *excusado* in the first place in *order* to remember, to bring off pat – it was perhaps also like Hugh's quotation from Matthew Arnold on Marcus Aurelius, like that little piece one had learned, so laboriously, years ago, only to forget whenever one particularly wanted to play it, until one day one got drunk in such a way that one's fingers themselves recalled the combination and, miraculously, perfectly, unlocked the wealth of melody; only here Tolstoy had supplied no melody.

'What?' Hugh said.

'Not at all. I always come back to the point, and take a thing up where it has been left off. How else should I have maintained myself so long as Consul? When we have absolutely no understanding of the causes of an action – I am referring, in case your mind has wandered to the subject of your own conversation, to the events of the afternoon – the causes, whether vicious or virtuous or what not, we ascribe, according to Tolstoy, a greater element of free will to it. According to Tolstoy then, we should have had less reluctance in interfering than we did...

' "All cases without exception in which our conception of free will and necessity varies depend on three considerations",' the Consul said. 'You can't get away from it.

'Moreover, according to Tolstoy,' he went on, 'before we pass judgement on the thief – if thief he were – we would have to ask ourselves: what were his connexions with other thieves, ties of family, his place in time, if we know even that, his relation to the external world, and to the consequences leading to the act ... Cervantes!'

'Of course we're taking time to find out all this while the poor fellow just goes on dying in the road,' Hugh was saying. 'How did we get on to this? No one had an opportunity to interfere till after the deed was done. None of us saw him steal the money, to the best of my knowledge. Which crime are you talking about anyway, Geoff? If other crime there were ... And the fact that we did nothing to stop the thief is surely beside the point that we did nothing really to save the man's life.'

'Precisely,' said the Consul, 'I was talking about interference in general, I think. Why should we have done anything to save his life? Hadn't he a right to die, if he wanted to? ... Cervantes – mescal – *no, parras, por favor* ... Why should anybody interfere with anybody? Why should anybody have interfered with the Tlaxcalans, for example, who were perfectly happy by their own stricken in years trees, among the web-footed fowl in the first lagoon – '

'What web-footed fowl in what lagoon?'

'Or more specifically perhaps, Hugh, I was talking of nothing at all ... Since supposing we settled anything – ah, *ignoratio elenchi*, Hugh, that's what. Or the fallacy of supposing a point proved or disproved by argument which proves or disproves something not at issue. Like these wars. For it seems to me that almost everywhere in the world these days there has long since ceased to be anything fundamental to man at issue at all ... Ah, you people with ideas!'

'Ah, *ignoratio elenchi*! ... All this, for instance, about going to fight for Spain ... and poor little defenceless China! Can't you see there's a sort of determinism about the fate of nations? They all seem to get what they deserve in the long run.'

'Well. ...'

A gust of wind moaned round the house with an eerie sound like a northerner prowling among the tennis nets in England, jingling the rings.

'Not exactly original.'

'Not long ago it was poor little defenceless Ethiopia. Before that, poor little defenceless Flanders. To say nothing of course of the poor little defenceless Belgian Congo. And tomorrow it will be poor little defenceless Latvia. Or Finland. Or Piddledee-dee. Or even Russia. Read history. Go back a thousand years. What is the use of interfering with its worthless stupid course? Like a *barranca*, a ravine, choked up with refuse, that winds through the ages, and peters out in a – What in God's name has all the heroic resistance put up by poor little defenceless peoples all rendered defenceless in the first place for some well-calculated and criminal reason – '

'Hell, *I* told you that – '

' – to do with the survival of the human spirit? Nothing whatsoever. Less than nothing. Countries, civilizations, empires, great hordes perish for no reason at all, and their soul and meaning with them, that one old man perhaps you never heard of, and who never heard of them, sitting boiling in Timbuktu, proving the existence of the mathematical correlative of *ignoratio elenchi* with obsolete instruments, may survive.'

'For Christ's sake,' said Hugh.

'Just go back to Tolstoy's day – Yvonne, where are you going?'

'Out.'

'Then it was poor little defenceless Montenegro. Poor little defenceless Serbia. Or back a little farther still, Hugh, to your Shelley's, when it was poor little defenceless Greece – Cervantes! – As it will be again, of course. Or to Boswell's – poor little defenceless Corsica! Shades of Paoli and Monboddo. Applesquires and fairies strong for freedom. As always. And Rousseau – not *douanier* – knew he was talking nonsense – '

'I should like to know what the bloody hell it is you imagine you're talking!'

'Why can't people mind their own damned business!'

'Or say what they mean?'

'It was something else, I grant you. The dishonest mass rationalization of *motive*, justification of the common pathological itch. Of the motives for interference; merely a passion for fatality half the time. Curiosity. Experience – very natural ... But nothing constructive at bottom, only acceptance really, a piddling contemptible acceptance of the state of affairs that flatters one into feeling thus noble or useful!'

'But my God it's *against* such a state of affairs that people like the Loyalists – '

'But with calamity at the end of it! There must be calamity because otherwise the people who did the interfering would have to come back and cope with their responsibilities for a change – '

'Just let a real war come along and then see how bloodthirsty chaps like you are!'

'Which would never do. Why all you people who talk about going to Spain and fighting for freedom – Cervantes! – should learn by heart what Tolstoy said about that kind of thing in *War and Peace*, that conversation with the volunteers in the train – '

'But anyhow that was in – '

'Where the first volunteer, I mean, turned out to be a bragging degenerate obviously convinced after he'd been drinking that he was doing something heroic – what are you laughing at, Hugh?'

'It's funny.'

'And the second was a man who had tried everything and been a failure in all of them. And the third – ' Yvonne abruptly returned and the Consul, who had been shouting, slightly lowered his voice, 'an artillery man, was the only one who struck him at first favourably. Yet what did he turn out to be? A cadet who'd failed in his examinations. All of them, you see, misfits, all good for nothing, cowards, baboons, meek wolves, parasites, every man jack of them, people afraid to face their own responsibilities, fight their own fight, ready to go anywhere, as Tolstoy well perceived – '

'Quitters?' Hugh said. 'Didn't Katamasov or whoever he was believe that the action of those volunteers was nevertheless an expression of the whole soul of the Russian people? – Mind you, I appreciate that a diplomatic corps which merely remains in San Sebastian hoping Franco will win quickly instead of returning to Madrid to tell the British Government the truth of what's really going on in Spain can't possibly consist of quitters!'

'Isn't your desire to fight for Spain, for fiddlededee, for Timbuktu, for China, for hypocrisy, for bugger all, for any hokery pokery that a few moose-headed idiot sons choose to call freedom – of course there is nothing of the sort, really – '

'If – '

'If you've really read *War and Peace*, as you claim you have, why haven't you the sense to profit by it, I repeat?'

'At any rate,' said Hugh, 'I profited by it to the extent of being able to distinguish it from *Anna Karenina*.'

'Well, *Anna Karenina* then ... ' the Consul paused.

'Cervantes!' – and Cervantes appeared, with his fighting cock, evidently fast asleep, under his arm. *'Muy fuerte,'* he said, *'muy terreebly,'* passing through the room, *'un bruto.'* – 'But as I implied, you bloody people, mark my words, you don't mind your own business any better at home, let alone in foreign countries. Geoffrey darling, why don't you stop drinking, it isn't too late – that sort of thing. Why isn't it? Did *I* say so?' What was he saying? The Consul listened to himself almost in surprise at this sudden cruelty, this vulgarity. And in a moment it was going to get worse. 'I thought it was all so splendidly and legally settled that it was. It's only you that insists it isn't.'

'Oh Geoffrey – '

– Was the Consul saying this? Must he say it? – It seemed he must. 'For all you know it's only the knowledge that it most certainly is too late that keeps me alive at all ... You're all the same, all of you, Yvonne, Jacques, you, Hugh, trying to interfere with other people's lives, interfering, interfering – why should anyone have interfered with young Cervantes here, for example, given him an interest in cock fighting? – and that's precisely what's bringing about disaster in the world, to stretch a point, yes, quite a point, all because you haven't got the wisdom and the simplicity and the courage, yes, the courage, to take any of the, to take – '

'See here, Geoffrey – '

'What have you ever done for humanity, Hugh, with all your *oratio obliqua* about the capitalist system, except talk, and thrive on it, until your soul stinks?'

'Shut up, Geoff, for the love of Mike!'

'For that matter, both your souls stink! Cervantes!'

'Geoffrey, please sit down,' Yvonne seemed to have said wearily, 'you're making such a scene.'

'No, I'm not, Yvonne. I'm talking very calmly. As when I ask you, what have you ever done for anyone but yourself?' Must the Consul say this? He was saying, had said it: 'Where are the children I might have wanted? You may suppose I might have wanted them. Drowned. To the accompaniment of the rattling of a thousand douche bags. Mind you, *you* don't pretend to love "humanity", not a bit of it! You don't even need an

354

illusion, though you do have some illusions unfortunately, to help you deny the only natural and good function you have. Though on second thoughts it might be better if women had no functions at all!'

'Don't be a bloody swine, Geoffrey.' Hugh rose.

'Stay where you bloody are,' ordered the Consul. 'Of course I see the romantic predicament you two are in. But even if Hugh makes the most of it again it won't be long, it won't be long, before he realizes he's only one of the hundred or so other ninney-hammers with gills like codfish and veins like racehorses – prime as goats all of them, hot as monkeys, salt as wolves in pride! No, one will be enough. . .'

A glass, fortunately empty, fell to the floor and was smashed.

'As if he plucked up kisses by the roots and then laid his leg over her thigh and sighed. What an uncommon time you two must have had, paddling palms and playing bubbies and titties all day under cover of saving me . . . Jesus. Poor little defenceless me – I hadn't thought of that. But, you see, it's perfectly logical, what it comes down to : I've got my own piddling little fight for freedom on my hands. Mummy, let me go back to the beautiful brothel! Back to where those *triskeles* are strumming, the infinite *trismus*. . .

'True, I've been tempted to talk peace. I've been beguiled by your offers of a sober and non-alcoholic Paradise. At least I suppose that's what you've been working around towards all day. But now I've made up my melodramatic little mind, what's left of it, just enough to make up. Cervantes! That far from wanting it, thank you very much, on the contrary, I choose – Tlax – ' Where was he? 'Tlax – Tlax – '

. . . It was as if, almost, he were standing upon that black open station platform, where he had gone – *had* he gone? – that day after drinking all night to meet Lee Maitland returning from Virginia at 7.40 in the morning, gone, light-headed, light-footed, and in that state of being where Baudelaire's angel indeed wakes, desiring to meet trains perhaps, but to meet no trains that stop, for in the angel's mind are no trains that stop, and from such trains no one descends, not even another angel, nor even a fair-haired one, like Lee Maitland. – Was the train late? Why was he

355

pacing the platform? Was it the second or third train from Suspension Bridge – Suspension! – 'Tlax –' the Consul repeated. 'I choose –'

He was in a room, and suddenly in this room, matter was disjunct: a doorknob was standing a little way out from the door. A curtain floated in by itself, unfastened, unattached to anything. The idea struck him it had come in to strangle him. An orderly little clock behind the bar called him to his senses, its ticking very loud: *Tlax: tlax: tlax: tlax:* . . . Half past five. Was that all? 'Hell,' he finished absurdly. 'Because –' He produced a twenty-peso note and laid it on the table.

'I like it,' he called to them, through the open window, from outside. Cervantes stood behind the bar, with scared eyes, holding the cockerel. 'I love hell. I can't wait to get back there. In fact I'm running. I'm almost back there already.'

He was running too, in spite of his limp, calling back to them crazily, and the queer thing was, he wasn't quite serious, running toward the forest, which was growing darker and darker, tumultuous above – a rush of air swept out of it, and the weeping pepper tree roared.

He stopped after a while: all was calm. No one had come after him. Was that good? Yes, it was good, he thought, his heart pounding. And since it was so good he would take the path to Parián, to the Farolito.

Before him the volcanoes, precipitous, seemed to have drawn nearer. They towered up over the jungle, into the lowering sky – massive interests moving up in the background.

Sunset. Eddies of green and orange birds scattered aloft with ever wider circlings like rings on water. Two little pigs disappeared into the dust at a gallop. A woman passed swiftly, balancing on her head, with the grace of a Rebecca, a small light bottle...

Then, the Salón Ofelia at last behind them, there was no more dust. And their path became straight, leading on through the roar of water past the bathing place, where, reckless, a few late bathers lingered, toward the forest.

Straight ahead, in the north-east, lay the volcanoes, the towering dark clouds behind them steadily mounting the heavens.

– The storm, that had already dispatched its outriders, must have been travelling in a circle: the real onset was yet to come. Meantime the wind had dropped and it was lighter again, though the sun had gone down at their back slightly to their left, in the south-west, where a red blaze fanned out into the sky over their heads.

The Consul had not been in the Todos Contentos y Yo También. And now, through the warm twilight, Yvonne was walking before Hugh, purposely too fast for talking. None the less his voice (as earlier that day the Consul's own) pursued her.

'You know perfectly well I won't just run away and abandon him,' she said.

'Christ Jesus, this never would have happened if I hadn't been here!'

'Something else would probably have happened.'

The jungle closed over them and the volcanoes were blotted out. Yet it was still not dark. From the stream racing along beside them a radiance was cast. Big yellow flowers, resembling chrysanthemums, shining like stars through the gloom, grew on either side of the water. Wild bougainvillea, brick-red in the half-light, occasionally a bush with white handbells, tongue

357

downwards, started out at them, every little while a notice nailed to a tree, a whittled, weather-beaten arrow pointing, with the words hardly visible : *a la Cascada* –

Farther on worn-out ploughshares and the rusted and twisted chassis of abandoned American cars bridged the stream which they kept always to their left.

The sound of the falls behind was now lost in that of the cascade ahead. The air was full of spray and moisture. But for the tumult one might almost have heard things growing as the torrent rushed through the wet heavy foliage that sprang up everywhere around them from the alluvial soil.

All at once, above them, they saw the sky again. The clouds, no longer red, had become a peculiar luminous blue-white, drifts and depths of them, as though illumined by moon rather than sunlight, between which roared still the deep fathomless cobalt of afternoon.

Birds were sailing up there, ascending higher and higher. Infernal bird of Prometheus !

They were vultures, that on earth so jealously contend with one another, defiling themselves with blood and filth, but who were yet capable of rising, like this, above the storms, to heights shared only by the condor, above the summit of the Andes –

Down the south-west stood the moon itself, preparing to follow the sun below the horizon. On their left, through the trees beyond the stream appeared low hills, like those at the foot of the Calle Nicaragua ; they were purple and sad. At their foot, so near Yvonne made out a faint rustling, cattle moved on the sloping fields among gold cornstalks and striped mysterious tents.

Before them, Popocatepetl and Ixtaccihuatl continued to dominate the north-east, the Sleeping Woman now perhaps the more beautiful of the two, with jagged angles of blood-red snow on its summit, fading as they watched, whipped with darker rock shadows, the summit itself seeming suspended in mid-air, floating among the curdling ever mounting black clouds.

Chimborazo, Popocatepetl – so ran the poem the Consul liked – had stolen his heart away ! But in the tragic Indian legend Popocatepetl himself was strangely the dreamer : the fires of his warrior's love, never extinct in the poet's heart, burned eternally for Ixtaccihuatl, whom he had no sooner found than lost, and whom he guarded in her endless sleep . . .

They had reached the limit of the clearing, where the path divided in two. Yvonne hesitated. Pointing to the left, as it were straight on, another aged arrow on a tree repeated: *a la Cascada*. But a similar arrow on another tree pointed away from the stream down a path to their right: *a Parián*.

Yvonne knew where she was now, but the two alternatives, the two paths, stretched out before her on either side like the arms – the oddly dislocated thought struck her – of a man being crucified.

If they chose the path to their right they would reach Parián much sooner. On the other hand, the main path would bring them to the same place finally, and, what was more to the point, past, she felt sure, at least two other *cantinas*.

They chose the main path: the striped tents, the cornstalks dropped out of sight, and the jungle returned, its damp earthy leguminous smell rising about them with the night.

This path, she was thinking, after emerging on a sort of main highway near a restaurant-*cantina* named the Rum-Popo or the El Popo, took, upon resumption (if it could be called the same path), a short cut at right angles through the forest to Parián, across to the Farolito itself, as it might be the shadowy crossbar from which the man's arms were hanging.

The noise of the approaching falls was now like the awakening voices downwind of five thousand bobolinks in an Ohio savannah. Toward it the torrent raced furiously, fed from above, where, down the left bank, transformed abruptly into a great wall of vegetation, water was spouting into the stream through thickets festooned with convolvuli on a higher level than the topmost trees of the jungle. And it was as though one's spirit too were being swept on by the swift current with the uprooted trees and smashed bushes in a débâcle towards that final drop.

They came to the little *cantina* El Petate. It stood, at a short distance from the clamorous falls, its lighted windows friendly against the twilight, and was at present occupied, she saw as her

359

heart leaped and sank, leaped again, and sank, only by the barman and two Mexicans, shepherds or quince farmers, deep in conversation, and leaning against the bar. – Their mouths opened and shut soundlessly, their brown hands traced patterns in the air, courteously.

The El Petate, which from where she stood resembled a sort of complicated postage stamp, surcharged on its outside walls with its inevitable advertisements for Moctezuma, Criollo, Cafeaspirina, Mentholatum – *no se rasque las picaduras de los insectos!* – was about all remaining, the Consul and she'd once been told, of the formerly prosperous village of Anochtitlán, which had burned, but which at one time extended to the westward, on the other side of the stream.

In the smashing din she waited outside. Since leaving the Salón Ofélia and up to this point, Yvonne had felt herself possessed of the most complete detatchment. But now, as Hugh joined the scene within the *cantina* – he was asking the two Mexicans questions, describing Geoffrey's beard to the barman, he was describing Geoffrey's beard to the Mexicans, he was asking the barman questions, who, with two fingers had assumed, jocosely, a beard – she became conscious she was laughing unnaturally to herself; at the same time she felt, crazily, as if something within her were smouldering, had taken fire, as if her whole being at any moment were going to explode.

She started back. She had stumbled over a wooden structure close to the Petate that seemed to spring at her. It was a wooden cage, she saw by the light from the windows, in which crouched a large bird.

It was a small eagle she had startled, and which was now shivering in the damp and dark of its prison. The cage was set between the *cantina* and a low thick tree, really two trees embracing one another : an *amate* and a *sabina*. The breeze blew spray in her face. The falls sounded. The intertwined roots of the two tree lovers flowed over the ground toward the stream, ecstatically seeking it, though they didn't really need it ; the roots might as well have stayed where they were, for all around them nature was out-doing itself in extravagant fructification. In the taller trees beyond there was a cracking, a rebellious tearing, and a rattling, as of cordage; boughs like booms swung darkly and stiffly about her, broad leaves unfurled. There was a sense of black conspiracy, like ships in harbour before a storm, among these trees, suddenly through which, far up in the mountains, lightning flew, and the light in the *cantina* flickered off, then on again, then off. No thunder followed. The storm was a distance away once more. Yvonne waited in nervous apprehension: the lights came on and Hugh – how like a man, oh God! but perhaps it was her own fault for refusing to come in – was having a quick drink with the Mexicans. There the bird was still, a long-winged dark furious shape, a little world of fierce despairs and dreams, and memories of floating high above Popocatepetl, mile on mile, to drop through the wilderness and alight, watching, in the timberline ghosts of ravaged mountain trees. With hurried quivering hands Yvonne began to unfasten the cage. The bird fluttered out of it and alighted at her feet, hesitated, took flight to the roof of El Petate, then abruptly flew off through the dusk, not to the nearest tree, as might have been supposed, but up – she was right, it knew it was free – up soaring, with a sudden cleaving of pinions into the deep dark blue pure sky above, in which at that moment appeared one star. No compunction touched Yvonne. She felt only an inexplicable secret triumph and relief: no one would ever know she had done this; and then, stealing over her, the sense of utter heartbreak and loss.

Lamplight shone across the tree roots; the Mexicans stood in the open door with Hugh, nodding at the weather and pointing on down the path, while within the *cantina* the barman helped himself to a drink from under the bar.

– 'No! . . . ' Hugh shouted against the tumult. 'He hasn't been there at all! We might try this other place though!'

' – '

'On the road!'

Beyond the El Petate their path veered to the right past a dog-kennel to which an anteater nuzzling the black earth was chained. Hugh took Yvonne's arm.

'See the anteater? Do you remember the armadillo?'

'I haven't forgotten, *anything*!'

Yvonne said this, as they fell into step, not knowing quite

what she meant. Wild woodland creatures plunged past them in the undergrowth, and everywhere she looked in vain for her eagle, half hoping to see it once more. The jungle was thinning out gradually. Rotting vegetation lay about them, and there was a smell of decay; the *barranca* couldn't be far off. Then the air blew strangely warmer and sweeter, and the path was steeper. The last time Yvonne had come this way she'd heard a whip-poor-will. *Whip-poor-will, whip-peri-will,* the plaintive lonely voice of spring at home had said, and calling one home – to where? To her father's home in Ohio? And what should a whip-poor-will be doing so far from home itself in a dark Mexican forest? But the whip-poor-will, like love and wisdom, had no home; and perhaps, as the Consul had then added, it was better here than routing around Cayenne, where it was supposed to winter.

They were climbing, approaching a little hilltop clearing; Yvonne could see the sky. But she couldn't get her bearings. The Mexican sky had become strange and tonight the stars found for her a message even lonelier than that remembered one of the poor nestless whip-poor-will. Why are we here, they seemed to say, in the wrong place, and all the wrong shape, so far away, so far, so far away from home? From what home? When had not she, Yvonne, *come* home? But the stars by their very being consoled her. And walking on she felt her mood of detachment returning. Now Yvonne and Hugh were high enough to see, through the trees, the stars low down on the western horizon.

Scorpio, setting ... Sagittarius, Capricornus; ah, there, here they were, after all, in their right places, their configurations all at once right, recognized, their pure geometry scintillating, flawless. And tonight as five thousand years ago they would rise and set: Capricorn, Aquarius, with, beneath, lonely Fomalhaut; Pisces; and the Ram; Taurus, with Aldebaran and the Pleiades. 'As Scorpio sets in the south-west, the Pleiades are rising in the north-east.' 'As Capricorn sets in the west, Orion rises in the east. And Cetus, the Whale, with Mira.' Tonight, as ages hence, people would say this, or shut their doors on them, turn in bereaved agony from them, or towards them with love saying: 'That is our star up there, yours and mine'; steer by them above the clouds or lost at sea, or standing in the spray on the forecastle head, watch them, suddenly, career, put their faith or lack of it in them; train, in a thousand observatories, feeble telescopes upon them, across whose lenses swam mysterious swarms of stars and clouds of dead dark stars, catastrophes of exploding suns, or giant Antares raging to its end – a smouldering ember yet five hundred times greater than the earth's sun. And the earth itself still turning on its axis and revolving around that sun, the sun revolving around the luminous wheel of this galaxy, the countless unmeasured jewelled wheels of countless unmeasured galaxies turning, turning, majestically, into infinity, into eternity, through all of which all life ran on – all this, long after she herself was dead, men would still be reading in the night sky, and as the earth turned through those distant seasons, and they watched the constellations still rising, culminating, setting, to rise again – Aries, Taurus, Gemini, the Crab, Leo, Virgo, the Scales and the Scorpion, Capricorn the Sea-goat and Aquarius the Water Bearer, Pisces, and once more, triumphantly, Aries! – would they not, too, still be asking the hopeless eternal question: to what end? What force drives this sublime celestial machinery? Scorpio, setting ... And rising, Yvonne thought, unseen behind the volcanoes, those whose culmination was at midnight tonight, as Aquarius set; and some would watch with a sense of fleeting, yet feeling their diamonded brightness gleam an instant on the soul, touching all within that in memory was sweet or noble or courageous or proud, as high overhead appeared, flying softly like a flock of birds towards Orion, the beneficent Pleiades ...

The mountains that had been lost from sight now stood ahead again as they walked on through the dwindling forest. – Yet Yvonne still hung back.

Far away to the south-east the low leaning horn of moon, their pale companion of the morning, was setting finally, and she watched it – the dead child of the earth! – with a strange hungry supplication. – The Sea of Fecundity, diamond-shaped, and the sea of Nectar, pentagonal in form, and Frascatorius with its north wall broken down, the giant west wall of Endymion, elliptical near the Western limb; the Leibnitz mountains at the Southern Horn, and east of Proclus, the Marsh of a Dream.

Hercules and Atlas stood there, in the midst of cataclysm, beyond our knowledge –

The moon had gone. A hot gust of wind blew in their faces and lightning blazed white and jagged in the north-east: thunder spoke, economically; a poised avalanche . . .

The path growing steeper inclined still further to their right and began to twist through scattered sentinels of trees, tall and lone, and enormous cactus, whose writhing innumerable spined hands, as the path turned, blocked the view on every side. It grew so dark it was surprising not to find blackest night in the world beyond.

Yet the sight that met their eyes as they emerged on the road was terrifying. The massed black clouds were still mounting the twilight sky. High above them, at a vast height, a dreadfully vast height, bodiless black birds, more like skeletons of birds, were drifting. Snowstorms drove along the summit of Ixtaccihuatl, obscuring it, while its mass was shrouded by cumulus. But the whole precipitous bulk of Popocatepetl seemed to be coming towards them, travelling with the clouds, leaning forward over the valley on whose side, thrown into relief by the curious melancholy light, shone one little rebellious hilltop with a tiny cemetery cut into it.

The cemetery was swarming with people visible only as their candle flames.

But suddenly it was as if a heliograph of lightning were stammering messages across the wild landscape; and they made out, frozen, the minute black and white figures themselves. And now, as they listened for the thunder, they heard them: soft cries and lamentations, wind-borne, wandering down to them. The mourners were chanting over the graves of their loved ones, playing guitars softly or praying. A sound like windbells, a ghostly tintinnabulation, reached their ears.

A titanic roar of thunder overwhelmed it, rolling down the valleys. The avalanche had started. Yet it had not overwhelmed the candle flames. There they still gleamed, undaunted, a few moving now in procession. Some of the mourners were filing off down the hillside.

Yvonne felt with gratitude the hard road beneath her feet. The lights of the Hotel y Restaurant El Popo sprang up. Over a garage next door an electric sign was stabbing: *Euzkadi.* – A radio somewhere was playing wildly hot music at an incredible speed.

American cars stood outside the restaurant ranged before the cul-de-sac at the edge of the jungle, giving the place something of the withdrawn, waiting character that pertains to a border at night, and a border of sorts there was, not far from here, where the ravine, bridged away to the right on the outskirts of the old capital, marked the state line.

On the porch, for an instant, the Consul sat dining quietly by himself. But only Yvonne had seen him. They threaded their way through the round tables and into a bare ill-defined bar where the Consul sat frowning in a corner with three Mexicans. But none save Yvonne noticed him. The barman had not seen the Consul. Nor had the assistant manager, an unusually tall Japanese also the cook, who recognized Yvonne. Yet even as they denied all knowledge of him (and though by this time Yvonne had quite made up her mind he was in the Farolito) the Consul was disappearing round every corner, and going out of every door. A few tables set along the tiled floor outside the bar were deserted, yet here the Consul also sat dimly, rising at their approach. And out behind by the *patio* it was the Consul who pushed his chair back and came forward, bowing, to meet them.

In fact, as often turns out for some reason in such places, there were not enough people in the El Popo to account for the number of cars outside.

Hugh was casting round him, half for the music, which seemed coming from a radio in one of the cars and which sounded like absolutely nothing on earth in this desolate spot, an abysmal mechanic force out of control that was running itself to death, was breaking up, was hurtling into dreadful trouble, had abruptly ceased.

The *patio* of the pub was a long rectangular garden overgrown with flowers and weeds. Verandas, half in darkness, and arched on their parapets, giving them an effect of cloisters, ran down either side. Bedrooms opened off the verandas. The light from the restaurant behind picked out, here and there, a scarlet flower, a green shrub, with unnatural vividness. Two angry-looking macaws with bright ruffled plumage sat in iron rings between the arches.

Lightning, flickering, fired the windows a moment; wind crepitated the leaves and subsided, leaving a hot void in which the trees thrashed chaotically. Yvonne leaned against an arch and took off her hat; one of the cockatoos screeched and she pressed the palms of her hands against her ears, pressing them harder as the thunder started again, holding them there with her eyes shut absently until it stopped, and the two bleak beers Hugh ordered had arrived.

'Well,' he was saying, 'this is somewhat different from the Cervecería Quauhnahuac ... Indeed! ... Yes, I guess I'll always remember this morning. The sky was so blue, wasn't it?'

'And the woolly dog and the foals that came with us and the river with those swift birds overhead – '

'How far to the Farolito now?'

'About a mile and a half. We can cut nearly a mile if we take the forest path.'

'In the dark?'

'We can't wait very long if you're going to make the last bus back to Quauhnahuac. It's after six now. I can't drink this beer, can you?'

'No. It tastes like gun-metal – hell – Christ,' Hugh said, 'let's – '

'Have a different drink,' Yvonne proposed, half ironically.

'Couldn't we *phone*?'

'Mescal,' Yvonne said brightly.

The air was so full of electricity it trembled.

'*Comment?*'

'*Mescal, por favor,*' Yvonne repeated, shaking her head solemnly, sardonically. 'I've always wanted to find out what Geoffrey sees in it.'

'*¿Cómo no?* let's have two mescals.'

But Hugh had still not returned when the two drinks were brought by a different waiter questioning the gloom, who, balancing the tray on one palm, switched on another light.

The drinks Yvonne had had at dinner and during the day,

relatively few though they'd been, lay like swine on her soul : some moments passed before she reached out her hand and drank.

Sickly, sullen, and ether-tasting, the mescal produced at first no warmth in her stomach, only, like the beer, a coldness, a chill. But it worked. From the porch outside a guitar, slightly out of tune, struck up *La Paloma*, a Mexican voice was singing, and the mescal was still working. It had in the end the quality of a good hard drink. Where was Hugh? Had he found the Consul here, after all? No : she knew he was not here. She gazed round the El Popo, a soulless draughty death that ticked and groaned, as Geoff himself once said – a bad ghost of an American road-house; but it no longer appeared so awful. She selected a lemon from the table and squeezed a few drops into her glass and all this took her an inordinately long time to do.

All at once she became conscious she was laughing unnaturally to herself, something within her was smouldering, was on fire : and once more, too, in her brain a picture shaped of a woman ceaselessly beating her fists on the ground . . .

But no, it was not herself that was on fire. It was the house of her spirit. It was her dream. It was the farm, it was Orion, the Pleiades, it was their house by the sea. But where was the fire? It was the Consul who had been the first to notice it. What were these crazy thoughts, thoughts without form or logic? She stretched out her hand for the other mescal, Hugh's mescal, and the fire went out, was overwhelmed by a sudden wave through her whole being of desperate love and tenderness for the Consul.

– very dark and clear with an onshore wind, and the sound of surf you couldn't see, deep in the spring night the summer stars were overhead, presage of summer, and the stars bright; clear and dark, and the moon had not risen; a beautiful strong clean onshore wind, and then the waning moon rising over the water, and later, inside the house, the roar of unseen surf beating in the night –

'How do you like the mescal?'

Yvonne jumped up. She had been almost crouching over Hugh's drink; Hugh, swaying, stood over her, carrying under his arm a long battered key-shaped canvas case.

'What in the world have you got there?' Yvonne's voice was blurred and remote.

Hugh put the case on the parapet. Then he laid on the table an electric torch. It was a boy scout contraption like a ship's ventilator with a metal ring to slip your belt through. 'I met the fellow on the porch Geoff was so bloody rude to in the Salón Ofelia and I bought this from him. But he wanted to sell his guitar and get a new one so I bought that too. Only *ocho pesos cincuenta* – '

'What do you want a guitar for? Are you going to play the Internationale or something on it, on board your ship?' Yvonne said.

'How's the mescal?' Hugh said again.

'Like ten yards of barbed-wire fence. It nearly took the top of my head off. Here, this is yours, Hugh, what's left of it.'

Hugh sat down: 'I had a tequila outside with the guitar *hombre* ...

'Well,' he added, 'I'm definitely not going to try and get to Mexico City tonight, and that once decided there're various things we might do about Geoff.'

'I'd rather like to get tight,' Yvonne said.

'*Como tu quieras.* It might be a good idea.'

'Why did you say it would be a good idea to get tight?' Yvonne was asking over the new mescals; then, 'What did you get a guitar for?' she repeated.

'To sing with. To give people the lie with maybe.'

'What are you so strange for, Hugh? To give what people what lie?'

Hugh tilted back his chair until it touched the parapet behind him, then sat like that, smoking, nursing his mescal in his lap.

'The kind of lie Sir Walter Raleigh meditates, when he addresses his soul. "The truth shall be thy warrant. Go, since I needs must die. And give the world the lie. Say to the court it glows, and shines like rotten wood. Say to the church it shows, what's good and doth no good. If Church and Court reply, then give them both the lie." That sort of thing, only slightly different.'

'You're dramatizing yourself, Hugh. *Salud y pesetas.*'

'*Salud y pesetas.*'

'Salud y pesetas.'

He stood, smoking, drink in hand, leaning against the dark monastic archway and looking down at her:

'But on the contrary,' he was saying, 'we do want to do good, to help, to be brothers in distress. We will even condescend to be crucified, on certain terms. And *are*, for that matter, regularly, every twenty years or so. But to an Englishman it's such terribly bad form to be a bona-fide martyr. We may respect with one part of our minds the integrity, say, of men like Gandhi, or Nehru. We may even recognize that their selflessness, by example, might save us. But in our hearts we cry "Throw the bloody little man in the river". Or "Set Barabbas free!" "O'Dwyer for ever!" Jesus! – It's even pretty bad form for Spain to be a martyr too; in a very different way of course ... And if Russia should prove –'

Hugh was saying all this while Yvonne was scanning a document he'd just skimmed on to the table for her. It was an old soiled and creased menu of the house simply, that seemed to have been picked up from the floor, or spent a long period in someone's pocket, and this she read, with alcoholic deliberation, several times:

'EL POPO'
SERVICIO A LA CARTE

Sopa de ajo	$0.30
Enchiladas de salsa verde	0.40
Chiles rellenos	0.75
Rajas a la 'Popo'	0.75
Machitos en salsa verde	0.75
Menudo estilo soñora	0.75
Pierna de ternera al horno	1.25
Cabrito al horno	1.25
Asado de pollo	1.25
Chuletas de cerdo	1.25
Filete con papas o al gusto	1.25
Sandwiches	0.40
Frijoles refritos	0.30
Chocolate a la española	0.60
Chocolate a la francesa	0.40
Café solo o con leche	0.20

This much was typed in blue and underneath it – she made out with the same deliberation – was a design like a small wheel round the inside of which was written 'Lotería Nacional Para La Beneficencia Pública', making another circular frame, within which appeared a sort of trade or hallmark representing a happy mother caressing her child.

The whole left side of the menu was taken up by a full-length lithographic portrait of a smiling young woman surmounted by the announcement that *Hotel Restaurant El Popo se observa la más estricta moralidad, siendo esta disposición de su propietario una garantía para el pasajero, que llegue en compañía* : Yvonne studied this woman : she was buxom and dowdy, with a quasi-American coiffure, and she was wearing a long, confetti-coloured print dress : with one hand she was beckoning roguishly, while with the other she held up a block of ten lottery tickets, on each of which a cowgirl was riding a bucking horse and (as if these ten minute figures were Yvonne's own reduplicated and half-forgotten selves waving good-bye to herself) waving her hand.

'Well,' she said.

'No, I meant on the other side,' Hugh said.

Yvonne turned the menu over and then sat staring blankly.

The back of the menu was almost covered by the Consul's handwriting at its most chaotic. At the top on the left was written :

Recknung

1 ron y anís	1.20
1 ron Salón Brasse	0.60
1 tequila doble	0.30
	2.10

This was signed G. Firmin. It was a small bill left here by the Consul some months ago, a chit he'd made out for himself – 'No, I just paid it,' said Hugh, who was now sitting beside her.

But below this 'reckoning' was written, enigmatically, 'dearth ... filth ... earth', below that was a long scrawl of which one could make nothing. In the centre of the paper were seen these words : 'rope ... cope ... grope', then, 'of a cold cell', while on the right, the parent and partial explanation of these prodigals, appeared what looked a poem in process of composition, an attempt at some kind of sonnet perhaps, but of a wavering and collapsed design, and so crossed out and scrawled over and stained, defaced, and surrounded with scratchy drawings – of a club, a wheel, even a long black box like a coffin – as to be almost indecipherable; at last it had this semblance :

> Some years ago he started to escape
> ... has been ... escaping ever since
> Not knowing his pursuers gave up hope
> Of seeing him (dance) at the end of a rope
> Hounded by eyes and thronged terrors now the lens
> Of glaring world that shunned even his defence
> Reading him strictly in the preterite tense
> Spent no ... thinking him not worth
> (Even) ... the price of a cold cell.
> There would have been a scandal at his death
> Perhaps. No more than this. Some tell
> Strange hellish tales of this poor foundered soul
> Who once fled north ...

Who once fled north, she thought. Hugh was saying :
'*Vámonos.*'

Yvonne said yes.

Outside the wind was blowing with an odd shrillness. A loose shutter somewhere banged and banged, and the electric sign over the garage prodded the night : *Euzkadi* –

The clock above it – man's public inquiry of the hour ! – said twelve to seven : 'Who once fled north.' The diners had left the porch of the El Popo ...

Lightning as they started down the steps was followed by volleys of thunder almost at once, dispersed and prolonged. Piling black clouds swallowed the stars to the north and east; Pegasus pounded up the sky unseen; but overhead it was still clear : Vega, Deneb, Altair; through the trees, towards the west, Hercules. 'Who once fled north,' she repeated. – Straight ahead of them beside the road was a ruined Grecian temple, dim, with two tall slender pillars, approached by two broad steps : or there had been a moment this temple, with its exquisite beauty of pillars, and, perfect in balance and proportion, its broad expanse of steps, that became now two beams of windy light from the garage, falling across the road, and the pillars, two telegraph poles.

They turned into the path. Hugh, with his torch, projected a phantom target, expanding, becoming enormous, and that swerved and transparently tangled with the cactus. The path narrowed and they walked, Hugh behind, in single file, the luminous target sliding before them in sweeping concentric ellipticities, across which her own wrong shadow leaped, or the shadow of a giantess. – The candelabras appeared salt grey where the flashlight caught them, too stiff and fleshy to be bending with the wind, in a slow multitudinous heaving, an inhuman cackling of scales and spines.

'Who once fled north ...'

Yvonne now felt cold sober : the cactus fell away, and the path, still narrow, through tall trees and undergrowth, seemed easy enough.

'Wl once fled north.' But they were not going north, they were going to the Farolito. Nor had the Consul fled north then, he'd probably gone of course, just as tonight, to the Farolito. 'There might have been a scandal at his death.' The treetops made a sound like water rushing over their heads. 'At his death.'

Yvonne was sober. It was the undergrowth, which made sudden swift movements into their path, obstructing it, that was not sober; the mobile trees were not sober; and finally it was Hugh, who she now realized had only brought her this far to prove the better practicality of the road, the danger of these woods under the discharges of electricity now nearly on top of them, who was not sober : and Yvonne found she had stopped abruptly, her hands clenched so tightly her fingers hurt, saying :

'We ought to hurry, it must be almost seven,' then, that she was hurrying, almost running down the path, talking loudly and excitedly : 'Did I tell you that the last night before I left a year ago Geoffrey and I made an appointment for dinner in Mexico City and he forgot the place, he told me, and went from restaurant to restaurant looking for me, just as we're looking for him now.'

> 'En los talleres y arsenales
> a guerra! todos, tocan ya;'

372

Hugh sang resignedly, in a deep voice.

' – and it was the same way when I first met him in Granada. We made an appointment for dinner in a place near the Alhambra and I thought he'd meant us to·meet *in* the Alhambra, and I couldn't find him and now it's *me*, looking for him again – on my first night back.'

> ' – todas, tocan ya;
> ¿morir quién quiere por la gloria
> o por vendedores de cañones?'

Thunder volleyed through the forest, and Yvonne almost stopped dead again, half imagining she had seen, for an instant, beckoning her on at the end of the path, the fixedly smiling woman with the lottery tickets.

'How much farther?' Hugh asked.

'We're nearly there, I think. There's a couple of turns in the path ahead and a fallen log we have to climb over.'

> 'Adelante, la juventud,
> al asalto, vamos ya,
> y contra los imperialismos,
> para un nuevo mundo hacer.

I guess you were right then,' Hugh said.

There was a lull in the storm that for Yvonne, looking up at the dark treetops' long slow swaying in the wind against the tempestuous sky, was a moment like that of the tide's turning, and yet that was filled with some quality of this morning's ride with Hugh, some night essence of their shared morning thoughts, with a wild sea-yearning of youth and love and sorrow.

A sharp pistol-like report, from somewhere ahead, as of a back-firing car, broke this swaying stillness, followed by another and another. 'More target practice,' Hugh laughed; yet these were different mundane sounds to hold as a relief against the sickening thunder that followed, for they meant Parián was near, soon its dim lights would gleam through the trees: by a lightning flash bright as day they had seen a sad useless arrow pointing back the way they'd come, to the burned Anochtitlán : and now, in the profounder gloom, Hugh's own light fell across a tree trunk on the left side where a wooden sign with a pointing hand confirmed their direction.

Hugh was singing behind her ... It began to rain softly and a sweet cleanly smell rose from the woods. And now, here was the place where the path doubled back on itself, only to be blocked by a huge moss-covered bole that divided it from that very same path she had decided against, which the Consul must have taken beyond Tomalín. The mildewed ladder with its wide-spaced rungs mounted against the near side of the bole was still there, and Yvonne had clambered up it almost before she realized she had lost Hugh's light. Yvonne balanced herself someway on top of this dark slippery log and saw his light again, a little to one side, moving among the trees. She said with a certain note of triumph :

'Mind you don't get off the path there, Hugh, it's sort of tricky. And mind the fallen log. There's a ladder up this side, but you have to jump down on the other.'

'Jump then,' said Hugh. 'I must have got off your path.'

Yvonne, hearing the plangent complaint of his guitar as Hugh banged the case, called : 'Here I am, over here.'

> *'Hijos del pueblo que oprimen cadenas*
> *esa injusticia no debe existir*
> *si tu existencia es un mundo de penas*
> *antes que esclavo, prefiere morir prefiere morir ...'*

Hugh was singing ironically.

All at once the rain fell more heavily. A wind like an express train swept through the forest; just ahead lightning struck through the trees with a savage tearing and roar of thunder that shook the earth...

There is, sometimes in thunder, another person who thinks for you, takes in one's mental porch furniture, shuts and bolts the mind's window against what seems less appalling as a threat than as some distortion of celestial privacy, a shattering insanity in heaven, a form of disgrace forbidden mortals to observe too closely : but there is always a door left open in the mind – as men have been known in great thunderstorms to leave their real doors open for Jesus to walk in – for the entrance and the reception of the unprecedented, the fearful acceptance of the thunderbolt that never falls on oneself, for the lightning that always hits the next street, for the disaster that so rarely strikes at the disastrous likely hour, and it was through this mental door that Yvonne, still balancing herself on the log, now perceived that something was menacingly wrong. In the slackening thunder something was approaching with a noise that was not the rain. It was an animal of some sort, terrified by the storm, and whatever it might be – a deer, a horse, unmistakably it had hooves – it was approaching at a dead run, stampeding, plunging through the undergrowth : and now as the lightning crashed again and the thunder subsided she heard a protracted neigh becoming a scream almost human in its panic. Yvonne was aware that her knees were trembling. Calling out to Hugh she tried to turn, in order to climb back down the ladder, but felt her footing on the log give way : slipping, she tried to regain her balance, slipped again and pitched forward. One foot doubled under her with a sharp pain as she fell. The next moment attempting to rise she saw, by a brilliant flash of lightning, the riderless horse. It was plunging sideways, not at her, and she saw its every detail, the jangling saddle sliding from its back, even the number seven branded on its rump. Again trying to rise she heard herself scream as the animal turned towards her and upon her. The sky was a sheet of white flame against which the trees and the poised rearing horse were an instant pinioned —

They were the cars at the fair that were whirling around her ; no, they were the planets, while the sun stood, burning and spinning and glittering in the centre ; here they came again, Mercury, Venus, Earth, Mars, Jupiter, Saturn, Uranus, Neptune, Pluto ; but they were not planets, for it was not the merry-go-round at all, but the Ferris Wheel, they were constellations, in the hub of which, like a great cold eye, burned Polaris, and round and round it here they went : Cassiopeia, Cepheus, the Lynx, Ursa Major, Ursa Minor, and the Dragon ; yet they were not constellations, but, somehow, myriads of beautiful butterflies, she was sailing into Acapulco harbour through a hurricane of beautiful butterflies, zigzagging overhead and endlessly vanishing astern over the sea, the sea, rough and pure, the long dawn rollers advancing, rising, and crashing down to glide in colourless ellipses over the sand, sinking, sinking, someone was calling her name far away and she remembered, they were in a dark wood, she heard the wind and the rain rushing through the forest and saw the tremors of lightning shuddering through the heavens and the horse – great God, the horse – and would this scene repeat itself endlessly and for ever? – the horse, rearing, poised over her, petrified in mid-air, a statue, somebody was sitting on the statue, it was Yvonne Griffaton, no, it was the statue of Huerta, the drunkard, the murderer, it was the Consul, or it was a mechanical horse on the merry-go-round, the carrousel, but the carrousel had stopped and she was in a ravine down which a million horses were thundering towards her, and she must escape, through the friendly forest to their house, their little home by the sea. But the house was on fire, she saw it now from the forest, from the steps above, she heard the crackling, it was on fire, everything was burning, the dream was burning, the house was burning, yet here they stood an instant, Geoffrey and she, inside it, inside the house, wringing their hands, and everything seemed all right, in its right place, the house was still there, everything dear and natural and familiar, save that the roof was on fire and there was this noise as of dry leaves blowing along the roof, this mechanical crackling, and now the fire was spreading even while they watched, the cupboard, the saucepans, the old kettle, the new kettle, the guardian figure on the deep cool well, the trowels, the rake, the sloping shingled woodshed on whose roof the white dogwood blossoms fell but would fall no more, for the tree was burning, the fire was spreading faster and faster, the walls with their millwheel reflections of sunlight on water were burning, the flowers in the garden were blackened and burning, they writhed, they twisted, they fell, the garden was burning, the porch where they sat on spring mornings was burning, the red door, the casement windows, the curtains she'd made were burning, Geoffrey's old chair was burning, his desk, and now his book, his book was burning, the pages were burning, burning, burning, whirling up from the fire they were scattered, burning, along the beach, and now it was growing darker and the tide coming in, the tide washed under the ruined house, the pleasure boats that had ferried song upstream sailed home silently over the dark waters of Eridanus. Their house was dying, only an agony went there now.

And leaving the burning dream Yvonne felt herself suddenly gathered upwards and borne towards the stars, through eddies of stars scattering aloft with ever wider circlings like rings on water, among which now appeared, like a flock of diamond birds flying softly and steadily towards Orion, the Pleiades . . .

12

'MESCAL,' said the Consul.

The main bar-room of the Farolito was deserted. From a mirror behind the bar, that also reflected the door open to the square, his face silently glared at him, with stern, familiar foreboding.

Yet the place was not silent. It was filled by that ticking: the ticking of his watch, his heart, his conscience, a clock somewhere. There was a remote sound too, from far below, of rushing water, of subterranean collapse; and moreover he could still hear them, the bitter wounding accusations he had flung at his own misery, the voices as in argument, his own louder than the rest, mingling now with those other voices that seemed to be wailing from a distance distressfully: '*Borracho, Borrachón, Borraaaacho!*'

But one of these voices was like Yvonne's, pleading. He still felt her look, their look in the Salón Ofelia, behind him. Deliberately he shut out all thought of Yvonne. He drank two swift mescals: the voices ceased.

Sucking a lemon he took stock of his surroundings. The mescal, while it assuaged, slowed his mind; each object demanded some moments to impinge upon him. In one corner of the room sat a white rabbit eating an ear of Indian corn. It nibbled at the purple and black stops with an air of detachment, as though playing a musical instrument. Behind the bar hung, by a clamped swivel, a beautiful Oaxaqueñan gourd of *mescal de olla,* from which his drink had been measured. Ranged on either side stood bottles of Tenampa, Berreteaga, Tequila Añejo, Anís doble de Mallorca, a violet decanter of Henry Mallet's '*delicioso licor*', a flask of peppermint cordial, a tall voluted bottle of Anís del Mono, on the label of which a devil brandished a pitchfork. On the wide counter before him were saucers of toothpicks, chillies, lemons, a tumblerful of straws, crossed long spoons in a glass tankard. At one end large bulbous jars of many-coloured *aguardiente* were set, raw alcohol with different flavours, in which citrus fruit rinds floated. An advertisement tacked by the mirror for last night's ball in Quauhnahuac caught his eye: *Hotel Bella Vista Gran Baile a Beneficio de la Cruz Roja. Los Mejores Artistas del radio en acción. No falte Vd*. A scorpion clung to the advertisement. The Consul noted all these things carefully. Drawing long sighs of icy relief, he even counted the toothpicks. He was safe here; this was the place he loved – sanctuary, the paradise of his despair.

The 'barman' – the son of the Elephant – known as A Few Fleas, a small dark sickly-looking child, was glancing near-sightedly through horn-rimmed spectacles at a cartoon serial *El Hijo del Diablo* in a boy's magazine. *Ti-to*. As he read, muttering to himself, he ate chocolates. Returning another replenished glass of mescal to the Consul he slopped some on the bar. He went on reading without wiping it up, however, muttering, cramming himself with chocolate skulls bought for the Day of the Dead, chocolate skeletons, chocolate, yes, funeral wagons. The Consul pointed out the scorpion on the wall and the boy brushed it off with a vexed gesture: it was dead. A Few Fleas turned back to his story, muttering aloud thickly, '*De pronto, Dalia vuelve en Sigrita llamando la atención de un guardia que pasea. ¡Suélteme! ¡Suélteme!*'

Save me, thought the Consul vaguely, as the boy suddenly went out for a change, *suélteme*, help: but maybe the scorpion, not wanting to be saved, had stung itself to death. He strolled across the room. After fruitlessly trying to make friends with the white rabbit, he approached the open window on his right. It was almost a sheer drop to the bottom of the ravine. What a dark, melancholy place! In Parián did Kubla Khan ... And the crag was still there too – just as in Shelley or Calderón or both – the crag that couldn't make up its mind to crumble absolutely, it clung so, cleft, to life. The sheer height was terrifying, he thought, leaning outwards, looking sideways at the split rock and attempting to recall the passage in *The Cenci* that described the huge stack clinging to the mass of earth, as if resting on life, not afraid to fall, but darkening, just the same, where it would go if it went. It was a tremendous, an awful way down to the bottom. But it struck him he was not afraid to fall either. He traced mentally the *barranca*'s circuitous abysmal path back through the country, through shattered mines, to his own garden, then saw himself standing again this morning with Yvonne outside the printer's shop, gazing at the picture of that other rock, La Despedida, the glacial rock crumbling among the wedding invitations in the shop window, the spinning flywheel behind. How long ago, how strange, how sad, remote as the memory of first love, even of his mother's death, it seemed; like some poor sorrow, this time without effort, Yvonne left his mind again.

Popocatepetl towered through the window, its immense flanks partly hidden by rolling thunderheads; its peak blocking the sky, it appeared almost right overhead, the *barranca*, the Farolito, directly beneath it. Under the volcano! It was not for nothing the ancients had placed Tartarus under Mt Aetna, nor within it, the monster Typhoeus, with his hundred heads and – relatively – fearful eyes and voices.

Turning, the Consul took his drink over to the open door. A mercurochrome agony down the west. He stared out at Parián. There, beyond a grass plot, was the inevitable square with its little public garden. To the left, at the edge of the *barranca*, a soldier slept under a tree. Half facing him, to the right, on an incline, stood what seemed at first sight a ruined monastery or waterworks. This was the grey turreted barracks of the Military Police he had mentioned to Hugh as the reputed Unión Militar headquarters. The building, which also included the prison, glowered at him with one eye, over an archway set in the forehead of its low façade : a clock pointing to six. On either side of the archway the barred windows in the Comisario de Policía and the Policía de Seguridad looked down on a group of soldiers talking, their bugles slung over their shoulders with bright green lariats. Other soldiers, puttees flapping, stumbled at sentry duty. Under the archway, in the entrance to the courtyard, a corporal was working at a table, on which stood an unlighted oil lamp. He was inscribing something in copperplate handwriting, the Consul knew, for his rather unsteady course hither – not so unsteady however as in the square at Quauhnahuac earlier, but still disgraceful—had brought him almost on top of him. Through the archway, grouped round the courtyard beyond, the Consul could make out dungeons with wooden bars like pigpens. In one of them a man was gesticulating. Elsewhere, to the left, were scattered huts of dark thatch, merging into the jungle which on all sides surrounded the town, glowing now in the unnatural livid light of approaching storm.

A Few Fleas having returned, the Consul went to the bar for his change. The boy, not hearing apparently, slopped some mescal into his glass from the beautiful gourd. Handing it back he upset the toothpicks. The Consul said nothing further about the change for the moment. However he made a mental note to order for his next drink something costing more than the fifty centavos he had already laid down. In this way he saw himself gradually recovering his money. He argued absurdly with himself that it was necessary to remain for this alone. He knew there was another reason yet couldn't place his finger on it. Every time the thought of Yvonne recurred to him he was aware of this. It seemed indeed then as though he must stay here for her sake, not because she would *follow* him here – no, she had gone, he'd let her go finally now, Hugh might come, though never she, not this time, obviously she would return home and his mind could not travel beyond that point – but for something else. He saw his change lying on the counter, the price of the mescal not deducted from it. He pocketed it all and came to the door again. Now the situation was reversed; the boy would have to keep an eye on *him*. It lugubriously diverted him to imagine, for A Few Fleas' benefit, though half aware the preoccupied boy was not watching him at all, he had assumed the blue expression peculiar to a certain type of drunkard, tepid with two drinks grudgingly on credit, gazing out of an empty saloon, an expression that pretends he hopes help, any kind of help, may be on its way, friends, any kind of friends coming to rescue him. For him life is always just around the corner, in the form of another drink at a new bar. Yet he really wants none of these things. Abandoned by his friends, as they by him, he knows that nothing but the crushing look of a creditor lives round that corner. Neither has he fortified himself sufficiently to borrow more money, nor obtain more credit; nor does he like the liquor next door anyway. Why am I here, says the silence, what have I done, echoes the emptiness, why have I ruined myself in this wilful manner, chuckles the money in the till, why have I been brought so low, wheedles the thoroughfare, to which the only answer was – The square gave him no answer. The little town, that had seemed empty, was filling up as evening wore on. Occasionally a moustachioed officer swaggered past, with a heavy gait, slapping his swagger stick on his leggings. People were returning from the cemeteries, though perhaps the procession would not pass for some time. A ragged platoon of soldiers were marching across the square. Bugles blared. The police too – those who were not on strike, or had been pretending to be on duty at the graves, or the deputies, it was not easy to get the distinction between the police and the military clear in one's mind either - had arrived in force. *Con* German friends, doubtless. The corporal was still writing at his table; it oddly reassured him. Two or three drinkers pushed their way past him into the Farolito, tasselled *sombreros* on the backs of their heads, holsters slapping their thighs. Two beggars had arrived and were taking up their posts outside the bar, under the tempestuous sky. One, legless, was dragging himself through the dust like a poor seal. But the other beggar, who boasted one leg, stood up stiffly, proudly, against the *cantina* wall as if waiting to be shot. Then this beggar with one leg leaned forward: he dropped a coin into the legless man's out-stretched hand. There were tears in the first beggar's eyes. The Consul now observed that on his extreme right some unusual animals resembling geese, but large as camels, and skinless men, without heads, upon stilts, whose animated entrails jerked along the ground, were issuing out of the forest path the way he had come. He shut his eyes from this and when he opened them someone who looked like a policeman was leading a horse up the path, that was all. He laughed, despite the policeman, then stopped. For he saw that the face of the reclining beggar was slowly changing to Señora Gregorio's, and now in turn to his mother's face, upon which appeared an expression of infinite pity and supplication.

Closing his eyes again, standing there, glass in hand, he thought for a minute with a freezing detached almost amused calm of the dreadful night inevitably awaiting him whether he drank much more or not, his room shaking with daemonic orchestras, the snatches of fearful tumultuous sleep, interrupted by voices which were really dogs barking, or by his own name being continually repeated by imaginary parties arriving, the vicious shouting, the strumming, the slamming, the pounding, the battling with insolent archfiends, the avalanche breaking down the door, the proddings from under the bed, and always, outside, the cries, the wailing, the terrible music, the dark's spinets : he returned to the bar.

Diosdado, the Elephant, had just entered from the back. The Consul watched him discard his black coat, hang it in the closet, then feel in the breast pocket of his spotless white shirt for a pipe protruding from it. He took this out and began to fill it from a package of Country Club el Bueno Tono tobacco. The Consul remembered now about his pipe : here it was, no doubt about that.

'*Sí, sí, mistair,*' he replied, listening with bent head to the Consul's query. '*Claro.* No – my ah peeper no *Inglese.* Monterey peeper. You were – ah – *borracho* one day then. *¿No señor?*'

'*¿Como no?*' said the Consul.

'Twice a day.' 'You was dronk three times a day,' Diosdado said, and his look, the insult, the implied extent of his downfall, penetrated the Consul. 'Then you'll be going back to America now,' he added, rummaging behind the bar.

'I – no – *por qué?*'

Diosdado suddenly slapped a fat package of envelopes fastened with elastic on the bar counter. '*¿ – es suyo?*' he asked directly.

Where are the letters Geoffrey Firmin the letters the letters she wrote till her heart broke? Here were the letters, here and nowhere else : these were the letters and this the Consul knew immediately without examining the envelopes. When he spoke he could not recognize his own voice :

'*Sí, señor, muchas gracias,*' he said.

'*De nada, señor.*' The Godgiven turned away.

La rame inutile fatigua vainement une mer immobile ... The Consul could not move for a full minute. He could not even

383

make a move toward a drink. Then he began to trace sideways in spilled liquor a little map on the bar. Diosdado came back and watched with interest. '*España*,' the Consul said, then his Spanish failing him, 'You are Spanish, *señor*?'

'*Sí, sí, señor, sí*,' said Diosdado, watching, but in a new tone. '*Español. España*.'

'These letters you gave me – see? – are from my wife, my *esposa*. ¿*Claro*? This is where we met. In Spain. You recognize it, your old home, you know Andalusia? That, up there, that's the Guadalquivir. Beyond there, the Sierra Morena. Down there's Almería. Those,' he traced with his finger, 'lying between, are the Sierra Nevada mountains. And there's Granada. That is the place. The very place we met.' The Consul smiled.

'Granada,' said Diosdado, sharply, in a different, harder pronunciation to the Consul's. He gave him a searching, an important, suspicious look, then left him again. Now he was speaking to a group at the other end of the bar. Faces were turned in the Consul's direction.

The Consul carried another drink with Yvonne's letters into an inner room, one of the boxes in the Chinese puzzle. He hadn't remembered before they were framed in dull glass, like cashiers' offices in a bank. In this room he was not really surprised to find the old Tarascan woman of the Bella Vista this morning. Her tequila, surrounded by dominoes, was set before her on the round table. Her chicken pecked among them. The Consul wondered if they were her own; or was it just necessary for her to have dominoes wherever she happened to be? Her stick with the claw handle hung, as though alive, on the edge of the table. The Consul moved to her, drank half his mescal, took off his glasses, then slipped the elastic from the package.

– 'Do you remember tomorrow?' he read. No, he thought; the words sank like stones in his mind. – It was a fact that he was losing touch with his situation . . . He was dissociated from himself, and at the same time he saw this plainly, the shock of receiving the letters having in a sense waked him, if only, so to say, from one somnambulism into another; he was drunk, he was sober, he had a hangover; all at once; it was after six in the evening, yet whether it was being in the Farolito, or the presence of

384

the old woman in this glass-framed room where an electric light was burning, he seemed back in the early morning again : it was almost as if he were yet another kind of drunkard, in different circumstances, in another country, to whom something quite different was happening : he was like a man who gets up half stupefied with liquor at dawn, chattering, 'Jesus this is the kind of fellow I am, Ugh! Ugh!' to see his wife off by an early bus, though it is too late, and there is the note on the breakfast table. 'Forgive me for being hysterical yesterday, such an outburst was certainly not excused on any grounds of your having hurt me, don't forget to bring in the milk,' beneath which he finds written, almost as an afterthought : 'Darling, we can't go on like this, it's too awful, I'm leaving – ' and who, instead of perceiving the whole significance of this, remembers incongruously he told the barman at too great length last night how somebody's house burned down – and why has he told him where he lives, now the police will be able to find out – and why is the barman's name Sherlock? an unforgettable name! – and having a glass of port and water and three aspirin, which make him sick, reflects that he has five hours before the pubs open when he must return to that same bar and apologize ... But where did I put my cigarette? and why is my glass of port under the bathtub? and was that an explosion I heard, somewhere in the house?

And encountering his accusing eyes in another mirror within the little room, the Consul had the queer passing feeling he'd risen in bed to do this, that he had sprung up and must gibber 'Coriolanus is dead!' or 'muddle muddle muddle' or 'I think it was, Oh! Oh!' or something really senseless like 'buckets, buckets, millions of buckets in the soup!' and that he would now (though he was sitting quite calmly in the Farolito) relapse once more upon the pillows to watch, shaking in impotent terror at himself, the beards and eyes form in the curtains, or fill the space between the wardrobe and the ceiling, and hear, from the street, the soft padding of the eternal ghostly policeman outside –

'Do you remember tomorrow? It is our wedding anniversary ... I have not had one word from you since I left. God, it is this silence that frightens me.'

The Consul drank some more mescal.

'It is this silence that frightens me – this silence –'

The Consul read this sentence over and over again, the same sentence, the same letter, all of the letters vain as those arriving on shipboard in port for one lost at sea, because he found some difficulty in focusing, the words kept blurring and dissembling, his own name starting out at him : but the mescal had brought him in touch with his situation again to the extent that he did not now need to comprehend any meaning in the words beyond their abject confirmation of his own lostness, his own fruitless selfish ruin, now perhaps finally self-imposed, his brain, before this cruelly disregarded evidence of what heartbreak he had caused *her*, at an agonized standstill.

'It is this silence that frightens me. I have pictured all sorts of tragic things befalling you, it is as though you were away at war and I were waiting, waiting for news of you, for the letter, the telegram ... but no war could have this power to so chill and terrify my heart. I send you all my love and my whole heart and all my thoughts and prayers.' – The Consul was aware, drinking, that the woman with the dominoes was trying to attract his attention, opening her mouth and pointing into it : now she was subtly moving round the table nearer him. – 'Surely you must have thought a great deal of *us*, of what we built together, of how mindlessly we destroyed the structure and the beauty but yet could not destroy the memory of that beauty. It has been this which has haunted me day and night. Turning I see us in a hundred places with a hundred smiles. I come into a street, and you are there. I creep at night to bed and you are waiting for me. What is there in life besides the person whom one adores and the life one can build with that person? For the first time I understand the meaning of suicide ... God, how pointless and empty the world is! Days filled with cheap and tarnished moments succeed each other, restless and haunted nights follow in bitter routine : the sun shines without brightness, and the moon rises without light. My heart has the taste of ashes, and my throat is tight and weary with weeping. What is a lost soul? It is one that has turned from its true path and is groping in the darkness of remembered ways –'

The old woman was plucking at his sleeve and the Consul –

386

had Yvonne been reading the letters of Heloise and Abelard? – reached out to press an electric bell, the urban yet violent presence of which in these odd little niches never failed to give him a shock. A moment later A Few Fleas entered with a bottle of tequila in one hand and of mescal Xicotancatl in the other but he took the bottles away after pouring their drinks. The Consul nodded to the old woman, motioned to her tequila, drank most of his mescal, and resumed reading. He could not remember whether he had paid or not. – 'Oh Geoffrey, how bitterly I regret it now. Why did we postpone it? Is it too late? I want your children, soon, at once, I want them. I want your life filling and stirring me. I want your happiness beneath my heart and your sorrows in my eyes and your peace in the fingers of my hand –' The Consul paused, what was she saying? He rubbed his eyes, then fumbled for his cigarettes : Alas; the tragic word droned round the room like a bullet that had passed through him. He read on, smoking; 'You are walking on the edge of an abyss where I may not follow. I wake to a darkness in which I must follow myself endlessly, hating the I who so eternally pursues and confronts me. If we could rise from our misery, seek each other once more, and find again the solace of each other's lips and eyes. Who is to stand between? Who can prevent?'

The Consul stood up – Yvonne had certainly been reading *something* – bowed to the old woman, and went out into the bar he'd imagined filling up behind him, but which was still fairly deserted. Who indeed was to stand between? He posted himself at the door again, as sometimes before in the deceptive violet dawn : who indeed could prevent? Once more he stared at the square. The same ragged platoon of soldiers still seemed to be crossing it, as in some disrupted movie repeating itself. The corporal still toiled at his copperplate handwriting under the archway, only his lamp was alight. It was getting dark. The police were nowhere to be seen. Though by the *barranca* the same soldier was still asleep under a tree; or wasn't it a soldier, but something else? He looked away. Black clouds were boiling up again, there was a distant breaking of thunder. He breathed the oppressive air in which there was a slight hint of coolness. Who indeed, even now, was to stand between? he thought desperately.

Who indeed even now could prevent? He wanted Yvonne at this moment, to take her in his arms, wanted more than ever to be forgiven, and to forgive : but where should he go? Where would he find her now? A whole unlikely family of indeterminate class were strolling past the door : the grandfather in front, correcting his watch, peering at the dim barracks clock that still said six, the mother laughing and drawing her *rebozo* over her head, mocking the probable storm (up in the mountains two drunken gods standing far apart were still engaged in an endlessly indecisive and wildly swinging game of bumblepuppy with a Burmese gong), the father by himself smiling proudly, contemplatively, clicking his fingers, flicking a speck of dust now from his fine brown shiny boots. Two pretty little children with limpid black eyes were walking between them hand in hand. Suddenly the elder child freed her sister's hand, and turned a succession of cartwheels on the lush grass plot. All of them were laughing. The Consul hated to look at them ... They'd gone anyway, thank God. Miserably he wanted Yvonne and did not want her. '*¿Quiere María?*' a voice spoke softly behind him.

At first he saw only the shapely legs of the girl who was leading him, now by the constricted power of aching flesh alone, of pathetic trembling yet brutal lust, through the little glass-paned rooms, that grew smaller and smaller, darker and darker, until by the *mingitorio*, the '*Señores*', out of whose evil-smelling gloom broke a sinister chuckle, there was merely a lightless annex no larger than a cupboard in which two men whose faces he couldn't see either were sitting, drinking or plotting.

Then it struck him that some reckless murderous power was drawing him on, forcing him, while he yet remained passionately aware of the all too possible consequences and somehow as innocently unconscious, to do without precaution or conscience what he would never be able to undo or gainsay, leading him irresistibly out into the garden – lightning-filled at this moment, it reminded him queerly of his own house, and also of El Popo, where earlier he had thought of going, only this was grimmer, the obverse of it – leading him through the open door into the darkening room, one of many giving on the *patio*.

So this was it, the final stupid unprophylactic rejection. He could prevent it even now. He would not prevent it. Yet perhaps his familiars, or one of his voices, might have some good advice : he looked about him, listening; *erectis whoribus*. No voices came. Suddenly he laughed : it had been clever of him to trick his voices. They didn't know he was here. The room itself, in which gleamed a single blue electric bulb, was not sordid : at first sight it was a student's room. In fact it closely resembled his old room at college, only this was more spacious. There were the same great doors and a bookcase in a familiar place, with a book open on top of the shelves. In one corner, incongruously, stood a gigantic sabre. Kashmir! He imagined he'd seen the word, then it had gone. Probably he had seen it, for the book, of all things, was a Spanish history of British India. The bed was disorderly and covered with footmarks, even what appeared bloodstains, though this bed too seemed akin to a student's cot. He noticed by it an almost empty bottle of mescal. But the floor was red flagstone and somehow its cold strong logic cancelled the horror; he finished the bottle. The girl who had been shutting the double doors while addressing him in some strange language, possibly Zapotecan, came toward him and he saw she was young and pretty. Lightning silhouetted against the window a face, for a moment curiously like Yvonne's. '*Quiere María*,' she volunteered again, and flinging her arms round his neck, drew him down to the bed. Her body was Yvonne's too, her legs, her breasts, her pounding passionate heart, electricity crackled under his fingers running over her, though the sentimental illusion was going, it was sinking into a sea, as though it had not been there, it had become the sea, a desolate horizon with one huge black sailing ship, hull down, sweeping into the sunset; or her body was nothing, an abstraction merely, a calamity, a fiendish apparatus for calamitous sickening sensation; it was disaster, it was the horror of waking up in the morning in Oaxaca, his body fully clothed, at half past three every morning after Yvonne had gone; Oaxaca, and the nightly escape from the sleeping Hotel Francia, where Yvonne and he had once been happy, from the cheap room giving on the balcony high up, to El Infierno, that other Farolito, of trying to find the bottle in the dark, and failing, the vulture

389

sitting in the washbasin; his steps, noiseless, dead silence outside his hotel room, too soon for the terrible sounds of squealing and slaughter in the kitchen below – of going down the carpeted stairs to the huge dark well of the deserted dining-room once the *patio*, sinking into the soft disaster of the carpet, his feet sinking into heartbreak when he reached the stairs, still not sure he wasn't on the landing – and the stab of panic and self-disgust when he thought of the cold shower-bath back on the left, used only once before, but that was enough – and the silent final trembling approach, respectable, his steps sinking into calamity (and it was this calamity he now, with María, penetrated, the only thing alive in him now this burning boiling crucified evil organ – God is it possible to suffer more than this, out of this suffering something must be born, and what would be born was his own death), for ah, how alike are the groans of love to those of the dying, how alike, those of love, to those of the dying – and his steps sinking, into his tremor, the sickening cold tremor, and into the dark well of the dining-room, with round the corner one dim light hovering above the desk, and the clock – too early – and the letters unwritten, powerless to write, and the calendar saying eternally, powerlessly, their wedding anniversary, and the manager's nephew asleep on the couch, waiting up to meet the early train from Mexico City; the darkness that murmured and was palpable, the cold aching loneliness in the high sounding dining-room, stiff with the dead white grey folded napkins, the weight of suffering and conscience greater (it seemed) than that borne by any man who had survived – the thirst that was not thirst, but itself heartbreak, and lust, was death, death, and death again and death the waiting in the cold hotel dining-room, half whispering to himself, waiting, since El Infierno, that other Farolito, did not open till four in the morning and one could scarcely wait outside – (and this calamity he was now penetrating, it was calamity, the calamity of his own life, the very essence of it he now penetrated, was penetrating, penetrated) – waiting for the Infierno whose one lamp of hope would soon be glowing beyond the dark open sewers, and on the table, in the hotel dining-room, difficult to distinguish, a carafe of water – trembling, trembling, carrying the carafe of water to his lips,

but not far enough, it was too heavy, like his burden of sorrow –
'*you cannot drink of it*' – he could only moisten his lips, and
then – it must have been Jesus who sent me this, it was only He
who was following me after all – the bottle of red French wine
from Salina Cruz still standing there on the table set for breakfast, marked with someone else's room number, uncorked with
difficulty and (watching to see the nephew wasn't watching)
holding it with both hands, and letting the blessed ichor trickle
down his throat, just a little, for after all one was an Englishman,
and still sporting, and then subsiding on the couch too – his
heart a cold ache warm to one side – into a cold shivering shell
of palpitating loneliness – yet feeling the wine slightly more, as if
one's chest were being filled with boiling ice now, or there were
a bar of red-hot iron across one's chest, but cold in its effect, for
the conscience that rages underneath anew and is bursting one's
heart burns so fiercely with the fires of hell a bar of red-hot iron
is as a mere chill to it – and the clock ticking forward, with his
heart beating now like a snow-muffled drum, ticking, shaking,
time shaking and ticking toward El Infierno then – the escape !
– drawing the blanket he had secretly brought down from the
hotel room over his head, creeping out past the manager's nephew – the escape ! – past the hotel desk, not daring to look for
mail – 'it is this silence that frightens me' – (can it be there ? Is
this me ? Alas, self-pitying miserable wretch, you old rascal) past
– the escape ! – the Indian night-watchman sleeping on the floor
in the doorway, and like an Indian himself now, clutching the
few pesos he had left, out into the cold walled cobbled city, past
– the escape through the secret passage ! – the open sewers in the
mean streets, the few lone dim street lamps, into the night, into
the miracle that the coffins of houses, the landmarks were still
there, the escape down the poor broken sidewalks, groaning,
groaning – and how alike are the groans of love, to those of the
dying, how alike, those of love, to those of the dying ! – and the
houses so still, so cold, before dawn, till he saw, rounding the
corner safe, the one lamp of El Infierno glowing, that was so like
the Farolito, then, surprised once more he could ever have
reached it, standing inside the place with his back to the wall,
and his blanket still over his head, talking to the beggars, the

early workers, the dirty prostitutes, the pimps, the debris and detritus of the streets and the bottom of the earth, but who were yet so much higher than he, drinking just as he had done here in the Farolito, and telling lies, lying – the escape, still the escape! – until the lilac-shaded dawn that should have brought death, and he should have died now too; what have I done?

The Consul's eyes focused a calendar behind the bed. He had reached his crisis at last, a crisis without possession, almost without pleasure finally, and what he saw might have been, no, he was sure it was, a picture of Canada. Under a brilliant full moon a stag stood by a river down which a man and a woman were paddling a birch-bark canoe. This calendar was set to the future, for next month, December: where would he be then? In the dim blue light he even made out the names of the Saints for each December day, printed by the numerals: Santa Natalia, Santa Bibiana, S. Francisco Xavier, Santa Sabos, S. Nicolas de Bari, S. Ambrosio: thunder blew the door open, the face of M. Laruelle faded in the door.

In the *mingitorio* a stench like mercaptan. clapped yellow hands on his face and now, from the urinal walls, uninvited, he heard his voices again, hissing and shrieking and yammering at him: 'Now you've done it, now you've really done it, Geoffrey Firmin! Even we can help you no longer ... Just the same you might as well make the most of it now, the night's still young...'

'You like María, you like?' A man's voice – that of the chuckler, he recognized – came from the gloom and the Consul, his knees trembling, gazed round him; all he saw at first were slashed advertisements on the slimy feebly lit walls: *Clinica Dr Vigil, Enfermedades Secretas de Ambos Sexos, Vías Urinarias, Trastornos Sexuales, Debilidad Sexual, Derrames Nocturnos, Emisiones Prematuras, Espermatorrea, Impotencia. 666. His* versatile companion of this morning and last night might have been informing him ironically all was not yet lost – unfortunately by now he would be well on his way to Guanajuato. He distinguished an incredibly filthy man sitting hunched in the corner on a lavatory seat, so short his trousered feet didn't reach the littered, befouled floor. 'You like María?' this man croaked again. 'I send. Me *amigo*.' He farted. 'Me fliend Englisman all tine, all tine.' '¿Qué hora?' asked the Consul, shivering, noticing, in the runnel, a dead scorpion; a sparkle of phosphorescence and it had gone, or had never been there. 'What's the time?' 'Sick,' answered the man. 'No, it er ah half past sick by the cock.' 'You mean half past six by the clock.' 'Sí señor. Half past sick by the cock.'

606. – The pricked peetroot, pickled betroot; the Consul, arranging his dress, laughed grimly at the pimp's reply – or was he some sort of stool pigeon, in the strictest sense of that term? And who was it had said earlier, half past tree by the cock? How had the man known he was English, he wondered, taking his laughter back through the glass-paned rooms, out through the filling bar to the door again – perhaps he worked for the Unión Militar, squatting at stool all day in the Seguridad jakes eavesdropping on the prisoners' conversation, while pimping was just a sideline. He might have found out from him about María, whether she was – but he didn't want to know. He'd been right about the time though. The clock on the Comisaría de Policía, annular, imperfectly luminous, said, as if it had just moved forward with a jerk, a little after six-thirty, and the Consul corrected his watch, which was slow. It was now quite dark. Yet the same ragged platoon still seemed to be marching across the square. The corporal was no longer writing, however. Outside the prison stood a single motionless sentinel. The archway behind him was suddenly swept by wild light. Beyond, by the cells, the shadow of a policeman's lantern was swinging against the wall. The evening was filled by odd noises, like those of sleep. The roll of a drum somewhere was a revolution, a cry down the street someone being murdered, brakes grinding far away a soul in pain. The plucked chords of a guitar hung over his head. A bell clanged frantically in the distance. Lightning twitched. Half past sick by the cock ... In British Columbia, in Canada, on cold Pineaus Lake, where his island had long since become a wilderness of laurel and Indian Pipe, of wild strawberry and Oregon holly, he remembered the strange Indian belief prevailing that a cock would crow over a drowned body. How dread the validation that silver February evening long ago when, as acting Lithuanian Consul to Vernon, he had accompanied the

search party in the boat, and the bored rooster had roused himself to crow shrilly seven times! The dynamite charges had apparently disturbed nothing, they were sombrely rowing for shore through the cloudy twilight, when suddenly, protruding from the water, they had seen what looked at first like a glove – the hand of the drowned Lithuanian. British Columbia, the genteel Siberia, that was neither genteel nor a Siberia, but an undiscovered, perhaps an undiscoverable paradise, that might have been a solution, to return there, to build, if not on his island, somewhere there, a new life with Yvonne. Why hadn't he thought of it before? Or why hadn't she? Or had that been what she was getting at this afternoon, and which had half communicated itself to his mind? My little grey home in the west. Now it seemed to him he had often thought of it before, in this precise spot where he was standing. But now too at least this much was clear. He couldn't go back to Yvonne if he wanted to. The hope of any new life together, even were it miraculously offered again, could scarcely survive in the arid air of an estranged postponement to which it must now, on top of everything else, be submitted for brutal hygienic reasons alone. True, those reasons were without quite secure basis as yet, but for another purpose that eluded him they had to remain unassailable. All solutions now came up against their great Chinese wall, forgiveness among them. He laughed once more, feeling a strange release, almost a sense of attainment. His mind was clear. Physically he seemed better too. It was as if, out of an ultimate contamination, he had derived strength. He felt free to devour what remained of his life in peace. At the same time a certain gruesome gaiety was creeping into this mood, and, in an extraordinary way, a certain lightheaded mischievousness. He was aware of a desire at once for complete glutted oblivion and for an innocent youthful fling. 'Alas', a voice seemed to be saying also in his ear, 'my poor little child, you do not feel any of these things really, only lost, only homeless.'

He started. In front of him tied to a small tree he hadn't noticed, though it was right opposite the *cantina* on the other side of the path, stood a horse cropping the lush grass. Something familiar about the beast made him walk over. Yes – exactly as he thought. He could mistake by now neither the number seven branded on the rump nor the leather saddle charactered in that fashion. It was the Indian's horse, the horse of the man he'd first seen today riding it singing into the sunlit world, then abandoned, left dying by the roadside. He patted the animal which twitched its ears and went on cropping imperturbably – perhaps not so imperturbably; at a rumble of thunder the horse, whose saddlebags he noticed had been mysteriously restored, whinnied uneasily, shaking all over. When just as mysteriously those saddlebags no longer chinked. Unbidden, an explanation of this afternoon's events came to the Consul. Hadn't it turned out to be a policeman into which all those abominations he'd observed a little while since had melted, a policeman leading a horse in this direction? Why should not that horse be this horse? It had been those *vigilante hombres* who'd turned up on the road this afternoon, and here in Parián, as he'd told Hugh, was their headquarters. How Hugh would relish this, could he be here! The police – ah, the fearful police – or rather not the real police, he corrected himself, but those Unión Militar fellows were at the bottom, in an insanely complicated manner but still at the bottom, of the whole business. He felt suddenly sure of this. As if out of some correspondence between the subnormal world itself and the abnormally suspicious delirious one within him the truth had sprung – sprung like a shadow however, which –

'*¿Qué hacéis aquí?*'

'*Nada,*' he said, and smiled at the man resembling a Mexican sergeant of police who had snatched the bridle from his hands. 'Nothing. *Veo que la tierra anda; estoy esperando que pase mi casa por aquí para meterme en ella,*' he brilliantly managed. The brasswork on the amazed policeman's uniform buckles caught the light from the doorway of the Farolito, then, as he turned, the leather on his sam-browne caught it, so that it was glossy as a plantain leaf, and lastly his boots, which shone like dull silver. The Consul laughed : just to glance at him was to feel that mankind was on the point of being saved immediately. He repeated the good Mexican joke, not quite right, in English, patting the policeman, whose jaw had dropped in bewilderment and who was eyeing him blankly, on the arm. 'I learn that the world goes round so I am waiting here for my house to pass by.' He held out his hand. '*Amigo*,' he said.

The policeman grunted, brushing the Consul's hand off. Then, giving him quick suspicious glances over his shoulder, he fastened the horse more securely to the tree. In those swift glances there was something serious indeed, the Consul was aware, something that bade him escape at his peril. Slightly hurt, he now remembered too, the look Diosdado had given him. But the Consul felt neither serious nor like escaping. Nor did his feelings change as he found himself impelled by the policeman from behind towards the *cantina*, beyond which, by lightning, the east briefly appeared, in onrush, a towering thunderhead. Preceding him through the door, it actually struck the Consul that the sergeant was trying to be polite. He stood aside quite nimbly, bidding, with a gesture, the other go first. '*Mi amigo*,' he repeated. The policeman shoved him in and they made for one end of the bar which was empty.

'¿*Americano, eh?*' this policeman said now firmly. 'Wait, *aquí. ¿Comprende, señor?*' He went behind the bar to speak with Diosdado.

The Consul unsuccessfully tried to intrude, on his conduct's behalf, a cordial note of explanation for the Elephant, who appeared grim as if he'd just murdered another of his wives to cure her neurasthenia. Meantime, A Few Fleas, temporarily otiose, and with surprising charity, slid him a mescal along the counter. People were looking at him again. Then the policeman confronted him from the other side of the bar. 'They say there ees trouble about you no pay,' he said, 'you no pay for – ah – Mehican whisky. You no pay for Mehican girl. You no have money, hey?'

'Zicker,' said the Consul, whose Spanish, in spite of a temporary insurgence, he knew virtually gone. '*Sí*. Yes. *Mucho dinero*,' he added, placing a peso on the counter for A Few Fleas. He saw that the policeman was a heavy-necked handsome man with a black gritty moustache, flashing teeth, and a rather consciously swashbuckling manner. He was joined at this moment by a tall slim man in well-cut American tweeds with a hard sombre face and long beautiful hands. Glancing periodically at the Consul he spoke in undertones with Diosdado and the policeman. This man, who looked pure-bred Castilian, seemed familiar and the Consul wondered where he had seen him before. The policeman, disengaging himself from him, leaned over with his elbows on the bar, talking to the Consul. 'You no have money, hey, and now you steal my horse.' He winked at the Godgiven. 'What for you ah run away with Mehican *caballo*? for to no pay Mehican money – hey?'

The Consul stared at him. 'No. Decidedly not. Of course I wasn't going to steal your horse. I was merely looking at it, admiring it.'

'What for you want to look at Mehican *caballo*? For why?' The policeman laughed suddenly, with real merriment, slapping his thighs – obviously he was a good fellow and the Consul, feeling the ice was broken, laughed too. But the policeman obviously enough was also quite drunk, so it was difficult to gauge the quality of this laughter. While the faces of both Diosdado and the man in tweeds remained black and stern. 'You make a the map of the Spain,' the policeman persisted, controlling his laughter finally. 'You know ah Spain?'

'*Comment non,*' the Consul said. So Diosdado had told him about the map, yet surely that was an innocently sad enough thing to have done. '*Oui. Es muy asombrosa.*' No, this wasn't Pernambuco: definitely he ought not to speak Portuguese. '*Jawohl. Correcto, señor,*' he finished. 'Yes, I know Spain.'

'You make a the map of the Spain? You Bolsheviki prick? You member of the Brigade Internationale and stir up trouble?'

'No,' answered the Consul firmly, decently, but now somewhat agitated. '*Absolutamente no.*'

'*¿Ab-so-lut-a-mente hey?*' The policeman, with another wink at Diosdado, imitated the Consul's manner. He came round to the correct side of the bar again, bringing the sombre man with him who didn't say a word or drink but merely stood there, looking stern, as did the Elephant, opposite them now, angrily drying glasses. 'All', he drawled, and 'right!' the policeman added with tremendous emphasis, slapping the Consul on the back. 'All right. Come on my friend –' he invited him. 'Drink. Drink a all you ah want to have. We have been looking for you,' he went on in a loud, half bantering, drunken tone. 'You have murdered a man and escaped through seven states. We want to found out about you. We have founded out – it is right? – you desert your ship at Vera Cruz? You say you have money. How much money a you have got?'

The Consul took out a crumpled note and replaced it in his pocket. 'Fifty pesos, hey. Perhaps that not enough money. What are you for? *¿Inglés? ¿Español? ¿Americano? ¿Alemán? ¿Russish?* You come a from the you-are-essy-essy? What for are you do?'

'I no spikker the English – hey, what's your names?' someone else asked him loudly at his elbow, and the Consul turned to see another policeman dressed much like the first, only shorter, heavy-jowled, with little cruel eyes in an ashen pulpy clean-shaven face. Though he carried sidearms both his trigger finger and his right thumb were missing. As he spoke he made an obscene rolling movement of his hips and winked at the first policeman and at Diosdado though avoiding the eyes of the man in tweeds. *'Progresión al culo,'* he added, for no reason the Consul knew of, still rolling his hips.

'He is the Chief of Municipality,' the first policeman explained heartily to the Consul. 'This man want to know ah your name. *¿Cómo se llama?*'

'Yes, what's your names?' shouted the second policeman, who had taken a drink from the bar, but not looking at the Consul and still rolling his hips.

'Trotsky,' gibed someone from the far end of the counter, and the Consul, beard-conscious, flushed.

'Blackstone,' he answered gravely, and indeed, he asked himself, accepting another mescal, had he not and with a vengeance come to live among the Indians? The only trouble was one was very much afraid these particular Indians might turn out to be people with ideas too. 'William Blackstone.'

'Why ah are you,' shouted the fat policeman, whose own name was something like Zuzugoitea, 'What ah are you for?' And he repeated the catechism of the first policeman, whom he seemed to imitate in everything. *'¿Inglés? ¿Alemán?'*

The Consul shook his head. 'No. Just William Blackstone.'

'You are Juden?' the first policeman demanded.

'No. Just Blackstone,' the Consul repeated, shaking his head, 'William Blackstone. Jews are seldom very *borracho*.'

'You are – ah – a *borracho*, hey,' the first policeman said, and everyone laughed – several others, his henchmen evidently, had joined them though the Consul couldn't distinguish them clearly – save the inflexible indifferent man in tweeds. 'He is the Chief of Gardens,' the first policeman explained, continuing; 'That man is Jefe de Jardineros.' And there was a certain awe in his tone. 'I am chief too, I am Chief of Rostrums,' he added, but almost reflectively, as if he meant 'I am only Chief of Rostrums'.

'And I – ' began the Consul.

'Am *perfectamente borracho*,' finished the first policeman, and everyone roared again save the Jefe de Jardineros.

'*Y yo* – ' repeated the Consul, but what was he saying? And who were these people, really? Chief of what Rostrums, Chief of what Municipality, above all, Chief of what Gardens? Surely this silent man in tweeds, sinister too, though apparently the only one unarmed in the group, wasn't the one responsible for all those little public gardens. Albeit the Consul was prompted by a shadowy prescience he already had concerning the claimants to these titular pretensions. They were associated in his mind with the Inspector General of the State and also as he had told Hugh with the Unión Militar. Doubtless he'd seen them here before in one of the rooms or at the bar, but certainly never at such close quarters as this. However so many questions he was unable to answer were being showered upon him by so many different people this significance was almost forgotten. He gathered, though, that the respected Chief of Gardens, to whom at this moment he sent a mute appeal for help, might be even 'higher' than the Inspector-General himself. The appeal was answered by a blacker look than ever: at the same time the Consul knew where he'd seen him before; the Chief of Gardens might have been the image of himself when, lean, bronzed, serious, beardless, and at the crossroads of his career, he had assumed the Vice-Consulship in Granada. Innumerable tequilas and mescals were being brought and the Consul drank everything in sight without regard for ownership. 'It's not enough to say they were

at the El Amor de los Amores together,' he heard himself repeating – it must have been in answer to some insistent demand
for the story of this afternoon, though why it should be made at
all he didn't know – 'What matters is how the thing happened.
Was the peon – perhaps he wasn't quite a peon – drunk? Or
did he fall from his horse? Perhaps the thief just recognized a
boon companion who owed him a drink or two –'

Thunder growled outside the Farolito. He sat down. It was
an order. Everything was growing very chaotic. The bar was
now nearly full. Some of the drinkers had come from the grave-
yards, Indians in loose-fitting clothes. There were dilapidated
soldiers with among them here and there a more smartly dressed
officer. He distinguished in the glass rooms bugles and green
lariats moving. Several dancers had entered dressed in long
black cloaks streaked with luminous paint to represent skeletons.
The Chief of Municipality was standing behind him now. The
Chief of Rostrums was standing too, talking on his right with
the Jefe de Jardineros, whose name, the Consul had discovered,
was Fructuoso Sanabria. 'Hullo, qué tal?' asked the Consul.
Someone was sitting next him with his back half turned who
also seemed familiar. He looked like a poet, some friend of his
college days. Fair hair fell over his fine forehead. The Consul
offered him a drink which this young man not only refused, in
Spanish, but rose to refuse, making a gesture with his hand of
pushing the Consul away, then moving, with angry half-averted
face, to the far end of the bar. The Consul was hurt. Again he
sent a mute appeal for help to the Chief of Gardens: he was
answered by an implacable, an almost final look. For the first
time the Consul scented the tangibility of his danger. He knew
Sanabria and the first policemen were discussing him with the
utmost hostility, deciding what to do with him. Then he saw
they were trying to catch the Chief of Municipality's attention.
They were breasting their way, just the two of them, behind the
bar again to a telephone he hadn't noticed, and the curious thing
about this telephone was that it seemed to be working properly.
The Chief of Rostrums did the talking: Sanabria stood by
grimly, apparently giving instructions. They were taking their
time, and realizing the call would be about him, whatever its

nature, the Consul, with a slow burning pain of apprehension, felt again how lonely he was, that all around him in spite of the crowd, the uproar, slightly muted at a gesture from Sanabria, stretched a solitude like the wilderness of grey heaving Atlantic conjured to his eyes a little while since with María, only this time no sail was in sight. The mood of mischievousness and release had vanished completely. He knew he'd half hoped all along Yvonne would come to rescue him, knew, now, it was too late, she would not come. Ah, if Yvonne, if only as a daughter, who would understand and comfort him, could only be at his side now ! Even if but to lead him by the hand, drunkenly homeward through the stone fields, the forests – not interfering of course with his occasional pulls at the bottle, and ah, those burning draughts in loneliness, he would miss them, wherever he was going, they were perhaps the happiest things his life had known ! – as he had seen the Indian children lead their fathers home on Sundays. Instantly, consciously, he forgot Yvonne again. It ran in his head he could perhaps leave the Farolito at this moment by himself, unnoticed and without difficulty, for the Chief of Municipality was still deep in conversation, while the backs of the two other policemen at the telephone were turned, yet he made no move. Instead, leaning his elbows on the bar, he buried his face in his hands.

He saw again in his mind's eye that extraordinary picture on Laruelle's wall, Los Borrachones, only now it took on a somewhat different aspect. Might it have another meaning, that picture, unintentional as its humour, beyond the symbolically obvious ? He saw those people like spirits appearing to grow more free, more separate, their distinctive noble faces more distinctive, more noble, the higher they ascended into the light ; those florid people resembling huddled fiends, becoming more like each other, more joined together, more as one fiend, the farther down they hurled into the darkness. Perhaps all this wasn't so ludicrous. When he had striven upwards, as at the beginning with Yvonne, had not the 'features' of life seemed to grow more clear, more animated, friends and enemies more identifiable, special problems, scenes, and with them the sense of his own reality, more *separate* from himself ? And had it not turned out that the farther down he sank, the more those features had tended to dissemble, to cloy and clutter, to become finally little better than ghastly caricatures of his dissimulating inner and outer self, or of his struggle, if struggle there were still? Yes, but had he desired it, willed it, the very material world, illusory though that was, might have been a confederate, pointing the wise way. Here would have been no devolving through failing unreal voices and forms of dissolution that became more and more like one voice to a death more dead than death itself, but an infinite widening, an infinite evolving and extension of boundaries, in which the spirit was an entity, perfect and whole : ah, who knows why man, however beset his chance by lies, has been offered love? Yet it had to be faced, down, down he had gone, down till – it was not the bottom even now, he realized. It was not the end quite yet. It was as if his fall had been broken by a narrow ledge, a ledge from which he could neither climb up nor down, on which he lay bloody and half stunned, while far below him the abyss yawned, waiting. And on it as he lay he was surrounded in delirium by these phantoms of himself, the policemen, Fructuoso Sanabria, that other man who looked like a poet, the luminous skeletons, even the rabbit in the corner and the ash and sputum on the filthy floor – did not each correspond, in a way he couldn't understand yet obscurely recognized, to some fraction of his being? And he saw dimly too how Yvonne's arrival, the snake in the garden, his quarrel with Laruelle and later with Hugh and Yvonne, the infernal machine, the encounter with Señora Gregorio, the finding of the letters, and much beside, how all the events of the day indeed had been as indifferent tufts of grass he had half-heartedly clutched at or stones loosed on his downward flight, which were still showering on him from above. The Consul produced his blue package of cigarettes with the wings on them : Alas! He raised his head again; no, he was where he was, there was nowhere to fly to. And it was as if a black dog had settled on his back, pressing him to his seat.

The Chief of Gardens and the Chief of Rostrums were still waiting by the telephone, perhaps for the right number. Probably they would be calling the Inspector-General : but what if they'd forgotten him, the Consul – what if they weren't phoning about him at all? He remembered his dark glasses he had removed to read Yvonne's letters and, some fatuous notion of disguise crossing his mind, put them on. Behind him the Chief of Municipality was still engrossed; now once more, he could go. With the aid of his dark glasses, what could be simpler? He could go – only he needed another drink; one for the road. Moreover he realized he was wedged in by a solid mass of people and that, to make matters worse, a man sitting at the bar next him wearing a dirty *sombrero* on the back of his head and a cartridge belt hanging low down his trousers had clutched him by the arm affectionately; it was the pimp, the stool pigeon, of the *mingitorio*. Hunched in almost precisely the same posture as before, he had apparently been talking to him for the last five minutes.

'My friend for my,' he was babbling. 'All dees men nothing for you, or for me. All dees men – nothing for you, or for me! All dees men, son of a bitch ... Sure, you Englisman!' He clutched the Consul's arm more firmly. 'All my! Mexican men : all tine Englisman, my friend, Mexican! I don't care son of a bitch American : no good for you, or for me, my Mexican all tine, all tine, all tine – eh? – '

The Consul withdrew his arm but was immediately clutched on his left by a man of uncertain nationality, cross-eyed with drink, who resembled a sailor. 'You limey,' he stated flatly, swivelled round his stool. 'I'm from the county of Pope,' yelled this unknown man, very slowly, putting his arm now through the Consul's. 'What do you think? Mozart was the man what writ the Bible. You're here to the *off* down there. Man here; on the earth, shall be equal. And let there be tranquillity. Tranquillity means peace. Peace on earth, of all men – '

The Consul freed himself : the pimp clutched him again. Almost for succour, he gazed about him. The Chief of Municipality was still engaged. In the bar the Chief of Rostrums was telephoning once more; Sanabria stood at his elbow directing. Squeezed against the pimp's chair another man the Consul took for American, who was continually squinting over his shoulder as though expecting somebody, was saying to no one in especial : 'Winchester! Hell, that's something else. Don't tell me. Righto!

The Black Swan is in Winchester. They captured me on the German side of the camp and at the same side of the place where they captured me is a girls' school. A girl teacher. She gave it to me. And you can take it. And you can have it.'

'Ah,' said the pimp, still clutching the Consul. He was speaking across him, half to the sailor. 'My friend – was a matter for you? My looking for you all tine. My England man, all tine, all tine, sure, sure. Excu. This man telling me my friend for you all tine. You like he? – This man very much money. This man – right or wrong, sure; Mexican is my friend or Inglés. American god damn son of a bitch for you or for me, or for any *tine*.'

The Consul was drinking with these macabre people inextricably. When he gazed round on this occasion he met, cognizant of him, the Chief of Municipality's hard little cruel eyes. He gave up trying to understand what the illiterate sailor, who seemed an even obscurer fellow than the stool pigeon, was talking about. He consulted his watch : still only a quarter to seven. Time was circumfluent again too, mescal-drugged. Feeling the eyes of Señor Zuzugoitea still boring into his neck he produced once more, importantly, defensively, Yvonne's letters. With his dark glasses on they appeared for some reason clearer.

'And the *off* of man here what there will be let the Lord be with us all the time,' bellowed the sailor, 'there's my religion spoke in those few words. Mozart was the man that writ the Bible. Mozart wrote the old testimony. Stay by that and you'll be all right. Mozart was a lawyer.'

– 'Without you I am cast out, severed. I am an outcast from myself, a shadow' –

'Weber's my name. They captured me in Flanders. You would doubt me more or less. But if they captured me now! – When Alabama came through, we came through with heels flying. We ask nobody no questions because down there we don't run. Christ, if you want 'em go ahead and take 'em. But if you want Alabama, that bunch.' The Consul looked up; the man, Weber, was singing. '*I'm just a country b-hoy. I don't know a damn thing.*' He saluted his reflection in the mirror. '*Soldat de la Légion Étrangère.*'

– 'There I met some people I must tell you about, for perhaps

the thought of these people held before us like a prayer for ab-
solution may strengthen us once more to nourish the flame
which can never go out, but burns now so fearfully low.'

– 'Yes sir. Mozart was a lawyer. And don't dispute me no
more. Here to the off of God. I would dispute my imcompre-
hensible stuff !'

' – *de la Légion Étrangère. Vous n'avez pas de nation. La
France est votre mère.* Thirty miles out of Tangier, banging in
pretty well. Captain Dupont's orderly ... He was a son of a
bitch from Texas. Never will tell his name. It was Fort
Adamant.'

' – ¡*Mar Cantábrico!* – '

– 'You are one born to walk in the light. Plunging your head
out of the white sky you flounder in an alien element. You think
you are lost, but it is not so, for the spirits of light will help you
and bear you up in spite of yourself and beyond all opposition
you may offer. Do I sound mad? I sometimes think I am. Seize
the immense potential strength you fight, which is within your
body and ever so much more strongly within your soul, restore
to me the sanity that left when you forgot me, when you sent
me away, when you turned your footsteps towards a different
path, a stranger route which you have trod apart. . .'

'He turreted out this underground place here. Fifth squadron
of the French Foreign Legion. They give 'em the spreadeagle.
Soldat de la Légion Étrangère.' Weber saluted himself in the
mirror again and clicked his heels. 'The sun parches the lips
and they crack. Oh Christ, it's a shame : the horses all go away
kicking in the dust. I wouldn't have it. They plugged 'em too.'

– 'I am perhaps God's loneliest mortal. I do not have the companionship in drink you find, however unsatisfactory. My
wretchedness is locked up within me. You used to cry to me to
help you. The plea I send to you is far more desperate. Help me,
yes, save me, from all that is enveloping, threatening, trembling,
and ready to pour over my head.'

' – man what wrote the Bible. You got to study deep down to
know that Mozart writ the Bible. But I'll tell you, you can't
think with me. I've got an awful mind,' the sailor was telling
the Consul. 'And I hope you the same. I hope you will have

good. Only to hell on me,' he added, and suddenly despairing, this sailor rose and reeled out.

'American no good for me no. American no good for Mexican. These donkey, these man,' the pimp said contemplatively, staring after him, and then at the legionnaire, who was examining a pistol that lay in his palm like a bright jewel. 'All my, Mexican man. All tine England man, my friend Mexican.' He summoned A Few Fleas and, ordering more drinks, indicated the Consul would pay. 'I don't care son of a bitch American no good for you, or for me. My Mexican, all tine, all tine, all *tine*: eh?' he declared.

'*¿Quiere usted la salvación de México?*' suddenly asked a radio from somewhere behind the bar. '*¿Quiere usted que Cristo sea nuestro Rey?*' and the Consul saw that the Chief of Rostrums had stopped phoning but was still standing in the same place with the Chief of Gardens.

'No.'

– 'Geoffrey, why don't you answer me? I can only believe that my letters have not reached you. I have put aside all my pride to beg your forgiveness, to offer you mine. I cannot, I will not believe that you have ceased to love me, have forgotten me. Or can it be that you have some misguided idea that I am better off without you, that you are sacrificing yourself that I may find happiness with someone else? Darling, sweetheart, don't you realize that is impossible? We can give each other so much more than most people can, we can marry again, we can build forward . . .'

– 'You are my friend for all tine. Me pay for you and for me and for this man. This man is friend for me and for this man,' and the pimp slapped the Consul, at this moment taking a long drink, calamitously on the back. 'Want he?'

– 'And if you no longer love me and do not wish me to come back to you, will you not write and tell me so? It is the silence that is killing me, the suspense that reaches out of that silence and possesses my strength and my spirit. Write and tell me that your life is the one you want, that you are gay, or are wretched, or are content or restless. If you have lost the feel of me write of the weather, or the people we know, the streets you walk in, the altitude. – Where are you, Geoffrey? I do not know where you are. Oh, it is all too cruel. Where did we go, I wonder? In what far place do we still walk, hand in hand?' –

The voice of the stool pigeon now became clear, rising above the clamour – the Babel, he thought, the confusion of tongues, remembering again as he distinguished the sailor's remote, returning voice, the trip to Cholula: 'You telling me or am I telling you? Japan no good for U.S., for America ... *No bueno*. Mehican, *diez y ocho*. All tine Mehican gone in war for U.S.A. Sure, sure, yes ... Give me cigarette for me. Give me match for my. My Mehican war gone for England all tine –'

– 'Where are you, Geoffrey? If I only knew where you were, if I only knew that you wanted me, you know I would have long since been with you. For my life is irrevocably and for ever bound to yours. Never think that by releasing me you will be free. You would only condemn us to an ultimate hell on earth. You would only free something else to destroy us both. I am frightened, Geoffrey. Why do you not tell me what has happened? What do you need? And my God, what do you wait for? What release can be compared to the release of love? My thighs ache to embrace you. The emptiness of my body is the famished need of you. My tongue is dry in my mouth for the want of *our* speech. If you let anything happen to yourself you will be harming my flesh and mind. I am in your hands now. Save –'

'Mexican works, England works, Mexican works, sure, French works. Why speak English? Mine Mexican. Mexican United States he sees *Negros – de comprende* – Detroit, Houston, Dallas ...'

'¿Quere usted la salvación de México? ¿Quiere usted que Crsto sea nuestro Rey?'

'No.'

The Consul looked up, pocketing his letters. Someone near him was playing a fiddle loudly. A patriarchal toothless old Mexican with a thin wiry beard, encouraged ironically from behind by the Chief of Municipality, was sawing away almost in his ear at the Star Spangled Banner. But he was also saying something to him privately. '¿Americano? This bad place for

407

you. Deese *hombres, malos, Cacos.* Bad people here. *Brutos. No bueno* for anyone. *Comprendo.* I am a potter,' he pursued urgently, his face close to the Consul's. 'I take you to my home. I ah wait outside.' The old man, still playing wildly though rather out of tune, had gone, way was being made for him through the crowd, but his place, somehow between the Consul and the pimp, had been taken by an old woman who, though respectably enough dressed with a fine *rebozo* thrown over her shoulders, was behaving in a distressing fashion, plunging her hand restlessly into the Consul's pocket, which he as restlessly removed, thinking she wanted to rob him. Then he realized she too wanted to help. 'No good for you,' she whispered. 'Bad place. *Muy malo.* These man no friend of Mexican people.' She nodded toward the bar, in which the Chief of Rostrums and Sanabria still stood. 'They no *policía.* They *diablos.* Murderers. He kill ten old men. He kill twenty *viejos.*' She peered behind her nervously, to see if the Chief of Municipality was watching her, then took from her shawl a clockwork skeleton. She set this on the counter before A Few Fleas, who was watching intently, munching a marzipan coffin. '*Vámonos,*' she muttered to the Consul, as the skeleton, set in motion, jigged on the bar, to collapse flaccidly. But the Consul only raised his glass. '*Gracias, buena amigo,*' he said, without expression. Then the old woman had gone. Meantime the conversation about him had grown even more foolish and intemperate. The pimp was pawing at the Consul from the other side, where the sailor had been. Diosdado was serving ochas, raw alcohol in steaming herb tea : there was the pungent smell too, from the glass rooms, of marijuana. 'All deese men and women telling me these men my friend for you. Ah me *gusta gusta gusta* ... You like me like? I pay for dis man all *tine,*' the pimp rebuked the legionnaire, who was on the point of offering the Consul a drink. 'My friend of England man ! My for Mexican all ! American no good for me no. American no good for Mexican. These donkey, these man. These donkey. No savee *nada.* Me pay for all you drinkee. You no American. You England. O.K. Life for your pipe ?'

'*No gracias,*' the Consul said lighting it himself and looking meaningly at Diosdado, from whose shirt pocket his other pipe was protruding again. 'I happen to be American, and I'm getting rather bored by your insults.'

'¿Quiere usted la salvacion de México? ¿Quiere usted que Cristo sea nuestro Rey?'

'No.'

'These donkey. Goddamn son of a bitch for my.'

'One, two, tree, four, five, twelve, sixee, seven – it's a long, longy, longy, longy – way to Tipperaire.'

'Noch ein habanero –'

' – Bolshevisten –'

'Buenas tardes, señores,' the Consul greeted the Chief of Gardens and the Chief of Rostrums returning from the phone.

They were standing beside him. Soon, preposterous things were being said between them again without adequate reason: answers, it seemed to him, given by him to questions that while they had perhaps not been asked, nevertheless hung in the air. And as for some answers others gave, when he turned round, no one was there. Lingeringly, the bar was emptying for la comida; yet a handful of mysterious strangers had already entered to take the others' places. No thought of escape now touched the Consul's mind. Both his will, and time, which hadn't advanced five minutes since he was last conscious of it, were paralysed. The Consul saw someone he recognized: the driver of the bus that afternoon. He had arrived at that stage of drunkenness where it becomes necessary to shake hands with everyone. The Consul too found himself shaking hands with the driver. '¿Dónde están vuestras palomas?' he asked him. Suddenly, at a nod from Sanabria, the Chief of Rostrums plunged his hands into the Consul's pockets. 'Time you pay foi ah – Mehican whisky,' he said loudly, taking out the Consul's notecase with a wink at Diosdado. The Chief of Municipality made his obscene circular movement of the hips. 'Progresión al culo –' he began. The Chief of Rostrums had abstracted the package of Yvonne's letters: he glanced sideways at this without removing the elastic the Consul had replaced. 'Chingao, cabrón.' His eyes consulted Sanabria who, silent, stern, nodded again. The Chief brought out another paper, and a card he didn't know he possessed, from the Consul's jacket pocket. The three policemen put their heads together over the bar, reading the paper. Now the Consul, baffled, was reading this paper himself:

Daily ... Londres Presse. Collect antisemitic campaign mex-press propetition ... textile manufacture's unquote ... German behind ... interiorwards. What was this? *... news ... jews ... country belief ... power ends conscience ... unquote stop Firmin.*

'No. Blackstone,' the Consul said.

'*¿Cómo se llama?* Your name is Firmin. It say there: Firmin. It say you are Juden.'

'I don't give a damn what it says anywhere. My name's Blackstone, and I'm not a journalist. True, *vero*, I'm a writer, an *escritor*, only on economic matters,' the Consul wound up.

'Where your papers? What for you have no papers?' The Chief of Rostrums asked, pocketing Hugh's cable. 'Where your *pasaporte?* What need for you to make disguise?'

The Consul removed his dark glasses. Mutely to him, between sardonic thumb and forefinger, the Chief of Gardens held out the card: *Federación Anarquista Ibérica*, it said. *Sr Hugo Firmin.*

'*No comprendo,*' the Consul took the card and turned it over. 'Blackstone's my name. I am a writer, not an anarchist.'

'Wrider? You *antichrista. Sí*, you *antichrista* prik.' The Chief of Rostrums snatched back the card and pocketed it. 'And Juden,' he added. He slipped the elastic from Yvonne's letters and, moistening his thumb, ran through them, glancing sideways once more at the envelopes. '*Chingar.* What for you tell lies?' he said almost sorrowfully. '*Cabrón.* What for you lie? It say here too: your name is Firmin.' It struck the Consul that the legionnaire Weber, who was still in the bar, though at a distance, was staring at him with a remote speculation, but he looked away again. The Chief of Municipality regarded the Consul's watch, which he held in the palm of one mutilated hand, while he scratched himself between the thighs with the other, fiercely. 'Here, *oiga.*' The Chief of Rostrums withdrew a ten-peso note from the Consul's case, crackled it, and threw it on the counter. '*Chingao.*' Winking at Diosdado he replaced the case in his own pocket with the Consul's other things. Then Sanabria spoke for the first time to him.

'I am afraid you must come to prison,' he said simply in English. He went back to the phone.

The Chief of Municipality rolled his hips and gripped the Consul's arm. The Consul shouted at Diosdado in Spanish, shaking himself loose. He managed to reach his hand over the bar but Diosdado struck it away. A Few Fleas began to yap. A sudden noise from the corner startled everyone. Yvonne and Hugh perhaps, at last. He turned round quickly, still free of the Chief : it was only the uncontrollable face on the bar-room floor, the rabbit, having a nervous convulsion, trembling all over, wrinkling its nose and scuffing disapprovingly. The Consul caught sight of the old woman with the *rebozo* : loyally, she hadn't gone. She was shaking her head at him, frowning sadly, and he now realized she was the same old woman who'd had the dominoes.

'What for you lie?' the Chief of Rostrums repeated in a glowering voice. 'You say your name is Black. *No es* Black.' He shoved him backwards toward the door. 'You say you are a wrider.' He shoved him again. 'You no are wrider.' He pushed the Consul more violently, but the Consul stood his ground. 'You are no a de wrider, you are de espider, and we shoota de espiders in Mejico.' Some military policemen watched with concern. The newcomers were breaking up. Two pariah dogs ran around in the bar. A woman clutched her baby to her, terrified. 'You no wrider.' The Chief caught him by the throat. 'You Al Capón. You a Jew *chingao*.' The Consul shook himself free again. 'You are a spider.'

Abruptly the radio, which, as Sanabria finished with the phone again, Diosdado had turned full blast, shouted in Spanish the Consul translated to himself in a flash, shouted like orders yelled in a gale of wind, the only orders that will save the ship : 'Incalculable are the benefits civilization has brought us, incommensurable the productive power of all classes of riches originated by the inventions and discoveries of science. Inconceivable the marvellous creations of the human sex in order to make men more happy, more free, and more perfect. Without parallel the

411

crystalline and fecund fountains of the new life which still remains closed to the thirsty lips of the people who follow in their griping and bestial tasks.'

Suddenly the Consul thought he saw an enormous rooster flapping before him, clawing and crowing. He raised his hands and it merded on his face. He struck the returning Jefe de Jardineros straight between the eyes. 'Give me those letters back!' he heard himself shouting at the Chief of Rostrums, but the radio drowned his voice, and now a peal of thunder drowned the radio. 'You poxboxes. You coxcoxes. You killed that Indian. You tried to kill him and make it look like an accident,' he roared. 'You're all in it. Then more of you came up and took his horse. Give me my papers back.'

'Papers. *Cabrón*. You har no papers.' Straightening himself the Consul saw in the Chief of Rostrum's expression a hint of M. Laruelle and he struck at it. Then he saw himself the Chief of Gardens again and struck that figure; then in the Chief of Municipality the policeman Hugh had refrained from striking this afternoon and he struck this figure too. The clock outside quickly chimed seven times. The cock flapped before his eyes, blinding him. The Chief of Rostrums took him by the coat. Someone else seized him from behind. In spite of his struggles he was being dragged towards the door. The fair man who had turned up again helped shove him towards it; and Diosdado, who had vaulted ponderously over the bar; and A Few Fleas, who kicked him viciously on the shins. The Consul snatched a machete lying on a table near the entrance and brandished it wildly. 'Give me back those letters!' he cried. Where was that bloody cock? He would chop off its head. He stumbled backwards out into the road. People taking tables laden with gaseosas in from the storm stopped to watch. The beggars turned their heads dully. The sentinel outside the barracks stood motionless. The Consul didn't know what he was saying: 'Only the poor, only through God, only the people you wipe your feet on, the poor in spirit, old men carrying their fathers and philosophers weeping in the dust. America perhaps, Don Quixote –' he was still brandishing the sword, it was that sabre really, he thought, in María's room – 'if only you'd stop interfering, stop walking in your sleep, stop sleeping with my wife, only the beggars and the accursed.' The machete fell with a rattle. The Consul felt himself stumbling backwards until he fell over a tussock of grass. 'You stole that horse,' he repeated.

The Chief of Rostrums was looking down at him. Sanabria stood by silent, grimly rubbing his cheek. '*Norteamericano*, eh,' said the Chief. '*Inglés*. You Jew.' He narrowed his eyes. 'What the hell you think you do around here? You *pelado*, eh? It's no good for your health. I shoot de twenty people.' It was half a threat, half confidential. 'We have found out – on the telephone – is it right? – that you are a criminal. You want to be a policeman? I make you policeman in Mexico.'

The Consul rose slowly to his feet, swaying. He caught sight of the horse, tethered near him. Only now he saw it more vividly and as a whole, electrified: the corded mouth, the shaved wooden pommel behind which tape was hanging, the saddle-bags, the mats under the belt, the sore and the glossy shine on the hipbone, the number seven branded on the rump, the stud behind the saddlebuckle glittering like a topaz in the light from the *cantina*. He staggered towards it.

'I blow you wide open from your knees up, you Jew *chingao*,' warned the Chief of Rostrums, grasping him by the collar, and the Chief of Gardens, standing by, nodded gravely. The Consul, shaking himself free, tore frantically at the horse's bridle. The Chief of Rostrums stepped aside, hand on his holster. He drew his pistol. With his free hand he waved away some tentative onlookers. 'I blow you wide open from your knees up, you *cabrón*,' he said, 'you *pelado*.'

'No, I wouldn't do that,' said the Consul quietly, turning round. 'That's a Colt ·17, isn't it? It throws a lot of steel shavings.'

The Chief of Rostrums pushed the Consul back out of the light, took two steps forward, and fired. Lightning flashed like an inchworm going down the sky and the Consul, reeling, saw above him for a moment the shape of Popocatepetl, plumed with emerald snow and drenched with brilliance. The Chief fired twice more, the shots spaced, deliberate. Thunderclaps crashed on the mountains and then at hand. Released, the horse reared;

413

tossing its head, it wheeled round and plunged neighing into the forest.

At first the Consul felt a queer relief. Now he realized he had been shot. He fell on one knee, then, with a groan, flat on his face in the grass. 'Christ,' he remarked, puzzled, 'this is a dingy way to die.'

A bell spoke out:

Dolente ... dolore!

It was raining softly. Shapes hovered by him, holding his hand, perhaps still trying to pick his pockets, or to help, or merely curious. He could feel life slivering out of him like liver, ebbing into the tenderness of the grass. He was alone. Where was everybody? Or had there been no one? Then a face shone out of the gloom, a mask of compassion. It was the old fiddler, stooping over him. '*Compañero* – ' he began. Then he had vanished.

Presently the word *pelado* began to fill his whole consciousness. That had been Hugh's word for the thief: now someone had flung the insult at him. And it was as if, for a moment, he had become the *pelado*, the thief – yes, the pilferer of meaningless muddled ideas out of which his rejection of life had grown, who had worn his two or three little bowler hats, his disguises, over these abstractions: now the realest of them all was close. But someone had called him *compañero* too, which was better, much better. It made him happy. These thoughts drifting through his mind were accompanied by music he could hear only when he listened carefully. Mozart was it? The Siciliana. Finale of the D minor quartet by Moses. No, it was something funereal, of Gluck's perhaps, from Alcestis. Yet there was a Bach-like quality to it. Bach? A clavichord, heard from far away, in England in the seventeenth century. England. The chords of a guitar too, half lost, mingled with the distant clamour of a waterfall and what sounded like the cries of love.

He was in Kashmir, he knew, lying in the meadows near running water among violets and trefoil, the Himalayas beyond, which made it all the more remarkable he should suddenly be setting out with Hugh and Yvonne to climb Popocatepetl. Already they had drawn ahead. 'Can you pick bougainvillea?' he heard Hugh say, and, 'Be careful,' Yvonne replied, 'it's got spikes on it and you have to look at everything to be sure there're no spiders.' 'We shoota de espiders in Mexico,' another voice muttered. And with this Hugh and Yvonne had gone. He suspected they had not only climbed Popocatepetl but were by now far beyond it. Painfully he trudged the slope of the foothills toward Amecameca alone. With ventilated snow goggles, with alpenstock, with mittens and a wool cap pulled over his ears, with pockets full of dried prunes and raisins and nuts, with a jar of rice protruding from one coat pocket, and the Hotel Fausto's information from the other, he was utterly weighed down. He could go no farther. Exhausted, helpless, he sank to the ground. No one would help him even if they could. Now he was the one dying by the wayside where no good Samaritan would halt. Though it was perplexing there should be this sound of laughter in his ears, of voices : ah, he was being rescued at last. He was in an ambulance shrieking through the jungle itself, racing uphill past the timberline toward the peak – and this was certainly one way to get there ! – while those were friendly voices around him, Jacques's and Vigil's, they would make allowances, would set Hugh and Yvonne's minds at rest about him. *No se puede vivir sin amar,* they would say, which would explain everything, and he repeated this aloud. How could he have thought so evil of the world when succour was at hand all the time? And now he had reached the summit. Ah, Yvonne, sweetheart, forgive me ! Strong hands lifted him. Opening his eyes, he looked down, expecting to see, below him, the magnificent jungle, the heights, Pico de Orizabe, Malinche, Cofre de Perote, like those peaks of his life conquered one after another before this greatest ascent of all had been successfully, if unconventionally, completed. But there was nothing there : no peaks, no life, no climb. Nor was this summit a summit exactly : it had no substance, no firm base. It was crumbling too, whatever it was, collapsing, while he was falling, falling into the volcano, he must have climbed it after all, though now there was this noise of foisting lava in his ears, horribly, it was in eruption, yet no, it wasn't the volcano, the world itself was bursting, bursting into black spouts of villages catapulted into space, with himself falling through it all, through the inconceivable pandemonium of a million tanks, through the blazing of ten million burning bodies, falling, into a forest, falling –

Suddenly he screamed, and it was as though this scream were being tossed from one tree to another, as its echoes returned, then, as though the trees themselves were crowding nearer, huddled together, closing over him, pitying . . .

Somebody threw a dead dog after him down the ravine.

¿LE GUSTA ESTE JARDÍN?
¿QUE ES SUYO?
¡EVITE QUE SUS HIJOS LO DESTRUYAN!